About the Author

TERÉZIA MORA was born 1971 in Sopron, Hungary. In 1990 she moved to Berlin, where she studied theater arts and Hungarian literature at Humboldt University and screenwriting at the German Film and Television Academy. She has worked as a translator of contemporary Hungarian literature and freelance writer since 1998. Her first collection of stories, *Strange Matter* (*Seltsame Materie*, 1999), received rave reviews, and one of its stories won the prestigious Ingeborg Bachmann Prize (1999). Her first novel, *Day In Day Out* (*Alle Tage*), was chosen as the best German novel of the year at the Leipzig Book Fair in 2004. She is widely recognized as one of the most noteworthy voices of her generation.

About the Translator

MICHAEL HENRY HEIM is Professor of Slavic Languages and Literatures and Comparative Literature at the University of California, Los Angeles. His many translations include works by Milan Kundera, Anton Chekhov, and Günter Grass, and his recent translation of Thomas Mann's *Death in Venice* won him the Helen and Kurt Wolff Translator's Prize in 2005.

DAY IN DAY OUT

ALSO BY TERÉZIA MORA

Strange Matter (Seltsame Materie, 1999)

DAY IN DAY OUT

Terézia Mora

Translated by Michael Henry Heim

ecco
7

HARPER ● PERENNIAL

NEW YORK ● LONDON ● TORONTO ● SYDNEY

HARPER ● PERENNIAL

Originally published in German under the title *Alle Tage* by Luchter-hand Literaturverlag.

FIRST U.S. EDITION

Designed by Laura Kaeppel

Library of Congress Cataloging-in-Publication Data
Mora, Terézia.

[Alle tage. English]

Day in day out / Terézia Mora ; translated from the German by Michael Henry Heim.
    p. cm.
  ISBN: 978-0-06-083264-3
  ISBN-10: 0-06-083264-9

07 08 09 10 11 DT/RRD 10 9 8 7 6 5 4 3 2 1

DAY IN DAY OUT

The tales I tell are heartbreaking andor droll. Extreme and preposterous. Tragedies, farces, genuine tragedies. Infantile, human, animal grief. Genuine intensity, parodied sentimentality, skeptical and honest faith. Disasters, of course. Natural and other kinds. And most of all—miracles. The demand for miracles is always enormous. We buy our miracles everywhere. Or they simply take us. There are miracles enough to go round. It is no accident we are called the time of miracles. They have their martyrs; we have our miracles. You understand.

The Latin countries are particularly productive. Good old Babylon. And Transylvania, of course. The Balkans, etc. Do you really know all those languages? All ten?

A man who looks like a beardless Christ cannot fail to be a liar, can he? Or a Rasputin. Rasputin is better. Let me call you that behind your back, all right? What's new with Rasputin? Not that it matters in the end, said the man, an editor, to Abel Nema, seeing him for the first and last time. *I don't care if you lie andor make it all up. The main thing is for it to be good. Understand?*

Good, good, good. Very good. Though there's no need to lie, actually. Life is full of horrific coincidences and countless events. *You understand.*

PART 0

NOW

Weekend

BIRDS

Let us call the time *now;* let us call the place *here.* Let us describe both as follows.

A city, a district somewhat east of the center. Brown streets, warehouses empty or full of no one quite knows what, and jampacked human residences zigzagging along the railway line, running into brick walls in sudden cul-de-sacs. A Saturday morning, autumn in the air. No park, just a tiny, desolate triangle of so-called green space left over when two streets came together in a point. An empty corner of land. Sudden gusts of early-morning wind resulting from the cleft-like layout of the streets—what you might call a *social* bite—rattle a playground carousel, an old or merely old-looking wooden toy at the edge of the green space. There is a ring nearby, the kind used to pull litter bins, but free-floating, with no bin attached; there is litter strewn over the nearby undergrowth, which tries to shake it off in attacks of the shivers, but what comes off are mostly leaves whooshing onto cement, sand, glass, and well-worn greenery. Two women and shortly thereafter another on their way to or from work. Taking a short cut, treading the trodden path that cuts the green into two triangles. One of them, corpulent, tugs at the edge of the wooden carousel with two fingers as she passes.

The stand it rests on gives a squawk. It sounds like a bird's cry, or maybe it was in fact a bird, one of the hundreds streaming across the sky. Starlings. The carousel twists and staggers.

The man looked something like a bird to us, or a bat, a giant bat hanging there, his black coattails fluttering now and then in the wind. At first they thought—they later said as much—that some-one had merely left his coat behind on that carpet-beating frame or whatever it was, jungle gym. But then they saw there were hands hanging out, white hands, the tips of the bent fingers nearly touch-ing the ground.

On an early autumn Saturday morning in a neglected play-ground not far from the railway station three women found the translator Abel Nema dangling from a jungle gym: feet wound round with silver tape, a long, black trench coat covering the head, swinging slightly in the morning breeze.

Height: approximately . . . (very tall). Weight: approximately . . . (very light). Arms, legs, torso, head: slender. Skin: white. Hair: black. Face: elongated. Cheeks: elongated. Eyes: small. Lachrymal sacs: incipient. Forehead: high. Hairline: heart-shaped. Eyebrow, left: drooping. Eyebrow, right: rising. A face that had grown in-creasingly asymmetrical with the years, the right side alert, the left side asleep. Not a bad-looking man. But *good*—that's something else again. A number of older, healing wounds plus a half dozen fresh ones. Yet apart from all that:

Something is different now, thought his wife Mercedes when she was summoned to the hospital. Though maybe it's just that I'm seeing him asleep for the first time.

Not quite, said the doctor. We've put him into an artificial coma. Until we know what's happening with his brain.

And since it was classified as a violent crime—no one, no mat-ter how skillful, could work himself into that position—they had been asking questions. When the last time was the wife had seen the husband.

Mercedes looked long and hard at the face.

I nearly said, Now that I think of it: never.

But instead she said, The last time was . . . It was at the di-vorce.

CHORUSES

On a Saturday slightly more than four years before, Abel Nema had arrived late for his wedding. Mercedes was wearing a tight-fitting black dress with a white collar and holding a bouquet of white daisies. He came in his usual crumpled black togs and took ages rummaging with trembling fingers for his identity card: at first it seemed he wouldn't find it, but find it he did and in the pocket where he had first looked. He was late for the divorce, on a Monday back in . . . I suspected as much: you can tell after a while, though there was still time, fifteen minutes before the deadline, when Mercedes was consulting with their lawyer.

Do you really want to go through with it? the lawyer asked when they hired her. That day he had shown up more or less on time, but then said not a word; all he did was nod after everything Mercedes said. Are you sure? the lawyer asked afterwards. Perhaps you should each . . . No, said Mercedes. We have no quarrel with each other. Plus the money we'll save.

So it was clear things would not go smoothly this time either: why should they? There they stood in the courtroom, the lawyer saying something, Mercedes saying nothing, both waiting. A roaring heat was gathering outside, as if the deep-red jaws of summer

were gaping wide to expel one last (Mercedes, this is her asso-
ciation) hot, supercilious breath, but here, indoors, a frosty cool
flowed through the long, greenish foyer.

When the lawyer's mobile phone rang just five minutes before
the deadline, it could have been nobody but him. Mercedes pricked
up her ears to hear what he had to say and the tone of his voice,
but there was nothing to hear, only the echoes of the foyer and the
lawyer's uh-huh's and okay's.

He had phoned, she reported, to let them know he was on his
way or, rather, pretty much, because there was a problem. I wonder why I'm not surprised. Whenever that man is about to be on
his way, no matter where, a problem comes up. The problem this
time was that he had to take a cab; no, that wasn't the problem;
the problem was that he couldn't pay for it, he had, sorry to say,
run out of money temporarily, but he had to take the cab or he
wouldn't make it to the court, or at least not in time.

I see.

They stood there in the foyer for a minute or so; then the lawyer
said she would go outside and wait for him in front of the courthouse. Mercedes nodded and went to the toilet. She didn't need to
go to the toilet, but she couldn't stand out there in the foyer either.
She washed her hands, stood in front of the mirror with her drip-
ping fingers, and looked at herself.

Female voice (singing): Do-o-na no-o-bis pa-a-cem pa-cem. Doooo-
naa no-o-bis paaaa-cem.

Male voice (singing with her): Do-o-na no-o-bis pa-a-cem pa-
cem. Doooo-naa no-o-bis paaaa-cem.

Other voices (singing with them): Do-o-na no-o-bis pa-a-cem
pa-cem. Doooo-naa no-o-bis paaaa-cem.

Unison: Do-na. No-bis. Pa-a-cem, pa-cem. Dooooo-naa no-o-bis
paaaa-cem.

Female voice: Do-o-na no-o-bis . . .

Male voice: Do-o-na no-o-bis . . .

Female voice (simultaneously): Doooo-naa no-o-bis . . .

Other voices (simultaneously): Do-o-na no-o-bis . . .

Male voice (simultaneously): Paa-cem, paa-cem.

Other voices: Paa-cem, paa-cem.

Male voice (simultaneously): Doooo-naa no-o-bis . . .

Female voice (simultaneously): Paaa-a-cem.

Other voices (simultaneously): Do-o-na no-o-bis . . .

Unison: Paaa-a-cem. (With a bit of concentration you can put it all together.)

None of this was audible in the foyer, only here. Somewhere in the vicinity or far away there was a choir, or whatever it was, rehearsing a prayer for peace, but why on Monday at noon, during lunch, why were they using their Monday lunch break to sing "Dona nobis pacem"? Who knew for how long, though they seemed tireless. Peace unto our soul, peace unto our soul, peace, peace.

The dark lipstick is strange. The pointy lip heart. What's the use of making up for a divorce? Other women come and go, looking at themselves in the mirror like her, looking at lips dark or lightish. Mercedes watches them through the mirror; they watch Mercedes or they don't; they go, Mercedes remains. Wiping your mouth with a tissue is a risky business: some red stays behind on the hairs. Raspberry-syrup mouth. Now it is turning down. I am less annoyed than sad. Peace, peace, peace.

Maria full of the grace of prison release, said Tatjana to Erik. Our friend Mercedes has married a kind of genius or something from Transylvania or somewhere, a guy she pulled out of the fire or something.

Actually, said Mercedes' mother Miriam, everything about him is just fine: he's a quiet, polite, good-looking young man. And at the same time everything about him is all wrong. Even if you can't put your finger on it. There's something *suspicious*. The *way* he's so quiet, polite, and good-looking. Though maybe that's what comes of being gifted.

What do you mean by *gifted*? Well, he can do things. He speaks a few languages. Or so they say. Because in fact he hardly says a word. Now that may be a symptom. But it's not the cause.

He has the same problems as any immigrant, Professor Tibor B. had said at an earlier point to his life partner Mercedes: he needs papers and he needs language. He's taken care of the latter: he's mastered the language, mastered ten, and to such perfection that you'd never believe he'd acquired most of his knowledge in the language lab, from tapes, so to speak. I wouldn't be surprised to learn he'd never spoken with a single living Brazilian or Finn. That's why everything he says is so, how shall I put it, *placeless*, so uniquely clear—no accent, no dialect, nothing: he speaks like a person who comes from nowhere.

The lucky duck, said a man by the name of Konstantin. I said to him, You're a lucky duck. And he stared at me as if he hadn't understood. And that's supposed to be what he's best at. Which makes me think the thing he's really best at is getting people to take an interest in him without lifting a finger. You think you've got a handle on him, but by the end you're upset because all the time you talked he looked only at your mouth, as if the only thing he cared about was how you produced your fricatives. And all the rest—the world, the whole caboodle—didn't concern him in the slightest. He's one of those types who are in the world and not of the world.

The persnickety type. A loner. But you don't fool me. Your name says it all: Nema, the mute, related etymologically to the modern Slav word for German, though originally for any non-Slav language or people, for the mute neighbors or, to put it differently, the barbarians. Abel the Barbarian, said a woman by the name of Kinga and laughed. That's who you are.

Trouble plain and simple, said Tatjana. You can tell from the start unless you're blind, unless you're Mercedes. In essence, she said, it's a fictive marriage. Those are her words: in essence, fictive. Which he used to solve both his problems. Congratulations. And as for her . . .

Now I'm not one to judge others. People have their reasons, reasons that are—and here she screws up her mouth in a way that makes the person sitting opposite her laugh—invisible from the outside, *outside*, where else than from the outside. So this Abel Nema is a promising young man, *the first free generation! the world at his feet*. And may he make the best of it while it lasts, since it could be over soon. Before you know it, something erupts, explodes, a civil war, say—I still can't comprehend it, practically *in front of our house*! *What* can't you comprehend?—so you say to yourself, That's it, I'm clearing out, starting over. Ten years ago—no, thirteen by now—A.N. was forced to leave his country, which wasn't easy, though since then everything has been pretty normal. So to speak. A man of remarkable talents, ten years, ten languages, learned and learnèd, a private person of *a certain esteem*, with wife, stepchild, citizenship, after all, who's found his niche, his quiet corner at one end of the party, and then a little more than a year ago, on a Saturday, no, it was Sunday by then, at the aforementioned party, up he stands, out he goes, and from then on *is basically unavailable*. Retreats into this *droll-to-preposterous* (all the italics are Mercedes') flat with this *fantastic* view of the station and nothing but a mattress and a telephone line and doesn't do a *thing* but sniff out droll-to-preposterous stories for a highly *dubious* agent for droll-to-preposterous *scandal sheets*, seven days a week. Need I say more.

Do-o-na no-o-bis. There comes a time when you've stared long enough in the mirror. You are what you are. On tiptoe—why?—to the little window. A gray courtyard with the mounting, characteristic smell of gray courtyards, cars parking below, sky above. Somewhat louder. Do-o-na no-o-bis. But you still can't tell where it's coming from. From everywhere it sounds like. There are bars on the window. This court takes normal cases. *Criminal* cases. I won't be able to escape through the lavatory window. Mercedes closes the window. The choir is still audible.

Then, back in the foyer, where there are other people, and, interestingly enough, all looking in the same direction, down the long greenish corridor. It's like standing on a train platform, all faces turned in expectation to the place where someone or something will make its appearance: him. You can already feel the air he is pushing before him.

When he actually did make his appearance, not more than a quarter of an hour late in all, he by no means looked so powerful as the wind he had generated in the field before him would have led one to assume. Tall, yes, but frail; not so much train as semaphore, a slash in the landscape: shut your eyes tight and he slips in from the sides. From head on he looked pretty much rooted to the spot. Stand there. Wait.

On a Saturday four years previous Abel Nema had been late to his wedding. He said he'd got *a little* lost, and gave a smile, though I can't say what kind. Mercedes smiled too and didn't ask why he couldn't have taken a cab. And *possibly* put on something else. The shiny sweat along the open collar is the clearest image Mercedes retained of her wedding. That and the smell mounting when in the middle of the speech by the official conducting the ceremony (at no particular point, because it was more or less impossible to make out what she was saying), when he—perhaps you could cut the speech short or do away with it entirely, said Mercedes, because we were late getting started, but the woman simply stared at her with blank eyes, caught her breath, and ran through it all again, higgledy-piggledy, love and law on the basis of civil arrangements, and all I could think was, I'm getting married, I'm getting married—when he suddenly: sighed. His chest and shoulders rose, then sank, causing a gale, a curious combination of the smell of the jacket, itself combined with dust and rain; the detergent-cum-sweat permeating the shirt; the skin beneath it; his soap, alcohol, coffee, and talcum powder preferences; and something like rubber, or, more precisely, latex, with a slight, synthetic, vanilla aroma, yes, that was it, the smell of a condom; plus the smell of a computer keyboard melting in the heat of a loft, with white circles in black dirt where the fingers came into contact with the keys; and so on; even more familiar smells, but they are merely incidental, as what was really important at the moment was something the bride could not name, something that smelled like a waiting room, like wooden benches, a coal-burning stove, warped tracks, a paper bag with bits of cement, salt, and ashes tossed into the bushes along an icy street, poison sumac, brass roosters, pitch-black cocoa powder, and most of all food: food of a kind she had never eaten, and so on, an endless variety for which she no longer had the words. He seemed to be carrying it in his pockets: the smell of foreign parts. She smelled *foreignness* on him.

Not that it was so surprising: he had had a certain *aura* about him before, the very first time, in fact, when he stood at her door looking slightly ridiculous in the passé black trench coat drooping from his shoulders, a diagonal stretched between the doorframe's two far corners. At that point I didn't know what to make of it. Years later, opposite the official conducting the ceremony, the sigh so overwhelmed her that she did not come to until he cracked his elbow while giving her a discreet poke in the side. She looked around, not at him but behind him, to the rows of chairs, where her son Omar sat next to Tatjana, the only people present in the empty hall, dear newlyweds, dear guests. Both Omar's eyes shone equally, the somewhat larger one of glass and the living one. He had just turned seven and was nodding: Say yes, go ahead . . .

Oui, yes, da, da, da, si sí, sim, ita est.

After that the smell returned and with increasing frequency: it could not be masked by the aftershave lotion she sprinkled throughout the apartment from time to time, and it grew so intense in the end that it was what made her realize the end had come.

So of course it was there when he finally showed. Despite the heat he was wearing the same old black trench coat, which was fluttering behind him (a draft?), though he was not in his usual flurry—long strides, torso bent forward. On the contrary: slow and stiff, dragging one leg, limping his way through the foyer with the sprightly lawyer on his heels. Drenched in sweat, as might be expected. New elements: the graze on the chin, the hematoma on the right cheekbone, the bump on the back of the head, and the aforementioned limp. The hair straggly, patches of stubble left after a quick shave, shiny spots on the ears and neck—all in all, he looked like someone who had just emerged from a street fight. But the voice was still the same, the only thing about him that counteracted the impression of general and growing desolation. Never had I heard my native language, which is not his, spoken so perfectly, though he never said a word more than was absolutely necessary, in this instance two:

Hello. Mercedes.

We have ten minutes, said the lawyer. We've got to hurry.

THE UNKNOWN QUANTITY

Just as his despair was at its height—after hours or even days of excruciating pain he would give in and kneel on the clammy linoleum between the bathtub and toilet bowl and pray to his God to forgive him what he would do before long and to help him do it—and on the eve of his long-contemplated suicide, the chaos scholar Halldor Rose disappeared from a plane, still in flight, that was bringing him home from a conference. Three days later he was sighted standing on a bridge. He was looking at the clouds floating by in a long wedge. When he waved after them, a psychiatrist by the name of Adil K., who happened to be standing on the other side of the street, crossed over after a short hesitation and accosted the physicist. Halldor R. stated that he had personally, physically gone to heaven three days before and had just been set down here on this bridge.

To the question what made him think he had gone to heaven, he responded, He didn't think, he knew.

To the question which heaven it was, he responded, What do you mean, which heaven?

To the question what it had been like there, he responded, He couldn't say, unfortunately.

To the question why he had gone to heaven, he responded, Because he was so peace-loving, of course. He was the most peace-loving man on earth.

To the question why he had returned, he responded, For the same reason. I returned as physical proof that the love which comes of peace is the highest good God has bestowed upon us and that any action to the contrary is an insult to Creation and an attempt to assassinate God.

To Father Y.R.'s question whether God had said anything else, he responded, God didn't *say* anything; God doesn't need language. God had merely placed that certainty in his consciousness.

To the question whether that was all, he responded, Yes. Though he should add that he had been completely conscious the whole time; indeed, his mind had been crystal clear, free from the usual chaotic turgidity of his thoughts and feelings. (Pauses to think.) As before birth or after death. Approximately. There had been no questions answered or, rather, there had been no questions asked. Nor had there been any of that imperfect entity time. He was amazed to learn that two whole days had passed while he was gone. The fact that time played no role was of particular importance to him as a scientist. He might have to rethink a good deal of it, so he would appreciate it if the gentlemen would let him get back to his work.

What was to become of the proclamation of the love that comes of peace?

He didn't know. He had been vouchsafed two things: the love that comes of peace and the non-existence of time. God grants man a free choice of what to devote his life to. He, as a scientist, had decided to study the problem of time. As to the love that comes of peace, perhaps the Reverend Father would . . .

Whereupon Father Y.R. replied . . .

Panic is not the condition of man; panic is the condition of this world. The unknown quantity P.

Actually, everything had been normal *until shortly before the end.* Abel had spent the weekend before his divorce the way he usually did: at home, basically. He got up at four in the morning, logged in, searched through the usual sources for the usual texts, then copied them and gave them titles. He slept a few hours in the afternoon, woke up as the sun was going down, and went out onto the balcony to take in the view.

If you stepped into the cramped metal cage through the narrow door in the roof of Abel Nema's apartment, the wind on a windy day would drive you back to the wall. You'd think you were on a trip, on a trip with a house—that's how strong the wind is—but of course everything stays where it was or travels with you, except that after a while, possibly as a result of the tears streaming down your temples, you can't see a thing anymore. A cul-de-sac at the edge of a narrow, tangled strip of small, old industrial buildings to the east of the station, Abel's street has houses only on one side. On the other side is a brick wall, behind which there are seventeen sets of tracks, behind which—the city stretching out endlessly along an endlessly flat landscape that disappears in the general haze before making contact with the horizon. It is open to everything that comes: man, beast, weather. At this point the tracks cover the broadest area, and although they cut through the city several times over they basically divide it in two: an elegant, prosperous, well-laid-out area to the west and the area known as the "Isle of the Brave," which one gains access to by means of the station's east exit. The "Isle of the Brave" had once been home to small industry, but after the industry gave out it was settled by a slaughterhouse, a beer factory, and a mill, together with the mentally disturbed, juvenile delinquents, and the aged, and if, in the short-lived "golden age," an attempt was made at gentrification to attract the yuppie crowd, in the end the area reverted to the down-and-outers, who then began streaming in as if someone were standing in the station saying, Take the east exit.

Anyway, on Saturday evening, his day's labor done, Abel would go out onto his balcony. Down below, on the other side of the brick wall, the trains would run back and forth like beads on an abacus. Later, when it got dark, the cars would start piling into the cul-de-sac, lining up bumper to bumper along the wall until not a single space was left. Latecomers had trouble turning around: the sound of hard rubber grating on cobblestone periodically drowned out the click-clack of heels crossing the street in front of the startled flashing headlights. The club at the end of the cul-de-sac was called The Loony Bin, and five days a week with a seemingly endless supply of energy people would party: workday, holiday, day after day, the waves of drumming would come and go like claps of thunder with the opening and closing of the door. And then it would suddenly fall silent again.

After he had stood on the dark balcony for a while, Abel would return to his single "preposterous" room, though the attic, having been tacked on as an afterthought—a presumably illegal afterthought—was a bit cleft-like. Whoever was responsible had tried to extract every inch of space, but all that came of it was more dead space: acute angles, worthless coves where dust and darkness gathered, unused objects kicked to the side or blown aside by a draft and lying immobile. Abel picked up a few black garments from the corners, stuffed them into a backpack together with his grimy bed linen, and climbed down the five flights of stairs to the street, where he was the only one heading not towards but away from the bar, and after a brief slalom between half-naked strangers dressed to the nines, made one right turn and then another: to a twenty-four-hour laundromat. There he had sat for several hours, staring into a porthole. Everything was black inside. A sock with a light-gray appliqué below the band kept falling back to the same place. Abel was all the way in the rear, where the rinse water spurted out into a cement tub in the corner and flowed off through a rusty iron pipe. When he was not looking into the churning black hole, he looked at the spinning white foam. He did not go home until the sun started coming up. Once more he fought against the current, this time the only one heading not away from the bar but towards it. Later the noise diminished and he sat down at the computer. Later the bells of two nearby churches rang and he pulled the blinds down to keep the light from making the screen hard to see. Later—the four figures in the lower right-hand corner of the screen gave a mid-afternoon reading and the words "zone unknown" flanked a (seemingly) rotating globe—the telephone rang.

Hello, Mother.

. . .

Her name is Mira. The last time they saw each other was thirteen years ago, shortly before she enabled him to escape conscription. Since then they had spoken once a month, mostly on Sunday afternoons.

I'll call you back.

Fine.

She hangs up. He calls back. Asks how she is.

She says she is fine.

They don't say anything for a while. There is a lot of clicking and squeaking on the line; it never stops. Click click, squeak squeak: a public telephone. He asks whether she had to wait long.

She says yes, but it's better now. The news is on. She can see three television sets behind curtains. Is it dark yet where he is?

Not completely.

Click, squeak, click.

Listen, Mira says. She needs to tell him something or, rather, correct something she'd told him before.

That is what she has been doing recently: calling and correcting things. My mother is a liar. Not a notorious liar. It's an imagination thing or a solidarity thing. She shows her compassion in the form of lies. Yes, I know what you're saying: we had Jews in the family too. We never had Jews in the family. I know, Abel says. No aviation pioneers either. No partisans. She had never been locked into a radioactive chamber by an evil professor or witnessed a shark attack. I know, Abel says, I know.

This time it's something different, she says. She's seen Ilia, she says.

Who?

Your friend Ilia.

No response.

In the beginning, she said, the town had basically remained as it was. Except for what had been destroyed—the hotel, the library, the post office, a few shops—everything was as it had been. Though not the people. You had the impression that there were more than before but that as the result of some miracle or bad joke the whole population had been replaced overnight. Unfamiliar young men everywhere. From the countryside. Or who knows where. Newborns.

It was wartime, says Abel.

Yes, I know.

Later she began talking about seeing friends more often. Some had been said to have died or gone to Germany, but she had seen them. He was walking along the street, carrying a paper bag. I was sure it was him, though he no longer lives where he used to.

Ilia had even talked to her, she says. In person. He came to her place. It must have taken some looking, because she didn't live where she used to either. He had a beard like a monk.

Hm, says Abel, adjusting his body in the chair. He says to his mother that Ilia was declared dead the previous year.

I know, says Mira. It was a mistake.

Pause.

And . . . what did he say?

He asked how I was. Then he asked about you. I told him where you live now. And he laughed and said, "Well, what do you know." He was about to fly there, tomorrow. Can you believe it? He could be there tomorrow.

. . .

Hello?

. . .

Aren't you glad? We thought he was dead, and it turns out he's alive. Isn't that wonderful?

TRIALS BY ORDEAL

There are times, said Ilia, when I feel myself brimming over with love and devotion. So much so that I am nothing more than that love and that devotion. The feeling lasts several minutes. Sometimes no more than seconds. When I emerge, I see: it was only a few seconds. Before I emerge, I see myself from the outside. I see myself in ecstasy and recognize it as a pose. In that moment, when I recognize it as a pose, I have changed from devotion to skepticism, in other words, from faith to the lack thereof. When in a state of skepticism, a state in which I often find myself, I recognize my former devotion as ridiculous and dim-witted, given the attendant superstitious rituals I perform alone or with others; when in a state of faith, in which I also find myself quite frequently, I feel repellent and dim-witted in my skepticism. Such are my two conditions. Either one or the other, and sometimes both together.

Back then, fifteen or twenty years ago they had lived in a town in the vicinity of three borders. A railway station that served as a terminus, approximately equidistant as the crow flies from the three closest capitals, a dark, quiet island amidst a former swamp. Climate: continental; soil: fertile; surroundings: the conventional beauty of hills, fields, woods, small lakes. Teachers, judges, and watchmakers with peasant roots provided the usual inveterate concert-subscription yawners of the provincial snobocracy. As if there were some remnants of a *bourgeois* way of life, be it ever so frail, circumscribed as it was by dictatorship, fear of the bomb, and economic decay. Was there a theater (for visiting companies), a hotel, a post office, an equestrian statue? There was. Were there Gothic, Renaissance, Baroque, eclectic, and postmodern peccadilloes? There were. Houses of worship serving the following denominations. Paving, lighting, green. Abel's parents were teachers; she was from a nearby village, he an alien orphan. They spent three of the four seasons in school; in summer Andor Nema packed wife Mira and son Abel into a sky-blue car and off they rode, up hill and down dale.

Andor would listen to pop music and sing along; Mira would turn the dial to classical music and ask if they couldn't stop at least once in a while and have a look at the sights. Andor usually did not wait for the end of the allegro movement to switch back and raced past all churches and most local history museums. Barbarian! Mira would shout over the combination of car noise, radio, and spousal crooning. Abel in the back seat did not take part in his parents' squabbles over the radio and cultural patrimony. He pressed his face against the side window and gazed up at the sky, which turned this way and that, though remaining the same color as the car, except that the clouds up there were white or, alternatively, black and the ones down here rust-colored. Also visible were: birds and treetops, bare or leafy, entire cities made up wholly of roofs, chimneys, and antennas. But most of all: vapor trails. Lots and lots of vapor trails. The sky was thickly populated at the time. And then would come the point at which you had to vomit.

I've had enough of this, said Mira to her son. Can't you sit up straight and face front?

He did sit relatively straight, but he did not face front. He went on observing the world above his forehead until his eyes ached, and the nausea situation did not improve appreciably.

Look here, said Mira. Look at us. Here we are.

Such were basically his first twelve years. Sky, earth. On the last day of school in his thirteenth year, eight hours before the summer holidays began, his father, Andor Nema, got up early and, careful to wake neither wife nor son, left the apartment never to return.

Mira and Abel spent the whole summer driving through the country and all the pertinent border countries. I met people I'd never heard of before. Besides "I love you" and "Will you kiss me?" Abel's mother could say nothing, so Abel interpreted and foreign women stroked his shiny, neatly parted hair. Then the summer was over, the money gone, and still no trace of Andor. They rolled back into the city on the last drops of gas.

Damn him! May he find no peace on earth! May fruit rot in his hands, iron rust, water turn bad, gold nuggets turn to horse dung! May he lose everything he fancies, and may he starve or, better yet, never die, suffer life eternal, the bastard! Bastard! Bastard!

There used to be a week at the end of the summer when his parents prepared their curriculums and Abel was sent to stay with Mira's parents in the village. A lonely week with frogs in the screaming heat. A chicken coop, lettuce bolting. Inside, in counterpoint to the loud tick-tock of the grandfather clock, the wheezy breathing of Grandfather, and, above all, the litany—with an undeviating rhythm all its own—of Grandmother's cursing, the put-put of the auxiliary engine she seemed to need to get through the day. She would mutter, complain, vituperate about and against pretty much all and sundry, summon God the Father, his Only Begotten Son, and the latter's Blessed Mother, the Virgin Inviolate, to wreak their just vengeance upon just about everyone possible. When Grandfather subsequently died—he had been managing with half a lung for quite some time—and shortly thereafter Abel's father—that bastard!—disappeared, Granny positioned herself on the orphaned side of her daughter's marital bed. Granted, that was not quite how Mira had pictured their *mutual support*, but I was nothing if not a coward my whole life. Abel slept, as he had always done, in a room of his own or, rather, in a large wall cupboard in the entry hall, where night after night he could hear his grandmother cursing her ex-son-in-law through the plywood: may his eyes, may his heart, until Mira forbade her ever to mention him again, *damnatio memoriæ*, which improved things somewhat. Then the school year began and Abel met Ilia.

The sun blazed down on the schoolyard, where the ceremony to open the school year went on *for ages*, and because those were the days when discipline still counted for something, they stood out there in their white shirts like trees in bloom until, as if the hot, windless day had rotted their roots, they started falling over. One by one they hit the hard cement surface, which turned into a number of gray-white pieces shimmering like a mirage. Abel looked first down at the pieces, then—until it made him dizzy—up at the sky.

Do you think there's something up there?

Abel lowered his gaze onto something small, dark, and round-headed. It folded its arms behind its back and assumed a stern expression.

What's that supposed to be? A test? An answer less friendly than it might be: And you?

The boy shrugged. Because his arms were folded behind his back, the shrug made his whole upper torso swing.

Abel thought about satellites, spaceships, rockets, bombs, UFOs. Are they good or bad? Will the junk fall out of our heads? Will it be the size of a whole city or only of a car?

What?

Satellites, said Abel. Though mostly you see just planes.

Mostly? The boy laughed.

Who are you? You arrogant, precocious little . . .

His name was Ilia, and what he had in mind was God. A minor misunderstanding. He laughed again. This time, clearly: at himself.

As if he had come, looked over the pickings, pointed at one, and said: You. Whereby the rest held no interest for him. Abel Nema, chosen from among four hundred and sixty-five human beings by Ilia Bor. Like the town. And Nema. You mean Nema as in "nothing"?

No, said Abel, blushing. Not like "nothing."

It's a . . . name.

I see, said Ilia, his eyes shining.

. . .

His mother was a piano teacher; his father managed the theater: pious, hardworking people, the Viennese classics resounding through their living room all afternoon, while two blocks away Mira administered filial aid between cupboard and couch. Ilia and Abel spent the time between the end of the school day and the beginning of darkness in the street playing a game called Trials by Ordeal. It was Ilia who had made it up.

It was based on the following: my father has come to God and yet failed to become a priest; now it is the duty of his only son to make him happy. Faith, as everyone knows, is hardly a prerequisite for becoming a priest. That is not the point. What he had in mind, said Ilia, was whether he would ever succeed in becoming a *true* believer. He seemed to be suffering from the disease known as skepticism—and when I say "suffering" I mean literally *suffering*— but from the disease known as superstition as well. He had thought up the game as blasphemy and prayer combined. Give me a sign.

They would leave school at about two in the afternoon and walk along Narrow Street, cross the Salt Market, enter Jew Street, cross the Main Square, and proceed through the Front Gate onto the Small Ring. At each intersection, fork, etc. they would stop and wait for a sign to be given them. They kept it up for a full five years yet never tired of it. Abel went wherever his friend felt summoned to go, through all the streets of the town. Abel said little; Ilia did most of the talking: about God and himself and possibly the world. They were known all over town as *the geezers*, *the eggheads*, and *the queers*. Somebody suggested ambushing them *for all that stuff* and a few agreed to meet at a certain place, but nobody showed. And that was the end of that.

At first they talked about Abel's interest as well—space travel and technology—but all that was child's play compared with the One Big Issue. By the time the five years were up—they were in their last year at school, the year of the comprehensive exam that would qualify them for the university—even Ilia had run out of words. They walked together in virtual silence. I still don't know where. Abel's head was reeling with plans for the future or, to be

precise, he had no plans: with languages and mathematics you can
do anything. There were other things at the time. Bodies. Ilia's was
slender, not particularly large but not frail either. Sometimes when
they stood at an intersection he scratched his nose. The frame of
his glasses would click; his hair would look moist and shiny. He
had beautiful hands. That was all you could see of him: hands and
face. Because Abel was so much taller, he would hunch his shoulders when walking next to him: he felt like a big hulk beside the
harmony of his friend's inner and outer proportions. He imagined
him a priest with the requisite priestess by his side and felt the
need to cough. They were standing at an intersection in the vicinity of the station. Abel coughed.

This last year had begun like the year before. It opened with an-
nouncements about price increases, of which more came in the following months. The first protests started in early April, though not
here. There were rumors of a latent crisis in the country, though
not here. A sense of identity among the minorities was stirring. Ilia
and Abel did not stir.

The intersection at the station was a T. Right or left. It basically
didn't matter: both directions eventually led home. In the old heart
of the town ring roads enveloped one another like onion layers
only to come together at the Main Square. For a long time nothing
happened. It grew dark. The streets emptied. Dogs howled. (Dogs
howling. He will always remember that of all things. The eerie,
homey feeling.) Then it fell quiet again, and Abel, suddenly overcome with longing, said into the silence, I love you.

I know, said Ilia without hesitation, matter-of-factly, as he said
everything. Then he went on. He knew and dismissed it. He even
felt a certain physical repulsion at the thought of it. That is why he
would leave the town and the country once the exam was over. He
would study abroad and break off all contact with Abel.

He must have known it for months. Applications had long since
been due. For months every one of his stirrings had been a lie. Everything he said, the usual things, the way he said them, the sound
of his voice, even the way he moved. Every time he stopped and
every time he started again. Lies.

Abel fell back against the rough, warm wall behind him. Leaned against the wall with its characteristic smell of summer-warmed walls on busy city streets, smelled the dog smell seep out and up to him. Tears were called for. It was dark; they were standing near a streetlight; Abel leaned against the wall. Did not cry. Ilia stood next to him, waiting or not. Just stood there, looking into space, his head cocked to one side. Hypocrite, thought Abel, noting he was starting to hate him and would soon have to cry: tears of hate. For being there. For encountering inner torment for the first time in his life on that street corner. It may not have been a bountiful harvest in terms of signs, but he was certainly none the poorer in terms of experience.

That is all. What came next was autumn, and Abel fled. Shortly after this final walk the fighting broke out, as if all that anyone had been waiting for was the summer.

POLICE REPORT

Stay at home, you hear? said Mira over the phone. Don't go out. He could turn up at any moment. Maybe even tomorrow.

Okay, said Abel. I'll wait for him.

He picked up his jacket and went out. And even though it was the night before the most important deadline of the last few years, after *that kind of thing* it was obvious: you had to go somewhere. The club at the end of the street was called The Loony Bin.

What sort of explanation can the owner of The Loony Bin, Thanos N. (What sort of name is that? A Greek name. The opposite of *thanatos*) give the police and media concerning the events that took place that Sunday in his establishment?

None.

So you'd say it was just another night at the club?

Depends on what you mean by that.

Smart ass.

The theme for the weekend was: An Orgy in Ancient Rome.

Orgy.

Right.

The main run was on Saturday night, of course, but it flowed seamlessly into Sunday: we never even closed the bar, though the place was filthy and you can't keep things clean with the hoi polloi underfoot (Can we strike that from the record?), which is why we're closed on Mondays and Tuesdays—if we make it through Sunday, that is.

So there was an almost uninterrupted flow of cars and platform shoes. Clickety-clack. The outer courtyards were as full as the main one—at least that's how it sounded: you can't see much. The Loony Bin proper is located in the rear courtyard of a former mill. The first courtyard gets a little light from the street, but the next is so black it could be a darkroom (Can we please . . . ?), and in the third the only light—a red lamp over the door—had a loose connection, so the people there would flash red, then vanish in the dark, and by the time they flashed back they were in completely different formations.

When Abel N. entered the third courtyard is unknown. At some point, though, he was standing there, leaning against the iron bar that held up the decrepit canopy over the entrance and doing: nothing. Later the steel door to the club opened and more red light and heat wafted out along with an unbelievable racket, from zero to a hundred. The fat, bald giant in the doorway was Thanos wearing tight lederhosen and a bed-sheet toga over his male tits and black chest hair. Given the noise, it was impossible to make out what he said.

What I said was, The party has a theme. Either you come in costume or you come in the buff. No jeans.

The people in the courtyard began divesting themselves of their clothing without further ado. A wavering stream of light appeared in the second courtyard: a pretzel vendor on his bicycle. He made the rounds of the people hopping on one foot—Pretzels anybody?—and ringing his bell. Some of them actually did stop undressing, bought something to eat, and remained in the courtyard; others danced their way into the club under Thanos' armpits. Before the door closed to the rest of them, a long, hairy arm reached out, grabbed the fully dressed, uncostumed man leaning against the iron bar, and dragged him through the fast-diminishing door opening.

Thanos subsequently disappeared, which was surprising, because people in the club were so pressed together it was nearly impossible to move. Suddenly (how?) Abel had a glass in his hand. He found a spot on the edge of a niche in the wall and took a seat.

At an hour when people are alone andor in the society of their spirits, in the night between Sunday and Monday, the decalingual translator Abel N. was sitting in the inner sanctum of a former mill on the edge of a niche in the wall on the edge of a bench. Deep in the niche, under the cover of a forest of glasses on the table, there was copulation going on. Senators with their mistresses, soldiers, gladiators, laurel-laden poets, noble ladies, but predominantly slaves, naked but for the luminous signs on their skin, dancing or looking on and so wedged together that it was like the bowels of a jam-packed ship and accordingly loud. A mechanical apparatus on the dark ceiling between galleries that seemed to proceed indefinitely and teem with people, a mechanism of indeterminate function and made of cogwheels and sails, flashed on and off in the changing light. It all might have been hanging on a piano wire and come crashing down at any minute.

Now or later—Abel's glass was in any case still or once more full—a curly-headed catamite mounted the stage, naked but for the gold dust covering him from head to toe, bent over, looked him deep in the eyes, and dropped a small white pill into his glass. It twisted and turned as it fizzed its way through the dark liquid. The boy's hairless member on a level with his glass. Abel emptied the glass in one gulp. Glittering cherub buttocks blurred by the glass's bottom. It had a number stamped on it: 1034. Then everything disappeared.

Tunne sa belesi houkutenel smutni filds.

What? asked the angel.

Abel had grabbed him by the ankle. What luck that he had happened past. The curls had slipped over the gilded ear. He looked down from great heights.

This mumbling idiot who wouldn't let his ankle go just shook his head. What's wrong with him?

The dancers tore Thanos' toga from his shoulders; it fell in Abel's face or, rather, on the back of his neck: his head was now hanging. Thanos pulled it away, then squatted, his lederhosen squeaking, and took the hanging head in his hands. Large, black pupils, rolling, elderberries in a reddish stock. Don't die. Please don't die.

He's not going to die from a little sweetener.

What . . . ?

It was just a little joke, that's all. I don't know what's wrong with him either.

I don't advise you to do my best customer in. Intentionally or not, he kept his hands over Abel's ears.

That's good, thought Abel and lost consciousness.

Sweetener, eh? And how do you explain the fact that nearly all those who, knowingly or unknowingly, took one of those tablets showed symptoms of a psychedelic high? Impaired sense of both time and memory as well.

Of both time and memory.

Pardon?

Never mind.

The next time Abel opened his eyes, he was no longer sitting on the bench or on the floor in front of it, to which he had slid. He lay in a strange room. Walls, floor, blanket red, air hot and powdery. I can't remember ever having been here before. He felt around him: his fingers disappeared in plush down to the first joint. He groped his way to the door. He saw: a corridor with other doors. Either it's very long, or I'm moving very slowly. Groaning, moaning, pounding, grinding everywhere, but no one in sight. A toe caught: he stumbled, fell against a wall; no big deal: he slid to the ground. He was back to where he had started from. Not quite. A couple next to him. He saw. A man and a woman. Copulating. Abel made believe he was watching them. The man laid his cheek against the woman's. Cheek-to-cheek they looked back at him, one grown-together head. Later Abel gathered his strength. Behind one door there was a tiny room in which men stood like brooms. Or vice versa. Behind the next: a mirror. Portrait of the artist as a skull. A sudden draft tore the door from his hand. Shut. A fat, belaureled Caesar passed, the shoulder of his toga fluttering, his lederhosen squeaking. He was soon gone, disappeared behind a (which?) door, only his smell remaining. It was no longer so hot here. That wakes you up a bit. That and noise. The pounding of machines and an endless scale thundering in the sky. That is where I must go.

Bare arms groping along the corridor in front of him. Look like mine. He looked down at himself and discovered that not only his arms were bare; his shoulders, chest, and belly were too. A little later he saw that not only his jacket and shirt were gone, his shoes and socks were too. The only piece of clothing he had left was a pair of black trousers. He made an about-face and started back to the place where he had lain, just around the corner, testing the floor underneath: maybe I've gone blind, but: no luck. He may well have gone to the wrong room because the naked couple from before was no longer there. He went back farther—hallways, doors, rooms—but could find nothing. He rummaged through the heads of a few mops and for a moment thought his shirt might be there, but all he came up with were gray rat's tails, the dirt that had collected there coming off on his fingers. Although he was now deeper into the labyrinth, the unbridled roar around him had grown even louder. The machines rumbled in his stomach. He made another about-face, out, find Thanos, ask what is going on, why am I half naked and where have the last few hours gone?

It was all a joke, he said.
Who?
The angel.
A naked man dressed as an angel?
Yes.
A joke.
Yes.
The blood of the people tested showed: aspartame.
Maybe the sweetener was actually a sweetener. Somebody put a sweetener into people's drinks.
What were the symptoms?

They produced it: mass hysteria. If you ask me. Like Pentecost.
Like what?
Pentecost.
What kind of crap is that?

Bellies, arms, armpits, shaved bodies, elbows. Blows to the ribs
from all directions. Abel had no choice but to shove back. Wine
sloshed out of a glass; a mouthful of liquid splashed against a net-
stockinged calf; the glass, reflex action, took a swing and hit him
on the cheekbone. He spun round. Gotcha! said a cheery bald man
and caught him under the armpits. Upsy-daisy! he said and tossed
him back, too small a catch. While he was in the air, the black light
went on and again he lost his orientation, was tossed blindly back
and forth until he fell into the outer room and onto the owner's
back. Thanos did not even look round. He had other things to
attend to. The room was packed with more or less naked people.
They were screaming, You said we should leave our clothes in the
courtyard. Now they're gone. Not only that. Their memory of the
last three hours was gone. It was an outrage, a scandal!

Excuse me, said Abel, pressing past Thanos' sweat and squeez-
ing through the other naked bodies, their skin sticking to his. Snail
tracks. The marks of two dozen strangers on me. Excuse me. He
had just time to see one of the men who was screaming the loudest,
lunge at Thanos. He sprang at him from a crouch, like a beast, the
strap of his G-string gleaming between his buttocks.

If a free-for-all breaks out in a crowd in which people can hardly
stand. Abel was first sucked back into the outer room, then spat
out into the courtyard. Once more he collided with someone.
Tinkle and steps followed each other almost immediately: first the
glass fell, then he stepped inside with his naked right foot, pain,
lost his balance, but of course now there is nobody there to catch
anybody, so he fell straight through the mass and onto the cobble-
stones. Hit his head, lay there. Lying on the ground, he saw the
naked men and women looking through the rudimentary piles of
clothing in the courtyard.

Could mass panic be said to have broken out?

Someone said something about the police, whereupon everyone started running like crazy through all three courtyards. Clacking high heels, buckling ankles. They ran with their necks in their shoulders, his G-string gold, hers silver, stumbling along, dragging the right heel over the stones. Trrrrrrrr. The next few were barefoot and one man with neon-green circles on his buttocks. Hopping. Cars starting up out in the cul-de-sac, a quarrel over a taxi, finally all four climb in, hectic twisting and turning.

Abel, a sharp heel having stabbed him in the side, crawled into a dark, quiet corner in the third courtyard, where he could not be seen and where he could not see what he had got into. His sense of touch said: a sack of cement next to a plastic pail with a sharp edge. A burnt child, he pulled his fingers away at once. Whether the cut on the bottom of the large toe was serious he would not know until later; now it was dark and slippery and painful. Later he discovered that although his money and ID were gone he still had his house key, because of having lain on his trouser pocket or for whatever reason. Which meant at least he did not have to go back into the club to ask Thanos for his things. Most likely futile anyway. He gathered his strength and limped, bleeding, after the others: the police threat was no laughing matter. I've got to be somewhere tomorrow or, rather, this morning.

Sorry. A woman getting into a car had bumped him with her naked hip. Abel stood flat against the brick wall; the car began a cautious U-turn. A police car swerved into the street, slamming on its brakes when the policemen saw the angel flying past. Wig in hand, his own hair glued dark and wet to the skin on his skull, he wore a black shirt much too large for him: it kept slipping off one shoulder and reached almost to his knees and looked vaguely familiar to someone (Abel). A policeman got out of the back seat, too late, he gave up immediately, and the angel disappeared down the side street. All that was left was the car with the naked couple. The man got out, went up to the policeman, his palms raised in front of his chest and a stupid grin on his face. A.N. slid unobtrusively along the wall past the blue lights. He opened the front door to his building and looked back to see traces of cement and blood in the street: white heels, red toes.

. . .

As far as the place of residence of the "angel" is concerned, Thanos, the club owner, hasn't a clue. But no matter where you are, I'll find you and rip your ass out. It's your stupid joke that got my club closed down. Some had only sweetener in their drinks, but others were high on ten or twelve kinds of junk. The DJ alone had three.

And that is basically how Abel Nema spent his weekend.

In comparison nothing spectacular had befallen Mercedes. Every-thing has become so nice and quiet around me lately. She had spent the week before the divorce date mostly by herself. Omar was away at camp, and half the city had gone with him. You could park. She listened to the summer through the open window, the sounds com-ing from the nearby park. There didn't seem to be fewer people there, but when you looked out here the streets were empty. Mer-cedes lived on one of those *nice* streets, lined on either side by leafy trees. The leaves glistened. It was beautiful.

On Saturday she got up: early, as usual. Birds were chirping. She made her customary rounds through the flat: bedroom, Omar's room—empty or, rather, full of things but without him. Mercedes had put the things where they were now: living *somewhere* as op-posed to living *life* left Omar cold. The only things he had brought in of his own free will were the two pictures over his bed: the color sonography of a brain and a drawing he had made with the help of compasses and a ruler—a square in a circle in a square in a circle, and so on. When asked what it was, he would answer, A circle in a square in a circle in a . . . (Omar was a clever child. A congenital defect. When asked where his left eye had gone to, he would answer, I traded it in for wisdom.)

Mercedes moved on into the bathroom, had a look at herself, as was to be expected, in the mirror. Standard height. Her head in the lower part, almost on a level with the shelf. Two toothbrushes showing approximately the same amount of wear came into sight: one red, one green. She decided in favor of *hers*: the red one. While brushing her teeth, she noticed a pimple forming on the tip of her nose, squeezed it out, opened *her* half of the medicine cabinet, disinfected the wound with aftershave. Then she replaced the used disposable razor with a new one; there were plenty of Band-Aids and aspirin with the *usual* signs of use. Though that didn't matter anymore. She slammed the door; the mirror shook.

Back through the bedroom with *his* smell in her nose, on into the kitchen to make tea, back into the bedroom. On the dresser between the two small wood statues—an African *Thinker* and a pair of two shiny, long-fingered hands—the set of family pictures: Omar, Omar and his mother, Omar and his stepfather, wedding picture. She put the cup down and dialed the emergency number for Omar's camp, but hung up immediately, because no sooner had she finished dialing than a great hubbub came in from outside, ruling out all possibility of talk.

Every day at noon and on Sundays and holidays all but nonstop—7:50, 8:15, 9:50, 10:15, 11:05, 12:00, 12:20, and so on—it was impossible to hear oneself talk in the park or its environs for a good fifteen minutes. Both churches bordering the park toll their bells. The Catholic church to the south sets it off; the Protestant church to the north chimes in about three minutes late. It is loud. So loud that the city should ban it. So loud that thoughts fall out of heads and objects out of fingers. For a quarter of an hour everyone puts down what they're doing: park denizens, music-school pupils, mental patients, visiting relatives, nursing-home residents, housewives, the homeless—they all put their hands in their laps and sit there numb waiting for the heavenly brouhaha to wind down.

Later—it was afternoon by then and the major clangor was over—Mercedes pulled herself together and went—simply to go somewhere, *because going somewhere is good*—out to the park.

Maybe there's a free bench somewhere. But there was no free bench, so on she went, on and on, twice around the whole dusty path circling the perimeter. Picnics, soccer balls, frisbees everywhere. The homeless camping at the south end of the park were still here. Other strollers, dogs, joggers passed her. A group wearing similar T-shirts with various peace logos appeared to be practicing sprinting: first they would race as if someone were after them, then jog along peacefully. You could hear them from a distance because they shuffled a lot, and they set a lot of dust swirling. Mercedes blinked. After the third time they showered her with dust and the second time she was sniffed by the homeless people's dogs, she gave up. Because she happened to be standing in front of a water fountain, she took a drink of water and set out for home.

In front of the mirror again, she discovered she had brought home a sunburn, but did not do anything about it. The rest of the afternoon she spent reading a manuscript she had to edit, until she got enmeshed in a fairly long sentence the meaning of which, as is only proper, unfolded from dependent clause to dependent clause only to tangle a bit just before the end, and suddenly you didn't quite know . . . She gave it a few tries, but each time the tangle moved farther forward, until it lost its clarity shortly after the beginning and she could no longer tell what it was about at all and whether there was any inconsistency in it.

Some friends had invited her for the evening. She picked up her friend Tatjana—You're bright red in the face. I know—and they drove together.

His name is Erik, an old friend and modest publisher of books dealing with contemporary history. Her boss, too, as it happens. His wife's name is Maya, and they have two delightful daughters and a house in the country. One minute after they returned from their holiday he was on the phone to her. He might have been asking her to come next door. Or down the street. Did you miss me? I missed *you*! I can't live without you! You must come immediately! If not today, tomorrow. Tomorrow is Saturday. You'll be able to see our idyllic cottage in all its rank but all the more enchanting end-of-summer luxuriance! And bring the boy along!

He's at camp.

Well then, bring the witch (Tatjana) if you like. Tell her she's my personal guest.

At last! he cried. A blue shirt stretching over his belly, strong brown arms sticking out of his sleeves, he pressed Mercedes to him; her face landed between the hills of his breasts; when she emerged, she was redder than ever. Maya gave her a smile.

They could none of them have said for the life of them what they went on about all evening: a typical summer party. Mercedes sat in an armchair opposite the door to the terrace and stared out into the darkness. The fresh wind had chased the mosquitoes from the garden, which was good: they didn't need to suffocate; they could open two windows and the terrace door to subsequent cricket chirps. So here they sat, inside, under the ceiling. Late, lazy mosquitoes. From time to time one of them pulled itself together or simply let go with a nose dive. Splat! Tatjana gave her arm a slap, pinched the mosquito corpse between two fingers, seasoned the floor with it. Erik lowered himself onto an arm of Mercedes' chair, his large, hot body bulging over hers.

What's wrong?

Nothing.

Later they drove back to town. Tatjana asked to be let off at a bar. Mercedes did not care for bars, and anyway she had to be on the road early the next morning. Then she lay awake until three o'clock, forgot to set the alarm, nearly overslept.

The city does not go on forever: somewhere you leave even the last warehouses behind and you can travel long distances between stands of trees, fields, and underbrush until slightly over an hour later you enter the woods. She noticed how scattered she was when she kept having the feeling she had just woken up: all at once she was somewhere else in the countryside. Then she thought she had lost her way, as a result of which she did in fact lose her way, took the turn before the one she should have taken, and ended up at a dilapidated old house. A pack of wild dogs sprang up and down behind the fence. Into reverse, past a small lake, a shooting gallery, a go-kart track, and farm equipment until the column of parents' cars coming in the other direction showed her the way to the camp.

Omar was all the way in the back: he sat on the steps of the cabin next to a fragile-looking boy, the son of one of the teachers. They were making Xs and Os in a grid with long twigs in the dust before the entrance. Mercedes apologized to all and sundry for being late; no one particularly cared.

On the way back they stopped off at Omar's grandparents' because it seemed the thing to do.

Your face is all red.

I know.

The garden was scorched, the kitchen a greenhouse, a hothouse. Mercedes went into the living room, where it was less bright.

Hello there, Felix Alegre—pseudonym: Alegria, an author of whodunits and Omar's grandfather—had said to his grandson at the door. Have a good morning? I didn't waste a second. I've concocted a new story for Pirate Om.

The reason I began to write, Alegria had once said—and had presumably said to Omar as well—was that from the outset I found life much too strenuous. Everything and everybody I came into contact with threw me off kilter and made me wonder whether life was worth living. I felt both listless and furious. Everything had this effect on me except the people I'd been making up for myself since early childhood. I am proud and happy to say that I eventually managed to regard everything I come into contact with as if I'd concocted it myself. Since then I can love everybody.

But he had never really made it until he concocted a one-eyed black detective by the name of Pirate Om who, when asked how he lost his eye, answers, I traded it in for wisdom. In his new case Pirate Om is asked to locate a politician of highly conservative, not to say extreme rightist views who disappears without a trace on the very day he has unexpectedly been elected mayor of a small town. To do so, he must review the entire electoral campaign, which he had tried to repress, by sitting through all the man's repellent speeches on video—you know these guys who appeal to our lowest instincts: envy, greed, fear, hate, and are so taken with themselves, with what good people they are. It will be one of P.O.'s toughest cases. Chapter after chapter he's forced into political discussions with friends and foes, that is, in both cases, hello there, darling!—Mercedes just gave him a wave and sat in a rocking chair in the corner—with potential murderers.

And where is he at the end of the story? asked Omar. The politician.

I don't know yet. It may never get cleared up. Understand? The guy himself is of no importance. Whether there's a murder or not is of no importance. Though political murders . . . What really matters is . . .

How did you like camp? Miriam came out of the kitchen and plumped a tray with lemonade down on the table.

That's just like her. I'm in the middle of a sentence, telling about my novel—which is going to feed and clothe us, mind you—and she comes and butts in.

Omar is not only clever and handsome; he is polite. He said . . .

Let me finish, said Alegria. Though I can't see why anyone, even a ten-year-old, would want to go gadding about in the depths of our woodlands, I hope I can get a story or at least a sentence out of it, as I do out of everything, so go to, boy, he said, picking up a pad and pencil.

What a ham. Makes a show of taking notes to show how hurt he is. How can he believe I do it on purpose? If I waited for him to come to a stopping point, we'd die of thirst.

We found a dead girl in a hollow tree, said Omar. She was naked. We stared a long time at her vagina.

Dead girl, hollow tree, vagina, his grandfather scribbled.

I can see there's no point talking to you, said Miriam. She wasn't sure whether to be hurt or not and threw a glance in the direction of her daughter. Is she with us? Sitting there in the darkest corner of the room. You can't tell what she's looking at.

I'm just making it up, of course, said Omar, but it was so interesting: flora, fauna, man, woman. The big farewell bonfire was canceled due to danger of forest fire, and when they thought I was asleep some kids raised my eyelid and shone a flashlight into the eye socket to see whether they could look through to the brain. That I didn't make up.

You didn't tell me that, said Mercedes. Her first words since the hellos.

Being gifted isn't easy, said Omar with a shrug.

We could build on that, said Alegria thoughtfully. In the next episode, chronicling our hero's youth. We would finally learn or fail to learn what he has or had under his eyelid. With the dead vagina as trigger mechanism. For something.

By the way, said Miriam, turning to her daughter, has anyone died?

???

How come you're wearing black in this heat? You're not a widow; you're just getting divorced.

Mercedes jumped up. The rocking chair gave a creaking rock.

Anything wrong? (asked Alegria with a sympathetic smile).

I'm getting a new eye tomorrow, said Omar.

On the way home they got caught in a jam, a frozen stream of returning day-trippers in the heat of the setting sun—but that's neither here nor there.

And now that.

Pardon? said Mercedes in the foyer of the courthouse. I didn't understand. What did you say?

RADIO

He could have asked his mother about the dogs. Whether the dogs still howled the way they used to when it was dark, or what had become of them. Instead, Abel N. had got mixed up in an orgy, was drugged, robbed and dragged into a free-for-all, made a trail of blood behind him all the way to his bathroom, which has no door—there is only a plaster wall with a bathtub and toilet behind it—and somewhere along the way lost consciousness for the second time that night.

It was still dark when he came to. There was a scab running along his right foot. He filled the tub, lay down in it, carefully positioning his foot on the edge of the tub, clotheslines overhead, and went back to sleep. All of a sudden he awoke with a start: somebody next to him was screaming. *We shall be redeemed! We shall enter a new age, and it will be an age of love and light! All the destructive energy of the previous centuries will be turned to good! The age of wars will give way to an age of peace! Man will be vouchsafed a new consciousness! Hate, envy, violence, oppression, and exploitation will flee the earth! Love, happiness, and joy will take their place!*

Poppycock! He sat up, splashing a cold wave onto the linoleum.

The injured foot fell into the water. He lifted it out at once. The scab did not come off. He laid his heel back on the edge of the tub.

There was nothing unusual about the screaming: *that damned clock radio.* Not his: it belonged to his neighbor, a physicist by the name of Rose, so it was on the other side of the wall, not that it made any difference. There had once been a passageway between the two apartments; later it had been closed off with laths and gauze. A kitchen cupboard now occupied the space. Which did not help. At least his neighbor tended to turn down the volume after a few seconds. This time he did not.

But woe unto us, the cupboard kept screaming to the chirping accompaniment of the two plates and single glass within, *for we have miscalculated! Astrologists have proved with the help of reliable star charts that entry into the Age of Aquarius will not take place between the years nineteen hundred and fifty and two thousand and fifty! We shall have to wait another three hundred and sixty years for the Golden Age!*

What kind of weekend have we had, for example? Weather and world politics robbing us of our sleep! Sand from the Sahara stinging our eyes and drying our throats! According to an official investigation so-and-so many liters of every possible abomination are being consumed a year! Is it any wonder that werewolves are reported roaming the streets? Though perhaps, yes, perhaps it was your neighbor from the local den of iniquity! On the night between Sunday and Monday a police raid on a sex bar known as The Loony Bin sent approximately twenty-five naked revelers into the street. Someone had slipped drugs into the revelers' drinks and then made off with their clothes! The depravity of it all! And at approximately the same time a group of unidentified vandals was feathering and tarring the white swans of peace in Municipal Park! Fly away home, o ye birds! Scarcely a week has passed since this fine work of art, an imitation of a porcelain sculpture of two swans from the collection of Pope Pius XI, was installed with due pomp at the northern end of the park! There they were, nestled between flowerbeds, shining peacefully in the sun, gazing out over the green water, when along came performance artist Igor K. and, planting his big feet on a camp chair at the edge of the water, roared, Down!

In other words, with lies and kitsch! My outrage is of a (1) aesthetic, (2) moral, and therefore (3) political nature. The moral and therefore political lie, illuminated as it is by the aesthetic lie, is all the more flagrant. But even without the moral and political lie I would be outraged by the moral lie alone. And outraged I am, said I.K. Then the artist went back to his basement and on with the hunger strike he had interrupted for the protest. The video documentation of the performance proves that the artist I.K. is not responsible for the tarring and feathering of the swans. The original of the sculpture may be seen unscathed in the Vatican Museum next to a display case exhibiting a sixteenth-century chasuble embroidered all over with six-armed seraphim!

The bathwater was cold; a film of grease had formed on the surface. Some of it was left in his eyes: it took a while before his vision began to clear. The grease was a golden color, and as far as he could tell, it covered his body. It was as if the angel, his whole body, had come off on him, though I can't remember having touched him. No, once, on the ankle. He looked at his fingers: shriveled, golden. He realized he would have to get rid of it and only later why it had become urgent. Renewed hectic splashing, no idea of the time, though much too late.

A shivery exit, a hasty dry. A smeary piece of mirror swaying over the tub on a string and showing a pair of smeary eyes behind bangles of plaster, blood in noble pallor, red and white: the colors of morning. The radio might have been five centimeters from his ear.

What else is there? What are the hospitals saying, the police stations, the suicide hotlines? On Saturday a man bought a chainsaw; on Sunday he sawed off his lower leg while his family was at church. He was counting on worker's compensation. He bled to death in the bathtub. What next? The same as always, by and large. Refugee ship sunk before landing, Indians attack village, fourteen dead, forest fires raging, water levels rising, back to the trees, witnesses at the H. Tribunal are gradually going free, junk bonds have been the undoing of five or six more companies, yet we face the new workweek full of hope and enthusiasm. Traffic is impossible. We hereby reaffirm our intention of using atomic weapons against the following states. You have been listening to Radio Paradiso. Welcome to the freak show, everybody, welcome, welc . . .

At this point Abel left the stairs.

Recounting the whole thing, especially in chronological order, would have been impossible and superfluous, so all he said to his wife was that he had been out the night before and had his jacket stolen. And everything in it: ID, money, credit card. Only now did it occur to him he had not yet frozen the account. All he had in his pocket were a few coins. It was a wonder he was actually there and with the only thing he had left to prove his good intentions: an expired passport.

What's that?

The only document left. There's a ten-year-old picture in it. If that helps.

Say it isn't so.

The judge looked at them, looked at the lawyer, Mercedes, the man with the black trench coat and the black eye, the passport, back to Mercedes, the lawyer.

This country no longer exists. She flipped the passport open and shut.

True, but, said the lawyer. Driver's licenses are valid too.

Not this one. The judge had another look.

The passport had expired not long after they had been married. Red spots on her face.

Look here, said the judge, I can't divorce a person who doesn't exist.

That's his original name. Before the marriage. The marriage certificate, prompted the lawyer.

Oh, said the judge and glanced at the document. I see.

Again she compared the picture and the man. It was the first time she had had a good look at him. Until then: his presence was not at all confirmed by *the data*. Height, color of eyes (the passport said blue, but the judge saw they were violet). Other distinguishing characteristics: None.

Well, said the judge.

All we want to do is declare intent, said the lawyer. We just want to say, yes, we wish to be divorced. The rest will come later anyway . . .

Still, I've got to know who is declaring the intention.

Grabbed off the street. Happens all the time. She looked at Mercedes. A pretty child. Scared. Sorry. You won't get rid of him. Not today.

She flipped the folder shut, then withdrew her thumb from the passport and gave it back to the presumed Abel Alegre, born Nema. What else could you do.

They left the building together: Abel, his still very-much-spouse Mercedes, and their mutual divorce lawyer. They stood on the steps before the entrance, twelve noon, traffic noise, sun, wind, a choir rehearsing "Dona nobis pacem," but Mercedes was the only one who heard it. The lawyer was in dark gray, the others in black: a mini mourner community.

Are congratulations in order? asked Tatjana.

What are you doing here? Mercedes looked at Omar. They had not arranged to meet. To be there when they came out. Dear divorcees, dear guests.

When she told him they would be getting a divorce, Omar did not look at Mercedes. He just said, Too bad.

He did not look at her this time either; he looked at Abel. I wanted to say good-bye. But instead of saying good-bye, he said, Hey there, spy.

What's up, Pirate?

My eye's too small. I'm getting a new one today. We're going straight to the clinic from here. Whenever the socket size changes, they've got to make a new eye. Eyes made of synthetic material don't break when they fall out, but they're more expensive to produce and require several visits to the eye doctor.

I see, said Abel.

Pause. Sun, wind, traffic, three women, one child, a man in black.

Well? Are you divorced?

Abel shook his head.

What did you do wrong?

I lost my ID. Somebody pinched it.

Tatjana laughed. Mercedes' glare.

You've got something on your neck, said Omar.

He made a grab for it.

On your ear.

He rubbed the balls of his fingers together. There was a flash of gold. Mercedes put a pair of sunglasses on.

Let's go.

Good-bye, said Omar and held out his hand to Abel.

Abel took the hand, pulled the boy to him, and kissed him on the cheek.

Give me a call when you get the new papers, said the lawyer and shook hands good-bye.

PART I

GODSEEKER(S)

Journeys

BROKEN WINDOWS

What happens after the end of things?

A new start! Now! Colleagues! Real life!

A graduation party or, rather, orgy, everyone roaring like . . . (on a spit) between the thick stone walls of the dungeon, currently the vault of the beer cellar below the main square, young men in black-and-white suits, soupy air, surrounded in the lime-speckled earth by the detritus of ancient times: heads, torsos, and feet made of stone. So this is the ritual end of our . . . (*golden*) youth: tedious sitting around massive tables in glad rags. We haven't got much to say, nor is there anything much to, to whom. The thing to do is to proceed as directly as possible to drunken stupor, even if it takes holding your puffy nose shut; you can force the stuff down some-how: yellow, red, sparkling, though best of all is the transparent stuff. Then comes the moment when you feel nerve and time come together to propel you onto a rustic table top and proclaim a phi-losophy of life! all your own.

Life! Standing, swaying on the table, shouting between two slurps, now laughing, now crying: Life! Real life! Friends! Now! You and me! Wedged between our fathers and sons. Our . . . What was I going to say? Wedged. Fathers. Oh, well. New! Old too! Everything's here! You and me! So let me say . . . I love you guys!

The stockinged legs of an unknown girl shining. I love you, she suddenly sobbed and put her arm around Ilia's neck.

Let's go, said Ilia to the boy on his right.

The arm slid down his back like something dead, white, and lay where it fell.

First they walked the town for five years—how many hours? how many kilometers? once around the globe? less? more? equal?— then they took the comprehensive exam. They left the traditional debauch early. They walked straight until the main post office stood in their way, turned right to circumvent the building, then proceeded in the direction of the station. They had been silent for a while, as had the city around them, or no, on the contrary, it was quite noisy—work, parties, fights—but always somewhere else, a block away. Everything where they were was empty and quiet. They went as far as the street leading off to the station. Ilia, the sign receiver, was always the direction giver. Now he came to a halt. The hour lines on the clock face shone white against the black sky. Abel counted the hours. Thirty-six. Then they'd be on their way, traveling all over the country for the rest of the summer. Destination: of no matter. Basic principle: trial by ordeal. We'll get lost. The proposal had come from Abel; Ilia nodded. They had no car or even driver's license, so we'll take the train.

Actually he'd meant to wait until they were at a better place, a coast, a panorama, something with atmosphere and meaning, but then Abel looked up at the floating clock and could not help thinking of the girl's arm, that completely meaningless arm, and said: I love you.

The minute hand on the station clock moved forward one notch.

I know, said Ilia.

Later he held out his hand. Abel had been leaning against the wall, Ilia standing in front of him, his head cocked, when—after a few minutes, most likely—he had extended his empty hand, palm up:

See? No weapon. But kept looking off to the side, into the distance. Abel began to slide down the wall towards the furry dirt of the pavement. Well! said Ilia, closing his outstretched hand into a fist before withdrawing it. Irritated, contemptuous: Well! That helped. Abel braked his slide, pushed away from the wall, and started walking. To the left. Ilia, one imagines, must have taken the opposite direction, or, who can tell, he may have just stood there. Abel never turned back.

A pinball run amok in the narrow corridors of the old town, he ran, stumbled, bumped into walls. Each time he stood still for a moment and looked around. Not to see whether *he* was following him. Ilia with his heart defect, exempt from PE, whether he could or not, run so fast, wasn't the point, he wasn't supposed to, if he did . . . He simply *looked around*, to see what was there, how things were. This moment, when things were becoming so strange. Until at a certain point he truly no longer knew where he was.

Can I be lost in streets I've walked through a thousand times? Is that possible? He made a few turns, listened to the noise made by the invisible others: what were they doing and where? In the main square perhaps, but in what direction is it now? After a while he had the feeling he was back on the route to the station. Fine. Then there it was again: his heart pounding. What if *he* was still there?

As the streets grew steeper, he realized: somehow or other he had ended up behind the station, crossed the tracks without noticing; now he was on his way into the hills. More and more the sidewalk consisted of steps; he ran up them as if he were in a hurry; the iron railing, where there was one, wobbled when he let go of it. Later the stairs and even the houses stopped, leaving only the bad, rough asphalt of the street with its sharp-edged, crumbling curbs. I know this way: it leads to a look-out point up above, the goal of numerous outings, though not in the middle of the night. It was pitch-black between the trees: some places you could easily have kept your eyes shut the way you do when you're running in a dream. He knew it was the way to the tower, but now it seemed endless: I can't imagine ever getting there. It was one of those endless dream rambles where the only thing that happens is that the hill gets steeper. He bent his upper body forward to compensate for the climb. His fingertips touched the asphalt. Crawling on all fours turned out to work well; he kept it up. The first really strange thing I've done in my life: crawling on all fours through a pitch-black wood. The stars shone down on the glossy material of his back. It was not until he reached the look-out tower that he straightened up.

What took place in the following minutes? hours? is not precisely known. He must have looked at the light of the town, because he had never before stood on the hill. He looked at the town from this new perspective and felt, apart from a raging pain that filled his entire body: nothing at all. A small town in the vicinity of three borders, terminus, as the crow flies, dogs. Have I ever been happy?

Yes. As long as he had him. And now? Spend the rest of my life here? The hermit of the look-out tower? A life among carved declarations of love and obscenities and other such proofs of existence? Spending every waking minute observing the maze of the streets? Because starting now everything is the rest and holds no interest for me as such.

A car drove up. The occupants, a couple, did not notice him: they were in too much of a hurry. They began to copulate. Abel waited until the windows had misted over, and walked past them. Later he lost his concentration and slipped on the crumbly edge of the street. He fell on his behind, crawled backwards on his palms and heels for a distance, stopped, remained sitting a while, then stood. His hands and the soles of his feet were in pain: tiny, bloody stones had lodged in the abrasions, though bit by bit they fell away, like the slowly drying soil from the woods on the back of his suit. No matter. He went back down to town.

Was *that* all there was now?

There was one thing. That window, ground floor, at the back of the theater, in that street without name because it was no street at all, just a ford with nothing in it but some parking places for designated vehicles, the artists' entrance, and the aforementioned window across the way. A windowsill so low that (at one time, sometimes) it was easier to knock on the window and climb into the room from there than to go around the corner and use the entrance. Abel came down from the hill, walked through the park and across the tracks: this was his street. He passed the house where Mother and Granny were sleeping, crossed two small squares, each with its own statue, walked around the theater, stood in front of the window. The bare bulb over the artists' entrance shone on his back; he saw himself as a silhouette in the dark windowpane. There was no sign of motion behind it. That made the thumping, banging, jangling, howling, cheering all the louder: it must have been one hell of a party, though perhaps it was just a hallucination, because there was still nothing to see. He waited a while, then gave his image two punches. First in the left, then in the right pane. The splinters tinkled in and rained down on the bed. He saw a grayish flash of bedclothes; nothing else stirred. Or he did not wait for stirrings.

At first lovers love each other as if nothing could be more natural; then they hate each other in the same way. The transition from one state to the other lasts the moment it takes to perceive it, and—this is the painful part—neither side takes it particularly hard. One said: I love you; the other: but I don't love you. Went off, wandered about, climbed a hill, walked back down, fell, stood, broke a window, went home, shut the wardrobe doors, and lay down. Later he awoke with a start, because a heart attack had hurled him out of the bed.

The bed was no bed, just a mattress in the hall wardrobe. He hit the plywood wall as he fell; it must have made a monstrous crash. He landed on his face on the wardrobe floor and lay there. He pressed his damp forehead to the rug on the floor: the grit crunched; he breathed as well as he could and listened—he could do nothing else—to his heart, heart, heart beat. The world is atremble from my gasps.

Anything wrong? Mira called out in front of the wardrobe.

He held his breath: it was easier that way. Unfortunately it increased the burning sensation in his breastbone. Concentrate on something else, on the outside noise: radio, pots and pans, a distant litany. Grandmother seems to be in the kitchen, so it's morning. Or evening again.

Abel?

Mira must be right in front of the wardrobe.

It'll be better soon, better soon, soon . . .

Maybe while he was asleep he just . . . said Mira, walking away. His arm against the wall. He really was getting too big for the thing.

There he lay—face, sweat, grit—waiting for the worst to pass, at which point he slipped in an *unobserved moment* into the bathroom, over to the mirror. He had bruised his cheekbone in the fall from the ten-centimeter-high mattress to the wardrobe floor (!)— only a red speck, but clearly visible.

And what is this?

As he came out of the bathroom, he found Mira in the wardrobe holding up his suit. Filthy from top to bottom. What is this? Soil? And Jesus—she had only then seen his face—you look like death warmed over.

What have you been up to?

Rampaging through town. Drinking, brawling, smashing bottles. (Grandmother) Couldn't sleep, couldn't help hearing.

Shop windows, said Vesna, Aunt Vesna, Mother's best friend. A lesbian! (Granny) Clever eyes, a big nose in a brownish face, a deep, coarse voice: They smashed shop windows.

Who smashed shop windows? (Mira)

It never changes, muttered Grandmother. They get rougher and rougher. Godless, tough, rotten to the core.

Who? asked Mira.

Why should good students do something like that? asked Vesna.

Not everything has a why, said Grandmother.

Vesna laughed. True enough.

Life can so easily go bad, said Mira.

She meant the remark for her son, the one with the bruise on his face. At least she assumed the speck was still there: she hadn't dared to look at *my only son* for several hours. I don't know. Something's changed. Overnight, as the saying goes.

Nor was Abel looking at anyone either. They were sitting in a restaurant, Sunday noon, as was their wont on special occasions, *the three Fates and I.*

Rougher and rougher, let me tell you. I can't understand how anyone could call that fun.

Later two policemen entered the restaurant, stood by the door for a long time, had a talk with the headwaiter, looked in. Abel looked out at them, but they were not interested. They went away.

Later, while they were eating, they heard a rumor—it might have been spirited through the room by the discreet waiters on their trays—to the effect that half the main shopping street had been seriously vandalized (Now don't you think of going there, for heaven's sake! They'll arrest you this time round. It's no tourist attraction), but the students were not the perpetrators or, rather, not the only ones; they were not there from the outset. When they staggered up out of their cellar, *it* had long been underway, and they were so far gone they had no idea what was going on; they just laughed hysterically and stomped around in the debris, the crackling fire in a salesroom mirrored in their eyes. But the fire went out later: the plastic floor burned poorly; all it did was make an awful stink, and apparently somebody had signed for the receipt of so and so many explosives and detonators.

What of it? asked Mira. And: Can't we change the subject?

After the meal the women drank liqueur; they wanted Abel to taste it; he picked up the glass and downed it in one gulp; it was sweet; no matter. Mira gave a sheepish smile; Grandmother clicked her tongue; Vesna laughed appreciatively and downed hers. Tsk, tsk, said Grandmother.

Mira opened her handbag, which contained an envelope with money she had just withdrawn for the meal and an envelope she gave Abel.

Thank you, said Abel.

I'd open it first, said Aunt Vesna.

It was a lottery ticket for a car. The lower category.

Oh, said Abel, who had no driver's license. Thank you.

He slipped the lottery ticket back into the envelope, put the envelope next to his plate, picked up the small fork, and went back to his dessert.

I'm sorry I can't buy you a car, said Mira.

After the summer they had spent riding around looking for Andor, Mira sold the sky-blue car. She also sold or gave away all his clothes and books and tore his pictures out of the albums.

A polite son would have said something at this point, but Abel said nothing.

Hey, said Mira, look at us. We're here.

A lottery ticket, said Vesna later. I can't think of anything better to send a child out into the world with. The world is a chancy place, my boy. If I were you, I'd have given him a pile of chips for the local casino: his chances would have been better. He could have met a few shady characters there; that would have upped his prospects. The underworld will definitely be taking over here in the future; you've got to stay on the right side of them; I personally would rather have a successful mafia boss as a son than . . .

As a what? Mira cried out.

Grandmother muttered curses: ugly witch, Gypsy, blabbermouth.

She's a great guy, said Mira.

Now it's my turn, said Grandmother. She unwrapped a box from a large man's handkerchief. It contained: Grandfather's medals, medals from the war and for achievements at work, a tin box full of tin, which made even Mira blush. Abel placed the lottery ticket over the medals, closed the cover, and announced that he would spend the rest of the summer traveling.

Three women's faces.

Who with? Ilia?

No.

Then who?

Nobody. Alone.

What about Ilia?

. . .

How?

By train.

And where?

He wasn't sure. (Lie.)

Silence.

He's a grown-up man, said Vesna, looking him—over her acne scars and cucumber nose—straight in the eye, and gave him what was for us a large foreign banknote. It would come in handy some day.

DOG DAYS

Disappeared: The mayor of a small community in D. during the ceremony celebrating his re-election. The chaos scholar returning from a conference. The former youth chorus conductor N.N., who so and so many days ago started out from Boca de Inferno in Portugal to cross the Eurasian continent on foot all the way to the Kola Peninsula. On 12 June twenty years ago: Abel Nema's father.

One half Hungarian, other half unclear: claimed he had the blood *of all the minorities in the region* in him; a newcomer, a Gypsy, a ventriloquist and adventurer who could play two flutes at the same time and the balalaika and who knows what else. There were always new things coming out about him. That was irritating and impressive, said Mira; as long as you want to believe in someone, that kind of thing is impressive. An alcoholic for sure or before you know it, said Granny when she saw how many Turkish coffees he could put away, but he wasn't one for prognoses: he remained unpredictable to the end.

Standing in front of the house, six A.M. on the first day of the summer holidays, the sunrays beating down on him along the street running from the station. A thick, gold arrow pointing at him, though with a radiance and intensity that made it feel like noon.

That it was actually quite a bit later, thought Andor Nema, and he presumably didn't have much time to lose. Or something to that effect. The last perception of him that Abel, lying in his wardrobe, had was the sound of the seven steps he needed to cross the entry hall. One-two-three-four-five-six-seven. The door. Quietly open, more quietly: shut. By one hour and forty minutes later, when he was scheduled to begin his first class, Andor had left the town. He went, as he had come, with empty pockets, except for some loose change, a packet of cigarettes, a handkerchief. He had left behind his empty clothes, a ramshackle car, and a box full of postcards.

Before he begat his only son, Abel, Andor Nema had had twelve loves. One of them had died by her own hand; one resided in a psychiatric hospital; with the others he exchanged postcards. He kept the latter in a box along with old love letters and photographs. Mira would laugh: The vain old goat!

Everything I know I've learned from women, Andor said. They are my teaching staff. They will always be with me.

Mira laughed: The twelve Norns.

Thirteen, my dear, said Andor, thirteen.

Mira turned red.

He had not told the truth. He did not take the box with him. Mira waited a week, then drove—poorly at first, not having driven for years (Abel, how do you feel? I'm about to throw up)—off in search of the ten relevant (non-dead, non-crazy) women. Ten women stood on nine thresholds (two were sisters who had eventually become friends again and were even living together), stared at the boy, and shook their heads.

The last woman she visited—we could actually have begun with her—was a woman called Bora. For Abel, at the time, Bora was a man's name, but a woman stood on the threshold. Andor's first love was the only one living alone, in the same tiny one-room flat as twenty years ago, in a building typical of Andor's city of birth: with internal balconies and gas fumes. The boy first looked through the rectangle of sky above the inner courtyard: empty; then down at the doormat. He saw the woman only from the waist down: the ocher raw-silk skirt from her mother's Sunday outfit ("You're a whore, my dear") which she wore around the house. Each side had an empty belt loop of heavy thread; you could look through them into the apartment (nothing, dark). Further down, legs and then feet in clogs: big, masculine feet. Bora the woman looked the boy over, as all the others had, and said, as all the others had, she didn't know where Andor was. It was so long ago. You've got to believe me.

Mira did not believe her but left. Just before she did, she asked if she could use her toilet.

Be my guest, said Bora, pointing to a small door in the far corner of the single room.

What's your name? she asked the boy when they were alone.

He said his name.

Thank you, said Mira. They went back to the car. Mira sat in the driver's seat, Abel in the back seat. And there they stayed two whole days. The height of summer. Thirty-five in the shade, twice as much in the car, and no wind coming through the open window, only the sluggish stink of man, animal, and machine. Either Mira was convinced she was right or she was clueless. They sat there in the car and kept their eyes peeled on the entrance to the house. Instead of Bora's toilet they used the toilet in a nearby cellar bar in which it was so dark and cold that the regulars caught colds in mid-August. They sat there sneezing. Well? they said to the skinny, timid boy. Well? they said to the well-built foreign woman. That somber look in her eyes was very becoming. The haughty way she paraded in and out.

They live in a blue car, one regular reported to the others. I wonder what's going on there; she looks real ladylike, could even be a teacher. What's she living in a car for? There's got to be a man behind this. A man from here she's come all this way to see. And the fruit of their love is in the backseat. When the men climbed back up into the heat after hours in the cold, their inebriation socked them in the face and they forgot all about the woman in the car, but next day the fine, wine-redolent, fountain-like cool of the cellar brought it all back, and they started up from where they had left off. The sky-blue car somehow offended their sensibilities. Somebody ought to be informed; somebody ought to come and see. But where did you go to and who did you go to in such a case? Later they came up with an idea: they posted a lookout at the door.

She's coming, said the lookout and stumbled down the stairs. They all took up their posts; in other words, they stayed where they were, miming the regulars they were. Mira came in, crossed the room, pressed the handle of the door to the toilet: occupied.

She looked around: a single, tiny room, glasses and men in the dark, still and shimmering like wax figures in different though very similar drinking poses, all eyes on her. All she needed was the slightest giggle, source unknown, to tell her it was a trap. A joke. She was certain—how?—that it was meant as a joke, nothing else, nothing, as it might well have been, more dangerous, yet for the first time in the summer she felt something other than rage and determination: frailty and fear. She pulled over an empty chair and sat on it. The wax figures suddenly came to life, moved closer, eyes glistening with joy, talking gibberish, pushing glasses and bottles of wine and soda water in her direction. The soda-water bottle glugged as if about to break out in tears.

I'm about to break out in tears. A pretty scene: a woman coming from nowhere pours out her grief over a faithless lover to agelessly drunken strangers, and though they do not speak her language they understand her because that language is universal, and even if they cannot help her they will at least share their feelings and curse the bastard roundly in their own language, because their lost drinker existence exhibits more moral sensibility than . . .

Two women's ankles-calves-knees passed before the gleaming rectangle of the entry, everything else vanishing into the dazzling white light. The boy out in the car.

Sorry, said Mira and stood up. The foreign tongue paralyzed the men again: mute, they watched her leave.

They began driving again. When they were well out of the city, Mira stopped the car and urinated behind a bush. Abel counted the cars coming in their direction. One thousand. One thousand and one.

A WOMAN BY THE
NAME OF BORA

Disappeared, seven years later, after leaving a graduation party and taking a walk: Ilia B. Abel waited a few days to see what would happen, whether he or *somebody* would turn up, but nothing came of it. It was not clear whether Ilia was still in town. Finally Abel left too.

He took the train, chugging along with people he did not know through regions he did not know. *Look at the trees walking.* Many villages seemed strapped down between power lines. Having little money to spare, he took locals but lost no time otherwise: he went straight to the right station.

It was summer, as it had been then, the station full of orange light. On both levels plus the basement there were people standing, squatting, lying amidst their baggage, waiting for a train or taking up residence. Careful not to step on a sleeper or upset a picnic basket, Bora made her way through them from the covered market to the trolleybus. There were floods of people with more baggage coming from the tracks; she kept having to alter her pace: it was a veritable migration of peoples. Later she thought they must have been on the same bus home, he perhaps among the troublemakers, because before she could unload the shopping bag, before the clogs she had slipped out of had cooled down, there was a ring at the door.

She stood barefoot on the threshold, second floor to the right, green door, small enamel plaque: No. 3.

Who did you want?

My name is . . . said Abel. I'm the son of . . .

Jesus, she said and curled her bare toes on the stone.

Why don't we start by sitting at the kitchen table, it's right here, next to the door, wait, I'll put the bag away. Not much natural light from the courtyard came through the glass in the door, though it did just make it to the table; the rest of the tubelike room was dark except for a patch of white, the shower curtain, at the far end.

It was not behind this curtain that Andor hid that day; it was in the tiny room next to the toilet Mira had used. He could hear his wife urinating. Bora had gone to work or shopping, making believe she did not notice the conspicuous sky-blue car parked a few buildings down the street. The boy seemed to be suffering from the heat and lay doubled up on the back seat. Two days later, when they were still there and she saw the woman going down into the bar while the boy stayed behind in the back seat, she tore open the door and said, Get out of my house.

What? said Andor. Now? This minute?

Damn it to hell, said Bora.

When Andor stepped into the street, he swayed and blinked from the heat. The boy in the back seat shut his eyes. Mira sat down on a cool chair. By the time she had stood up and come out, the street was empty.

I'm sorry, said the boy. I shut my eyes.

No, said Mira. I'm the one who's sorry.

Whether Andor saw the sky-blue car is unclear. His back in the side street, his bright bell-bottom trousers sparkled in the sun. Or maybe I merely dreamed it all. Look straight ahead, said Mira to Abel, or you'll be sick again.

. . .

Bora thinks it must have been a matter of seconds. I'm very sorry. The last time she'd heard about him he was working with a crew of forty in a French shipyard, but that was years ago, and who knew whether it was true or not. He had no idea about shipbuilding. Not that I know of. On the other hand. Anything's possible. Andor, the orphan with twelve mothers. One after the other and to some extent all at once.

She looks at the boy: a tall nineteen-year-old, somewhat thinner, paler, and more disheveled than usual. You can tell he's been on a train for twelve hours; not only that, he's brought the smell with him, the smell of the train; he'll never get rid of it. He has his father's eyes, which here in the dark look black, but Bora knows that they are actually the color of a raging sky: violet and gray. His mother is present too, in his features, sleepy as they are, but his overriding attribute is something else, something he is completely unaware of but Bora sees perfectly well. This there-is-no-word-for-it, this *provocation* that radiates from him, that calls forth an *excitement* in everyone who meets him, the compulsion to have something to do with him in one way or another.

As long as he was *with someone*, this—what shall we call it—flair did not make itself felt. The *other* shielded him from it. Besides, he may have been too young. But now, as Vesna said after the dessert, he's a man. During that first lonely train ride all eyes were automatically on him. He did his best to look out of the window, but no matter what you do, *read* (just one example), we simply won't leave you in peace. Nice people, fellow passengers, the older ones in particular, engaged him in intimate conversation: Who are you, young man? Where are you from, where are you going? Working his way— intentionally overdoing a bit his natural timidity, though always courteous—from truth to lie: From S. To see relatives. An *aunt*.

Really now, said the plainclothesman. This was the second time he had been checked on the train. In the meantime everyone in the car could have told the story every bit as well. What is your aunt's name and where does she live?

. . .

What's the matter? Didn't he understand the question? I'm sure he can make up a name and address.

Leave the young man alone, will you? said the old woman opposite him when the man came back a third time. He's just finished his exams. I know him. He's a good boy. Let him go and see his aunt.

The plainclothesman took a good look at his papers, then again at his face, as if to stamp its image precisely on his memory. When he had finally gone, the old woman gave Abel a piece of chocolate. What's your name, my boy?

That is how it went; that is how it would go from then on: love or kill. For Bora it was the former. There must be a family somewhere, she says by way of consolation, but even as she says it she is so jealous that her voice cracked. *She* wanted to keep him. She, she, she. Here and now bind him to her by caring for him, helping him, doing things for him . . . But that was mad.

Abel shook his head.

Thank you, he wasn't hungry.

Thirsty?

To that he does nod. There they sit, at the kitchen table; he with the door at his back, she facing him; she drinking wine, he schnapps and water. Evening came. Funny, thinks Bora, wasn't it just morning? She is still barefoot, but the infusion of alcohol in her body delivers regular doses of warmth. The boy in the chair facing her does not move. Let me put the kettle on for you. Did he nod or not? She sits back down. Evening noises. Neighbors, corridors, shoes, keys. Light switches, water, flowerpots. Cats, pigeons, a child crying, a children's song. A badly tuned in station, pop music, not enough bass. The streetlight in front of the house crackling as it goes on. Cars, car doors, curses, pedestrians. Women, men. The grill on the nearby grocery. A drill, a window opening. Men throwing their dogs plastic rings. Whistles over cement. A group of students who have finished their exams. Bodies, shouts, laughter. Later an orchestra rehearsing. The *New World Symphony*. Adagio. Later television. Later silence. Later drunks, then silence again. The boiler going on and off. You can undress now. The water's warm.

Her tongue is heavy from all the silence and drink: I'm going to bed.

She makes him a bed out of woolen blankets. There is room on the far shore of the rug, between the desk and the door to the toilet. She closes her eyes and wonders whether she should make believe she's sleeping when he comes in or, on the contrary, talk to him, and whether he has any idea she is sixty. Almost. Bora the woman thinks of sex with the son of the man whose first love she was and—the alcohol or whatever—tears well up in her eyes. Before they can reach her eyelids, though, she has fallen asleep.

Wake up! Wake up!

The door to the courtyard is open, as is the window in the room, but it makes no difference: cross ventilation is out of the question.

Wake up! Wake up!

She slaps his face wildly. He is still on the kitchen chair, his shoulders and head leaning against the wall.

Oh my God! Sobbing, she grabs the pot from the stove and a newspaper with the other hand, waves it, lets it go, pours out some water, washes his forehead. Ohmygodohmygodohmygod!

The water runs into his eyes. It is the water she used to boil the eggs the day before, with salt and vinegar, but that may actually help. The first time he stirs, he squeezes his eyes further shut and may have moaned as well. Everything in his face is the same color: wax.

Wake up! Bora shouts. You must wake up! I know it hurts, but you must open your eyes! We have gas! Can you hear me?

He doesn't stir, though he's breathing. Bora gives a cough, which turns into sobs, which she suppresses. Seizes him under the armpits, jerks him off the chair; chair topples, clatter echoes in the courtyard. She has to twist him to get him between the table and the stove. Gets caught on the pot handle; flings it to the floor. It hits Abel's ankle before landing: yesterday's water seeps into his trouser leg; a small piece of egg white sticks to the dark fabric.

The damned kettle she put on for him and then forgot. The flame must have gone out during the night. She could hardly open her eyes in the morning; the alarm clock rang, kept ringing; I usually wake up before it, and if she had forgotten to set it they might never have woken up, but she forced her eyelids open into a raging headache, everything—eyes, ears, nasal passages—burning as if chafed, mouth lined with metal, dizzy, down on all fours to the kitchen, then trying to wake him.

She drags him over the stone floor to the door. Groans, strains. It's only a few steps to the threshold, but I thought I'd never make it. Her fingers bore deeply into his armpits. Finally at the door she lets him down, carefully, his head in her hands. The threshold is now under his neck, his head outside the doorway, visible from the neighbor's door. Bora points at her, there, this head, lying here, would she please call an ambulance and fast.

And the gas company? the neighbor asks. Bora shakes her head.

You've got to notify the gas company in such cases, says another neighbor.

In the fifteen minutes it takes for the ambulance to come all the people who are at home have gathered on the galleries surrounding the courtyard and are looking down at the man in the doorway, on the mat, next to the flowerpot.

MIRACLE

Hello, I've killed your son.

No.

Ohmygodohmygodohmygod, said Bora, running all over the hospital—talk to somebody, the doctors have no time, a freckled medical student looks after him as best she can, takes his pulse and blood pressure, looks helpless, tries to calm her down—all over town, home, all over the house.

Looking through his things, she came up with a telephone number with a foreign prefix and, in parentheses after it, (school). She copied the number, crumpled up the slip of paper she had written it on, ran all over, smearing the penciled number. To phone or not to phone. In the end she realized that even if she managed to let Mira know there wasn't much she could do. Come here? It wasn't as easy as all that, not anymore it wasn't. Arrivals at the station had doubled in the two days he'd been out cold; if that was possible. There'd be a war if there wasn't one already. Ohgodohgodohgod.

She sat on the kitchen chair she had sat on when facing him. I don't need to let her know until he's dead. Hello. I've murdered your son.

. . .

Prime bjen esasa ndeo, said the boy. *Prime.*

What?

Songo. Nekom kipleimi fatoje. Pleida pjanolö.

What's he saying? You hear that, nurse?

Three men, any of whom could have been his father, and one his grandfather, standing around his bed. They are wearing pajamas, bathrobes, and bandages. Bending over him like weeping willows. The nurse parts the branches with her body, moves in closer, puts her hand on his forehead.

Just a fever, she says. He's a foreigner.

You think you understand what he's saying, and then you don't, said one of them, the youngest, who was wearing a striped bathrobe. German words, Russian words. I don't understand the others. Though there's something of ours in it too.

They stand there. Later the oldest man sits on the next bed, because he's tired. For a while the boy talks less. Later he starts in again. The three of them sit or lie in their beds listening. Sometimes they can pick out words, but on the whole . . .

Avju mjenemi blest aodmo. Bolestlju. Ai.

I wonder if this is the death chamber, says Mr. Stripes, his eyes gleaming in the direction of the other two. Well? What do you think? (Grinning.) You know the joke about the death chamber, don't you?

The other two mumble something. Grandpa pulls his blanket down over his bare feet.

Know the joke about the death chamber? Mr. Stripes asks the nurse.

The nurse does not respond: she is taking Abel's pulse.

Everybody knows the joke about the death chamber, says the Third Man.

Don't be ridiculous, says the nurse. Nobody's going to die here.

She pulls the blanket tight around him. As if it were necessary. As if he were moving.

What does he have?

The nurse shrugs.

Abel sighs.

That was a sigh.

Then: nothing more. He is asleep.

Three days during which his condition was basically stable. The fever rose and fell according to its lights. He spoke from time to time, but more at the beginning; towards the end he grew calmer, merely sighed, and, finally, on the third day he awoke to find three elderly men standing at his bed.

Hello, said the youngest in the striped bathrobe who spoke foreign languages. Awake, I see.

Blank stare.

Will you look at the eyes on him!

Do you understand what I'm saying? asked Mr. Stripes.

He hesitates, but nods. The three men literally break out in a cheer. He understands! They tried other sentences. During each he looked as if he were hearing a revelation, and at the end of each he nodded as if giving his approval. Yes, yes, yes, yes.

Don't say anything, said Bora, kissing him all over and pressing his head between her breasts. Don't say anything, anything, anything.

He said nothing. At first he merely listened. Over the last few years he had nearly forgotten his father's language; he had said no more to Bora than three broken sentences, and now he was internalizing every word, every sentence he heard, and even if he did not understand everything he could tell where they made a mistake; he could picture the constructions as if they grew out of his fellow patients' mouths in the form of branch-like patterns. He stared at them.

I don't know why, Grandpa muttered to the Third Man, but I don't like the way he keeps staring at a single point.

Later Abel asked Bora whether she could lend him the coins or a card for a long-distance call, and she was so happy that she failed to notice the change in his grammar and pronunciation.

Without knowing what he would say, he phoned Mira.

As if out of breath: Where are you? Have you found him?

Pause. Her frenzied breath.

No.

Goddamn him! Where are you? Are you with her? Stay there or move on; look for him, the son of a bitch, if you need him, but don't come back here. (She burst into tears:) Oh God, your studies! (She stopped crying. Continued in a frenzy:) You've been called up. They've been taking young men off buses and trams. Listen, have you got something to write with? Write this down.

She gave him a name. Unfortunately she had neither address nor telephone number. He lived in B. He'd have to find out in B.

A stranger's name on the back of Bora's slip of paper.

Have you got it?

Yes, said Abel.

Silence.

Everything okay?

Yes, said Abel.

He listened hard. He could hear ten or twelve other voices on the line. He also heard the voices in the hall and in the wards, the TV set in the TV room: it was tuned to an English-language station.

I think she's hung up, said Bora softly. She put her arm around his shoulder and led him back to his room.

What went on in Abel's brain during those three days is hard to ascertain. He himself has no recollection of it, just an idea along the lines of a Somebody who keeps pushing around the pieces of a puzzle until a completely new picture emerges. That is how he organized, reorganized the maze in Abel Nema's theretofore equally developed and undifferentiated aptitude for all school subjects until everything that had theretofore played a role in his life—the swarm of memory and projection, of past and future that blocked the passageways and filled the rooms with their hullabaloo—was stowed away, in secret closets somewhere, and he, now empty, was ready to accept a single brand of knowledge: language. Such is the miracle that befell Abel Nema.

I will donate a marble plaque and evermore be pious, said Bora and packed a lunch box for him.

PART II

THE VISITOR

Hysteria, Lamento

FOOD I. KONSTANTIN

They came out of the court together, the women considerately, unobtrusively, accommodating themselves to Abel's tempo. (No, I'm not angry; I just want to get it over with.) They had heard the last sequence of the noon bells in the foyer; it broke off just as they opened the door to the street. They stood on the steps, he slightly dizzy in the sudden bright light: it was some time since he had eaten last, plus the loss of blood, but then all of that receded into the background, because—an unearned pleasure it was—the boy was there. He threw his arms around him and kissed him. Then, because it was so close, he went, he *limped*, to the park: he had blood in his shoe but could make it that far.

A park like that is a good thing: you can sit on a bench, gather your thoughts for a moment. The homeless at the southern end who are here the whole summer: We're just gathering our thoughts for a moment. In the smell of the tortured grass, of the drought-ridden plants, the out-of-commission fountain, themselves, their dogs, the food they fetch daily at noon at the church's soup kitchen. Otherwise they budge not an inch. They sit there all day and all night in a semicircle of stone niches, more or less symmetrical, six to a side. In the middle sits a fat man in splendor, one knee to the southwest-west, the other to the southeast-east, the putative commander of this raggle-taggle Olympus, a paved sun at his feet with a fountain at its center. It is broken. The water splashes onto the ground. What the dogs do not lap up runs off between their masters' feet. To the left, behind the bushes, a public toilet; to the right two wire cages for soccer players and a bench no one sits on, not even now, during lunch hour, when the park is full of office workers: the Thai laundry with its broken, constantly wailing doorbell is right behind it and no one can stand the yowl for long. Abel did not seem to mind it, though: he fell asleep the moment he sat down.

Well, look at that, said Konstantin Tóti. Well, what do you know.

The day had started out miserably for Konstantin T. with his getting up: *miserable. It* was stuck in his head and kept everything else out. With the help of water—cold, rubbed into the eyes, and lukewarm, gargled—things slowly improved. So much for breakfast. Later he thought things would be better in the (fresh) air, but they weren't. It made him dizzy, and he had gone too far from home and the soup kitchen wasn't yet open. I may faint any minute now. He had to buy a pretzel at a stand. Something like that can ruin your whole day: the few pitiful pennies for that slimy thing. Furious and dying to sink his teeth into it and tear a piece off. Walking through the park.

At the northern end two convicts were working off their sentence by scraping the tar and feathers off the peace swans. The odor of all-purpose glue and solvent, bits of down floating like late seeds through the air. Pillow feathers, goose or duck, with a few white chicken feathers thrown in, but most of all polyester stuffing. They were being guarded by one male and one female police officer as well as two Russians from the nearby old people's home.

Where I come from, we'd have called it a student prank.

Worthy of Ulyanov the anarchist.

The two old Russians laughed.

You're Russians? asked Konstantin, pretzel in hand.

Bela—said one sullenly, the other merely giving him a suspicious look. Then off they went, still conversing, but in softer voices than before.

Other people came and went, taking pictures of the ever balder

swans. A dog-sitter stopped next to the police officers, her dogs
restless with the smell, the feathers. When the policewoman bent
over to pet a spaniel, the dog-sitter's shoulder grazed the policeman's upper arm. Lightly and just for a second, as if by chance,
as if she had lost her balance, but it was not by chance. One of
the young convicts and K.T., who was passing by, had noticed it.
The policeman was nearly two meters tall and blond, she scarcely
one meter fifty and dark. Her shoulder touched him just above the
elbow. By the time the policewoman had stood up straight, the girl
with the dogs was on her way. Konstantin stared after her open-
mouthed. Then over to the policeman. The giant saw he was being
looked at and glared back. The guy must hate me. Somewhere
behind the trees the church clock struck: four times bright, twice
dark, bong, bong. The cop finally gave up when the bells began to
chime. Relieved, a bit triumphant, then again somewhat anxious,
Konstantin wrapped the rest of his pretzel in the undersized and
now grease-soaked napkin that came with it, and stuck it in his
pocket. It looked ridiculous, but what can you do? He moved on.

He didn't arrive at the soup kitchen until the last bits were being
scratched out of the pots. He had taken his time: he was over the
worst of his hunger; besides, the big crush was something he
wanted to . . . For a while he lurked in the bushes, but he could
not get a good enough view from there, so he went over to the
broken fountain, spreading his legs to keep the water from falling
on his shoes. Though a few drops did. The sun shone on his green
sweater. Too warm. That's because I live in an apartment where not
even flies can survive. When I look out of the window, I can't tell
if we're having a heat wave or a cold alert. While he drank, he eyed
the remains on a plastic plate a homeless person had left on the
paved sun: noodles with a red sauce and salad. The plate was being
licked clean by a dog. The dog was eating the salad too. Two men
came up to him just before he reached the soup kitchen. One of
them was wheeling a rusty bicycle. Good, sweet, green tea, he said
to the other. The other nodded.

We've run out, said the woman with the food. Stern, but good-
natured.

Konstantin peered into a pot. Bits of noodle on an aluminum background.

They're cold, said the woman. Sauce is gone too.

Konstantin peered into another pot. There were patches of sauce along the sides, in the corners too.

Sizing up the situation herself, the stern woman finally (sigh) took a large ladle of noodles and plopped it into the nearly empty sauce pot, pushed the noodles around with the ladle, scratching aluminum against aluminum, until they were all to some extent red. Pulling them back together was another matter. They slipped and tore. A ladle of wounded noodles.

Where's your bowl?

My bowl?

Your plate, your mess kit, your plastic container.

Konstantin made a gesture of helplessness. Nothing. In one pocket a bulge of keys, in the other, oh yes, a crumpled handkerchief. And the pretzel. It crumpled too. Don't carry everything in your pockets.

The woman with the (heavy) ladle in her (arthritic) hand bent down and pulled a plastic plate out from under the table. A second, fluted disposable thingy was stuck to it; she tried to hold them with four fingers and use the fingernail of the fifth to separate them. The ladle still in the other hand.

Here, let me . . .

It's okay. She slopped the noodles into the two plates. Here.

Thanks.

Here, a plastic spoon, and here, in a plastic cup, lukewarm tea.

God bless you.

She gave him a look. She's not having any of my holy holy crap. She went back to her clean-up job. Konstantin stood there eating. Every once in a while he would pick up the cup and have a drink of tea. Good, sweet, green tea. Another woman and a Franciscan monk were helping the first woman tidy up. The monk had a long white beard; it practically covered his face, but the body and eyes were those of a young man. The women spoke, the monk did not. He merely nodded or shook his head, whichever was called for.

Has he taken a vow of silence?

Come again?

The monk.

No.

I didn't know this was a monastery.

It isn't. Have you finished? Was it good? Give me the plate.

Konstantin wiped his mouth.

Praise be to God.

He didn't even respond to that. The beard is split beneath the mouth. Red scar tissue beneath the split. Who sliced up his face? Konstantin looked him in the eye to see whether he had been good-looking. Before. Then he forgot about it.

I, that is, me, I've been toying with the idea—I apologize for disturbing you with my stammerings, my web of subjunctives and lies, but I, Konstantin Tóti, feel the urgent need to withdraw for a time to a monastery, it being a matter of both a scholarly project and a turn inward I find ever more necessary. I might even go so far as to become a monk, yes, I am seriously considering becoming a monk; it's an idea I once had as a child, when I was eleven or twelve; Fulbert had Abelard castrated; in short, I need a bit of rest, I need to collect myself and turn to God. The urgent issue is the choice faced by K.T. of whether to go underground or to stay above ground by acquiring false papers. He greatly fears acquiring false papers: he has committed an error and given his real name, but he had to do it, or not. Of course he doesn't mention a thing about it here—not that they think I'm a criminal, not yet. I could see myself being called Father Pierre, though I've heard there are fellowships available for young scholars and Christians . . .

Excuse me, said the stern woman. I'm sorry, Father. You've come to the wrong place. You might want to go and see . . .

By now I (Konstantin) am growing a little impatient: Excuse me. I'm talking to the Father now.

He looked over expectantly at the Father. As did the woman. There was a short pause.

Exoose, said the Father after a pause. Made the sign of the cross over Konstantin's bewildered face, left.

Satisfied?

What's with the guy?

Nothing. Did you hear what he said or didn't you.

What *did* he say?

That he's sorry, I assume. As am I. And now please leave.

What's with the guy? Why does he wear that white beard?

Must you know everything?

Is it a secret?

It's no secret. It's just none of your business. We're closing now.

It's no disgrace . . .

Time to go.

What did I do wrong?

She said nothing more, just waved him away with her hands: out, out. He moved backwards, still facing her.

Why must you be so hostile? Eh? Now you won't even talk to me. What . . .

Outside at the door. Trees gleaming in late-summer light, beauty. Konstantin realized he was full. Stuffed. He could have saved the money he'd spent on the pretzel. And the remains were making his pocket greasier and greasier.

The next thing he knew he was back at the fountain, a hundred meters away, and you're thirsty again and your shoes are getting splashed again, and then: Well, what do you know! A minute later he was back on the park bench near the Thai laundry with the wailing doorbell and next to him sat sleeping: the droopy-headed (nearly) divorced translator Abel Nema. Tóti waited until he woke up and said, So, you're still here too.

FOOD II. TIBOR

All he had was the name on the slip of paper. Standing on a bleak, dirt-colored platform, early in the morning, Abel Nema, nineteen, just off the train, *here*, holding a slip of paper with an unfamiliar name. A paper crumpled by time and space, the handwriting all but undecipherable partly because it had begun to dissolve in the underground and partly because it had simply become *different*.

At first it looked as if he would never wake up—he had slept a full three days through—and when he finally did regain consciousness there were all sorts of symptoms. It began with his losing his way on the way back to the ward from the toilet, and he had wandered up and down the hospital corridors—how long?—until Bora found him. Poor boy. Totally confused. Then there was the problem that since the time he had woken up he could hardly sleep—one or two hours a day—but that may have been only because he'd slept too much. Another symptom was that he might just as well have thrown the paper away or never even have written anything on it because from that time on he would never forget anything that was language and memorizable. Still he could not bring himself to throw away the paper: the new constellation in his brain and in the things around him seemed too fragile. He would—if he removed even the smallest piece of the new structure—be tearing up something that was not meant to be torn, that had just begun; whether it was good or bad nobody knew; it was what was possible.

Standing on the platform, a similar season, similar weather, the first cold ash-redolent wind from the east announcing autumn. A slice of the city on the far side of the platform: a sky riddled with wires, a few high-rises including one in which he would live the next four years, on the eleventh floor, though of course he did not know it yet. At the time the station was less shopping experience than loading platform, all reticent gray and malodorous. He accordingly saw no steps leading down from the tracks, only a ramp, a gigantic, fluted ramp designed for much more than the few early-morning travelers. Texas cattle. He walked down the ramp.

In the underpass he followed the signs through the usual station echoes and lights. Left and right numbers and stairs, then a row of eggshell-colored lockers, toilets, telephones. Finally he came to a small post office. He asked for a telephone book.

The name with a number. Write it down or not?

Excuse me, how do I make a phone call?

On his first day, his first hour, a sullen-looking somebody with a tendency to drink hard and fight hard gave him two coins without slowing his pace. Abel said a polite thank-you to his benefactor's overgrown neck, but he was out of earshot by then. Your good deed for the day.

Then he excused himself again. He was given your name. He was from S.

Oh, said the voice on the other end of the line. Sluggish, distant. Did I wake him? What time is it? Early.

And you've just arrived?

Yes.

Where are you?

At the station.

I see.

You take the metro, get off at such and such a station, then right, left, etc. Listening to the directions over the phone, Abel understood not a word, and the moment he hung up, even the chance scraps he had managed to hold on to for a few seconds faded away. The city had one of the most transparent systems of public transport in the world. Abel stared at the network, stared and stared. By now the ramps and stairways were full; suddenly it was noisier than it had ever been—*ye who come from quiet backwaters*—and there were so many people you could scarcely move. Sorry, he stammered. Sorry.

Where to? Middle-aged woman, wrinkled brow.

He said the name of the station.

Red line, said the woman, pointing as she walked.

Thank you, said Abel to nobody. The doors shut. During the ride he kept his eyes glued to the diagram over the door as if one could help the train to remain on course: red line, red line. It was a long ride. His backpack on the wrong side in the wrong place in the crowd. He had been swept away from any hold-on opportunity, but it made little difference from the point of view of balance: the other bodies pressing against his kept him upright. There was talk too: the windows misted over. I rode through the city without seeing a thing, entered a tunnel in the gray of dawn, emerged into a sunny day, at some other end of the city.

The man's name was Tibor; he was a professor at one of the local universities. What Mira's connection with him was, no idea; none at all perhaps: a note on a colleague's desk, an article set down by the wind between her feet. A distant son of our town.

My name is Anna. I'm his wife. Today, here, the first happy person.

A voice all but ecstatic, jubilation at the end of each word. We've been expecting you! Leave your things in the hall! The first door to your left! She fairly danced attendance on him.

My husband's study. Just what you'd imagine. The spartan variant. Bookshelves on three of the four walls; a desk; a table, which they will sit at; a window showing something green. Tibor has a bony face and skin that looks windburned, though he clearly spends most of his time at this desk. The yellow eyelids—curtains ready to fall; the voice hoarse from tobacco as if emerging from sleep; hesitant in speech. A pause before every question.

Pause.

So you're from S. How old are you?

Nineteen.

Pause. A cigarette lit. Rough yellow fingernails; hands that look accustomed to work.

I was younger than you when I left. Haven't been back for nearly fifty years. *Something* has always stood in the way.

At this point Tibor smiled for the first time. He did not want to ask the next question, but as it was he did: What are things like there?

Abel did not want to shrug, but.

I see, said Tibor. Another smile.

Yet another in the doorway. A fifty-year-old, gray-blond girl with a tray.

You must be starved!

Abel couldn't say.

See what a little coffee and cake will do for you, Anna said cheerfully and set the tray down on the table. Tibor waited patiently until she had left the room—on tiptoe, all solicitude and grace, even her fine back smiling—and then asked, Are you religious?

Why precisely that question with the bread and butter?

Abel looked around but saw nothing of help. He bit into a roll, had a gulp of the black soup, swallowed, and finally said, *There are times when I feel full of love and devotion* . . .

Pause. Tibor smiled. The eyelid curtains rose and fell. He nodded.

I'm not either. We are not redeemed. There are no ifs or buts about it.

Abel turned over the food in his oral cavity as quietly as he could. He had begun to sense it before, but now it was definitive: there was something wrong with his taste buds. Everything tasted like chalky wallpaper. The coffee like overly hot water. When he put a sugar cube in his mouth, there was something *there*, but it was too vague: he couldn't have said it was *sweet*. Tibor flicked the last ashes from his cigarette.

What plans did he have. For here. A circular motion with the cigarette butt.

Shoulders. Looks around again. Has a look at the *here*. Lots of books. Mira had got rid of Andor's things down to the last hand-kerchief, the books too, at the Saint George Street secondhand bookshop. He would have bought them back later and stored them in the trunk in Ilia's room, but Abel no longer remembers *which* they were . . . It would be perfectly possible to stay right here, stretch out on the rug in front of the shelves, and read one's way leisurely through the books. It would take some time of course. The man who lived in a library.

The sun shone through the green of the windowpanes; there he sat with his rolls and butter and coffee; what was going on in his head; was he paying attention at all?

Originally, he finally said, *at home* he was going to be a teacher. Of what?

Geography and history for no particular reason. But that was out of the question now. I could say everything and nothing about the First World War. Or deposits of raw materials . . . Maybe some-thing to do with languages.

Aha. Which do you know?

The roll in the boy's hand began to tremble; he put it down; this didn't mean anything anyway. He began to think. He thought: *Semmel*, *zsemle*, bread, roll, *bulochka*, *petit pain*. Thought: *Butter*, *vaj*, butter, *maslo*, *beurre*. Thought . . .

What to do with this new ability was not quite clear. There were high points—words, cases, syntagmas—but the languages kept getting mixed up: I start out in Russian and end up in French. That doesn't matter, he realized now: he couldn't prove or demonstrate anything; it was one big muddle. And then he said, My mother tongue, my father tongue plus three international languages.

Well, well, said Tibor. A good beginning.

Löffel, *kanál*, spoon. I have no sentences, just words. All the sen-tences were with *him*; I was just the audience, and today I'm . . .

What was your name again?

Ilia.

Ilia who?

Bor. No. Why not? Make believe you're him. A stranger rather than another stranger. And then? . . .

No, he said, not, sorry, I was in . . . Abel. Abel Nema.

Pause.

And? Are you furious too, Abel Nema?

Pause. The *old man* was still smiling. The *young man* just sat there.

Somewhere a fly was buzzing.

No, not a fly; the doorbell. Someone new has come: voices in the entry hall, moving towards the door.

May I?

Girl or young woman, big black eyes, short black hair, a few glimmering strands of beard.

Mercedes. Come in, come in. My assistant Mercedes.

Abel Nema. No function as of yet. His fingers were buttery: there was nothing for him to wipe them on. He stood there inept.

She glanced over at him. Her eyes looked as though she had been crying, but she had not. Some eyes simply look that way. They were both very young at this moment: she twenty-six, he nineteen. It was his first day, she one of his first people here. She had no reason to engage in such calculations; she smiled politely, detached.

I have an idea, said Tibor. Come to my office tomorrow. I'll be in, and we can talk things over.

Mercedes stepped aside to let him pass.

Good-bye.

The other woman, Anna, had disappeared. Was there water running somewhere? Abel picked up his things in the entry hall and left.

So we're back to where we started from: an unfamiliar city stretching out between now and tomorrow. By the second time we are old friends with the S-Bahn. A few of the stations have beautiful names, as do one or another of the streets when the train comes out into the open. Advertisements, ubiquitous promises. Christ is with you! Learn the language of your choice. Lawyers will help you solve your problems! Orthodontists will help you solve your problems! Winter is on the way! Take that trip while you can!

Later. I'll travel later perhaps. For the moment he has just arrived, a young man with a backpack; what is going on in his head? An elderly woman with a very big, brightly made up mouth gives him a curious look.

He was thinking: *Esszettbeekaefhaajoto. Esszettbeekaefhaajoto.* Or: the way Abel Nema registered this stretch of the red S-Bahn line, the way he would henceforth register each stretch by the first letter of the pertinent street or station, not as a tourist might but for practical reasons: the code that will let me decipher the city. In time you have enough of your faculties free to keep conscious track of: streets, shops, cars, how the buses work, what the ambulance siren sounds like, what's on in the cinemas, stadiums, shopping malls, supermarkets, flea markets, farmers' markets, and the people, of course, *people*, and the clouds of coal smoke over everything, more over some districts, less over others, and here and there, of course, vapor trails. When seen from close up, by the way, they are black, not white. Who told me that (when)?

Later a man came up to him and asked to see his ticket. Abel made believe he had trouble understanding him. Switching to hands and feet, he communicated that he had lost his way looking for the train, here was his ticket, a round-trip ticket, that's what you need, isn't it, my intentions are honorable. His reward was not long in coming. The friendly man turned a blind eye, actually shut an eye, or maybe just blinked; he nearly put his hand on the young man's arm, caught himself feeling a definite impulse to do so: love, don't kill. Luckily the train was pulling into the station, so get off while you can.

Now we're back to where we started from. Out of a cupboard have I come; onto a station bench have I landed. Alone in a city where you know nobody. Winter is on the way. You can get coal here and here. But first stop: Tibor's office for help. Not that he knew where it was. Forgot to ask, but that wasn't until morning. Had he any other thoughts on this autumn afternoon? Scenarios: what had happened so far; you didn't know where things would go from here. There wasn't much to see: a teenager on a bench, a tourist who had missed a train, his backpack perched next to him like a person.

Later a fellow who had been hanging around the ticket machines for a while eyeing him—brown pleated trousers, green sweater, greasy part in the hair, circles under the eyes—came up to him and said, Hi. My name is Konstantin. Looking for a place to stay?

How did he guess.

WELCOME

At first, and later, you are constantly in motion, though never getting anywhere. In a vehicle or not, you keep going round in circles. Your mother gives you instruction in science and day-trips, your father chimes in with the international hit parade, accompanying himself on the piano, the electronic keyboard, and once on a harmonium. His right foot taps in time to the music; his beige socks curl around his ankles. Later feet, ankles, calves—four altogether— play a major role, but then it all comes to an abrupt, even violent end, and you are back in new circles.

What can I say? These are *hysterical* times! The whole world seems to be playing musical chairs. Pushing, shoving, whimpering, shrieking. Everyone seeking a place for himself. Or any place. A safe place to put your—sorry—ass. Voluntarily or not. Life is hard everywhere, here and now, because they have nothing better to do than freeze all quotas as if there were no, as we put it so elegantly, *international situation*! Not a pretty picture. We all have our stories; on the other hand, we're only barely twenty years old and therefore as full of hope as never before and never again, said Konstantin as they were winding their way through the rush-hour traffic.

It was not necessary or even possible to say anything: he spoke nonstop, recounting the miraculous salvation *of our young hero*, gasping frantically for breath, as if swimming, moving his arms like a swimmer too.

We (wheeze, wave) can walk it! It's right over there! The clay-colored monstrosity you must have seen from the platform when you got off the train. We take the first twenty-floorer and then—here, here, here!—the first set of stairs and then, claustrophobia or no (more new things . . .) the elevator to the tenth floor. As soon as you get out, you see a (likewise) clay-colored door, and Konstantin Tóti, Ancient History—from then on he will always say Konstantintótiancienthistory—welcomes you to his humble abode, or, as I call it, the Bastille!

Voilà! The place where no darkness reigns. Or darkness reigns supreme. It's what you might call a *yes-and-no-affair* (the italics are Konstantin's). People here build buildings—*and even schools!*—that have rooms without windows. Abel's room-to-be does have a window, though it doesn't either, because the window there is opens onto a cramped and dark inner courtyard, so cramped and dark that you can't make out any details in it. A window to nothing. We might as well be living on the *equator* here: you can't see what's down in the pit (darkness) or going on along the sides (twilight) or, your head in your neck, up above, in the sky, because it's too bright. The voices of the house go up and down or from wherever to wherever: they're just there, *the sounds of life*. I hope you're not sensitive to noise. Anyway, you must be feeling pretty good now just to have a roof over your head other than the station's. Though it's probably less annoying there to hear somebody practicing the sax.

Actually the Bastille is more two buildings than one, two buildings pushed together, each reaching into the other's cavities. You wonder how it's possible: from outside it looks like a *colossal monument to the right angle*; inside, though, the most unexpected twists and turns open up. You sometimes have to take a circuitous route to get to what should be your next-door neighbor—if your progress isn't cut off entirely by fire doors and the like. Sinbad, alias Konstantin, had once tried to traverse this world in its entirety, but I can't say whether I made it to all the floors. Many parts of

the building seem totally inaccessible; many parts have Arctic tem-
peratures—they lie in the path of the wind tunnel, and *that* you
hear too, not now, no, but in winter it howls like a dog—and others are as hot and sultry as a greenhouse. There would even seem
to be something like a roof terrace: he had once spied the tips of a
kind of bamboo plant behind a small whitewashed wall, but the
skylight had unfortunately been filled in. As for the residents, they
were twice twenty stories of *humdrum existence.* Some floors had
been sublet to the university for student use, but there were many
civilians as well. Konstantin would strike up a conversation with
any he met in the hallway or elevator. He would tell them where
he lived, what he was *studying,* and found out from them who had
unoccupied rooms, but unfortunately most people aren't willing to
take in outsiders, even in cases of emergency. That's just the way
they are. Welcome to my world. All-embracing gesture.

The place where we're standing now is called—I, Konstantin,
call it—the *piazza.* In the beginning: the so-called common room,
to whose beige linoleum all roads of the *imperium* lead. Notice the
six doors: entrance and exit, kitchen, bathroom, plus the doors to
the three adjoining *coffins,* in which the *delinquents* are *domiciled.*
The piazza and one of the rooms have a view of the tracks; the rest
look out on the aforementioned inner courtyard. The room with
the view is inhabited by a person (sigh) we (Konstantin) call Blond
Pal, a fish-headed Scandinavian who is most likely an informant:
you've got to be careful around him. He doesn't happen to be in,
luckily. The second room belongs to Konstantin himself, and the
third, the smallest and darkest, is meant for an Algerian by the
name of Abdellatif El-Kantarah (or something like that) in theory,
at least, because in practice he's never shown up. Trustworthy
Konstantin has carried around the key to the room for two months
now, to hand it over if need be, but has not yet had occasion to do
so. And so: *Voilà, monsieur.* Your room.

That is how Abel met Konstantin. He seemed to have a preference
for the French, but apart from that there was not much to be had
from his monologue. Though having lived here a year, he had not
picked up much of the language. Just the basics.

You hungry? Eat? Eggs and this here?

Fatty bacon. A wire attached to one end to hang it up. From home. Konstantin ceremoniously sliced off a quivering sliver.

And you? he finally asked. What's your story? Where do you come from? Where are you going?

. . .

Holy smoke! So you're in for the long haul!

By the way, he went on, this is a *fantastic* town. If you haven't picked up on it yet, you will as soon as your belly is full and you've had a rest. You'll start thinking it's perfectly natural you're here, which it is, take it from me. But don't go thinking that just anybody would take you in off the street as if he'd been waiting for you, because Konstantin T. is not just anybody. No, let me tell you: the countryside will spit you out, the countryside won't give you the time of day, but you may well say to me in ten or twenty years, Remember when we lived in the *most pulsating metropolis of the hemisphere*? It has most of the features of the white world, East-West-South-North, with a pinch of Asia and even Africa. Religions! Nationalities! If only we could open the window and feel the famous air of the city on our skin, the air that—especially in winter, which traditionally begins here on 10 September, you'd best adjust to that right away—smells mainly of coal, but unfortunately the windows don't open: nobody understands the locks, and they're broken to boot. Broken on purpose: the last thing we need is promising young students sailing out of the upper stories. Because, no matter how you look at it, life for your garden-variety student, with or without scholarship, is little better than slow starvation. More eggs? More bacon? Take as much as you like. Sorry there's so little. In the first few days you'll buy the things you like: sausage, bread, milk, etc., but before long you'll realize the money won't hold out for more than ten days, and I'm just talking about breakfast. You can apply for more, bend over backwards, pester the hell out of people—reserve doesn't come naturally to me, and if it did I wouldn't be able to afford it (by the way, have you got any money? no?)—in ninety-nine cases out of a hundred it will get you nowhere. There are just too many of us. My recommendation for the *interim*: lots of pasta, lots of broth, tomato puree, and cabbage.

And in such and such an *eatery* you can get spinach with a hard-boiled egg for a song. There, now you know everything there is to know!

The male body does not reach maturity until the age of twenty-one, said Konstantin. The reason I'm always so hungry is that I must still be a growing boy.

He was especially pleased with *a growing boy* and let out a sputtering giggle. He did it all the time: he was a great sputterer. He fried everything *to give it some taste*. The tiles, clay-colored like everything else at the Bastille, grew tiny pockmarks of fat; the cupboards shone of it. As much as the light that made its way in allowed. The lower half of the window was taken up by an air-conditioning unit attached to the outer wall; the upper half was usually misted over. The place smelled of rancid bacon and crumbs and of the powder they used every few weeks to keep the cockroaches in line. Abel, on his first morning—Blond Pal came into the kitchen, saw him, may have nodded, he nodded back, Pal took something out of the refrigerator (milk), and was off—shook them out of his bowl and ate some rolled oats, which belonged to *nobody* and happened to be on a shelf, with water.

Take what you want.

Thanks. He didn't want anything.

Are you vegetarian?

No.

What's the matter? Are you doing penance for something or saving up for a sports car?

Konstantin laughed, though not quite so heartily as he had the previous evening. This new guy is strange: nothing phases him, nothing at all.

Not quite, my friend, not quite.

BEING AND HAVING

The stray oats lasted five days and were all Abel needed. After wandering a while through the maze of the university building—Want me to take you there? asked Konstantin. No need to, said Abel. I'll go with you, Konstantin insisted. No need to. Really—he landed in Tibor's office on the very next day.

To sum up, said Tibor, you need what everyone needs: a roof over your head, student status, and naturally money. You can't apply to your embassy for objective reasons. I'm right to assume you're a deserter, aren't I? (Good lad.) So you're at the mercy of foreigners.

Pause. The scrape of a match, frantic inhalation, smoke.

What I can do for you isn't much. I too am merely a . . .

He embellished his name with all his titles—people are fortunately! such snobs!—on a sheet of letterhead. Here, a letter of recommendation. And here's another. These people have money. Just be yourself. You'd have an easier time of it if you were religious, but you can't have everything.

Thank you, said Abel.

Don't mention it, said Tibor and went back to work. The whole thing took less than fifteen minutes.

What the letter basically said was that Abel Nema was a genius. *Given the extraordinary nature of Mr. A.N.'s talents it is in the interest of us all to use every means at our disposal to . . . ,* etc. Before the week was up, Abel had everything a man needs. Everything fine, he wired to his old address. Since the call in the hospital he had been unable to phone. There was no answer either at home or at the school.

Have I heard correctly? (Who from anyway?) Konstantin in the kitchen. You've received a scholarship from the S—— Foundation? Why didn't you tell me they were accepting applications? I let you live here free of charge and what do you do? Why are you all so selfish?

They aren't accepting applications, said Abel. It's a special grant for the gifted.

I see, said Konstantin, taking a seat on the side of the kitchen table and watching *the chosen one* eat: slowly, fastidiously, with dignity. Konstantin smacked his lips like an animal. When he was offered something. Of course *that* never entered his mind *here*. So you're gifted, are you?

Lucky dog, said Konstantin. So what are you going to do? Move out?

Pause. Abel ate on or, possibly, gave it some thought. Yes, he probably would try to find a place of his own.

Hm, said Konstantin. Everything costs so much. You can't imagine. Pause.

The toilets were out on the landing and froze in winter; the black toilet seats bore obscure white petrified traces of what the neighbors left behind.

What, Konstantin finally said, what—except that it's illegal and dangerous—is to prevent you from staying in the Algerian's room *for good*. Since he wasn't officially there, he would pay no rent and instead take over half of *his*, that is, Konstantin's; after all, he, Konstantin, had taken a considerable risk for him—the fish-headed Pal and so on—so it would only be fair and we'd be even, so to speak. (Looking him up and down.) Could you pass for an Algerian? Why not? What does an Algerian look like when you get down to it?

Abel said neither yes nor no, but stayed on.

Konstantin gave a hearty laugh: These *were* strange times!

Later, though, he had to admit that, this time as so often, he was disappointed. *Our fictive flatmate* appeared to have no interest *in anything*: was neither carried away nor disillusioned by *all this here*, uttered barely three words a day—you (Konstantin) saw his face as good as never, ate little, slept less, but studied practically nonstop and with a frenzy that . . . I don't know. You'd think he never looked out of the window. You'd think he didn't care what the out there looks like. A city, period. I can't accept that, said Konstantin. No one sees the world like that. In such *formal* terms.

At one time Abel had wanted to be or, who knows, *was preparing to be* a geography teacher; now the inside of his mouth was the only land whose landscapes he knew to the last detail: lips, teeth, alveoli, palate, velum, uvula, tongue, apex, dorsum, larynx. Voice onset time, voiced, voiceless, aspirated, distinctive or non-. Stops, fricatives, nasals, laterals, vibrants, taps and flaps. For four long years—years redolent of the male dormitory, of linoleum and neon lights—he followed basically one and one route only: dormitory to language laboratory and back. Three S-Bahn stations, a short walk. It is always dark in this picture, as if it were always winter, but that cannot be, of course: in the four years there must have been at least one summer. It made no difference: he wore the same clothes, the black, old-man's outfit that made him stand out even more here than *there*, if people here bothered to pay attention to such things. Ostentatiously (?) out of style. So what. When people did pay attention—and they did, because apart from the clothes and the unidentifiable hairstyle he was good-looking—he did not respond. He went nowhere he did not absolutely need to go, and went to the language lab mostly at night when he could be alone: a single hovering square of light in a dark building.

Abel N. had been granted or vouchsafed a miraculous gift, but one that needed fashioning. At first there is the mathematics, the web of the construction. Like a pop-up fairy-tale castle a glass forest arises out of two pages. Each of its trees is a sentence, the branches forming such and such an angle with the trunk, the

smaller branches likewise with the larger, with nice little syntagmas twinkling at the ends. Nature builds everything according
to a design. This is where a knowledge of fractals comes in handy.
Or simple, universal linguistic instinct. The forest stands for itself alone, in all its fatal clarity and beauty, though mute. In the
beginning Abel's mathematical understanding was insufficiently
connected to his tongue, that is, he understood everything and
could say nothing. He would have been hard put to give so much
as a demonstration of his gifts or, to be more practical, pass a single
examination, which one needs to do to keep one's documents. The
secret genius. I see, said Tibor, who was not *actually* there: he had
taken a year's leave to write a book, but all he had to do was em-
bellish another sheet of letterhead with his beautiful calligraphy.
Should any problems arise, contact my assistant. You remember
Mercedes, don't you? He did, but here and now that made no difference. He also got a key to the language lab.

What makes the whole thing even more unbelievable—no,
uncanny—the Modern Languages people said, is that he learns
sound by sound, analyzing frequency charts, rummaging through
phonetic codes, painting his tongue black to compare imprints. It's
starting to look like punishment: drinking ink or eating soap powder. The word *laboratory* appears in a new light: the technological
comes first, the human second. You'd think he was creating a ho-
munculus there in the night, except that his consists exclusively of
language, the perfect clone of a language between glottis and labia.
What kind of life is that?

What are you up to in there? Konstantin asked Pal, who was passing
through the piazza. Pal looked up and walked on, closing his door
behind him. He's another case. All night there's a blue light glimmering under his door: he never takes his eyes off the monitor (or,
rather, monitors: he has three computers); he sleeps in the morning, presumably attends a few lectures and such in the afternoon,
comes home in the evening, and then it starts all over again. I share
my digs with the most boring and the most bored person in the
world. Without the tight corset of their rituals I don't think they'd
be capable of producing even minimal signs of humanity, said

Konstantin to the windowpane, his conversation partner whenever he lacked a human one. He stood at the unopenable window facing the station, *lamenting* (the italics are Pal's), for *hours* on end, anything and everything: past, present, future; *this century, which has brought us all together here*! His breath formed a small, round cloud on the windowpane. He spoke into it: it was his microphone. You are listening to Radio Konstantin. Politics, panorama, weather. Fifty-thousand-year-old humans found; the Leaning Tower of P. is leaning lower and lower; the largest living organism in the world is a hundred-ton mushroom; armistice declared; republic founded; barricades erected; priest and standard-bearer murdered during wedding ceremony; star discovered and recognized as independent country (Congratulations!), taken hostage; bridge blown up, 427 years of history swallowed up by the ice-cold, blue-green waters of the . . . Pal's door flew open—Could you shut your trap for a minute? Thank you—and slammed shut. Plastic monster, K. muttered.

He does nothing of the sort. He is courteous and quiet: his steps on the linoleum scarcely audible, his face free of sadness or petulance or assent. I can't accept that, said Konstantin. How can you stand never listening to the news, not even asking me to give you an hourly report? You simply *can't* be uninterested in what is going on here and abroad. Haven't you been out of touch with your mother for a year? How is she?

I'm fine, said Mira when they spoke again for the first time. It was hailing mildly; three men were hunched forward in front of the booth; a wind was blowing leaflets from the marketplace: vegetables or politics; the right was said to be strong on this side of the tracks.

We lost the apartment, said Mira. I'm living at Vesna's. A basement room, but it's okay: there are only the two of us. Grandmother died. Hurt and angry, just as she lived. She was so hurt and angry that she'd stopped praying, stopped cursing even. Just pursed her lips hard, lay down, and . . .

Oh, said Abel.

Give your mother my warmest greetings. I want her to know who I (Konstantin) am, in case anything should happen to you.

. . .

Though the opposite was more likely. Whereas virtually nothing ever befell Abel or Pal and they did not appear to be unhappy about it—it was impossible to know *what* they were!—Konstantin was constantly embroiled in something.

He was pursued by the shell game con artists up and down the local shopping street, two kilometers—I didn't know I could run so far—after he had given a speech to the passersby in front of the station, warning them to beware of the scam. For days he had paced the piazza, trembling with fright: they said they knew where I live; they would kill me within my own four walls. He went on about the blood that would stick to the walls. Later he was stung by a wasp in the bathroom and his tonsils were so inflamed for a whole winter that for weeks and then months he could not make a sound. Weak immune system, the result of poor nutrition and nervous tension, and he couldn't stand drafts or air-conditioning. I basically always have a fever. Red cheeks, shiny eyes, the hot breath of pus and penicillin. Red and black pills. He carried them in his pocket and took way too many. When he finally stopped, his entire body was covered with pustules. Slowly but surely I'm turning into a monster. What have I done? Who has cursed me? Why don't you (Abel) ever get sick? Later spring came and he dared to go outside. The first thing he did was to get mixed up in an argument in a snack bar and the man sitting next to him, who hadn't said a word till then, stepped down hard on his ankle. The point of his shoe landed in a hollow just under it. Konstantin screamed and fell. When he opened his eyes, he was on a level with the snack-bar litter. Fuck off, said the tough men standing over him. Having to flee at a limp. Later he himself beat up a young woman when he noticed she had a penis. He threw up. He tore down a poster advertising a magazine with a naked man on the cover. He explained to a young woman he scarcely knew, screaming over the cafeteria racket, that in all cultures blessings come from above, that the sun god impregnated the earth goddess and not the other way around. He said he was going to put the following ad in the personal column: Seek eighteen-year-old innocent virgin from the old country. Have no riches to offer, only a true and honest heart.

Keep your eyes peeled! he called after Abel. A few days ago— did you hear?—a man was stabbed on the train because he was wearing left-wing glasses. Good thing it's winter again, coat and sweater: the knife went in under the kidney and only one centimeter deep. But what an atmosphere: frantic times, frantic!

Hm, said Abel and disappeared through the door.

Like preaching into a toilet bowl, said Konstantin to the window.

Such were the early years.

SALON

Intermezzo

Throughout this period, as far as Konstantin could tell, Abel was to be found in virtually no other contexts than those sketched above, though sometimes before going to the lab he would watch any undubbed film playing, for practice, and sometimes he stopped at the first available snack bar and ordered something to eat or drink. By pointing.

Once, not long after his arrival and against his better judgment, he attended a student prayer group recommended by Konstantin.

You might try a prayer group, said Konstantin. Are you Catholic or Orthodox?

Neither. I wouldn't dream of it. But then he went. It was only a brief episode, no more than a glance at the catacombs, here: a long typewriter room. There were not many people, ten or twelve. He saw that *he* wasn't there. It took only seconds. Sorry, he said, and left.

Another time he was the one who took Konstantin along. A dinner given by his sponsors. Konstantin was touched. Will S—— be there in person?

Abel didn't imagine so. Only people from the Foundation.

Members of the selection committee?

Possibly.

Thanks, said Konstantin. You're a true friend.

The hostess's name is Magda, a *native of their country* who has a gray bun and chain-smokes; her husband is a friendly, well-to-do native. She has struck it rich: he is mad about her culture.

Now you see how the other half lives! Our kind rarely even visits this part of the city. The rooms, the light, the parquet floors, the molding, the trimmings . . . no, I mean trappings!

As the guest of a guest Konstantin spent his time sniffing out everything: paintings, signatures, armatures! Oh, let us erect a tent by the stream of the rich! Hey, a buffet!

Finally something to eat. For a while things calm down. Abel finds himself a quiet corner.

And who have we here? Fresh blood!

Fresh blood . . . That's not quite what I would call my child.

Laughter. Most of the guests are the hosts' age, *started out together*, know one another, apart from the few unrevealed secrets, inside out. A little variety is always . . .

Can one still be so young? Twenty? At most. What's your name, my boy? Abel, a fine name. Today of all days we're wanting in young women. Give him a chance to eat first. He's no more than a *breath* . . .

(Few understood. Only a quiet giggle.)

Inviting young students to lunch once a week is a fine old tradition.

Once a *month*.

That was Aida, the hosts' only daughter, who wrote for the radio from time to time, manic depression permitting. Between times, now, she lived with her parents. The medicine made her bloated, and she was plump to begin with and always so sad, said her dainty mother: life is a torment for her. Lithium causes a calm tremble of the hands. The advantage of familial and historical catastrophes is that they bring people closer together. That has its good and bad sides. Eating your fill once a month is not to be pooh-poohed.

Oh, this embarrassing *community warmth*! Aida thinks as she studies the newcomer. The fresh blood. I wouldn't be surprised if he's said no more than three words altogether. Shy or arrogant? (Both?) Did he bring the other one to divert attention from himself? Does he know how beautiful he is?

Poor, ailing Aida. Can't tear her eyes off him. Out on stalks. If a beautiful young man like that could love poor, ailing, overweight Aida, it would be her salvation: I so wish I could come up with someone for her. He's just a child, that Abel! The food seems to take all his concentration. Aida smiles. I eat practically nothing and my weight stays the same. What would happen if I stopped eating altogether? I might turn out to be immortal.

He can't hold the men's attention for long. They're in a hurry to get to the next phase of what purports to be a forty-year conversation: *the old partisans*, caught in a time warp back in the sixties, since when they . . .

H. didn't get a visa, not until the conference was in progress; she didn't let it stop her . . . the perfect cosmopolitan, five languages, I met her once . . . It was on the twenty-first of October, nineteen hundred . . . On the twenty-third. On the twenty-first they hadn't yet . . . stood on the balcony while they marched past below, and all at once they all do this . . .

Makes a fist. A few laugh: if you're under fifty, you don't know why.

The ladies know the stories; they're more interested in the newcomers.

And you?

Konstantin.

Another one of our scholarship students? Oh, a friend of . . . Ancient history? Oh, how intere . . . What in particular? The migration of peoples?

Number one or number two? (One of the men calling over.)

The prehistorical migration can, with the help of a stomach bacterium known as Helicobacter pylori . . .

Oh, does your hand hurt? So you cut it with an electric knife yesterday while out on a job.

(Have you any experience? asked the man, himself a foreigner.

Yes, yes, said Konstantin. There less than half an hour. No money, of course. Out, out, get out, said the man, and take your blood with you. Just what we need! I may never be able to move it again. I may be an invalid all my life. I don't know if I can go to the dinner like *this*.

That man should be reported. Employs illegals, throws them into the street bleeding. Not so much as a napkin. I think it's beginning to smell.)

He does not want to go to the hospital.

Who does?

Luckily the good Dr. F. is present.

Let me have a look at it.

The good Dr. F., the one who knew about the stomach bacteria, has treated generations of patients, often free of charge. When my daughter was born, I laid the camping table with our four plates. The fourth was for the good doctor: he was the godfather; we were friends even then. He's retired now, but he always carries a little black bag with him just in case. Mostly for disinfection.

Come with me, young man. There's a quiet room next door. We'll see what the matter is. You've got a clean cut there except for possible infection from microscopic scraps of sausage that may have stuck to the knife. Flesh on flesh, there's nothing worse—it poisons the blood—but a splash of iodine should do the trick.

Will I have a blood-brown stain in the middle of my palm for the rest of my life? See ye my wound!

Your friend is wounded; he is gone; now all eyes are on you. Abel, Magda tells everyone, speaks five languages. Or is it six now? I have the impression the number grows weekly.

We're good at that. Not that we're more gifted: it's a matter of necessity.

The market's pretty full, I imagine. Must be.

Isn't it always full?

Since I'm immortal, Aida thinks, the fifteen-year age difference between us counts for nothing; besides, I have the right passport, and if I can keep my nerves under control you'll forget my body and come to appreciate my intelligence and sensitivity.

Tibor B. sent him to us.

Haven't seen him for ages.

His second wife was a dancer and choreographer. Beautiful, petite.

Jewish.

Wrong. Only her father. So she's not.

If push came to shove, every drop of blood that strayed into a side branch of the family fourteen generations ago would count.

A drop of blood encircles the globe!

Bloodwurst says: Come, liverwurst . . .

Can we stop talking about blood. I'm going to be sick.

Take a little schnapps, Aida dear.

She can't. The medicine.

At this point they feel a need for silence.

I hate you, Mother.

Now you turn back to *him*: How do you know Tibor?

Not at all. He had his name on a scrap of paper.

Oh . . .

The name of any one of us could be on a scrap of paper!

Magda had formerly been the *official* starting gate, the mother of all émigrés. That was no longer possible: there were simply too many.

Somebody hid twenty-five Jews. A woman.

I've launched hundreds of business cards into the world in my day. Who knows where they are now.

Our dear doctor is a saint too. May God bless you and grant you long life.

The man in question gives a sad smile. His hand has begun to tremble.

The iodine glimmering through his bandage, Konstantin listens bright-eyed to *it all*. Places himself so that he has contact with the partisans as well as the ladies; even attempts to take part in the discussion, as if that were necessary or possible: an interesting young man. The other boy: hard to tell. There are two besides him who are mostly silent: Aida and a tall, effeminate fifty-year-old with curly gray hair and a small, vain mouth. A former actor, the star of his provincial town, he would roar like a lion and brandish his fists: it wasn't yet in to be gay, but when they tried to pressure him into marrying he stood firm, a praiseworthy stance, *actually*. Now he thinks he can write—nice little human-interest books from home.

Human interest is high art, my dear. His name is Simon. He is observing them all, *a bountiful source*, including, of course, our handsome young hero.

Heeheehee, Aida thinks. Heeheehee.

Later her eyes fill with tears, and she goes to her room without the customary formalities, poor thing. The seat next to Abel having thus been vacated, the man by the name of Simon changes places.

Pause. Then, a soft, intimate, somewhat singsong voice close to his ear: What is your name?

He leaves shortly thereafter; Abel leaves with him. The dirty old man! Konstantin, who knows how to behave, offers to leave too.

No need, says Abel. He was just going to the language lab. Oh, when industry joins youthful energy and furtive glances turn to recognition! And you, dear friend, do stay a while. So Konstantin of the bandaged hand returned to his seat with dignity.

The next time he received his own invitation. He went alone. You were missed, he said with a giggle. At least two fair young maidens were invited specially for you!

Later it was less enjoyable. Why has the handsome young man stopped coming? I don't think he'll ever return.

The fair young maidens made a face.

Not only that, they dress like those child whores. To be honest, Konstantin said later to Abel, the closer you come to knowing *it*, the closer you come to revulsion, if you see what I mean. *True* solidarity? He dismissed it with a wave of the hand. I never got a grant either. All in all I (Konstantin) would classify this intermezzo under "The Edifying Loss of an Illusion."

TRANSIT

The good thing about having a youth with *ups and downs*, Konstantin said one day to the windowpane, is that there's practically nothing more that can happen to us. Nothing more can happen to us, he mumbled into the fog. In other words, he said after a short pause, *everything* can happen to us. Everything does. Everything will. Obviously. What is possible happens. That's not the point. The point is that while the pretty much most trifling of things can threaten us, our very existence, the pretty much most cruel of things has little more capacity to reach into our soul and shatter us.

He looked around. The piazza was empty except for a hideously upholstered sofa that had been there—who knows how it got there—since before the first of them had moved in. *Like God*, said Konstantin and laughed, though his face grew quite red. God as sofa. *Convertible* sofa! The blue light was glimmering under Pal's door, but all was quiet. Abel did not seem to be at home.

That's how it is, Konstantin said meaningfully to the sofa.

Later Pal came out of his room and noticed there was a dull spot in the windowpane where Konstantin's breath had touched it. That wouldn't usually have bothered him, but this time, after hours of mumbling from the living room, which had even put him off pissing, Pal also discovered the impression of an oily forehead and a nose on the window. With a *Disgusting!*—which he said in English, the language he preferred to curse in—he disappeared back into his room. But soon he realized that the thought of the grease spot would not leave him in peace, so he went out again, cursing all the while, and wiped it away. It wasn't easy: the grease was stubborn; so he rubbed around it, smearing it all over the place, then saw that the whole window was now thoroughly *sullied* and in a fit of anger polished the entire pane and! frame until they glistened. His forehead was covered with sweat.

Wow, said Konstantin when he came home. Look at that view!

His *hope in the establishment* thwarted, Konstantin turned back to his true *mission*. As a child I wanted to be a missionary. Why did I fail to become one? It's not too late, said a Lithuanian church musician, an Albanian poet, a Slovenian-Polish couple on their honeymoon, a former Hungarian prostitute, a student from Andalusia with her friend. Konstantin was in love with two of the last three. Later he stood by the window, calling them names, especially the former whore. Her of all people! And so on. Tatars, Chechens, Basques, the Irish. In the following months the comings and goings in the piazza practically never stopped. With the same intensity that Abel and Pal worked their way through their respective territories, Konstantin neglected his studies in favor of his *lamentations* on the one hand and his *expeditions* on the other. When not talking or eating, he was prowling the city. To meet them, if they were there to meet. In point of fact he spent virtually all his time at the station and its environs, because his true goal was to find people to whom he could offer shelter. He quartered his people on the sofa named God and treated them to what little he had. If *we* know anything, it is the supreme importance of the network. Here, in this tiny book, he noted the addresses of all his guests. Wherever I go, people will be glad to see me. The Abkhasians, Lapps, Estonians, Corsicans, and Cypriots nodded. One day my true calling may prove to be: the man who comes to visit.

Sitting cross-legged on God, he discussed the international situation with them. A veritable epidemic of new nation-states. Don't get me wrong now: I'm in full sympathy with everything that it entails as well. My field is the migration of peoples, by the way. Not surprisingly, xenophobia is a major theme here and elsewhere: young male lions kill the young of their predecessors, bite off their heads; our jaws may not be strong enough, but . . .

Enough! Blond Pal shouted every few weeks, when yet again you couldn't move for days! because somebody was always! in your way, blocking the TV! stopping up the toilet! cooking their stinking food! screwing forte on the sofa and howling! All night long! Some even bring instruments! Rice-cookers! Remote-controlled toys! And use them all! One day I'll come home to find a nice little bonfire! burning! in the middle of the room! Enough! he said, do you hear! with this goddamned transit point in my apartment!

But you have a TV set in your room, Konstantin whined. Standing in the piazza, on the desert-sand-colored floor covering, whirling his windmill arms, directing an invisible rush hour, the streams or trickles of through traffic—bands of people, herds of animals, columns of cars—nearly disappearing behind the dust he whirled up. Abel's curls fluttered as he swerved around him on his way to the door and thence to the lab.

Blond Pal would refer Konstantin to the words "to third persons" and "allow use of" and "forbidden" in the building regulations. The next time I catch anyone here from the world transit stream . . . There are people here who want to work, damn it!

Since I myself am in a *what might be called a precarious position*, said Konstantin to Abel, it would certainly be smarter for me to listen to Pal and comply with the regulations, but that would be (in a loud, theatrical voice that can be heard in all the rooms) tantamount to denying my *most basic humanity*.

Whether Pal knew about Abel is not clear: he never said anything about it. As long as he keeps his trap shut, I don't care. They hardly ever crossed paths. (Early one morning in the kitchen. They bump into each other in the doorway. Sorry, says Abel, his voice hoarse from practicing all night, while Pal stares at him, amazed and fascinated. Sorry, says Abel and removes himself from the doorway. That was it.) I consider him (Pal), honestly, capable of anything, said Konstantin, but he simply could not help himself.

He went on putting people up. If he could make no headway with his rudimentary language skills—bad grammar and *earsplitting* pronunciation, neither of which improved in the slightest over the years—he would knock on Abel's door. He's got somebody there whose language he doesn't speak. What is that? Polish?

No.

Czech triplets or, rather, two cousins and a friend, all equally faded: jeans, blond hair. Konstantin had found them wandering about in the U-Bahn.

Abel knew neither Polish nor Czech.

You're putting me on, said Konstantin in the spirit of pan-Slavism.

The spirit of pan-Slavism can lick my ass with a hundred tongues. I'm a pretty spirited guy myself when you get down to it. But that soon blew over. Before long Abel's brain was back to *normal* and he started picking up individual words, then syntagmas, then whole sentences. That's right. Sometimes it took a while, but in time I can understand everyone *somehow or other*. Adventure, he translated for Konstantin. They came for the adventure of it. They don't speak anything but their native language; the only foreign words they know are the names of rock bands Konstantin and Abel had never heard of. Later Konstantin was very hard on them. It had been a bad move. Adventure, bull! You've polished off all the bacon and all the eggs and left only a gulp of milk. That curbed his passion for *the project as a whole*, and things calmed down somewhat.

Later, during the year-end festivities, they got involved in something that put an end to the *Great Open House* (Pal).

EKA

How long will you be gone? Konstantin asked Pal, who was leaving for the holidays with an incredible amount of luggage.

None of your business, said Pal.

It's the fourth Christmas we're celebrating far from our near and dear ones, Konstantin said to Abel with great solemnity. The latter saw no need to interrupt his work schedule. By this time he had seven languages down pat and was *laboring* over three more.

What's your limit? asked Konstantin. The sky? I wonder what good they do him: he never talks to anybody.

It was Christmas as usual at the entrance to the station: no snow, much wind. The Bastille's intestines piped and boomed day and night. Konstantin stood at the window, watching the so-called hustle and bustle and Abel slaloming his way through shoppers and shopping bags without letting up speed. A string of ornaments blown over from the Christmas market came hurtling towards him, but he was too quick for it and it missed him by a few centimeters. Konstantin sighed.

When Abel came home early the next morning—or the morning after, in any case, just after Pal had closed the door behind him—

and went into the common kitchen, he found a black Madonna with a gigantic child nestled in her arm. There was a small pot of porridge warming on the stove; she was tasting it with a wooden spoon. For a moment he thought he was in the wrong apartment. Could it be?

Sorry, he said.

The Madonna dropped the spoon. Some of the porridge had stuck to her lips. Jesuschristalmighty, she said in her language, staring at the man in the doorway. Everything about him was black: hair, clothes, mouth, tongue, teeth. They've come to get us at last.

Sorry, Abel said again, holding his hand in front of the black pit. There they stood: he covering his mouth, she with porridge on her lips, the baby reaching for it, hitting her hard. Her teeth were chattering.

Excuse me, Abel mumbled, walking backwards out of the kitchen. He gave his teeth a good, long brush. Gray foam crawling down the greasy sink through leftover beard stubble. After that his teeth sat in small, black chalices and gave off a bluish glow.

Her name was Maria. Once she was over her initial shock, she gave him a friendly smile. The baby's look moved between indifferent and hostile.

Actually, said Konstantin, her name isn't Maria, it's Eka. But her passport says Maria. Her sister's passport, that is. She has her sister's passport.

Eka nodded and said the same thing. Abel noted the Georgian word for "sister." They wouldn't give her a passport. We look alike, though, don't we?

No. First there was the eight-year gap in their ages, then the fact that Eka, though twenty, looked like a thirteen-year-old: round eyes, braids down to the hips, and you had the feeling the baby was half as large as she was. Konstantin had not found her; she had come on her own: someone had given her the address. Proud: I'm known.

Eka's come to find her husband, said Konstantin by way of information. He hasn't seen the kid yet. She left him a note with someone: Am waiting at such and such a place for you. Her husband's name is Vakhtang. She'll be living in the piazza until he turns up.

Hm, said Abel and went to his room to sleep.

He's a little . . . —Konstantin gave his nose an apologetic twist and waved his hand back and forth in front of Eka—you know what I mean. But no fear. He may look formidable when you first lay eyes on him, but he's harmless *actually*.

Eka and the baby spent several days in the piazza. Konstantin never crossed the room without playing with it. It had a large, rectangular head, half of which was covered with dark fluff. Konstantin sang it Christmas carols. It pursed its lips and made not a sound. Eka washed its things by hand, took it for walks, did the shopping and cooking. Konstantin could not praise her enough; Abel was not hungry.

Konstantin, theatrical: But they're the most hospitable people in the world! Then, muted: Hungry or not, could Abel contribute a bit? After all, Eka and he couldn't be expected . . . You're the one with the genius grant.

Abel gave him what he had on hand, after which things quieted down for a while. Eka spruced up the piazza for Vakhtang's arrival. Konstantin helped her to pick up stray ornaments from the Christmas market: Whenever he bent down, she stuffed candles, dried fruit, and wooden toys into the pockets of her roomy coat. She tried on a red scarf, flinging it elegantly over her shoulder. Konstantin nodded and smiled approvingly; Eka smiled and nodded back and walked on. But you, but you didn't p . . . Here, said Eka, sorting out her treasures in the piazza. This is for you: dried fruit and another scarf. Konstantin's mouth fell open. I have to say I'm a bit shocked. Oh, said Eka with a smile, I forgot diapers. Diapers, she said, pointing. Right away, said Konstantin, rushing off. Don't bother paying me back.

Konstantin, Eka, and the baby celebrated Christmas without Vakhtang, from whom there had as yet been no word, and without Abel, who did not come home, and I really could have used you here. Konstantin spent half the evening trying to get worked up over his absence. He was so good at it that in the end he himself believed (a) that he was worried, and (b) that something had in fact happened to him. Maybe he'd been murdered; maybe he was lying somewhere nearby, right next to the Bastille, right under the windows, and nobody would discover the corpse until they came to take away the dried-out Christmas trees thrown down onto the street. A smiling Eka gave him the biggest knife in the house to carve the roast with, the roast she had again *seen to*, and Konstantin forgot the scenario he had just dreamed up.

When Abel finally did come home, Konstantin was ready and waiting at the door and pushed him into the kitchen.

In a whisper: Where were you, or no, it doesn't matter; I've got something to tell you, but first eat. We've been saving it for *him*, but it will just go bad.

What Konstantin had to say to him was that it could very well be that the reason this guy, this Vakhtang, hadn't come was that he had to go underground or was already *behind bars*. He, Konstantin, would certainly understand if Abel was annoyed with him for having involved them in this *affair*, which had a drug connection: When he'd gone to buy the diapers, he'd run into somebody who pretended he knew everything and grinned a malicious grin, and I thought it was just a nasty rumor, but maybe the time has come to *put our heads together*. What do we do, for instance, Konstantin asked glancing over at the leftovers—how come you're not eating?—if Vakhtang *never* shows?

But all *our genius* had to say was that he wasn't hungry, he was too tired. He went into his room, closed the door.

My (Konstantin's) first impulse was to sock him in the kisser: really now, the selfish, arrogant asshole; if we were married, I'd get a divorce . . . Look out, thought Konstantin.

During the next few days Konstantin kept a close watch on *things*. Wherever Eka and the baby went, he went with them; whatever they did that didn't cost money, he did with them. They took a walk through the park. Eka smiled her way into an extra portion of chestnuts. What a nice little family, said the chestnut woman. Look out, thought Konstantin.

Marry Eka, bring up Eka's child, have a son with Eka, do

everything for her, eat Eka's food, calm Eka down . . . I'm twenty-four years old; I've seen something of the world, though only indirectly—the media and personal accounts—but be that as it may I'm ready to start a family. She seems to have stopped pilfering, though there were two wrapped presents under the sofa, one for Vakhtang, the other for Abel: she hadn't had an opportunity to give him his. Konstantin would have liked to know what Eka thought of Abel, but she didn't understand the question. Much as I hate to say it, said Konstantin as they were strolling through the park, I've had this thought about him: The only thing he lacks is . . . He did not know the word. Had to form it from scratch: *humanity*. I don't know if you can put it that way: a human without humanity, know what I mean? Eka did not understand what he said, let alone know what he meant; she merely smiled and walked on.

The next night in the lab Abel lifted his head before three quarters of an hour had passed, in other words, just as he was getting started. Seven plus three equals ten, he thought. Seven plus three equals ten. Seven plus three, in all his languages, one after the other, then over and over. He grew dizzy. He staggered across the hall. He saw blinking lights in front of him as he made his way along it. He started with each blink, as if he had not expected it, as if it had ever been different. Blinded, he reached for the wall, felt his way to the toilet. There was no motion detector, nor did he look for the light switch. He let the door shut behind him, pressed his forehead and palms against the cold tiles, and stood there in the dark. He was near the door; had someone come, he might not have noticed him, a person behind an open door. How long he stood there, no sense of time. At a certain point the palpitations, the nausea, the sweating, the sensitivity to light receded: the tenth language was complete; one more and I'll vomit. He washed his hands and face and left.

He did not take the first train in the rising sun with the dozing workers; this time he walked, walked along the tracks, and even so he arrived home hours before the usual time. The piazza was pitch-black; it smelled of perfumed smoke. They must have cooked again, lighted candles. Abel, who had lost sense of taste and, to a large

extent, sense of smell, had only a vague inkling of it. So as not to
wake the baby he did not turn on the light. Although he made no
statement to that effect later, he bumped his shin against the open
convertible sofa. Something shifted in the dark, bodies in sudden
motion, then Eka, whispering something perhaps, then silence.

Later someone switched on the light in his room with a loud
clack and tore the curtains open. It was dark behind them: still or
again. The leathery smell of a uniform filled the room, so perme-
ated it that even *he* could smell it.

They forced us down to the floor—men, women, children—
noses in dirt, hands behind heads. They climbed over us, flung
our things about, yanked us up by one arm; we stood there in our
pajamas; they led us out as we were or pulled any old clothes over
us, pushed our heads down, shoved us into the car. They didn't
tell us where they were taking us; we were blindfolded; they drove
us here and there so we'd lose our orientation; they made us kneel
in sand and rubbed our noses in it; they made believe they were
going to shoot us. Then they let us go in our sopping-wet underwear . . .

Well, not exactly, but they did take everyone who was in the
apartment—Konstantin, Abel, Eka, the baby, and a man Abel had
never seen before—to a police station. To be precise, the only ones
he saw were Eka and the man, and that only for a moment, from
the head down, his angle of sight. Of Konstantin and the baby he
registered only the voices, the ways they reacted to the treatment,
before they disappeared into another car. For years that was the
last Abel heard of Konstantin Tóti.

QUESTIONS

Where you off to, boys?

Nowhere.

Nowhere? Is that possible? Aren't we always on our way some-where? Even if we're not sure where that somewhere is. Know what I mean?

Every afternoon two men our fathers' age leaned against the kiosk in the main square near the town hall, facing the plague monument, the fire tower, and the town's first pizzeria. They drank tea with wine from plastic cups with plastic stirrers, rain or shine. Since when they had begun observing Ilia and Abel is unclear, but the boys remembered first seeing them through a cloudburst. It was thundering when they emerged from the school gate. Later their classmates ran past them, faster and faster, plastered them-selves against the walls, gathered under courtyard entrances; only the two of them proceeded as if nothing were wrong. The awning the men were standing under had holes in it, and water was drip-ping onto the sleeve of one of them, yet all he did was move his elbow and the plastic cup slightly to the side. That was how they first saw each other, through the rain: two lounging plainclothes-men, two passing Gymnasium students.

The kind of moment when people suddenly turn visible. From then on, the men stood at the kiosk every time the boys passed through the main square—in other words, nearly every day—and watched them. One day the hand of one of them was bandaged and as he spread cream on his lips he held the dispenser carefully in the bandaged hand, looking over at them from under heavy eyelids, bandage dirty, lips shining. The day next only the cups were left, no men. They both noticed but said nothing. They never spoke about the men. Once you were in the main square, there was only one path to take: under the fire tower and out along an ill-smelling passageway to the city ring road. Hold your breath, then surface.

The men stood on the other side, under the man-sized iron key nailed to the city wall.

Where you off to, boys?

Nowhere.

Nowhere? Is that possible? Aren't we always on our way somewhere?

Pause. They blink. The sun was bright.

Even if we're not sure where that somewhere is.

Pause.

Know what I mean?

Pause.

Yes, Ilia said finally. That's true.

And started off, but the man with the heavy lids, bandaged hand, and shiny lips stood in his way. The other man stood behind him and said nothing.

From then on, it happened each time. Where you off to, boys?

Sometimes they answered, sometimes not. The men checked their IDs each time. Will you look at how dirty this ID is. As wilted as an old salad. Some patriots you boys are . . .

When Abel Nema came home from the language laboratory in the middle of the night, years later, different city, he was nearly shot to death by an invisible man in the pitch-black piazza. No one else would have heard, but he heard the presence of metal in the room, of skin and metal, of *reaching for*. Luckily Eka was there to whisper "He lives here." He never mentioned it. He said as good as nothing.

Nameaddressdateandplaceofbirthdocumentswhatisyourprofes
sionstudentwhatareyoustudyinglanguageswhendidyoufirstmeet
BlackVakhtangwhatsthatsupposedtomeanyoudontknowwhoheis
youthinkweredumborsomething?

I'm sorry, said Abel. I don't understand.

His *crony* in the next room, Konstantintótiancienthistory, more
than made up for his reserve. Lost his cool. There I was, sleeping
peacefully, when you break in and carry me off and now you ask
me: What's up? I mean really! I'm a respectable citizen! He was actually scared to death. Before long he had fallen back on the usual
poor-student-and-so-on laments, his lower lip moist and quivering.

Eka tried to get her hosts off. Just two nice guys who took in
me and my baby. But things went downhill when she insisted she
was Maria, a patent lie, so why should they believe what she said
about etc. After they had come back to this point several times in
succession and a whole day had passed, they asked Abel and Konstantin, who were obviously no more than a couple of blue-eyed
patsies, if they could come up with character references.

When Tibor B. received the phone call, he was in the bosom of his
closest friends or, rather, he was next door in his study taking care
of something urgent or, rather, he had lost all interest in society,
in everything, for that matter. His midlife crisis. Or the depression
that had been waiting to catch up with him from the outset. Never
quite out of sight. Standing there, waiting patiently, winking
whenever you glance in that direction.

It all began when after a hiatus of nearly twenty-five years
Tibor took to suffering again from being ugly. He despised himself for it. He was a smart man, a very smart man, and had a way
with women: they fell in love with him; they would do anything
for him. What more do you want? He took a year's study leave. I
want to write a book, and I will. The year had passed, the book
was unfinished, but that was no reason to make only sporadic appearances at the department. He had simply lost interest. He was
no longer excited by his students; to be frank, he had trouble telling them apart. Scarcely praiseworthy, to be sure, yet he could not
be dismissed from his post; besides, rumor had it that his second

wife, the Anna woman, had had a relapse (breast cancer), so people bothered him no more than necessary. Anna would prance through their rooms with a smile on her face, making things harder than they already were, while he, overwhelmed by the fear of her death, hardly left his study. His research assistant, Mercedes, came almost every day, brought his mail, looked things up for him, handled his students, represented him whenever possible. She was twenty-six, a single mother, and in love with him, her father's school friend. She devoted her every free minute to him. Most of the time she left the child with her parents. Tibor did not like children. They got on his nerves. When asked for help, he gave it, to this promising— though who could tell—young Abel N., for example, who shows up one day thinking that because he comes from the town we were forced to leave back then . . . Oh well, forget it. Still, he must be full of hope, at that age, in those circumstances. Helping him was the least he could do, so he helped, though the unknown quantity D is related to the unknown quantity P only insofar as one cannot truly muster interest in the lives and sufferings of others. Tibor was aware of that and despised himself for it: a decent person would have asked whether the young man had found a place to live; a decent person would have offered him one of his two guest rooms; a passionate person would have won him over and treated him henceforth as a son . . . *Scenarios*. One can't help *everybody*, he thought, and went back to work.

Anna had similar thoughts. She knew everything—about him, about herself, about the young woman—and thought it was impossible to help everybody. *For this brief period* she concentrated on a few things she liked to do. Once a month she invited people to a *jour fixe*: old friends, including Mercedes' parents, though they seldom came (to be perfectly frank, Miriam couldn't stand Tibor, and not only because he didn't welcome her grandson at the gathering; Alegria saw no reason why he should, by himself, etc . . .), his more tolerable colleagues, a sprinkling of his favorite former students. Once a month the head of the household can pull himself together, make himself available for a few hours, take part in the discussion, even chat like an ordinary person. Some people failed to notice what was happening: they spoke the way people speak about anything and everything. After Anna died, Mercedes moved in and took over her duties. By then the child was nearly six; he was beautiful and as bright as they come, the secret star of the convivial get-togethers, and Tibor caught himself looking at and listening to him with great pleasure. At a certain point he even realized he admired him, was grateful to him, and that—the fact that he could feel gratitude—made him almost happy. His health improved. He completed the book and started another. Four years had passed since Abel's arrival.

So there they were again, the friends of the house. Somebody, an ex-colleague, had recently survived a trip through Albania. A poet there had spoken to him at length about the beauty of the fatherland or about beauty and the fatherland: it was the duty of the poet—whose every other tooth was missing—to speak of the beauty of a fatherland in despair. Beauty despite despair, despair despite beauty. The meat is nondescript, the traveler continued. I mean, which animal.

The Japanese, said one of the former students whose name was Erik and who had just started a publishing venture and was always *amazingly up on things*, the Japanese, he said, have discovered an enzyme that makes it possible to put carved meat together again. It looks like normal meat. Except that you can't tell what part of what animal it comes from.

The Albania expert nodded: it's tough and doesn't smell very good. The gap-toothed poet had recited a poem in his native language. I didn't understand a word. But we were so drunk by then that we wept together.

Oh? said Omar. Why? His grandfather could not suppress a snicker. The Albania expert—his name was Zoltán, but that is of no consequence—eyed first one, then the other, annoyed.

Stop it, Miriam whispered to her husband (once the boy was allowed to go, she sometimes went along), really. Pull yourself together.

What do you mean? I haven't done anything.

Miriam shook her head: we've got to stick it out until midnight.

At this point the hall phone rang.

I'll be right back, said Mercedes and went next door to get Tibor.

I see, said Tibor into the receiver.

Oooh! said the guests in the living room. The host at last!

Right, said Tibor. I'm sorry. I've got to be going.

What? said Mercedes. Now? On New Year's Eve?

Right, said Tibor. He had to get somebody out of jail. He'd be back in a jiffy, or next year, he couldn't tell. One of his students had got mixed up in something to do with drugs or residence permits, and since he had no family he'd given Tibor B. as a reference. Don't wait for me.

What shall I do now? Mercedes asked her mother.

What would you have done?

Served the food?

Well then, said Miriam, I'll help you.

Who is it? asked Omar. Who's been arrested?

I don't know, said Mercedes. I don't know him.

We have no idea how much easier things were when we were students, said Zoltán. He'd received a state scholarship that enabled him to support his foreign wife and their child. Nowadays students had to deal drugs if they wanted to survive. Every night they made a pot of instant broth and added enough cheap noodles to soak it up.

May I use that? (Alegria)

Zoltán looked at him, annoyed.

Hey, it's got nothing to do with me. It's just a look he has.

It usually takes forty minutes to get into town; this time there was so much holiday traffic that it was an hour and ten minutes before Tibor arrived at the police station. Plus twenty minutes to find a parking space. He had tried to park in front of the building—there was room enough—but the policeman at the door shook his head, and when T.B. gave him a questioning, conspiratorial look (might it not be possible for him to hop in and out, he was just picking somebody up) he shook a begloved finger at him and waved him on. Which made Tibor fly off the handle, something he never ever did except when behind the wheel and confronted with uniforms.

A while back this had led him to resolve never to drive again: Mercedes did the driving when there was driving to be done. But that was out of the question today. As Tibor circled the block, cursing, he talked himself into believing that he had to save his *own son* from the abuse of state authority and that every minute counted.

Then he had to wait, minus the formalities that had to be gone through, a full two hours. At the end of each half hour he went out for a smoke. Four times altogether. No sooner had he lit the fourth cigarette than he threw it away, marched back in, and made a scene worthy of Hollywood. He screamed at the cops. What right did they have, etc. Did they have any idea whom they were dealing with, etc.

Calm down, professor, said the cops, unimpressed. That's not the way to behave with us.

Tibor stopped screaming and started pacing up and down the waiting room at breakneck speed.

Cut the shit, will you, and sit down.

He shot a glance in the direction of the voice. A fat slob. He resumed his pacing.

Sit down, I said. You're driving me up the wall!

But the squirt refused to listen, and the slob was sure he'd go out of his mind if the guy kept it up, so the only thing to do was to beat the living daylights out of him. He had placed his hands on his knees in preparation for hoisting himself up when the professor's name was called out and (practically) everybody was saved.

Since none of the influential people the other pain in the neck (Konstantin) had listed as references could be located, they asked Professor B. whether he happened to know him. Tibor shook his head impatiently. Are you letting my student out or aren't you?

Everything okay?

Yes, said Abel.

Those were the last words they said.

Now that *it was all over*, any feelings Tibor may have had about standing up for the foreign student had faded. What do I really know about him anyway? Tibor took him as near as he could get to the Bastille and dropped him off.

Thank you, said Abel.

Don't mention it, said Tibor and drove off.

Back in the apartment the chirping had returned together with the blue strip of light under Blond Pal's door. He must have heard the door open if he was there, but he gave no sign. As if every single object in the place—food included, his food included—had not been turned upside down, as if the edges of the linoleum in the common room had not been torn up, as if the sections of the sofa were not sticking up towards the ceiling with the remains of the two last, decimated Christmas presents strewn among them.

He said he would betray us, Konstantin later told someone, and betray us he did.

But hadn't he left for the holidays? asked Konstantin's later conversation partner. He wasn't even there.

Konstantin: They've got everything now. My fingerprints, my name. They know I exist and I'm here. And I've still got to live with *him*. Can you imagine that?

As for Abel: he went to his room, gathered up his belongings, and left the Bastille, never to return.

PART III

ANARCHIA KINGANIA

Folklore

IN THE WOODS

Taking a cab was out of the question. He walked. In the twenty minutes it had taken him to pack, the streets and weather had changed radically. The streets were fog-bound. He could see almost nothing, yet he could hear everything, and it all seemed so close—the murderous traffic: cars, buses, trains, trams; were there any tracks?—and even something that sounded like a ship's siren. Above it all, amidst it all: rockets whistling, pistol salvos, as if a battle were in progress: the gods were sore afraid. He couldn't tell about the men: they scurried here and there, oddly dressed, some cheerful, some not, suddenly popping up in front of him, bumping into him, clinging to his backpack when he paused every few blocks to compare street signs with street map.

Later, when the streets were as good as empty, the noise so subsided that one, he, could hear his own footsteps and those of the remaining pedestrians. They were few; they tried to steer clear of their echoes by hugging the walls. Sleeves and pockets took on white stripes.

Later he groped his way along a staircase. Here it was once more pitch-black, cold, and quiet; somewhere up ahead he could sense the opposite: noise, heat, light. The concrete walls all but vibrated beneath his fingers.

He had forgotten to count the steps, thought it must be another flight up, when suddenly a door swung open before him, *tsing*, iron striking concrete. Out came a stranger. Walked from right to left and vanished behind a small door across the way. The first door remained ajar.

The smoke could be cut with a knife, the visibility resembling that outside, though it was warm. There seemed to be many people, belly to belly, a dense wood of bodies. Abel stood hesitant before the crack made by the door. Was there any room at all or would he be the last drop before the glass overflowed if he set foot . . . All at once the man appeared again; the sound of water came from behind him; without a word he walked at the same speed, this time from left to right, shoving Abel before him.

The wood was dense. The wanderer bumped into the trees with his bundle—sorry, excuse me—but they didn't mind: he might as well not have been there; they just kept jabbering: . . . *and that's what really gets my goat a whole generation virtually cleaned out we're the new germans stigmatized for a hundred if not more well I say wealth may be at the bottom of it it's heartbreaking to think you could die from a ruptured appendix or breech delivery the bloody ignorance of those people it's all on account of their self-satisfied hold it the whole thing was and is a bald-faced lie that's what drives me up the wall and when I ask them if it gives them nightmares they look at me like I was crazy but that was the way things were they make it look like everyone can strike it rich but I don't stand a chance not in this life and it can be downright humiliating if you can't afford beans because that's what matters most isn't it beans or glug glug* . . . A woman wearing a gold cardboard helmet was elbowing her way through the crowd, tilting a bottle she was holding like a lance, pouring schnapps into beaks that opened as she passed: glug glug, gargle talk. Suddenly she paused, pushed the sweaty helmet up from her eyes to give her a better view, of whom, of *him*, and took a running jump: *Kurva*, Abelard, where have you been keeping yourself?

. . .

I set off on my own, rambling through strange regions with strangers. We grew to such numbers that we grew numberless. The heating got stuck on high, the windows got stuck halfway, and heat came from above, cold from below. The train rattled, the heating rattled, the wind roared, everything roared, the train was one big roar. The locomotives and the people froze, quarreled, wept, or cried out, *KURVÁK*, GIVE ME SOMETHING TO DRINK! Everything was sticky from spilt alcohol; you could walk on the ceiling like flies; your fingers made little slurping noises when you groped your way over people's heads to what passed for toilets but had no water: there wasn't a drop of water on the train. Everything was in constant motion, from one end to the other and back again: *Kurvák*, give me water! Somewhere along the way, where the smoke was the thickest, there was a dining car, but all it had was an overheated coffee machine, there being no water after all. Retching bile into a waterless toilet just as two trains, one of which is yours, fly screeching past each other, Abel Nema, Gymnasium graduate and future deserter, bumped his head against the raised toilet seat. His forehead made a slurping noise as he disengaged it from the seat.

And now a spot to drink, said the woman outside the door, not yet helmeted, after smearing his forehead with schnapps from the bump out.

He thanked her politely and said he didn't drink.

So you do-hon't dri-hink. Something wrong with you? Something's wrong with you. Smoke? You don't smoke either. No vices. How about sex? Or is that out too?

She laughed. None of her teeth had any effect on its neighbors. Lips the color of blackberries under large, hairy nostrils, but magnificent cheekbones, eyes, and a forehead topped by dark, unruly, and uncombed locks. Still laughing.

Hey, are you a monk or something? He just stares. And those eyes! The sky before a storm. Or maybe you just have a source for violet contact lenses.

He stood with his feet wedged between suitcases, she with

her back to the dining car. People kept pushing past her. The gap between cars was covered with two iron plates that clattered whenever you set foot on them. There was a new bottleneck every minute. The spot that drives people mad the moment they board a train. Excuse me. She moved closer until the bottle was pressing into his stomach. It hurt. My heart was about to do a trampoline jump onto my stomach. She moved even closer, the faded-jeans curve of her thigh pressing into his. He was glued to the toilet door, it was impossible to move, there was no out, they were squashed into their corner. She leaned against him and laughed, reeking of alcohol.

If you'd stayed back there in your monastery, Abelard, you'd have been nice and comfortable now.

She harped so long on his seminary ways that at last he asked her, not curtly, no, wearily, that if at all possible he'd rather talk about something other than religion.

At this point a bit of space opened up and she could move away and look him over.

Well, well, my little heathen. The fire blazes wild 'neath the glowering brows.

Once more he is stymied. He is only eighteen.

Nineteen.

Name?

Abel.

. . .

No, really. It is.

She poured some schnapps onto her fingers and—what was that she was doing?—sprinkled it over the baffled boy. In the name of the Father, the Son, and the Holy Ghost I solemnly baptize you Abel Fromthethicket.

Baptized with schnapps in a crowded sleeper. He pressed his eyes shut. She wiped a drop from the tip of his nose.

By the way, my name is Kinga. Which means lady warrior. Today—in other words, right now, starting a minute ago—is my name day, and since I've lost my friends, three musicians, some-where here on the train, you're the only one I have to drink a toast to me. To my health! I want to see you drink. Make a man of you.

Later, not even halfway, he got out to look for somebody by the name of Bora. Kinga waved to him from the window. See you at six when the war is over!

Later he asked her whether she remembered what her last words to him were then.

I talk a lot when the day is long.

And now he was staggering under the weight of his suitcases and of her. A plastic iguana she had stuck between her breasts was pressing against his chest, and a transparent liquid issuing from its red plastic mouth was soaking his collar. She laughed and licked it away, her large, dark teeth sliding over his neck. It still felt sticky later. Every time he moved his head.

She jumped up and raised the bottle to his mouth: Where have you been keeping yourself? Here, have a slurp. But in so doing she jerked him back and they bumped into the people around them, glug, glug, bottle scraping tooth enamel. How can it be so packed, you can hardly see where you are, the windows seem painted black, but it is just the night and the smell of so many bodies. There was a man in the kitchen whose name was Janda, with a face that made you think he had not slept in three days and a cigarette dangling out of the corner of his mouth. With one hand he was stirring something in a pot; with the other he was releasing a red-powder snow into it, some of which fluttered into the eyes, noses, and mouths of new arrivals. Kinga coughed.

They hadn't arrived until this morning! (Cough.) Hadn't slept a wink for three nights. Their last gig had been a wedding. Mixed it all together in tubs—meat, drinks, *real* spices! They could pick up some money by playing again today, but they won't, because New Year's Eve belongs to the Café Anarchia—to me, in other words.

Hello, said Abel.

Hi, said Janda. The cigarette wobbled; the ashes fell into the pot. He stirred them in.

Jesus! Kinga screamed, looking into Abel's mouth for the first time. You look like Dracula! What's wrong with your teeth?

He'd forgotten his teeth were black again today, the whole day.

What happened? Here, rinse your mouth out.

Only now did she seem to notice he was there with bag and baggage.

How come you've got all this stuff with you.

Can I stay a few days?

Why? What's this? She turned his palms up.

Black fingertips. What have you been up to?

Nothing. Fingerprints.

Now they were all looking at him, the three in the immediate vicinity, that is. Janda must have got paprika in his eyes: he was blinking.

What for?

A mistake.

And how did your teeth get that way? Did they make you lick the ink?

No, it was a phonological procedure.

Pause.

Come on, come on. Are we going to have to drag it out of you?

He can tell them nothing more. The story of the past two days in brief. He himself could make out nothing of what had gone on. And then I left my flatmate behind so I could move on unencumbered. He doesn't tell them that.

The bastards, said Kinga.

Poker-faced Janda tasted the brew and, tapping the spoon on the pot, called out, To the trough!

Kinga would have asked more questions, but a flood of newcomers kept her from it. Making for the pot as if on the point of starvation. Abel was washed away by them. Found a quiet mattress corner to settle on. It had been a wild few days: I'll view *the rest* from here. Kinga came swimming up. Stroked the hair out of his eyes. Everything okay?

Yes.

Later Janda and two others began to play; people danced, bouncing in place for want of room. Later somebody opened the skylight, and everyone sober enough clambered up the rusty iron ladder to a rather uncomfortable tar roof. Abel knew it from earlier, warmer days and stayed where he was. A *water*fall of cold air streamed in through the skylight. He sat right there in the train;

clearly it didn't bother him. Hours in the same position, backed against the corner, it couldn't have been comfortable, but he: Like a statue, said a woman who had observed him for a while because she found him good-looking; a black-and-white *wooden* statue, a little eerie, though . . . Something you couldn't put your finger on seemed to emanate from him. Far-off places and . . . was it strength or weakness? You feel like lying at his side—when if not now, when you're New Year's drunk—yet you were afraid to go up close. Kinga didn't have that problem. She rushed up to the roof, rushed back down, flung herself on him, kissed him, rubbed against him, then jumped up and called for music or drink. Later, when pretty much everyone was drunk, they blew glassy-eyed into their cardboard trumpets until it hurt so much they had to open their mouths wide and scream AAAAAAAAAAAAAAAAAAAAAAAA AAAAAAAAAAAAAAAAAAAAAAAAAAAAAAAAAAAAAA AAAAAAAAA to keep from going deaf. That was in the last night of the year 199–. In the corner next to the window Abel Nema closed his eyes.

THE GODMOTHER

Who is that guy, anyway? asked Janda. He was suspicious.

They had met again, accidentally or not, a little more than a year after he had got off the train. How he had ended up at a gourmet restaurant with cultural pretensions catering to the university community was unclear. Perhaps he had heard about it on Radio Konstantin; perhaps he simply needed a toilet. He stood sheepish—it was not his *milieu*—at the drafty entrance and watched the usual tumult: tables, chairs, people, a bar to the left, and—straight ahead at the other end of the room—a low, dusty podium with instruments and men on it. He would have to thread his way through it all. He finally made his mind up and was about to turn around when he suddenly heard, *KURVÁK*, GIVE ME SOMETHING TO DRINK!

He said not a word, stood stock-still, right where he was, stargazing again, just the way we like him. A premeditated elbow where it hurts the most, between spleen and ribcage, an elbow belonging to an anatomically sophisticated someone. *Someone* has a way of life or perhaps merely a character that for days has sent him out spoiling for a fight. These are . . . times, and he has pegged Abel Nema for the ideal candidate. Bad choice. The mooncalf takes no notice, just stands there gaping at the tousled old woman who bends to slip a tray with four full glasses of beer onto a nearby table, then slowly straightens up. It was as yet unclear whether she recognized him or not. The man standing behind Abel was still hopeful. Hey! He gave him another shove. You deaf or something? But at that point she took a running jump and arms around neck, legs around thighs, pelvis thrusting. Twisting to keep from falling, moving away from the man at Abel's back, who, resigned to the snub, withdrew. Still in her clutches, Abel kept flailing—what else could he do with his arms?—until fortunately she jumped back.

To get a good look!

No changes. Still the sheepish monk. The same clothes—though the hair was a year longer, framing his face like a girl's—and my, how skinny! A breeze and you're gone! But it's a nice smell you've got. She smelled of smoke, alcohol, and something more. Maybe, say, a train, yes, she smelled in her own secret way of train.

It might have been only yesterday. The day before yesterday. Good friends. An elementary-school teacher from B.—I once spent twelve hours with her and her bulky luggage—told me her whole life story from My grandfather was an anarchist and one day I'll write a story about him and name a pub after him to interpretations of poetry (he had just finished school and could, to some extent, follow. You're a clever boy, a good boy, too, and good-looking. Your mother must be proud of you. How old do you think I am? Quiet and polite too . . .) down to the latest *scandals* with a violent lover, after which, of course, she had to get out of town. Off on a summer holiday and then stuck here, like you. How good it is to see you again, my boy! How's life been treating my godson?

All kinds of things have happened. Miraculous new skills, good luck among other things, side effects included. No, don't say that. Just say, Very well, thank you. And you?

Plenty to complain about, more to curse.

She laughed. She began to pinch him, everywhere, pinch his cheeks, his side, his penis. The tingle lasted the whole evening. The next day his back hurt too, but he had forgotten why.

Kinga had come with the musicians, the men on the stage who moved so carefully among the instruments. You can peek between the boards. The fellows from the train—had he actually met them? Not that I recall. Let me introduce you. She dragged him through the crowd, a large backpack through a jam-packed metro, though here things were calmer.

Meet Janda, Andre, and Kontra, percussion, cimbalom and guitar, and, as you can tell by the name, contra- or double bass. And this is Abel Fromthethicket, my godson. Yes he is, yes he is. My godson. Be nice to my godson!

That is how Abel and Kinga met again.

The fox-faced Janda, the friendly, stocky Andre with his rectangle of a forehead, and Kontra the taciturn played; Kinga danced. Abel spent the entire evening in the *musicians' corner*, id est, a worn-out couch draped with whatever articles of clothing the musicians happened not to be wearing—here too, *that* smell, its masculine variant, leather and pre-shave—the royal box, apart from the others.

How come you're in the musicians' corner? Konstantin called to him. The hall is sold out. *Men* are grabbing chairs away from *women*! Can you imagine? Got room for me? Don't be an asshole. He squeezed in beside him. Shove it over a little, can't you?

Sorry, said Abel. A large metal can was pressing into his side. It's an instrument.

Konstantin, drinking his Grüne Wiese and talking. About this kind of music: wolves howling in folklore run through a jazz mill, the usual crap. Until Kinga came back from her dance: Make way for the queen what have we here up you go pal up and out.

Konstantin stared at the curly-headed dragon. Who was that? My godmother. Your *what*? He blinked, then drank down the Grüne Wiese in silence, at *moderate* speed, and went *to order another*. He got into a conversation with a woman at the bar and never went back. Kinga plonked herself down in the now-empty space, landing on Abel's hand. Her bottom was hard; his hand gave a crack. A tingle reaching up to the elbow. She turned to him and draped a knee over his thigh. It too was hard: now the tingle reached down into his thigh.

Tell me, she shouted. Still a virgin? Me too. 31 August. She laughed and wiped the moisture out of the indentation above her upper lip.

Everything about her is loud. When she speaks, but even when she does things others do noiselessly: opening a beer can, dropping a napkin. When she does it: bang.

Abelard smiled in silence.

Right. An eloquent, meaningless smile. You are completely and utterly depraved, you know that?

She took his head between her hands and pressed his temples with her thumbs.

You're just a sad, sad . . .

She slapped him with both hands and shouted, Why are you always so sad, eh?

I'm not sad.

What would you call it then?

He shrugged.

Don't even know, do you?

Pause. Then softly: And you?

And me what?

What are you?

What am I?

Sad? Happy?

She looked him in the eye. What do you mean?

She laughed, then grew serious, sat up, shoulder to shoulder. For a while she just leaned against him, jiggling her foot in time to the music. The room had long since vanished behind the sweat, dust, and noise, as if they had never got off, as if it were still the same rattling, stinking train, so she had to roar: When I was your age, Janda was my husband. I'm still living off him, when you get down to it. More or less. More or less we live on more or less. (She laughed.) And you? Making ends meet?

Yes.

Papers in order?

I've a student visa.

So you're a student now.

Yes.

What are you studying?

Languages.

Which ones?

He named four.

Well, well. What about money?

I have money.

What do you do for it?

Nothing. It's a scholarship.

Who gave it to you?

He named the foundation.

I see. Only the gifted need apply, eh? How much do you get?

Nine hundred.

What? A month?

Yes.

Hm, she said. She flopped back, bumping him again with her shoulder. Another round of pins and needles, this time down to the fingers. Her arms were crossed. She was looking over at the dance floor or at least in that direction. Every time a dance was over Abel caught Janda's eye. He returned it. That was all. Kinga hummed. Hummed, hummed, hummed.

At the end of the evening she asked if he could lend her a hundred and fifty. Could they go to the money machine then and there? There was one on the corner. The musicians waited a little way off. She protected him from prying eyes by nestling up to his back. She was heavy. She hooked her thumbs into one of his belt loops; he hoped the trousers wouldn't rip.

Thanks. She flicked her thumbs free of the trousers and gave him a wet kiss on the cheek near the mouth. Thanks, kid.

Half Armenian, her mother called her the little whore and made her eat her own vomit. In the home, where she willingly went to live, there were fourteen girls to a room. All her pocket money went for cotton. Actually just small, scratchy cotton plants fresh from the field: when she walked they made a soft squeaky noise between her legs. At twelve she began to collect bottles and cigarette stubs: smoking is supposed to hinder the flow, but it hinders growth as well. Even so, I got these little what-d'you-call-its. She was called the artist lady, which in those parts was about as much of a compliment as what my mother called me, but nobody could drink, brawl, or recite poetry like Kinga. Her first lover was a post-

man by day and a poet by night. I always remember him in connection with the ashes on the slab of metal in front of his stove: I
would stare at them while he lay behind me. The seventies were a
pretty good time, except that you threw up every day on account
of the Pill and my own gynecologist called me a whore. On the
other hand, the sea was sky-blue and we had the best passport
in the world. Let me tell you, we were somebody back then! She
wanted to become a writer; I became a muse. Didn't I, darling? I am
a muse, aren't I?

Sure, said Janda. What else.

They had met while students, a passionate affair, kissing and
fighting while three other girls in the room feigned sleep. She had
had trouble with a guy and he with the law; they were both basically fed up. Still, it was meant only as a summer interlude, a trip
to dispel the gloom, and now.

The most important thing is not to get pinned down. Get
pinned down and you're done for. Hold on to your independence,
no matter what. Her apartment was actually a rehearsal space she
gave the musicians for practically nothing, out of the goodness of
her heart. It was L-shaped. The short leg was for sleeping mostly,
the long leg for everything else. At the far end there was a cooking
stove and a sink; the toilet was on the landing. Kinga had taken it
all in and decided to live there. New countries were popping up all
over the place; why shouldn't I have one of my own? In honor of
my grandfather Gabriel I hereby declare the independence of Anarchia Kingania. Down with all despots, generals, slaveholders, and
the media! Long live free spirits, hedonism, and tax evasion!

She laughed; everybody smiled except Janda, who was no
smiler: he had the mouth of a skeptic.

Kinga pointed straight in his face: Every people makes a contri-
bution to world culture. Ours is—see the illustration—pessimism
combined with depression.

Oh, said Janda. I thought it was paranoia combined with rage.
What we have here, he said, is a dictatorship based on a cult of personality. He called her *the field marshal* and was about the only one
who occasionally stood up to her.

Skeptic! said Kinga.

. . .

So it is not true to say that Abel kept completely to himself during the first four years. Once they had found each other again, they actually met quite regularly. Sometimes she asked for money, sometimes she did not.

Be nice to my godson, she would say to the others. Be friendly. After all, he's keeping us in food.

She chortled. In fact, they had all kinds of ways to keep going: the musicians' pay and whatever she earned cleaning houses and babysitting. At home I'd have been a teacher, a day laborer of the nation; my afternoons would have been just about as they are now. My body, she was wont to say, is the only capital I have left. Bereft of my mother tongue, I have only two roles to play: old gray nag or sexual object. After Janda she had taken up with Kontra and then Andre, then gone back to Janda, then had a young clarinetist who did not belong to the band, and so on down the line, most of them young. The names were unimportant. At first the musicians thought *he* was one of them—who knows where she'd picked him up; in the train the day we lost each other—but this time it seemed different. You don't need to worry, she said to Janda. I could have him if I wanted to. If I don't, it's because I don't want to. I don't believe it, said Janda. It was not clear which part of her statement his referred to. The fact was, he'd been seen with neither women nor men—apart from *her*. I'm not worried, said Janda, who had not the slightest intention of being nice to the boy.

What's the matter?

Nothing.

You never say a word to him. None of you do.

What do you want me to say to him?

How should I know? Where are you from? Have you had your appendix out? Do you collect anything?

Does he *collect* anything?

You know what I mean.

No, said Janda. I haven't a clue. I know where he comes from. And I'm not interested in his appendix.

Pause. Then, softly: What do you want from him?

What do you think? Nothing.

And what does he want?

What do you think he wants? What do *you* want?

I want, he started counting on his fingers: to make music every day of my life, for myself and for others, so I can earn money, be famous, keep my friends, love a woman, be loved by a woman; I want tenderness, looking after, good and regular sex, delicious and nutritious food—at this point he ran out of fingers and began again—good drink, and eventually I'd like to find a place not too familiar or unfamiliar, a place where I can settle down in peace with all the things I've just enumerated and live a painless life until I die amidst kith and kin, die a death not too sudden, so I have a chance to say good-bye, but not long and drawn out, so I'm not a burden on anyone. That's what I want.

Well, that's exactly what he wants.

Janda shrugged. Sure. Doesn't everybody. It doesn't bring him any closer. We can't stand him, that's all.

You're jealous, said Kinga.

Ha, said Janda.

Kinga danced around him, chanting, Jealous, you're jealous!

He's not one of us, that's all.

He said it softly, but even in her rollicking she heard him and stopped. Wrinkled forehead, deep voice: I'm the one who determines who's one of us, get it?

AFTER THE FROST

The night after New Year's Eve Kinga had a dream about frost. The whole city was ice. Only the five of them were here; the rest had gone, and Kinga shouted, To the sea! On New Year's morning the sea's the place! The boy's never been out of the city! Don't be an idiot, Kinga, said Janda. It's all ice. But they went anyway. The windshield was a prism of hoarfrost: they had to squint through it to see where they were going. They were the only ones on the road: the city was empty and white. They crawled along, snow crunching under the tires. They had taken the van the guys took on their tours. It was hot and cold at the same time: biting drafts made their way through the windows, yet the air smelled musty plus the stench of a heater going full blast. The ice flowers on the windows refused to melt: they could see nothing but the narrow tunnel directly in front of them. We'll never see the sea, said Andre; we'll go blind first. Kontra scratched away at the ice flowers in his window. Scrape, scrape; scratch, scratch. I don't know why, but I had the feeling it was wrong, he shouldn't be doing it. A *hole* in the *whole*. That's just like us, said Janda. He was drinking black coffee and vodka out of a thermos. Let me drive! Kinga shouted. You've been driving the whole time! True. Then it's okay; then there's nothing more to stop us. She laughed. A second later they were crunching their way through the frosty sand. Look, look! cried Kinga. See that? See that? Frozen waves! Frozen waves! She noticed she was saying everything twice, and laughed. But she also laughed for joy. Ever seen the likes of it, boy? she shouted at Abel, pulling him over to her. What do you think, said Andre, if he's never left the city. Then they stood there, all five of them, arms linked: Janda, Kinga, Abel, Andre, Kontra—in that order. There was nobody but them on the beach. They looked at the frozen sea. I love you all, Kinga wanted to add, but then she woke up.

Opened her eyes, looked over at the window: everything really was white; so there's a chance, on my knees, window wide open, shivering with fear, joy, cold, like when you've just woken up. But then she saw it was only fog, the dirt below dark and wet, a slight smell of gunpowder, the party stench unfurling to the left and right of her, and I realized: I'd dreamed it all.

She told her dream to the musicians. There was a new smell in the kitchen now: slightly over-roasted coffee. Abel opened his eyes. The window under which Kinga had rolled up and slept at his feet was open. Fog was flowing in, slithering across the flotsam and jetsam of the previous evening: food mixed with ashes, paper, and the like. *As if the bomb had fallen.* Only now that the crowd was gone was it visible. The furnishings in Kingania consisted basically of mattresses, suitcases, and cardboard boxes stuffed with all the things you need to live or don't: clothes, books, musical instruments, pots. Scattered among the containers lay moraines of odds and ends, from an aluminum soup ladle to a fly swatter, though there were never flies to swat.

Christ, what a pigsty! Kinga, elated, trod through the mess as if it were newly fallen snow, a preserving glass with coins and banknotes in her hand. As is only meet and proper, the quite considerable number of invitees who bring along people of their own, people nobody knows but who make themselves perfectly at home, help to defray the cost of the drinks. We live on the edge of an abyss. The minuscule benefit left over at the end! Don't say I'm running a speakeasy.

Morning, kiddo!

A kiss redolent of a long night. She sat down next to him on the mattress, crossed her legs, shook the money out of the glass, and began to count it. Kontra and Andre were tidying up; Janda took the toilet key and went out. The *boy* stayed where he was.

When all is said and done, nothing earth-shaking had happened: not even thirty-six hours in police custody. But then, shortly before they were released—Tibor had been waiting for quite some time by then—a fatherly type came up to Abel or whatever your name is. A thin forty-year-old but, as I say: a fatherly type. Came up and sat down facing him, the desk lamp radiating palpable heat and a diffuse light from high on the right, as in paintings with Biblical subjects; half the man was illuminated, and the way his hands lay crossed on the desk had something of the Let us pray about it. Then, too, his intonation, reserved and respectful, respect for something not present in the room or, rather, for something higher, which we call law and order here. And then he commenced to speak in the following terms.

You are young, *my son*, young and alone. Life, which first led you to believe it is a bowl of cherries, has proved anything but. The countries that first kept you in their iron grip have spat you out into the world. Now you are spread over all God's earth like dandelion seeds [sic!], said the man on the opposite shore of the desk, and one never knows where a seed will land: in fertile soil, perhaps, or on a mound of dog's muck, in the gutter, or worse. You come into contact with people you would never have come into contact with earlier, *under normal circumstances*. The question is: How can the individual one has become under the circumstances hold his own, that is, stick to the straight and narrow, the path leading eventually from the A where we are to the B where we all want to be. You probably have no idea of how tricky it is, especially for people of your age, to progress from A to B. Fate has a way of catching up with someone on his own, and you are as much on your own as it is possible to be: your professor, who asked Who? over the phone, is your closest contact. The importance of community is often underestimated: team players tend to prove more useful to the commonweal than individualists, though of course it depends on the nature of the community. But I'm running on. We wonder how best to handle someone with the talents your professor told us about—it may well be his genius that makes you find him so suspicious!—this Abel Nema, who looks like a reasonable young man and who from the start or at least from relatively early on struck us as innocent, though we kept waiting for him to come out and proclaim it. It's hard to work for a paternalistic state: we don't punish; we transmit values, get people to think for themselves. He hoped he'd had some success with Abel. Now it was time for us to go along home and think over how best to manage our future. Exceptional talent is a privilege one must not claim exclusively for oneself; besides, all the talent in the world is useless unless one's papers are in order.

Pause. The *genius* had never been particularly forthcoming, but now the room was so quiet you could hear breathing. And something like a whiny lament coming through the wall. For hours on end. The fatherly type sighed. We know where we can find you, he said, and let him go.

It might have been worse, of course, yet Abel could no longer stay at the Bastille or exchange a single word with Konstantin, for that matter. Not that it was really his fault. Once more his life to date was wrenched a world away, and from one hour to the next. But it was time to look for something new anyway: ever since he had mastered the tenth language, his life had lost direction. Except for the certainty that there was no reason to report anybody or anything for any matter, you pigs.

But you don't know any pigs, said Kinga during a breakfast of leftovers. Except for us. And nobody gives a damn about us.

They just wanted to give him a scare, said Kontra, licking one end of a cigarette paper. One of their strong-arm tactics.

Watch out, said Janda. He's been working with them for ages.

Asshole, said Kinga.

No one spoke for a while.

I mean it, said Kinga. How can you be such an asshole?

He was just kidding, said Andre. Would you do me a favor and not start the new year off with a fight.

Kinga mumbled something, moved over to the boy, stroked his face, kissed him. Poor kid! But never took her eyes off Janda. Janda pretended to watch the level of coffee in the coffeemaker rise. Kontra lit a joint.

Now that they've finally signed a peace treaty after four years of shoot-outs, they'll probably send us back, said Kinga. Anybody given any thought to the matter?

Kontra handed her the joint: Here. Cannabis eliminates unpleasant emotional memories.

The saliva-soaked stub made its way to Abel via Andre and Janda. Their hands touched. Janda looked him in the eye.

Later the musicians left. Kinga laid her head on Abel's thigh, a hard head on a firm thigh: uncomfortable. She repositioned herself in his lap and fell asleep. For a while he stayed under her; later he carefully rolled her head onto a pillow and put water on to boil in the kitchen.

Later she awoke or, no, earlier, from the bubbling: she had only pretended to be asleep. Waited until he was squatting in the blue plastic bathtub, three days without a wash, the water now up to his ankles. She stood, walked over to him, helped him to pour water over his head, scrubbed his back. On your feet, she said. He stood up dripping in the cold; she washed him with her washcloth, wiped him dry, ordered him back into bed. brought him hot, somewhat too bitter tea. You can stay as long as you like, kiddo.

Thank you, said Abel.

He stayed the rest of the winter.

IN THE ENCLAVE

This place is an enclave, said Kinga. Which means? Which means for one thing that everything is *now*. We can make statements about the future all right, but they're just so many coffee-bean prognostications. Today four beans fell out of the mill. Does that tell us anything about my day? Or birds. How many—and how many varieties—flew past my window while I was trying to wake up?

Another thing it means is our lack of customary creature comforts: after the fully automated Bastille there were temporary power outages, or the water suddenly turned coffee-brown. The hotplate warmed a radius of approximately one meter: so much for the heating. True, there was an old iron stove filled with paper, but it was not attached to a chimney. Kinga stuffed her own papers into it, *failed love letters*, and there was room for more. Lo! the Magic Black Hole in the middle of my universe. In case of emergency there was always the Ice Age ventilating system, which noisily circulated the stink of burnt dust around the room, and whenever you put it into action you had to turn off all other electric appliances: refrigerator, light bulbs, etc. Luckily it had been a mild winter, no trace of the ice she had dreamed of. It was customary for Kinga to move in with one of the musicians—they had places with various heating arrangements—but it was clear, though never said, that no one had room for the *boy*, so hard-nosed Kinga stayed put too: we'll keep each other warm, won't we, kiddo?

Life in Kingania was not so bad, all in all. The first weeks of the new year were quiet: what looked like chaos was in fact a series of similar days. On the days when she cleaned houses or babysat for people *crazy enough* (Janda) to trust her, she would leave early. Abel was by himself until afternoon. Had it been up to him, he would never have left the short leg of the L. Hibernate. Winter it out. An increasingly human-smelling mattress by the window, which you were free to look through or not, a lair—what more does a man need? When I was young, I lived in a wardrobe. The musicians would come later in the day. Kontra first and most regularly, the youngest, the organized music student. He would spend several hours practicing his classical double-bass repertory. Abel sat in the corner listening; they did not speak. Once they had said hello, the musicians never exchanged a word with him. They practiced or took breaks to cook, smoke, drink, or when there was sports or news on television (a small black-and-white set with a makeshift antenna). The coffeemaker constantly hiccupped on the stove; the mulled wine simmered. The room and stairs were filled with effusions. Later Kinga came home, and they sat in a circle to eat. They spent a good deal of money—*for people in our circumstances*—on food: good food is the most important thing. Later in the evening drinking became the most important thing: Kingania's official currency was the *slivo*, and the extent of their boozing defies description. They could hold so much alcohol, each of them, that it took a lot of work to make them drunk. Except for Kontra, who drank only to intensify the effect of the grass, and Abel, who simply never got drunk. Apart from everything else the guy is a medical miracle. Kinga laid an ear to his chest and listened. Perfectly normal, she said to the others. He's human.

Andre had a birthday at the end of January, and a new flurry of activity commenced. You would think the party guests had never gone home or gone home only to catch their breath before the next night: familiar faces and faces repetition had begun to make familiar, though many new faces as well. We've gained a certain notoriety, my boy, a proud Kinga would say. Open rehearsals, salon, call it what you will. Not that we're doing anything but what we've done forever or at least the last ten years. The eighties weren't bad either, though things were a bit darker then, which may have its roots in the basement hole that we—that is, I, Kinga—lived in at the time. It was a small town, and at a certain point *everybody* started gathering at her place to talk politics: everything is politics in our country. We criticized from both left and right, talked about nothing the whole time but how impossible it was to live *there*, and now? Can you believe we thought the main problem was that our nationalities were oppressed, and look what's going on now.

It's not the simple people, said Andre. It's a pronouncement by the academy. Everybody knows that.

Bullshit, said Janda. And I say that as a man of the people.

But it's different in your case, said Andre. You had no political motives.

Sigh, sighed Kontra. Oh for the good old days, when people went out on a limb for personal motives.

Janda laughed with a snort.

Kinga to Kontra: You too, my son? You too a cynic?

Is that a question? (Janda)

Man is not good! he cried out later, when he had had more to drink. Can't you get that through your head!

Andre merely shook his big head.

As for Abel: he said not a word. Looked on while everyone around him got drunk or high. The men's euphorias were soft, except for the accordion that Andre insisted on playing on such occasions; Kinga's high pushed her mood swings, which were not what you might call mild to begin with, over the top.

At times she was melancholic, at times motherly: Look what I've swiped for you! An orange. Want me to peel it for you? When she was drunk, she would hassle everyone in sight. Pull total strangers to pieces, people she had seen only in passing. I go into a department store, take the escalator, ladies apparel; what do I see but one of those painted cows handing out advertising to everybody, everybody but: me. Won't buy a thing, that one. Just looking, like in a museum. Well, at least I've been to a museum, you perfumed cunt. Thinks her shit don't stink. Let me see, shall I learn these forty new love positions or go on a diet or take a trip around the world? Or shall I do something about being so endlessly bored with myself and have a child?

I wouldn't mind having a child, said the truthsayer Janda, thereby transferring the conflict from the street into the heart of the hearth.

Kinga: *You?* A child? Poor kid.

There was a brief pause before she let loose again. Conjecturing. And of course he wants the mother to be a dumb blonde, the dumber the better; it makes things easier: the IQ of a mustard seed is all it takes to be the queen of our hearts!

Could you cut the crap, please. I (Janda) would be much obliged.

And what would you have to offer her? Take a good look in the mirror. You can't even take care of yourself. You think we need you here?

Janda: In the name of our friendship may I ask you to shut your trap!

Cut it out, will you. Both of you. (Andre, the voice of reason)

Sometimes that stopped her, and she would squat in the blue plastic bathtub and shave wherever she could.

There, she would say then. There!

To Abel: Am I beautiful?

Yes, said the shy ex-student. (Your upper lip is a rasp, but I worship you.)

She laughed—she was flattered—and put her arm around his neck: Would you like me to have your child?

Let the kid be, will you. (Janda)

Kinga laughed and cooed Kiddle, kiddle, kiddle into his neck.

Or it didn't stop her, in which case—it wasn't what Janda wanted, but we all have our tempers—it ended in a shouting match. Asshole! Whore! Cut it out, will you! Sometimes they made peace before Janda left, sometimes not. Never say die; door slams. The next day he was back and did not refer to the issue.

. . .

But nights were the crux of the matter.

However late it got and however tired they were, the musicians never spent the night in Kingania. If we spent the night together, we would *regularly* beat each other's brains out. That's why I hate sleeping alone. But now, said K., you're here.

She lodged herself in his armpit, caressed him, touched him all over, rested her hand on his chest: How does it feel? Played with his hair, explored his skin, counted his moles (nine on the right underarm, five on the left). For hours on end. Those were the better nights. On the others she would roll into a ball on her mattress after a wordless evening and rock, mumbling to herself. Later, in the middle of the night, she would crawl over. Sometimes she told him her dreams, nightmares and sweet, but most of the time she said nothing comprehensible; she only whimpered, moaned, cried, wrestled with the body next to her, pulled it over her, tossed and turned with it. With all the others the sequence had been sex first, squabble later: let me be, will you, let me sleep, why won't you let me sleep! He roars, she sobs, doubled up, two nudes. But *the boy* is something else: he doesn't fuck her, he doesn't push her away. Am I the woman who knows your body better than any other? Yes. Kiss me! she said the first time in the train and thrust her tongue into his mouth. She was tasting him: Hm, not bad. He let her do whatever she liked with him, wrestled with her patiently until their bones cracked. Now I see why she's so covered with black-and-blue marks. After a few nights he had them too; it was as if he had caught them from her. Once she gave him a love bite on the neck. It wasn't easy: he may not look it, but he has a thick skin; she had to work long and hard before a small reddish blotch began to appear. He made sure his shirt collar covered it, but it didn't seem to bother him otherwise. It sometimes peeked out when he moved. Little bastard, Kinga whispered up close to his face. It was getting dark; she stroked him. Do you love me, little bastard? Then she fell asleep, snored. When she awoke, she was as cheerful and loud as always. She threw the window open: I smell wet poplars. What a lucky girl!

WHERE FROM, WHERE TO

After watching and hearing all this for several weeks, Abel needed to find himself a new occupation. Since he had given up his studies, he had time for aimless activities: all he needed to do was fill up the time and not be *there*. There are advantages to not needing sleep or much sleep, but *something* was too much. I've overdosed on Kinga, said Janda from time to time; I need air. Abel waited for Kontra to finish his practicing—he never said anything, but he clearly enjoyed it—then went out.

Where do you come from, where do you go, in winter, even a mild winter, which *here* means a virtually permanent drizzle, when for some reason you can't stay at home? He had formerly spent only so much time in enclosed space as was absolutely necessary. He could easily have lived in a village, on a tiny island: he never walked more than two or three routes. I can see all your inner organs you're so pale! (Kinga) Now he started roaming through the city.

Hands in the pockets of his trench coat, shoulders hunched— does he own a scarf? probably not; the drizzle lands on his hair, runs down his forehead—with long strides and bent torso, as if battling a gale. Either he followed his nose or found a person to follow. The latter was connected with something that had concerned him for years, to be precise, since the day he had left his death chamber. The fact that no matter how often I have taken a certain route, if I don't concentrate hard and sometimes even when I do: I get lost. When there was no perceptible improvement after much concerted effort, he came to terms with having no more than a vague idea of where he was most of the time. He would use significant landmarks—the park, the station, the insane asylum, one or another church tower—as points of orientation. Pretty much everything in between looked as if he had just been there. It was like walking through a permanent déjà vu. On the other hand, a route he had taken a hundred times often looked—just before what he was positive was the last turn—as though it could not possibly be right. The points of the compass seemed to have made a last-minute shift.

Luckily or not, the extent to which he could stray had physical limits (his). Basically his movements were limited to the three districts east of and adjoining the station, as much as an individual can cover. Some days were colder than others. Christophoros S.— once a miller, now better known as the fat Zeus in the park—knew good spots for the cold days in the abandoned workshops along the tracks. Should I make friends with him for the sake of a toasty fire? Later perhaps. Meanwhile there are still waiting rooms (definitely not), pubs (too expensive in the long run), and libraries, as well as museums on their free-entrance days (for a change). (My mother set great store by culture as a bulwark against barbarism. After selling the car, Mira would take her son to one of the three neighboring capital cities by train. They had eight hours until the last train home, and during that time they visited as many museums and churches as was humanly possible. If I weren't so well-mannered a child, I would stop now at this corner, take my socks and sandals off, and see whether I have—as I must—any black-and-blue marks on the soles of my feet. Who do you think I'm doing all this for?!?)

In the *winter of the void*, when Abel, despite months of mattress-sitting and navel-gazing could not for the life of him come up with a plan for what he should do now that he could no longer study— If you want to unload trains or sell newspapers, Andre can get you a job. Thank you, said Abel; I'll think it over—he read more books and saw more works of art than ever in his life, before or after. Besides the artist and a young woman who was writing a thesis about the artist, he was the only person who in an installation consisting of forty-two talking heads listened to each of the stories in its entirety. An installation is a good place to sit: the earphones bob peacefully up and down; the temperature is constant; the air, well ventilated, minimalizes the smell of a life spent in anarchy, with the result that we are less conspicuous. Occasionally an attendant pulls open the curtains and peers in. Black heap of clothes in the corner. Chinese peasant children learn to play ping-pong in the hope of a better life.

For several weeks nothing unusual happened: art is normal. Later an incident came to light.

A stern-looking, elderly gentleman, small and round, the chief guard or something—what could have been going on in his head? Anyway, ten minutes before closing time he strides through the rooms, clapping his hands and saying, Closing time, ladies and gentlemen, closing time! . . . Well, I'll be! If he isn't fast asleep. Fast asleep!

He claps again, a martial kindergartener. You there! Wake up! He can't sleep here! This is a museum, not the Salvation Army! Why, I've never seen such a thing!

But is the fellow in black in the installations room actually asleep? He is sitting on a stool in front of the screens, back straight, hands on knees, eyes shut, earphones on; maybe he just didn't hear the old man. Two young guards hovering curiously in the background. Now he opens his eyes, not so much like someone getting up as like a doll or a monster that has just been awoken: that is, his eyelids went up.

Does he hear me? Finito!

The old man, who is now in plain sight, starts waving his formerly clapping hands in the air; makes a slicing motion in front of his neck; jerks his forearms forward as if directing traffic: There's the exit. Up! Up!

The fellow takes off the earphones, stands, is suddenly much larger. Frightened, the old man takes a step back, though he is far out of range in any case; says no more, just waves his arms; directs in silence.

Abel sees him or does not; goes. No sooner does he leave the room than the little man rushes out to the main gallery, where he can look down at the top of the head making its way down the stairs, crossing the ticket desk, and approaching the revolving door. By now the old man has recovered his voice.

The nerve of some people! Coming here to sleep! Looks the part too! This isn't the circus, you know! Coming here on the free day to sleep! This associ . . .

The rest is lost: Abel is out in the street.

I should have had him searched, thinks the little old man, absurd as it is: none of the objects is small enough. Nevertheless, he rushes back into the installations room to check, check *something*. Twenty-four black headsets bobbing up and down from a white ceiling. He grabs at one irresolutely and puts it to his ear: maybe the fellow siphoned the text into his ear. He would mention the incident in his retirement speech. The man who came to sleep. General amusement.

Had it happened to Kinga . . . inconceivable. *Jawohl, mein Führer!* Or I won't stand for it, you midget, you fascist, you fascist midget, you bureaucratic asshole, chauvinist swine, you can talk that way to your wife, but I am a lady, so scram, make tracks: a report would be more than fatal. Then—from a distance, in the security of autonomous Anarchia Kingania—there would have been much waving of clenched fists, much laughing and crying. He here, Abel, said nothing; he simply stopped going to the museum. It was the day of the official spring opening; by then he had seen everything that was to be seen anyway, and was close to a decision, a decision he apparently made several hours later in the university computer room, where he was observed sitting at a monitor on that day until midnight. What exactly he was doing there we do not know; we do know that he scarcely touched the keyboard, merely sat there staring at the screen as if sunning his face.

Later his eyes burned; he went home. It was dark and quiet in Kingania: the guests had left; the sole inhabitant was asleep.

Or was she? No, she was hiding behind the door: Huaaaaaaa! There, did I scare the shit out of you? She laughed, but she was not happy. Stopped immediately. Serves you right, you bastard. Out whoring on me again, eh? Don't you think of anyone but yourself? What if I was worried about you? What if I needed you for something? How can you be such an egoist?

Sorry.

And such a liar. You're never sorry. What are you doing there?

He thought, Going to bed.

Oh, yes, obviously, stupid question: we've had a hard night; we need our beauty sleep. You don't care if I'm bad company. I'm too wound up to sleep. First too wound up to worry and now . . .

Furious because nothing had happened to the little bastard, he'd had a great time, we're just his hotel!

I was in the computer room. Working.

Now she is ready to be quiet. Awaits further information with interest.

He had decided, said Abel, to write a dissertation in the field of comparative linguistics.

No! said Kinga, sinking to her knees next to him. How proud I am! The boy—a PhD! She grabbed his head and kissed his hair. I'm so happy . . .

The start of a new

CRISIS

So you're back! said Tibor. We've been worried. Everything all right? Everyone's been looking for you. (Well, not quite.)

When an ill-humored Tibor came home on New Year's Eve, he found all his guests waiting patiently. Oh, you're still here.

Where is he? Where is he?

Who?

The drug dealer. How come you haven't brought him back?

He's no . . . There was never any question of his coming here. What for? Why should I bring him the next time, though it wouldn't do any harm. All right, all right, said Tibor to the guests (who were in high spirits and—some, at least—tipsy), if that's what you want, I'll invite him; the general curiosity requires it, plus common decency: somebody's got to keep an eye on *these young people* after all. But now: I'm old and I'm tired. Gossip your fill and go home and come back in a month or whenever the new lady of the house invites you. I bet you'll have forgotten him by then.

Several days later a person by the name of Konstantin showed up at the department and made a big scene: they had *made off with* his flatmate. Come and taken his things and . . . A fanciful and

long-winded thriller. They grabbed people off the street and spirited them off God knows where. It was a case for conspiracy theo-
rists and human rights organizations. I'm going to borrow money
for leaflets.

Calm down, said Tibor. Don't worry. I had your friend released
from custody on New Year's Eve.

Konstantin blinked: On New Year's Eve?

Right.

Pause. Blink.

And where is he now?

I don't know, said Tibor. I dropped him off where he lives.

And where is he now?

I don't know, Tibor repeated.

Then three more times, the same circle. Where? Don't know. But
where? Mutual looks, blinks.

A.N. is coming next Monday.

Who? Oh, yes, of course, said Mercedes.

To be frank, she had only a vague memory of him. The first and
last time they had stood facing each other was four years before,
on his first day, approximately two hours after the border crossing.
The butter had ruled out even a handshake: just hello and good-
bye. If they did see each other subsequently, it was only from a distance. Should you have any trouble, go to Mercedes. But he had no
trouble or at least did not go to her with it. She had heard a thing
or two about him—department gossip: coat pockets brimming
with tiny dictionaries, wandering lost through the corridors—but
she had never been particularly interested. And now he stood in
the doorway.

Improbably thin and tall, one shoulder pad of the trench coat
at half-mast: everything seemed to have been tossed onto him;
even his white hands dangled listlessly out of sleeves too short—
the same dangle as later, *here and now*. She held out her hand.
Welcome, my name is Mercedes. The moment the fingertips met,
there was—rubber soles on the matt—an unexpectedly loud and
visible spark. Ohsorry. He jerked his hand back and stood there
as before, though now apparently so abashed that he would have

been unable to take a step without assistance. Perhaps that—the putative helplessness—was what now, four years later, immediately won her over. There was something heart-rending about him. And (to a certain extent) something ridiculous. Mercedes gave him an encouraging smile. Tibor had work to do, she knew, but he, Abel, would want to go in with the others, wouldn't he? Into the *sarong*.

Ohsorry. She laughed and covered her mouth with her hand. That's what my son always says. What I mean is the . . . Oh, there you are, Omar. Come over here. This is Omar, my son.

Height: four feet five inches. Build: slender. Skin color: milk coffee. Shape of face: egg. At this point Omar was six years old, and everything about him—except for a minor deviation in the amber of the artificial iris in the right eye—was in perfect equilibrium.

Good evening, he said. My name is Omar. I have only one eye. (Pause. He gave his interlocutor a serious look.) I traded the other in for wisdom.

Abel reacted with neither surprise nor compassion; his helplessness had suddenly vanished. His voice sounded different from what the last, hoarse *Ohso* . . . would have led one to expect: full, manly, warm.

Most people, he said, would not be so bold.

The boy looked up at him—how? surprised? impressed? I often find myself looking like that—then smiled.

This is Abel, Omar, said Mercedes, a student of Tibor's. He knows ten languages.

Omar stopped smiling. How come?

Well, said Abel, nine seemed too few, eleven too many.

Whereupon Omar nodded, took him by the hand, and led him away from the sarong. As if he had come, looked around, and pointed straight at him. Abel Nema, chosen by Omar Alegre. The given name is Arabic and means: solution, means, exit.

He might have been taking him through a museum. There's nothing new in that. Except that *there* nobody held your hand. When were we, was he, was I in physical contact with someone for so long?

Ever? The boy stopped at many objects, both art and household, to explain their history and function or to draw his attention to a specific detail in the design. This Chinese vase belonged to Anna, Tibor's wife. She's dead. Unfortunately its value is diminished by the fact that its pair is missing; in other words, what you see here is not so much a vase as half of a set of vases. Interesting, isn't it? said Omar. Two identical vases are worth more than one or three. Because what if you had three identical vases? What would happen if one of them broke? Would the two be worth less? Pause. The boy, his hand in Abel's, gave Abel a questioning look.

Your question, said Abel, is the most that can be said on the matter.

Omar nodded. They moved on. This is *nearly* the strangest thing that has happened to me till now. Not only that, there is something indescribably *good* about it. After a while their palms began to sweat, and it was hard to follow the boy's small steps without stumbling, yet they did not let go.

The house belongs to Tibor, Omar went on. Mercedes—that's my mother—was his student and later his research assistant. Later she gave up her job at the university so we could move in here. Now she's a schoolteacher. This is part of the library. Most of the books are in Tibor's study—he needs them for his work; we can't go in now—though there are a few downstairs in the sarong. The most valuable ones.

I wonder how old he is.

I'm six, said Omar, as if he had heard. I skipped the first year of school by special dispensation. This is Mercedes' room. Please note the red motorcycle helmet on the lemon-yellow wardrobe: you might not have expected to see something like that here. The pink ballet slippers hanging on the wall next to the wardrobe are size thirty-five. If I want to try them on, I'd better hurry: in a few months they'll be too small for me. A black boy in pink ballet slippers. Looks up to see how the new guest reacts to the image. Abel smiles. Not too little, not too much, just right.

The rest are family pictures, mostly of me or of her when she was younger. There are also terracottas from Mexico, wooden statues from Africa, fabrics from India. Mercedes is a collector. My father was a prince. He came from G. He disappeared before I was born. The mask is not of him, by the way. Mercedes bought it.

And now, said Omar once they had sat on his bed, say something.

Njeredko acordeo si jesli nach mortom, Abel said. *Od kuin alang allmonpend vi slavno ashol.*

I see, said Omar. I'd like to learn Russian. Do you know Russian too?

Well now, do you know everything there is to know? A beautiful, elderly woman in the doorway to the sarong. I am Miriam the grandmother. Omar's grandmother, she added, as he did not seem to have understood.

And that man there is my grandfather. Omar pointed to the masculine edition of the hostess: a filigree of a man in a floral armchair. He writes whodunits. His pen name is Alegria. That means happiness. He's based one of his characters on me. His name is Om the Pirate. Pirate as in pirate and om as in the sacred syllable, get it? My grandparents are old friends of Tibor's. He's known my mother since she was a child. The woman on Grandfather's left is Tatjana, my mother's oldest friend. They say she's very beautiful and very cynical; she has hair like Snow White and crosses her slim white legs first this way, then that. And the tall *fat* man over there, the one who's talking so loud, that's (he seems to heave a sigh) . . .

Erik, said Tibor, who had suddenly turned up behind them, this is Abel. He's writing a dissertation in the field of universal grammar.

. . . . , said Erik. No idea what it was, because Omar had just let Abel's hand go and gone off somewhere, disappeared into the crowd. Abel's empty palm felt moist. The man facing him, this Erik, was listing names, evidently writers he published. Much to his regret Abel knew not a single one. And you really speak all those languages? All ten?

Abel nodded and was instantly surrounded, enclosed in a cluster, the center of attention, all sorts of questions: where are you from, I've just been to Albania. Monosyllabic responses: Hm . . . I think . . . I don't know.

What gives? (Erik to Tibor.) Can't he speak?

Brilliant discovery! said Tatjana. Took you ten minutes, didn't it? The first time you stopped to come up for air.

She gave him a sweet smile and shifted her legs. Erik made a face.

Abel looked around for the boy. He was standing at the far end of the room saying to his mother, I'd like to learn Russian. Abel's going to give me Russian lessons. Thursdays.

Fine, said Mercedes and sent Abel a friendly smile across the room.

Thus did Abel meet his future stepson Omar.

THE TICK

It was light by the time he got back to Kingania. The door was locked, not a sound anywhere. There had been another party that night; maybe people were still asleep.

They were not. Through the concrete and steel Abel began to hear soft voices conversing. He knocked. For a while nothing happened; then he thought he heard, Go and look; maybe it's the boy, in Kinga's voice. Shortly thereafter Janda opened the door.

Morning, said Abel.

Janda left the door open without saying anything.

Kinga: Is that you? Thank God. Or, rather, what kind of jokers are you trying to saddle me with?

There had been, as noted, another open house, Abel having left before the first visitor came. An invitation from his professor. I see, said Kinga. Well, well. On your way then. She was hurt or simply in a bad mood. It was the kind of night—we all have them—when nothing wants to take shape or go anywhere: hours of boredom and irritation. You don't know if it's better to forge on or give up: everything's getting on my nerves today. The musicians fumbled around on their instruments; nothing seemed to come of it. And the company this time seemed to consist entirely of strangers, who didn't know the customs: the preserving glass was as good as empty while the alcohol disappeared faster than usual. And then they leave me with this godawful mess. Kinga marched into the kitchen and *made a demonstration* of washing glasses. Washed and washed and suddenly there's this joker standing next to her. One of the new crowd, but I had a feeling I'd seen him somewhere before. Parted his hair on the side. He was one of the first to arrive; you (Abel) had just gone out of the door, half an hour. She had dubbed him the tick from the word go. A griper and cadger who'd come to eat his fill, always a glass in one hand and a greasy appetizer in the other, eyes scanning the terrain, taking everything in. Thinks he's as clever as they come, goes up to people and says with much smacking of lips, *Anarchia Kingania*. What's that supposed to mean? Kingdom of the Arachnids? He laughed; you could see the bread in his mouth. This some kind of a drug hangout?

You got it, said Kinga and moved off, though she had not yet finished her washing. Pisser!

Janda raised his head as she flew past, seething, saw it was nothing special, lowered his ear back to the neck of the guitar, and plucked on. Later they perked up and did some real playing.

There were two new girls, two whorelets wearing microminis in x degrees below weather and sitting cheek by jowl the whole time, still in school no doubt, still impressed by the smoky tedium of it all, ogling at the musicians, whispering to each other.

What do you think, my little chickapeas? Take a good look at them. I've had each at least four times. (She didn't say the last part, of course.) A little more to drink, my girls?

Kinga, blood-sweet, with schnapps bottle in hand; Andre, shaking his head and laughing: Let them be.

Which she did, and sat down. The tick stayed mostly in the kitchen, eating bread as long as there was any. When there wasn't, he went over to the girls, sat down, and started talking, on and on without a break, blahblahblahblah. Andre and Kontra no, but Janda—it made him furious. He looked around. Who was blabbing away like that?

Ssssssssh. Kinga had bent over and whispered something into the tick's ear: You. A rest is music too.

He stopped in the middle of a word, stared at her open-mouthed; the microminis giggled. Kinga gave them a wink. Later she went to the toilet, and on her way back she passed the tick leaning next to the door. You, he said. (Aping me?) I've seen you before.

Is that so.

She moved on, he clumping on her tail. Janda looked over.

Yes, said the tick. Years ago. Such and such a club.

Is that so.

I believe we have a mutual friend. A Hungarian. Half-Hungarian. Nema. Abel.

Hm.

A tall guy, dresses in black.

Black, you say?

She looked around. The microminis were white with gray squares. But . . . A split-second decision: make believe the name means nothing to her. But at the same time I thought, Shit, who is this guy? Don't look him in the face. She turned; he followed.

He disappeared. A complaint from behind her back: left me high and dry; reckoned he'd been picked up; it happens, you know, people disappear from the street, done nothing wrong, held in custody, interrogated, and ever since . . .

Sorry, said Kinga. I haven't the slightest idea what you're talking about. Sorry.

She didn't kick him out, but from then on she kept an eye on him. Not an easy thing to do when you want to avoid eye contact and the person in question is staring at you.

What's going on? asked Janda.

Nothing. A pain in the ass.

Later her attention flagged briefly: a short respite from the strenuous peripheral spying, and the guy's voice shrieking suddenly, That's his bag! I'd recognize it any . . .

Ssssssssh! The musicians are playing again.

But the tick was not to be subdued: How come you're doing this? How come you're like this? Who are you anyway? I've never done anything to you, I'm a friendly kind of guy, always ready to help, the caring type, full of compassion and solidarity, a good man, a good man, and you, and you . . .

It was at about this point that Kinga took aim, grabbed the tick by the shoulder, and ran him through the room like a ramrod all the way to the door, which, as luck would have it, was open, so she could push him straight into the hallway, no, chuck him out with a veritable kick in the behind. The guy was so taken aback he kept jabbering for a while; it wasn't until he saw the door that he began to screech: Heeeeeey! Kinga raised her knee, kicked him out, slammed the door shut behind him, and pulled the bolt. She laughed.

A few others laughed with her; still others never noticed anything was wrong. The musicians gave her a questioning look; she waved it off. Even so, I had this crazy feeling the whole time.

A few minutes thereafter the microminis decided to hit the road. It was almost too much for them to address Kinga, though they managed, quite courteously: Would she please unbolt the door. Unbelievable as it may seem, Kinga had forgotten the tick by then. It was like I'd pushed him off the face of the earth. The microminis left and returned.

He's crying, they reported.

Who?

The man you just—you know. Sitting in the hallway and crying.

The microminis just stood there, embarrassed. Finally the sharper of the two shrugged and off they went a second time.

Sorry. High-heeling their way carefully past the sniffling man.

Kinga stuck her head into the hallway. Well, what do you know. I even felt a little sorry for him, though . . . She closed the door softly.

A little later there was a loud roaring noise in the courtyard. At first they had trouble establishing exactly where it came from. Then somebody opened the window, and everything was clear: the tick. Standing down in the courtyard and shrieking up, beside himself, echoing like crazy: I'll turn the whole lot of you in! For running an illegal drinking establishment!

Kinga laughed, but she was nervous. She did not dare to look into the preserving glass, which in fact was nearly empty.

The whole lot of you. Do you hear me! (Whimpering, but even

that was good to hear: the courtyard was like a fountain.) You bastards!

Janda stood up and went to the door as if on his way to the toilet, but he didn't take the key.

What do you have in mind?

No response. He went out.

You'll be sorry! (Roar down in the courtyard.)

Then: silence.

It was dark down there; you couldn't see a thing. They turned off the lights so they couldn't be seen either. Stood at the window, listening: nothing. Later steps and what sounded like talk; later still, Janda came back.

What happened?

Nothing, said Janda.

What did you . . .

Nothing! By the time I got downstairs, he was gone.

But when everyone had left, Kinga felt a shiver go down her spine.

Don't get all worked up about it, said Janda. Nothing's going to happen.

Will that rat really turn us in? Kinga asked Abel *now*. Who was he anyway? Do you really know him?

I don't think so, said Abel. That he'll turn us in, that is. Not likely.

Hey, what are you doing there?

Packing his things, he said.

How come you're packing your things?

He'd found a new place to live.

What?

A new room.

When?

Just then. On his way home.

How? Out of the blue?

What do you say to that? You (Kinga) are speechless. How can you do *such a thing*? Go? Now? She looked over to the musicians for help. Kontra shrugged. The other two did not react at all.

Sorry, said Abel. But he'd promised the man who offered him the room that he'd be back within the hour.

He kissed Kinga on the cheek and gave her some folded banknotes. For his stay there. She glanced down at them. For a moment it looked as though she would drop them, balancing them as she was on her stretched-out fingers; then she stuck them in her pocket after all. He was already out of the door.

PART IV

MEAT

Affairs

could do it. He may have strayed a few times, but maybe not: you could spend days wandering through a big city after all. He could have taken the main streets, followed the station signs, the station being his constant point of orientation, but no one really wants to do that, so he stuck to the small streets, using his ear to keep himself parallel to the main ones. Sometimes he lost his way—that was inevitable—but found it again or a new one later. It took five hours in all before he reached a neighborhood that looked familiar. It didn't feel so long to him: basically once he had *woken up*, he was—*there*. A pharmacy, a junk shop, a tobacconist's, a nail salon, a travel agency, a flower shop. Each unfamiliar on its own, but together . . . Two pubs, clothing, household goods, flowers, drugs, paper. Deliveries were being made to a few of the shops: picturesque scraps of meat sailing over the sidewalk. The early stroller could have squeezed past the two sides of pork propped against the back of the van, but for some reason he paused and watched. The owner of the butcher's shop, a young fellow with a beard and soft belly, came out several times and looked at him each time. The plastic-aproned deliverymen looked over at him too. Then the van pulled away, and the butcher was left standing next to Abel.

Where are you coming from?

Names the district.

Is it snowing there?

???

You're all white.

He reached for his hair. Hoarfrost. On his eyebrows too. Young man with white hair. So that's why they were all staring at him. Probably.

The butcher's name was Carlo, and he had trouble keeping his head above water. The disappearance of the working class signals the decline and fall of the local butcher. It's all in the lunch-box sausage. I don't know if we'll pull through. You don't happen to know of anyone looking for a room, do you?

A room, a toilet. The bed a convertible armchair that did not look the part, a humming fridge with a coffeemaker on it in a corner, a hot plate on a shelf. The walls reeking of smoked meat, the sound

CARLO

Pleading the long trip home, he had left the get-together relatively early.

See you Thursday, said Omar and his mother.

See you Thursday, he said.

See you four weeks from Monday! the guests called out.

Wait, said Tibor, going into the room next door, and without ever having seen a line of Abel's work and without batting an eyelid wrote an updated letter of recommendation, this time for a dissertation fellowship—*it is in the interest of us all*, etc.—thereby taking care of the next three years.

Thank you.

Don't mention it.

When he finally stepped into the street, it was covered with hoarfrost. Crunching steps and the white pennants of his breath. A miniature soul each time. Observing their brief flight was engaging. He felt a bit nauseous. What from was not clear: he hadn't drunk anything unusual, just something with a high percentage of alcohol and some water. As a result, or not, he decided to walk the entire fifteen? twenty? (I have no way of judging) kilometers *home*.

He simply wanted to see what would happen, whether he

of a sausage maker coming from next door. Then there was the tele-phone, which had originally been here and was now just outside in the passageway. You could hear Carlo's voice whenever he made a call. He also took emergency messages for his subtenants, in which case a red-and-white-aproned member of his all-female workforce would knock—shyly or energetically, according to her nature—and deliver whatever news there was to be delivered. He usually sent the apprentice—her name was Ida—who from the first day to the last was so in love with him that she did not dare glance at him and in his presence turned redder than the goulash she chopped the meat for.

Occasionally, to Ida's relief and distress, the butcher put in a personal appearance—apron, rubber boots, and all—and stayed a while. Naturally enough, he had things to do in his office now and then. He shouldn't really have rented it out as living quarters, which is why it had no bell. If anybody asks, he said on the morn-ing of their first meeting, just say you're renting the room as an of-fice. Abel nodded and went back to Kingania for his things.

What are you working on? asked Carlo with a glance at the Stone Age laptop Abel had bought some time between the night in the computer room and the visit to Tibor. There was not much else: two or three books.

A dissertation in the field of comparative linguistics, said Abel in response to his landlord's question.

I see, said the butcher.

Himself, he had few interests besides meat. No matter what subject came up, he always brought it back to meat. You're not a vegetarian, I hope. He was always working on prototypes for new sausages, marinating and roasting meat and asking the foreigner in the most considerate terms whether he would be willing to taste it and tell him if he thought his people would like it. *His people* were the *gratifying number of foreigners* who had come lately: Carlo val-ued them highly because they complained less, not at all, actually, and not about the sausage smell in the hallways, and because they liked meat, and Carlo *for his part* wanted to give them meat they liked to eat. He was currently experimenting with the minced meat and hot spices he tucked away in his memory when he'd gone to this snack-bar place to sample the food. What do you think of it? *It* was always the meat. When he said: *it*, he meant: *meat*.

Abel Nema moved the bits of meat around his mouth with his famous decalingual tongue. It was instantly numb.

Too spicy?

To tell the truth, I have practically no sense of taste.

The butcher merely stared at him.

It's the truth, said Abel. I can taste only the strongest flavors. So it isn't too spicy.

Which would explain why the guy looked like a pipe cleaner. Though Carlo couldn't quite believe him. Had he always been like that?

I don't remember. I never used to pay attention to it.

There was not much to say after that. He would leave *it* with him in any event, said Carlo. It is and always has been a prime source of protein.

At this point Abel was twenty-six and living on his own for the first time in his life. True, with a sausage machine, Carlo, Ida, and the other rubber boots close at hand, but still.

The drizzly winter was followed by an unusually warm spring, which he mostly used to set up a new daily schedule. He applied for and received a dissertation fellowship and found five or six families willing to take him on as a language tutor for their children.

Here we must record something of a scandal. For a while there was a *regular furor* (Mercedes, in retrospect) surrounding him and originating in the mind of a now-forgotten mother of two daughters. Don't you feel it? There's something wrong, something very wrong: those eyes, that reserve, the hands, the way they move when he explains something, white, tender hands, and the way he has with children. He doesn't seem to do anything, and they just sit there, talk, jot something down from time to time. He's neither too lax nor too strict. At least as long as the lesson is in progress. Before and after and when he's with parents—mothers, mostly—he's back to his old helpless self, like a teenager, says basically nothing, leaves with a slight bow. I may be crazy, but it, *the whole thing*, makes me feel almost (in a whisper) *sexy*.

Mercedes shrugged, yet said, keen observer that she was, that he and Omar were clearly kindred spirits. Though unfailingly polite, Omar had had true confidence in only three closely related individuals. And now in him: took him by the hand, led him through the flat, then said (this is a boy who could read and write fluently before he was six): I want to learn Russian.

Russian? Really?

Yes. Abel said something to me in Russian. I like it.

What did he say to you in Russian?

How should I know? I don't know Russian.

The grown-ups—mother, grandmother—laughed; the two *men* remained serious.

Well, why not? said Mercedes.

Precisely what they had done since then Mercedes was not in a position to say: she was busy with other things (Tibor). The most she had to do with the tutor was to open the door when he rang the bell and pay him once a month. At first she looked in on the lesson in Omar's room occasionally. There was nothing to see. And there was no way of testing whether they were making progress, whether he could really *do* what he *said*. Tibor's circle included a few who claimed proficiency in Russian, but Omar saw no reason to display his knowledge.

Switching back to the local language, they asked, Why do you want to learn a language if not to communicate with others?

But I communicate with others as it is, said Omar.

Whereupon they gave up on him. Talking to that child is like . . .

Here, at least, Abel did not create a stir; on the contrary. Tibor once stood at the door, saw the two of them sitting there, and thought, What if the boy—the bigger one, Abel—stayed on *forever*, and what makes that such a *comforting* proposition?

Well, well, said Kinga, when Abel finally phoned a few weeks after moving out. Getting on well, eh? I thought as much. We are too, thanks for asking. For the time being we've even been sleeping.

(At first she seemed to have calmed down, but the night after the boy moved out she had another breakdown: she sobbed, shivered, begged the musicians not to leave her alone; she was afraid of leaving Kingania, refused to leave, and huddled in a corner until Janda started screaming, Stop it, take a good look at yourself, you're wallowing in filth!)

Glad to hear it, said the boy.

Dial tone.

Not much happened after that for a while. The usual transition between two installations. Later something came about quietly: he got to know that boy. He said his name was Danko. He fell into my lap like a ripe apple.

GAMES

In fact, they were half rotten to begin with: they had found them among the rubbish behind the covered market. He was late again, and as he rounded the corner they were waiting for him, ready to pelt him. He grinned and walked on, dodging the apples right and left, but you only have so many arms. Some of the apples were hard and hurt; others were soft and burst: a stinking mush.

Shit! Danko shouted. Stop! But the others kept aiming and throwing, careful and focused, wasting no ammunition. Danko cursed, twisted, to no avail, and as he twisted he was hit by an apple, the most rotten yet, at the base of the spine: an explosion of brown sauce. They all laughed, but as he was about to twist back to them with a grin—bastards, assholes—they started pelting him again. I've had enough of this. He turned on his heel and set off. Until the next big tree, where he crouched and took cover, his back against the trunk. Now he's mad.

There were seven of them. It just happened that way, but it worked well. We'll never have more. Nothing in particular had brought them together: they were a gang, that's all. Played hooky, roamed the streets, took what they needed or wanted from the shops. Can't say I *ever* bought me nothing. They would crush Coke cans and kick them across the asphalt in the classic way, smoke like chimneys, play soccer on the fenced-in field at the southern end of the park. Or what they called soccer. Christophoros S., homeless, who had a clear view of everything from his niche, would have called it mass slaughter. They gave it everything they had, slamming into the fences, tackling one another mercilessly, writhing in piles; they moaned and shouted curses in a language unknown to the homeless gentlemen (and ladies—it was often hard to determine which was which). The man in black on the bench between the tramps' semicircle and the soccer field: every word.

Eventually during the spring, presumably on the recommendation of someone in Tibor's clique, Abel had found another job: simultaneous interpreting at a nearby conference center, though he was called in only for emergencies on the butcher's hotline.

You're a disgrace! the Irishman roared.

You're a disgrace, said the small woman with the pageboy in the booth next to him.

You're the disgrace! the Serb roared back.

You're the disgrace, said Abel into the microphone.

The small woman smiled at him through the glass.

After work he went on with the walks he had initiated in the winter. His rambles through the afternoon were arbitrary as usual, but he passed the park relatively often, because it was so centrally located. Whenever he came to it, he would sit on the bench in front of the laundry, the one no one else sat on. The broken doorbell at his back did not seem to disturb him. He appeared to be sleeping. Later he was visited by a wild roar in which all his ancestors and descendants were cursed, and he woke up or, who knows, maybe he just decided to lift his chin off his chest. He looked over at the cages.

It would be wrong to say that he had been *observing them for quite some time*. He did not come regularly enough for that in the first place, and in the second place, watching them did not mean anything: given the noise they made, you *couldn't help* noticing them. He would stay a while, then move on. In general, he went unnoticed, except by Christophoros S., who sees all but says nothing. None of the gang members had picked him out before the day of the apples, and even now, though they were crouching/sitting practically shoulder to shoulder—trunk, bench—it was a long time before the boy took note of him. The only thing he was interested in was what was happening on the soccer field or whether anyone had come to get him. But all that came were apples. As soon as his head stuck out from behind the tree, sirrrrr, paff. Not today.

It's not the pain that makes me cry; it's that I don't understand. What have I done? Why are they all behaving like maniacs?

An apple hit the tree and rolled over to Abel's feet. Both looked first at the mangled apple, then at each other; then the boy looked away quickly. He started wiping the remains of the apples from his clothes insofar as he could see and reach them. His hand was swollen. That's something else, he said later.

Maniacs, mumbled the boy. I'm surrounded by a bunch of maniacs. My father is the mother of all maniacs. Maybe I should go to a crazy house. Maybe that's where normal people live.

He was sure he'd only thought the last part, but he must have said it because suddenly the guy on the bench said, The man at the gate of the psychiatric hospital greets everybody with, Freedom!

The boy (Danko. His name is . . .) stopped wiping apple bits from his clothes. He sneaked a look up at the bench.

What?

The guy grinned.

What're you grinning for?

He wasn't grinning. That was his face.

Danko looked at the face; then he looked back at the cage. They had chosen up teams and begun to play as if nothing had happened. He turned his head back.

What do you mean he greets them with freedom?

In the spirit of the French Revolution.

???

Because he's crazy too.

Now *he* finally grins. The first black down above his lip.

Where are you from? the guy asked.

What do you mean?

Dark skin. Accent. He looked over at the tramps' semicircle: the broken fountain sloshing, the dogs playing, the doorbell yodeling.

Letting their filthy tomcats run loose, he mumbled. Bet they've got rabies.

Pause.

We're Roma, he then said.

Your friends are looking in this direction, said Abel.

Really? He grinned, still squatting.

And what are they doing now? What are they doing now?

Playing, stopping, looking over, talking, walking, the spy reported.

And now?

Nothing. I can't see them anymore. What's your name?

No answer. Leaves.

That was his first encounter with Danko.

What kind of guy is he?

They were waiting around the next corner for him, standing there like a block with Kosma out in front: Kosma was the boss, an animal; he claimed to have started fucking. What kind of guy is he? asked Kosma.

Danko gave a mysterious grin.

Kosma threw the ball in his face. It bounced back and landed in his hand. Wipe that grin off your face, cocksucker!

As random as their makeup was—*scum finds scum*—they had to have some degree of organization, because a gang without laws, everybody knew that, was worth shit, said Kosma. Most of the time they were children playing silly games, but there were times something would come over him and he would scream *for hours* at them: You scumbag, you! I'll set your toenails on fire, I'll turn your dick into minced meat and stuff it in your mouth, I'll stick your head down the toilet till you drink your own puke, you shithead! His tirades gave them the creeps, but they loved them: it was his consummate skill at making them feel threatened that had made him boss.

Danko's nose tickled. Don't scratch.

No idea. Just a guy. Sitting on a bench.

A pervert. Or a spy. Look what he's wearing.

The usual babble: spy, pervert, etc. Sitting on a bench watching us. Danko turned (why?) red.

Bull, said Kosma. And: Who gives a shit about the bumfucker? You, man. (Don't say that.)

Kosma was the one who said, Who gives a shit about the bench queer, but the truth was that he (why?) had left his mark on them all. They never talked about it, but when he was sitting on the same bench the next time, Kosma stopped the game and looked over at him. The guy on his bench made believe he was sleeping, but *everybody* knew it was just a show.

There he is again.

Danko, who sensed something was up, concentrated on twirl-ing the ball between his feet, wasn't particularly good at it, wasn't good at soccer in general, nearly fell; the ball flew off and hit the fence: *tsing*! Kosma stepped on it. That's it for now.

You talked to him, didn't you. What did you talk about?

Danko couldn't remember. Really. Not a thing.

Liar! I saw you, you cocksucker!

Kosma rolled the ball under his foot, kicked it onto his toes, balanced it for a moment, then kicked it away, as if it were the guy himself. That guy gives me a royal pain.

Then they went back to the match, slamming into the fences, etc., yelling, laughing extra loud. Danko laughed the loudest. The apple thing—it was just fun, see? Everybody does it. They looked over at him out of the corner of their eyes to see if he was watching them. They were playing *for him*. Later, leaning against the fence, out of breath, smoking like chimneys, they didn't look over. Nor did Kosma stir when the guy got up and walked off: he just stood there—the cigarette between thumb and index finger, the foun-tain sloshing, the trees rustling, a police siren in the distance—for about a minute. Then he flicked the stub away and walked off too. We go where we please. And if it's to tail the guy, then it's to tail the guy. He goes on making believe he doesn't know we're there, but the pace he sets proves the opposite. Try to look like you're just out for a stroll with your pals even if you've got a pain in your side from walking so fast.

They did not know his name, so with their usual horseplay-and-laughter they tried a few of the buttons at the entrance of the building he had disappeared into. Nobody answered at first, then a woman: Who is it? Horseplay, laughter, then Kosma pushed through the crowd to the microphone and took over: Did such and such a man live there? But by then the woman was no longer at the other end of the line. The buzzer went on; they shoved the door open and were in.

They made for the waste containers, peered in—you never knew what you might find—pressed their faces up to the grills covering the dark windows on the ground floor, as if there were machines inside. They looked through the office window as well, but they did not see him: he was in the toilet. And then Carlo came out of the shop: Hey! What're you doing here? They gave him the finger and ran.

Nothing to get upset about, said Carlo to Abel. Just a few stupid kids. They had written something illegible with their fingers in the window dirt. Motherfucker, Abel read. That was the last they saw of the guy on the bench.

The creep, said Kosma. Good riddance.

A LONG DAY'S NIGHT. ABEL

What did he (Abel) have in mind? Start a conversation, throw in a few psychiatric-hospital anecdotes picked up somewhere, ask, What's your name? Most likely he had nothing in mind. He had simply had many conversations with children lately, and it worked well.

I can ask him any question as long as it's in Russian, said Omar to his grandfather in confidence.

Any? Really?

Any that comes to mind.

And does he answer?

As far as I can tell . . .

Hm, said Alegria. (I'm a little jealous, I must admit.)

But *this thing*—where was it going? At first you can't account for it; it's almost sociable: the curses, the brutal games. Later it starts moving in an unpleasant direction: they follow you home, write Motherfucker in the grime of the butcher's window. It looks so normal, said Mercedes years later, that it takes a while before you realize it's actually a magnet attracting things strange, absurd, and depressing. Once your fate goes off the rails, you bear the sign, said Kinga. He just laughed as if he didn't believe her. But this time he did notice something in the air and did his best to steer clear of it.

Which wasn't easy. Make every effort to keep your distance from a place—in this instance, the park—and you'll keep ending up there. Eliminating one of his main landmarks meant limiting his freedom of movement, and when that happens, sooner or later everything goes out of kilter. Troubles and misunderstandings multiply.

One day a woman noticed he was following her. What had her day been like? She was on her way home from work, office attire, making tracks in her stilettos, then slowing down: the distance between them remained the same. So she took either fright or offense and went up to a policeman who happened to be coming out of a bakery.

Are you following this woman? the policeman asked Abel N.

Yes. (Don't say that; say another non-lie:) I'm lost.

You're what?

Lost.

And that's why you're following her? May I see your ID? Looks it over, off duty, wouldn't he just like to have a look at the guy's record. The most unbelievable things can come out of innocent situations like this. But then he let it slide. Get yourself a map. I will, said A.N.

Later, another day, he was stopped three times, one right after the other. The first two times it was for no apparent reason: they were looking for someone; he was not it. The third time he had had a drink in a beer garden. It was the first day that year when tables could be moved outside. He was about to leave when a man with matted white hair and rattly teeth appeared and started singing (= cawing) in such a way that you couldn't tell whether he just wanted to get on people's nerves. Because they were sitting there. Scram, said the waitress with a tray full of glasses in her hand.

You there! the newcomer roared, pointing at her. You shall be cursed forever! You shall be plagued with bad luck! You shall never have children! Hear that? Never have children!

The waitress laughed and spun on her heel. The glasses slid off the tray. Glass and drink sprayed into the air, a sliver lodging in a woman's calf. She leaped up, overturning the table, and a beer glass fell into her companion's lap; he leaped up as well, lost his balance, swept the change off the next table—the change Abel had just put down—and poked Abel in the face with his elbow.

Hahahahaha, said the newcomer, pointing to the waitress, who was standing in a pool of glass, the woman and her companion, and Abel. He did not laugh; he *said*, Hahahahaha!

Abel put his hand to his nose. You all right? the woman's companion asked. Abel nodded and hurried off before the police got there. He tried waving down a taxi; it did not stop. Only now did he laugh. Hahaha. Two police cars arrived. One drove on; the other stopped. His papers were checked. What happened to your face? Abel laughed. What's so funny? They almost put him through a drug test, but he managed to pull himself together in time.

The moment he was out of their range, he felt dizzy. He leaned a slippery hand against the wall. Someone, a passerby, was watching: drunk or something. He pulled himself together again and moved on. Later he was seen at The Loony Bin.

Much as he had been burned, he was so hopelessly embroiled that he had no choice. He picked out a gay couple and followed them for several blocks. Both of them noticed him and looked back occasionally but did not seem particularly concerned. They had reached the second courtyard of the former mill by the time Abel realized he was no longer in the street. He stopped. The other two moved on, unperturbed, until they came to a door, then turned, expectantly: Well, are you or aren't you? He quickly closed the gap and followed them into the club, which at this relatively early hour was as good as empty.

Welcome, said a portly middle-aged man. I'm the owner. My name is Thanos. What are you drinking?

Later he watched a boy with a weeping-willow-switch of a frame wind his body—sallow, supple, smooth—around a rod. Two couples in the immediate vicinity—two women, two men—were making love or pretending to. Most of what went on in The Loony Bin was mere show, people playing at erotic activity. Most of the bodies were older than our hero's, though a few were younger.

The boys were largely professionals, but since that was prohibited in The Loony Bin they made believe they were students who had climbed out of their windows at night and had to catch the first morning train back to their homes and gardens. Abel, who would later be dubbed *The Spy*, was the only one buttoned up to the collar. Just looking on. Who would have thought it. That he would feel most at home in a place like that. He stayed until dawn.

Then for the first time he showed up at the conference center visibly groggy, with a swollen nose. Look at that, thought the woman with the pageboy, whose name was Ann. A-N-N: she would spell it out at the first opportunity. They had met, as they often did, in the courtyard, she having a smoke, he sipping a hot chocolate from the machine: her third break, his first.

I thought you never got tired, said Ann. He must get tired some time or other, I said to myself. Or hungry or thirsty.

He lifted the plastic cup and smiled. She glanced at his hand. White, bony. He's as thin as can be, all over. Could that hot chocolate be the only thing he partakes of all day? More or less. Though we earn a pretty decent salary. Has he got a family to support? He doesn't wear a ring. Suddenly (how come, because she's the motherly type—she could in fact be his mother, just barely—and would be only too happy to take care of *him* specifically) she had the idea of inviting him home. For a bowl of soup. You've got to eat something. A good, healthy bowl of soup.

Later, when, still silent, they were climbing the stairs together on their way back to the booths, Ann had a sexual fantasy involving a kitchen chair. They said good-bye with a smile and a nod.

She could easily have asked; he wouldn't have said no, not to the soup. If he had gone with her then and there, one consequence, besides other advantages we will never know, would have been that he might never have met Danko again. A bowl of soup, a violent affair—such are the options at this point.

But Ann did not ask, so he could not answer. The soles of his feet were tingling; he had been away for two days; he wanted to go right home. On the way he bought a book in a secondhand bookshop and put it in his coat pocket. It was a bit too big and stuck out. Go right home, skim through it.

All the way to the psychiatric hospital things were normal. But one block more and everything was wrong. What's going on? Nothing he did after that improved matters: he progressed farther and farther into the evening and a part of town he had never seen before. Not that I recall at least.

His old elegance was gone, and speed: he had been on his feet for two days and evening was approaching. He stumbled his way through radio chatter, drilling blasts, dog-, gas-, and cooking odors and—was it fatigue?—everything seemed his enemy. The people who stared and the people who looked away. The two men there in the door.

He took a few more wrong turns and ended up at a small, gray, urine-soaked intersection, stood there motionless.

Hey! said Danko. What are you doing here?

A LONG DAY'S NIGHT. DANKO

They had been out of school for three days by then; there was no point in going back for the rest of the week: What am I doing there anyway? I don't understand a thing all day. But there are always those people who all they do is look important. One evening he came home to find a man and a woman laying into his old man for not sending his son to school.

What can I do? his old man whined, wringing his hands. What can I do with you? Eh? No sooner did Danko come through the door than he seized him by the ear and shook him as if the ear were a handle: What can I do with you?

That's enough, said the man and the woman. He should let him go. But he didn't; he kept jerking him up and down. What, tell me, what can I do with you?

Later the man and the woman left and the old man let him be after giving no more than a smack, almost in passing. He wasn't really concerned in the least. The ear burned; it felt twice as large. Danko lay on it, pressing his head into the pillow so it would go down during the night.

The next morning the gang met in the park as usual. Two men were dunking the head of a third in the fountain. The water had been standing in it for weeks. The man had wheat-colored hair curling in tiny, hard locks around his head. Claimed to be a shampoo tester. Would go up to girls in the park and ask if he could wash their hair. He carried a leather bag with two plastic four-liter bottles of lukewarm water and two kinds of shampoo, supposedly the product of his beauty salon. One he called Citron. First we've got to comb the hair to see if the skin is uniformly pink. The color must be uniform for the test to work. He would take the women into the bushes and comb and wash their hair. Forwards or back. Mostly forwards, so no water ran down their collars. He never got spots on their clothes. Afterwards he would take a long time towel-drying and combing out their hair to return them to the state he had found them in. State you found me in is good, the woman would say with a giggle. He would compliment them on their hair and their intelligence: he was sure they had brilliant futures before them. Really? the middle-aged women would ask. The young ones just nodded placidly.

Now he had surfaced arm in arm with two muscular young men. They flanked him left and right and were bobbing his angel hair up and down. Later they kept his head under water for a long time. If he saw any coins down there, the young men said, he was to pick them up with his teeth: we'll split them fifty-fifty. They grabbed the shampoo bottles out of his bag and emptied the contents into the water. The lemony smell lasted the whole day. The basin looked like a large dessert plate: lemon froth with green wafers—algae that had come loose from the edge. In the end he looked like a fountain statue, the foam and algae sticking to his hair, his eyes pressed shut, his mouth open wide. A woman with a pram and another with a number of dogs in tow were protesting in strident tones: he isn't doing anything to you, they were going to call the police. We are the police, said the young men, wiping their hands on their jeans and grinning. The women then picked the algae out of his hair, rinsed him off with clean water from his bottles, and dried him with his towel. He was sitting dazed on the fountain's edge, letting the women clean him up and spitting out shampoo when enough accumulated in his mouth.

Fucking fantastic, said Kosma. They were standing with their faces against the wire mesh. Fucking geniuses those guys. He laughed. Giving that pervert a taste of his own medicine! Then he turned serious: Oh, how I hate all those freaks and kiddyfuckers.

Later it was noon, and they went—as they sometimes did for the fun of it—to the homeless kitchen. The bona fide homeless made groveling way for them. Yuck! said Kosma, spitting out the green tea. What kind of cat's piss is that!

Then they went to a gambling den. Kosma's father, uncle, or brother had won something there the day before and given them a handful of coins to play around with. They used them in the slot machines—mostly Kosma, of course—until they had lost them all. When they had lost them all, the owner kicked them out. Gamble or scramble. Kosma turned deep red. Add that guy to our list. He'll get his. Like all the freaks and bums and other cocksuckers. I'll shoot lead up your fat ass, you piece of shit, split your nostrils open, fuck your daughters in all their holes! At this point—he had been cursing for nearly half an hour—his mood suddenly shifted: suddenly he was in a rush, shook them off, said he had to leave or, rather, said, Fuck off, I've got something important to do, and he was gone.

It was not very late, they could have done something else, but without Kosma nothing occurred to them. Can't you do anything on your own, you fucking cocksuckers? They hung around the street in a loose cloud for a while, then tried out the kiddy equipment in a playground, but one or another of them gradually dropped out of the picture till you realized you were the only one left. Not the worst thing in the world, to be honest.

Since the tirade in the gambling den Danko had had something of a headache; he kept wrinkling his forehead. Nor did a concrete plan of action occur to him: he just plunged his fists into his pockets and took off through the neighborhood. It was getting dark. In a billiard parlor a one-armed man, urged on by his pals, was clearing off the tables one by one with a cue lodged under his armpit. Danko looked on through the open door for a while. A one-armed billiard champ. Not bad.

Turning from the door to the piss-soaked intersection, he saw the guy from the park. The guy in black. No mistaking him.

. . .

Is he staring at me or am I crazy? He held back for a while, then said, "Hey!"

Not very loud and there was the intersection between them, but you'd think the guy would react one way or another. No, stands there like a statue.

Hey, what are you doing here?

Finally he looks over, but you'd think he was looking at a stranger.

It's me. Danko.

It's not getting through. We haven't been introduced. Should have kept my mouth shut. What's he to me? Should have let him be and told the gang, Guess what, you cocksuckers. That guy from the park, he's following me. Standing at an intersection, ogling me. Trying to look like he's waiting to cross, but what he really wants . . . How come none of you guys have seen him here? Just when I happen to be here by myself . . .

Finally the guy looks up, looks around, crosses the intersection cautiously. You'd think he was scared something might appear out of nowhere and run him over.

Hello.

How come his (Danko's) heart is suddenly pounding? What should he say? Good evening? It's dark.

Is this your neighborhood?

Danko nods.

Could he tell him how to get to the station?

??? There's no station here.

The train station.

The *train* station?

Now we both have stupid looks on our faces.

Or the park, said the guy. The park's just as good.

(Station or park doesn't matter?) Don't know, the boy says. (He's lying. He just wants to come up with something that would make Kosma proud of him:) But the insane asylum's in that direction.

He grins. Hands in pockets, he points his chin in the direction he himself is going. The guy is facing the other way, grins too.

Thanks, he says. The asylum's just as good.

The weirdest voice in the world. It sends shivers up your spine. He's going now.

No, he's turning back. Asks if the boy, if Danko would go with him a way. Just till he's sure he won't get lost again.

You got *lost*? Danko laughs a hearty laugh, calls out to the neighborhood at large, an invisible audience, here, up front, there, all the way in the back, everywhere: He got lost! What kind of freak are you anyway?

The guy gives him a blank look. Shrugs, sets off.

Shit, what a weird feeling. The boy looks around: apart from the billiard parlor on the corner there's nothing much going on. People are having dinner. You can smell the schnitzel, almost hear the sizzle.

Damned if I know what it is. Danko sets off after the guy. Catches up with him, walks alongside him; doesn't look up, doesn't know how the guy is reacting. He hasn't said a word. You get a good whiff of a person when you walk beside him. He smells like a barbershop. Plus alcohol, hot chocolate, and Plexiglas, though young Danko lacked the terms. The guy has something bright and rectangular in his coat pocket. A book without a cover, just the book. It's too warm for a coat actually. I never wear a coat. I don't even own one. Which do you like more? Summer or winter? I like summer more. In summer we go to the seaside. Have you ever seen the sea?

They are coming to an intersection. The guy slows down. Danko, hands in pockets, makes a demonstrative swivel in the right direction. The guy follows. When they are back in a straight line, he asks, "What's your name?"

Danko, says Danko to his feet.

How old?

(What's it to you?) Fourteen. (Liar.) And you?

Abel.

What?

That's his name. Abel.

What kind of name is that?

Hebrew.

He doesn't seem to have understood. He keeps having to ask

people to repeat things, as if there were something wrong with his ears, or maybe he just doesn't know the words.

My name is Abel, and I'm six and a half.

???

Right, says the guy. I was born on the twenty-ninth of February. So I've only had six birthdays. I have my next in two years.

When he tells that to his pupils, they're all thrilled: I'm older than you! This boy doesn't get it. Could he possibly not know what a leap year is?

The twenty-ninth of February, he explains, using his hands to help make the point, comes only once every four years. When there's a leap year.

Hm. Danko casts a furtive glance to the side. The *other* side, not the direction *he* is going in. No response. Pause. There's something funny about him: the guy talks and moves in a way that he (Danko) has never seen before. You might call his movements electric: each one seems to cause the opposite physical reaction. Light blows in the side.

They are silent again until the next corner, where the boy takes a step ahead of him again, which again makes peace between them. After a bit of stuttering, what . . . um . . . what . . . he asks what Abel does.

I'm an interpreter.

???

I translate from one language into another.

Which one?

Abel lists them. He leaves out their common mother tongue. So there are nine.

Hm, says the boy. What about Chinese? You know that too?

No.

Well, I know two: the language of this country and the language of my country.

And neither very well, I must say. A noun-based approach. Quite common. Hear it all the time. Amazing how little you need to get along. Abel has pupils half Danko's age with twice his vocabulary. To say nothing of Omar. (Picture the two of them in a room together. What would they have to say to each other?)

They proceed in silence. A corner with a used car dealer's. They set off the automatic-lighting switch. For a moment they are bathed in a garish light. Small pennants on strings give off a metallic gleam. The boy, suddenly excited, grabs onto the chain-link fence and drinks in the sights on the other side. The guy had kept going, but now stops, waits.

Have you got a car?

No.

What?

No.

We had one . . .

Aha.

I'll buy that one when I've got money.

The guy does not approach to get a closer look at *that one*. The boy lets go of the fence and catches up with him.

And take it on joy rides.

Hm.

Have you ever been to the sea?

Hm.

What?

Yes.

The sea's awesome. I'm going to buy a house by the sea. On a rock.

Hm.

Pause. Another topic down the drain. The guy is losing his patience—he wants to move faster—but the boy is in the clouds, in a dream world, ambling along, peering into every shop window. I want that and that. The guy three steps ahead of him now.

Hey! the boy shouts. Not that way!

He had turned on his own. In the wrong direction, of course. The boy runs up to him laughing. You don't know anything, do you. You don't know anything, you don't have anything, right? You're nothing. Look, there it is. Up ahead. The trees. Danko laughs.

What's made him so happy?

They are standing near a streetlamp, the boy's dark profile backlit: Nubian lips, fuzz under the nose. Abel holds out a white hand.

Thank you, he says, for accompanying me.

The boy's fist is balled up tight in his pocket. Open it? The solution never occurs to him, nor would it clearly have been the right one. He merely gives a twitch, then remains as he was. The fingers, his fingers, feel warm and sticky. He knows how they smell too. He mutters something. The guy obviously doesn't understand but nods, withdraws the hand with a friendly expression on his face, and takes two steps back before he turns. He does not look back after that.

Danko turns on his heel, sharply, and, without knowing why, cannot stop himself from running. He runs.

NIGHT

Young Danko was not the only one who was confused that day, during the last hour of which, when they had begun walking together, all fatigue and vexation had flown and he (each of them) could have gone on walking till dawn. Which is strange. Because what do people actually want from one another? The one can scarcely understand what the other says. To say nothing of the context. Disgusting. On the one hand. On the other he's beautiful.

When Abel came home and opened the front door, he almost expected to find something behind it; there was nothing behind it but the dark. He turned on the light, walked through the entry, and opened the door to the courtyard, again expecting to find something, but found nothing, only the smell of sausage and the dark bodies of the trash cans. He opened the office door: dark, then light; he threw off his coat together with the book. Later, before he went out again, he pulled the book out of the pocket and threw it somewhere, in a drawer. In between he sat under the shower for half an hour; it was cold and smelled of the nearby toilet bowl. Later, in a corner with the third glass in his hand, things got better. He forgot the boy or made believe he had.

Days—which he had spent mostly at The Loony Bin—later he returned home to find him on his doorstep. At first he failed to notice him, the front door being pitch-black. Fumbling for his keys—where is the lock anyway—he came up against something soft. It gives you the creeps, stepping on a lump of flesh. A (drunken) body.

Ssssss, went the darkness.

What is it?

Finally he got the key into the lock; the door opened; he felt along the wall in the entry until he found the light switch. The boy was blinking in the sudden flash of light.

It's you. What are you doing here?

Sss, said Danko, holding the foot Abel had stepped on.

The day had begun like any other: they had gone off with the ball, but instead of going to the park they took the bus to the sea. Except that the bus didn't go all the way to the sea; it stopped who knows where, on some back road: a post at the edge of a ditch, the remains of a faded poster wound round it, the ditch full of stones and thistle, opposite a relay station. Not a matchstick of shade. Last stop, said the driver, and when they asked what time the next one came he said he only gave information to paying customers. Doors closed. You goddamn motherfucking asshole, you! I'll bust all your teeth and stuff them down your throat! roared Kosma running after the bus, which was luckily well on its way. The only thing left was the empty road, the heat, the forced march. Should they start off at once? Going back without having seen the sea was out of the question. They kicked the ball along for a while, then carried it. First they outshouted one another with opinions about where the sea was; later they laid into one another because somebody had kicked the ball into the brush and suddenly nobody had the strength to retrieve it. Where is that shitty sea anyways? Later they stopped talking altogether and just stared at the bland dandelions underfoot: following the dusty heels of the boy in front of them took the least energy.

It was afternoon before they found it. Low tide: brown muck, stench, litter, quivering yellow foam; warm pools in the ground

with sharp edges. They splashed about for a while, played at low-
flying bombers, droning and roaring for all they were worth to
hide their disappointment. Covered with muck from head to toe
and thirsty, they sat in the sand looking out to where the water was
supposed to be. Later it came back and with it some people: families with blond daughters in pink bathing suits. They had brought
food and drink and kept glancing over at the Gypsy youths, who
sat there glancing back. One was actually brave enough to venture up to them and ask for water. The woman handed over a
half empty bottle without a word. The others followed, of course,
taking turns, each drinking a little more than the last, because he
thought the one before him had drunk too much. As soon as the
first round was over, they wanted to start in on a second, but the
woman said, That's enough, and took the muck-covered bottle
back. It was as good as empty anyway. They never even thanked
her; they just zoomed off—some in their underpants, others fully
clothed—into the advancing water, and at last it was just the way
they'd imagined it.

The trip back was a piece of cake: they got another driver luckily.
But he too glared daggers into the rearview mirror at the back seat
where they were sitting, knees bouncing and mouths wide open.
Danko was the only one who kept quiet, did not howl or bounce:
he sat at the window and looked out as long as there was something to see. What was so bad about going to the sea?

What's so bad about going to the sea? thought Danko going
home on the bus as the sun went down outside. What's wrong with
wanting to be where you feel good? Why did they call us collabo-
rators to get rid of us because we're Roma, why does my father hate
me so much that he looks at me with eyes I dream of at night, why
does he knock me around the kitchen till my bones crack?

(Whatthehellhaveyoudone?! Huh? What are you up to?! Huh??
What are you up to? Shoves to the shoulder. What, what, what?
Slaps. What are you up to? What???!!! He shoves him in front of
him. You little bastard! What?! What kind of shit are you into?
Who are you running around with? None of your lies, you little
cocksucker! . . . has seen you! He didn't catch the name: he had to

cover his head, plus the sobs. Sticky all over. The blows rain down on his underarms raised high. Whathaveyougoneanddone?! What are you up to? What are you up to, the lot of you? Let me see! He yanks his sweatshirt up, his head gets stuck, so what, he jerks him this way and that to view him from all sides, and when all he sees is skin he yanks down his pants: Let me see, you little bugger! Let me see what you've been up to. What, what. Go ahead. Scream to high heaven, kick up a storm. He'll be naked soon, sweatshirt around the neck, pants around the ankles. You turn fairy on me and I'll cut your throat. He goes out for a piss; Danko lies there; five others look on from the door. Which is how *that* long day came to a close.)

This time, thought Danko as the bus crossed the city line, this time he'll *really* cut my throat. He's done it before. The guy lying under the cement in the pigsty. The sty stayed back there in the old country. But I know. It's a matter of life and death.

The bus made straight for the bus station, the same one, though a different platform. Nobody crabbed about anyone or anything: they were unusually content and empty, even Kosma. They went back to the soccer field from the station because that was where they had started out from and you go back to where you started out to learn what to do next. The soccer field was dark and empty. They stood around for a while, one of them bouncing the ball a few times, which you could hear even though the Saturday night din of bars and traffic was all around them. And then it was simple: they all went home except Danko.

He just kept walking, ambling along, taking it all in: Saturday night. Bar after bar, tables jammed together, chair legs intertwined, sidewalks packed to the parking cars, only a narrow path, can't stop, got to keep going, heels clicking forward and back. Hands in his pockets, he looked at the people, men and women; they looked back at the Gypsy kid: Wonder if he's a pickpocket. Somebody was flambéing something behind a pane of glass, meat or a sweet of some kind. Sorry, said a man, taking him by the shoulder and putting him out of harm's way. Don't stand in the middle like that. Two young Russian women in national costume began singing nearby; he quite liked it; they had good voices; "Kalinka"; he'd heard it somewhere before. A waiter was removing a salted fish skin; a clump of salt rolled up to Danko's feet; he scooped it up from the sidewalk, popped it into his mouth; the taste of salt and dirt. I'm happy. I'm happy and I don't know what time it is. When he thought, I don't know what time it is, he had to move on until he forgot it. He walked on and on—how slowly time passes when all you want to do is spend it—until he got bored and found himself back at the soccer field. The homeless were bedding down for the night. You could sleep on a bench or in the grass; I've slept in the grass a lot. But it didn't appeal to him for some reason; everything was losing its appeal, the burning in the gullet, and what should he do now, where should he go. He drank some water from the water fountain, watched by the homeless and their dogs; he watched back. I don't like dogs, I don't like bums, and wiped his mouth, shook the water off the back of his hand, and set out as if he knew where he was going. He'd show them.

Eventually he was standing in front of the butcher's, and since he didn't know where the bell was he sat in the doorway in the corner where the dirt collected and the pigeon feathers, gazed up at the stars, listened to what there was to hear. Eventually he fell asleep.

What are you doing here? asked the guy, though he did not wait for an answer. As if it didn't matter: he knew everything. He walked in front of him into the office.

Are you thirsty? Do you want something to drink?

Danko was in fact thirsty, a bit hungry too. Got any Coke? Sorry, no. Tap water. Danko drinks it under the light hanging from the ceiling; the chalky residue on the glass is shining. The guy stands next to him, watching, curious. Finished? He takes the glass, puts it down.

I can't go home, the boy says. Can I crash?

For the first time he has a good look around: a desk, a chair, an armchair. A coffee machine, its glass turned brown: maybe it's got a teabag in it. Nothing else. Is this your life? How come Danko thought the guy was rich? No TV, no stereo, not even a picture. Though there was a laptop on the desk.

Anywhere. On the floor.

You can have the bed, said the guy. May I?

Danko happens to be standing in front of the armchair, takes a step to the side. So that's the bed. A modest bed for an unexpected guest. Only one sheet, unfortunately, and used, but that's all there is. (And you?)

The boy stays where he is, under the light. The back of his neck is the brightest point in the room. Abel sits down at the computer.

What are you doing?

Working.

He writes something.

You write?

Yes.

What? Whodunits?

No. A dissertation.

Hm.

Danko inspects the armchair. It's pretty big and comfortable as armchairs go. He lowers himself carefully onto the edge of the seat.

What's that there?

The guy looks over.

Whiskey.

Will you give me a glass?

The guy gets up, takes the nearly empty bottle off the shelf, and pours: two fingers, straight; stands as close to him as before; waits. Danko presses his thighs together, drinks. Smoky, sharp, not bad. Abel takes the glass back, walks over to the door, turns out the light, goes back.

Good night.

He sits down at his laptop again, sometimes typing a bit but mostly staring at the screen. Danko slips further into the armchair, the blanket under him, his shoes still on: tar, sand, thistles sticking to the soles. Later he stretches out properly; he does not know what to do with his hands; folds them over his chest; looks up at the ceiling: a water stain.

For a time all is still. Only the hum of the laptop. The boy in the convertible bed moves a little. A rustle. Eventually he begins to speak.

. . .

One time, says Danko, he locked me in the cellar for five days. I came home, back entrance. He was standing in the dark, in the kitchen; didn't say a word, just grabbed me and threw me against the wall. It made a rattle like dice in a shaker. It was so loud that Danko thought for a moment he had gone deaf. Then he shoved him out of the door he had come in, and through the courtyard to the cellar door, down the cellar stairs, into a corner, and kicked him for good measure. Door shut. He lay there on the wet floor. It was cold, but pain keeps you warm. He could still hear the rattle in his head, but later it went away, only a soft whistle—still there, by the way.

Pause. The boy listens. Far off, true, but still there.

Later he carefully shifted his position, testing whether the painful rib had entered the lung, but it had not. He tried to pass the time by thinking of anything and everything. It's not so easy. When he searched his memory for reminiscences, he did not find much. The day he smoked his first cigarette. There's a picture: not the village as such but its reflection in the pond, trees, a few slanting wooden gables, a half-naked man fishing in the right foreground, and at the left edge, out of focus, proud—Danko with the cigarette stub in his mouth. The rest of the time he thought about cars. When I was little, I thought a donkey cart was the greatest thing a man could own. Later a scooter, a motorcycle, a Mercedes, a sports car: pull up, roll the window down, wave. At who? Whoever's there. (No one is there. Nobody.) If it had been now, he would have thought about planes. Or ships maybe. Stowing away between containers. With survival bars and water in a backpack. Writing a letter to the world leaders at sixty-five below. Or not. Fuck the world leaders.

The next day the door opened, and his father's silent silhouette placed a plate on the top step. A soup plate with the leftovers of the rest of the family watered with soup. That's *his* way. Nothing is bad at sea. That's not the problem. He'll kill me because he can.

Later that day he crawled cautiously up the stairs; slurped up some of the goo, not all: he didn't want it to look like he'd eaten anything. It was salty, and the congealed fat stuck to his teeth. He used his tongue to spread it around; then everything was greasy, his whole mouth, so he had to drink some more; in the end, it was pretty much all gone. It was harder to get down the stairs.

The third day was given over to the stench of the excrement and to despair; on the fourth he pulled himself together and made plans. Stretch a wire across the door; the fall will break his jaw. But that wasn't enough. Take a brick—painful though the broken rib would make it—and good-bye teeth, good-bye fucking nose, fucking cheekbones, eye sockets, forehead—everything, everything, your bloody brain in your bloody skull . . . !!!

The boy spoke poorly at first; later he stopped caring: he spat out whatever came into his head, and that made things better. How strange it is. I don't want to talk; I don't want to tell stories; I want to kill and then say not a word about it—that's what I want! Abel sat motionless at his desk. Behind his back there was whining and wailing and spouting of blood until nothing was left but a blood mush seeping into the earth below the cellar, a frightful—correction—fruitful sacrifice. By dawn the worst had passed: the spouting had given way to a blood-satiated bubbling, and finally, in the middle of a sentence, the boy fell asleep. Abel listened to his breathing for a while, a few minutes, before he turned to have a look at him—or what was left of him.

He was utterly overwhelmed: by his *beauty*. The radiant skin, the forehead, the cheeks, the eyelids, the lips, brittle when he arrived, now full and moist. One of the most beautiful faces I have ever seen.

He bent over him. The breath coming out of the nose did not smell good.

DAY

It was almost light when Danko fell asleep only to wrestle with a dream for the rest of the brief night. He dreamed that a big face hovered over him, only a face. At first it was like the mask of a monster from a game they had played in the casino, but at the same time it looked like somebody else, especially the lines between the nose and mouth, while the eyes and forehead seemed to belong to yet another person, and that is how it was the whole time: the monster's features kept merging with those of the boss, the father-of-all-madmen, and the man in black, or, no, it was more like they were fighting, fighting for hours on end, and no one could gain the upper hand. At times it was so frightening he was afraid he would die; at times it was almost beautiful, even when the blood flowed out of his eyes into his mouth. They fought the night through until the rising wave of an orgasm jerked him out of his sleep.

Hhhhhhh! He shot up, his hands in the air; he gasped for breath, a fish on dry land, until finally it was over.

The guy was not there, nor was the laptop humming. There were no sounds at all: it was Sunday, no butcher. Danko struggled out of the over-soft nest.

No sooner did he move than he felt hungry. *The last time I ate—when was it?* He was so hungry the world went black before his eyes even though he had not closed them. Wet basement cold combined with the acute heat of nausea. Salt burning everywhere: the eyes, the stomach. *If I don't eat something right away, I'm going to barf all over the chair. It's your own fault: you shouldn't have left me all alone. And now I feel an attack of diarrhea coming on. Where's the damned toilet?*

Bent over, he made his way to the main entrance, though he knew it couldn't be *there*. If he could only get out to the courtyard and the trash cans. But the door was locked. He was overcome by another wave of nausea. *Trapped*, drenched in sweat. He bent even more, hopped up and down. Then it occurred to him that he could take advantage of the guy's not being there to have a look around. He felt better instantly.

There wasn't much to see: a few wall cupboards. In one he found a packet of crispbread, which he ate. That was it. An empty coffee tin. No. It had money in it. You never knew when it would come in handy. He took one banknote and put the rest of the previous month's earnings for tutoring back in the tin, which he returned to the cupboard. Next to it there was a book in a bright, battered cloth binding. Whether he remembered it or not, he at first passed over it, then picked it up and leafed through it.

A picture book. Old photographs or photographs made to look old. Brownish. Fake Greek landscapes: studio skies, papier-mâché pillars, stuffed foxes, purposely cracked amphoras, and scattered here and there—holding a sandal or a flute—a collection of naked youths. Boys. Kids. True, a few wore old-fashioned white underpants or leather loincloths, but most were naked with adult penises that looked stuck onto their slim, olive-colored bodies. *Why you . . . !* Danko shoved the book back into the cupboard; it hit the wall. He grabbed it again and took it out, though who could remember the position it had been in before.

It was then he finally noticed the freshly painted green door in the corner. Well, well: a sink, a toilet, even a squeezed-in shower. There was a twitch in his stomach from the saltwater. He sweated on the green toilet seat. At one point everything had gone bad. A book full of pricks.

By the time he came out, the guy was back. The boy hadn't washed his hands—he would have heard it—and had plunged them, rolled into fists, into his pockets. Abel had brought back some food, whatever he could pick up nearby: bread, milk, carrots. (*Surrealities* for breakfast, Omar says, and laughs.) I don't like carrots. Then don't eat them. A file cabinet turned out to be a refrigerator, and Abel took out something wrapped in paper. Sausage. He said he'd had some.

The boy eats like a pig, his mouth open: you can see his large, pink tongue at work. He breathes through the food, slurps and gurgles as if making a show of it, though it may just be that he's ravenous: his fingers tremble when he breaks off a piece of something. He has dirt under his nails, his hair is greasy, his clothes are stained saltwater-white, his neck is covered with scratches and streaks of dirt, ditto his feet, and his rolled-up trouser legs are full of sand, shell bits, and sticky grass seeds.

Abel turns on the laptop. Keeping his back to him, keeping on clicking—What are you doing there? Working—so as to keep from seeing or hearing it. But of course he could hear it all too well. The same as yesterday: a raging sea.

Eventually it was over.

Finished?

The boy nodded, suppressing a belch: spicy sausage in milk and saltwater.

And now?

I'll walk home with you if you like, said Abel.

The boy did not move. Fists in pockets, eyes on floor. What does he want?

I'll just stand here under this light: this is my place. I don't really want to stay here, though I must admit I haven't given it too much thought . . . —Are you all right? Abel asked, going up to him—and to be honest you've been a terrible disappointment, although . . .

Danko?

The boy seemed on the point of tears. A comforting touch could help. On the arm, for instance. Who was the last person I (Abel) touched like this? No sooner was contact made than the boy let himself fall, his forehead landing on Abel's shoulder, his tears seeping through his shirt. What can I say? Hold him, stroke his back maybe. A minute or so. Then the boy pulled himself up. On tiptoe he was almost my height; our lips were at the same level. Lips to lips, his breath, he was resting; then with a new, timid flair he presented his tongue. Abel felt it: moist and cool; for a brief and perhaps merely imagined moment he even tasted: poplars, village pond, smoke, sand, shell bits, the cheap lemon sherbet they had shared at a filling station, saltwater, sausage, and crispbread. He took a step back. The boy had not yet closed his lips entirely. There was something glittering in the pit between upper lip and nose.

Sorry, said Abel. It won't work.

Asshole! Danko hisses, yanking open the door and slamming it shut immediately—Careful now or you'll bump your forehead on that board—storms through the trash cans and their rotting offal into the entryway and onto the street. The terrible heat nearly bowls him over: on a day like this hearts stop beating by the thousands. At the same time the bells began to chime: it is Sunday. Danko staggers a bit, then runs on, the laptop cord (revenge or habit?) trailing behind him.

Prickly sweat, a stitch in the side, the food, a load of crap to begin with, lying all chunky in his innards, though not so much in the stomach—maybe it had gone down the wrong way—as sliding here and there under the skin: a chunky pressure in the intestines. Sooner or later I'll have to stop and shit. He regains his grip on the laptop. The plug starts banging against his shin. That hurts and makes him even madder. I should have taken *all* the money. He looks back: twenty meters of hot sidewalk, then the guy, running after him, his stupid face all twisted with the effort.

He crosses a six-lane street with an island in the middle; you push the button twice for the light; Danko doesn't push the button; he darts through a none too spacious gap between the cars. The chiming finally stops on the other shore. The wind reels from house to house in low gusts carrying unlocalizable noises—a drill, a piece of music—and foreign odors—spices, stenches—as if from afar. A pot-and-pan racket sails out of an open window: the kitchen of the psychiatric hospital. On the wall of the hospital garden someone has written FUNNY on one side of the gate and FARM on the other: FUNNY-gate-FARM. The gate is ajar. There is a sign on the porter's lodge: WELCOME. The faces of people at bus stops near prisons and insane asylums. The boy slaloms between them. He is at the southern end of the park, not far from the soccer field; maybe the others are there, but no, he shifts direction and runs past the kiosks. People all over. Horrible Sunday. Horrible Sunday people. Old and young, blacks, bums, Chinks. Women wagging their rear ends like the backs of double buses, their men trotting flatfoot two steps behind, hands in pockets, their children in knee socks running ahead or holding meekly onto their hands. I could mow down every last one of them. He runs through them, shoving aside the old people, the women, the little kids. Not the men and the big kids: they might knock his block off. When he thinks about it: fury again. At this moment he hates every living being on earth. This city. Kosma and the other wankers. Everyone everywhere. Why was it that pathetic gambling den, the one he'd been kicked out of like a dog, why was it the only place he'd like to be? A riddle. There and in the village with the poplars.

He looks back. The guy is still on his tail. Ask for help. That cop there. That man is following me. No, never ask a cop.

Turning back, he slips on a half-eaten candy apple someone has dropped, twists his ankle, sugary gook on his shoe, struggles to keep balance. Someone, a man, pushes him away. Hey, I'm no leaning post. My, my, that kid can look bullets! Well? What do you want?

Thanks to the *incident* Abel has nearly caught up with him. They eye each other—one face, the other—standing in the middle of the path, a Sunday in the park going on around them, the boy with the laptop under his arm. He starts off again.

Hey, the policeman shouts. The light was red! Stop!

Danko does not stop; he runs like the devil, swinging his free arm, his aching elbow. And Abel? He does something he has never done before: feints to the right and runs past the cop to the left.

What's got into me? When have I ever run like this? Never. Danko
looks back, shakes his head, puts on speed. Passersby, obstacles.
He'll shake him soon, that's clear—the distance between them
is growing with every step—but Abel won't give in. It's not the
laptop anymore—though it's the laptop as well—it's the pointless,
childish running. He is no longer concentrating on the boy's back;
he is looking in all directions, seeing the world from a runner's
perspective, the sky. He is even on the point of laughing out loud
when something lands between his legs, a rope or something, a
hand swishes past him as he falls, he fails to catch it, he sinks
through a tangle of squat bodies onto the hard, dirty asphalt.

Caught in a pack of dogs. There he lies, the animals swarming all
over him: legs, stomachs, testicles, whimpering. Their smell. Buried under dogs. The asphalt vibrating between their teeth. Hit his
head. Let me close my eyes, just for a moment.
    You okay?
    The voice of the dog walker, her worried face pushing through
the bodies, a patch of sky opening behind her, a small but noisy
plane flying through it, low. She gives him her hand, helps him to
sit up. The dogs sniff him; the dog walker gives the leashes a yank:
No! Come!
    Passersby stop to look. A policeman too. Stern:
    You okay?
    Yes, says the dog walker. Come!
    Luckily it is another policeman.
    Why were you running so fast? Did the boy steal something?
Somebody said he was carrying something.
    He stole something from him!
    Can you stand? Are you bleeding?
    Yes. No. He fights his way out of the leashes.
    Since there is no blood, most of the people move on. His lungs
have stopped hurting for the time being. Dusting of his clothes.
Stern looks. Doesn't anybody want to see my papers?
    Do you want to file charges?
    Abel shakes his head. It hurts a little. He apologizes to the dog
walker.

That's all right. She untangles the leashes and leaves.

Well then, the policeman says. Watch where you're running. Even better, don't run at all. Walk. Nice and slow. Okay?

The patient laughs to show: Right. You're right. Everything's fine.

He looks around. An unfamiliar street. He looks up the street and down. Unfamiliar. The policeman is watching him from the corner; he comes back.

You okay?

Yes, says Abel.

I just don't know this neighborhood. I'll just go on, mingle unobtrusively in the unobtrusive crowd. His head is cocked: he looks deep in thought. Or is it a stiff neck. Sheepish. He probably wants to run his hand through his hair, surreptitiously feeling the bump.

MEN THE RIGHT AGE

When he got home, he found the door to the butcher's office locked and had no key with him.

It was open, said Carlo. I locked it for you.

Thank you, said Abel.

Good thing I happened past.

Yes.

Something wrong?

Abel looked over at the desk. No laptop.

No, no, he said. Thank you.

Later, the next day, he went to the soccer field. It was empty. Not on the same day but the day after, he brought himself to go back and look for the intersection where they had met, but of course if it means so much to you, you never succeed: the same corner bar over and over and any number of billiard parlors. He went into two secondhand shops. They gave him suspicious, even hostile looks. The laptop was not there. Try one or two of the corner bars maybe: stand around a while, blend in. Somebody's looking for a laptop. How come? Important files? Do I say yes or no?

No results. Eventually he just walked around, looking for men who might be the right age, who could be the boy's father. How do you propose to recognize him, and if you do what then? Later he kept his eyes on the ground; the sidewalk was indescribably filthy: feces (dog, human, bird), a condom here and there (thrown out of a window?), and finally—it was nearly daybreak—in a corner, on a bed of pigeon feathers: a hard disk, all shiny green and silver. Suddenly it dawned on him: time to give up. He gave up, went back to the butcher's.

A few days later there was a knock on the door: three short raps. That was how Carlo always knocked. Maybe everybody knocks that way. He pressed the door handle without thinking. The door obliged with great intensity: they forced it open with their combined weight, as if they were a single body, and entered the room, spreading out to all corners wordlessly and quick as lightning, as if they had done so a hundred times before—a special unit—turning every object upside down and scattering them over the room.

The guy said not a word, just stood there looking on as a horde of half-children vaporized the contents of his room. They tore pages out of books, ripped shirts in two, tugged at the pillowcase buttons with their teeth so they could slice them off with their knives, and then of course slit the pillows open: bits of yellowish foam rubber flying through the air. They dumped the contents of the fridge onto the floor: meat all over the linoleum plus broken glasses stained with whatever happened to have been in them. They slid through marmalade and butter goo as if the kitchen nook were a skating rink and each chunk of meat a puck. As if it were all a game. Squeezed soap bubbles out of the detergent bottle. We hereby declare this zone our amusement park. The whole thing took no more than ten minutes. When they had finished, when everything was shattered, smashed, torn to bits, they came back into formation. The courtyard's never-ceasing sausage stench wafting in through the open door.

And now, said one of them, slightly out of breath . . . And now: to you. Where is he?

Abel merely looked at him. Had they been looking for someone in his cupboards and food and failed to find him?

You know very well who we mean, you bugger!

They were like a seven-headed dragon. No, six. Slowly things fell into place for me. You know very well. A draft set the scattered papers in motion. Something in the room was cracking and creaking, something crumpled unfolding, something buried emitting one more puff of air. Good question: where was he?

They lay on their stomachs, peering into the cellar, pressing their ears to the ground: they might see something, hear something.

We hear something! one of them shouted. His name was Atom. They all went and lay there, their cheeks in the filth, because Atom claimed to have heard something underground.

It's only cars.

No, said Atom. Voices.

They listened.

You morons! said Kosma. Voices underground?

Maybe he's murdered him. His father. He's murdered somebody else.

Kosma shook his head skeptically. If anybody's murdered him . . .

I really didn't want to, but instead of saying I don't know, nor do I know where the boy Danko might be, which was the truth, Abel simply shrugged.

Kosma grew red and started screaming. You bugger you, he screamed. Want me to slice you up? Well, do you? Want us to slice you up, you asshole? You pervert, police spy, murderer! Slice his ass up for him. Bite his balls off. Yuck! Kosma spat or, rather, he made believe: nothing came out.

He didn't know why it happened; he couldn't do anything about it, hold himself back: while that boy was screaming, Abel started laughing.

The guy must have a screw loose, laughing like that. Kosma could feel the dragon behind him beginning to drift. Because of the guy laughing. But the guy stopped laughing and was only smiling when he said, in his mother tongue and that of the gang: Sorry. I don't know where he is.

They stared at him. Some thought they were hallucinating, but not Kosma. He went up to the guy, very close, the way the other person the other time had done; he did not have his hands in his pockets, but otherwise it was the same, their lips very close. From here on: not a sound. Kosma said not a word; he merely raised his fist and punched him in the solar plexus. Abel doubled up and sank to the ground. The gang gathered round and kicked him, all in the same way, with the toe of the shoe: we're a fair machine.

Hey, Carlo shouted from the doorway. What's going on here? What are you doing? Get out! He waved his arms as if chasing crows, but with a cleaver in one hand. Get out of here! He swung the cleaver but of course did nothing more, and the gang, unperturbed, shoved him aside as they ran past, Kosma bringing up the rear at an almost measured pace. He bent over him and said in a hiss, Asshole. We know where you live. You hear? We know where you live.

Then they were gone. It might have been a dream; it was not: I never dream. Carlo stood in the door, cleaver in hand, surveying the devastation.

I had better move out, said Abel.

The butcher could not even nod.

PART V

ROAD MOVIE

Unfinished

AMERICAN AS APPLE PIE

A gang of Gypsy kids broke into your room, robbed you, and beat you up? How come? Kinga asked. What's your connection with them? What's behind it? Some dirty secret? Or did they just happen in, off the street? Is that possible?

Maybe we should make the rounds of the markets over the weekend, she said later. There are booths with stolen goods galore. Or put an ad in the paper: Will buy back computer. That's what they do back home. People buy their stolen cars back.

Hey, don't look at me. I've given up dealing in stolen goods. I'm a musician now. (Janda)

I wasn't looking at you, and even if I was, I look where I like.

Abel dismissed it all with a wave of the hand: he had tried everything.

Poor kid. Poor, poor kid. She showered him with kisses. Everything gone. Everything, everything.

What do you plan to do now? (Andre the compassionate)

He'd brought his things, wondered if he could leave a few of them in Kingania.

How come?

All the time he'd been here—how many years was it now? seven, even eight—he'd never left the city. He felt the time had come to do a little traveling.

Where to?

A shrug.

Ah, said Kinga. M-hm.

As for me, she said, I've been pretty moody lately. For weeks actually. You'd have noticed if you'd kept in touch. I've got a job for the summer. What kind? A teaching job, believe it or not. A music teacher in a summer camp. She dances around the kitchen table. Ring around the rosy! Janda's taking it hard, of course. Not because he's losing a driver when they're on tour: the three of them can spell one another. No, what gets his goat is I've got something of my own. *That* he can't accept. Clearly. (All I said was, Just don't get your hopes up . . . Oh, forget it. A dismissive wave of the hand. She:) It's almost like working in my field again! Know what I mean? She sat in Abel's lap and gave him a happy choke. Know what I mean? I may go back to my field again. She squeezed his face together in the middle and planted a smack of a kiss on the protruding lips.

They were having dinner by then, sitting in a circle. Janda had made the noodles too hot; the fire extinguisher, homemade currant wine (Where did we pick the currants? Can't remember), was scratchy and its alcohol content astronomically high. It made even Kinga clear her throat.

Actually—hhrm—the boy could take my place. You need a driver, don't you? You can drive, can't you?

Abel shook his head.

Janda: Well, that's that.

Kinga: What do you mean! It's never too late to learn! Whereupon she declared herself willing to teach the boy to drive before she left for her job.

Out of the question, said Janda. We're not going to put an unlicensed driver behind our wheel, especially if *you* are the one who taught him.

He could borrow Kontra's license. Look at you, you could be

cousins! Besides, *they* think we all look alike. (She laughed.) All you have to do is memorize each other's family history.

What for? said Kontra. Nobody here knows them.

Later. Country road, outside, day, scorching sun. Andre and Kontra.

Things can't get any crazier, said Andre.

Sure they can, thought Kontra.

Janda had refused to come with them—This is the most hare-brained thing you've ever . . . —and they were standing just the two of them at the side of the road watching the minibus bumping its way through the potholes. On both sides of the road the wind was whipping up wisps of dust from the fields. Andre shut his eyes tightly.

Andre: Is this the way we used to be? I can't remember. I'd play the guitar in an old people's home or a youth club, and sometimes I could only think of dirty songs. But that was it. And now? We've clearly crossed a border of sorts, and I don't quite know what's behind it all.

Sure you do, said Kontra. Of course you do.

Later. Kingania.

Out of the question, said Janda. He can't have learned to drive in one afternoon on a country road.

Take it from me.

J. waved his wave of dismissal. You're talking through your hat. But Andre and Kontra confirmed Kinga's words: the boy could handle the bus. After he and Kinga had spent a few hours criss-crossing the fields, they disappeared for nearly a half hour into a terrain as flat as a sheet—a valley or something—and when they came back into sight he seemed to be managing all right. He drove them back into the village and parked the bus in front of the bar between a blue compact and the motorcycle of the village police-man, who was sitting in the bar watching them first while he parked, then while they sat on the curb sipping their soft drinks (!) and licking their ice-cream bars (!!). One of those uneven curbs that border bumpy village thoroughfares. The leaves weighed down with dust. The sun going down.

A pretty picture, Janda admitted. But nonetheless: No. It would be madness.

Kinga put her arms around him and whispered into his ear, All he needs is someone to keep an eye on him.

I suppose you could look at it that way.

She kissed him on the stubbly cheek: Take good care of my godson.

Ts, said Janda with a shrug.

Later Janda and Abel sat alone on the roof on either side of a giant candle that had survived one of the parties and melted into a bizarre shape. For years the two of them had looked at each other in silence. Not this time, though: they were looking straight ahead at what they called *the forest*, a vine-covered windowless wall in the adjacent courtyard, where birds were battling over a place for the night.

Janda was smoking. It was clear he would never utter a word to Abel. But had the boy ever initiated a conversation? Hrrum, said Abel. Just take me out of the city, drop me anywhere. For her peace of mind.

Janda stared fixedly at the forest or, alternately, the sky above it. The city was invisible from this angle. You could hear it somewhat, but not much by this time of day. We could *take* you farther than that. It's up to you, though. I don't care.

I don't either.

Then he does look at him. Beady, fox-like eyes. A grin: Well, that's that.

Long pause. Smoke.

Is it true you once killed a man? Abel finally asked.

Janda put the cigarette out on the tar roof. Carefully. Over and over. Black tar, black ashes. A grinding noise. The birds were getting louder. Who had first talked about it could no longer be reconstructed: it had *seeped out*, as things have a way of doing. Janda the teacher, Janda the youth-organization leader, Janda married (Just to show me, Kinga, he can do without me! Ha!) and divorced—the usual—and he goes and—was it before the divorce or after?—bumps a guy off.

No, it's not. Just bashed his head in: he didn't die.

Why did you do it?

He was a neighbor. We didn't get along.

(Not quite, said Kinga. They fought over me. No, not what you think. He insists you can't make him jealous. But he's got enough of a sense of honor to stand up for a woman at the hands of a brutal idiot.

To be precise, said Andre, it was over the diaries. Nine notebooks she'd written over the years. Who knows. One day. A novel or something of the sort. The diaries of a muse. She turned the guy on, the way she does, then laughed in his face; he slammed the door behind him but came back the next day when she was off somewhere: he had a key and he burned all the notebooks, in the kitchen. The heat made the sink crack. Ashes all over the place. Kinga roared like a . . .)

What had he used? Abel asked on the roof.

Used for what?

What had he, Janda, used to bash the man's head in? Janda's thin lips trembled slightly. They were surrounded by a trace of dark stubble: he had to shave often. The boy's skin milky, like that of a teenager. So we want to know all the gruesome detail, do we.

With a frying pan, said Janda. It was on the stove. Bits of omelet sticking to the rim. A little oil, still warm, ran over his hand as he struck the man. An everyday cast-iron frying pan. (Pause, then fast:) He had police connections, relatives. I've got a few false teeth, and when the weather changes, the bridge on the upper right-hand side gets inflamed. And I was in jail. I couldn't teach when I got out, didn't feel like it either; felt like traveling, at least for the summer. I told the others. They started gunning each other down. You know the rest.

The birds had fallen silent. Janda took the tobacco out of his pocket, looked at it, hesitated: should he have another smoke *with him*? He put it away. Listen, he said. We'll never be friends. If you know what I mean.

That is all right, said the boy. It was dark by then: his face was scarcely visible. His voice sounded perfectly normal. Or what was normal for him. Its peculiar, bisexual resonance. Janda couldn't help laughing. That's *all right*?

He stood and brushed off his trousers.

We're on our way. The day after tomorrow.

That was the conversation with Janda. He left the roof; Abel stayed behind. Later he lay down.

Stars.

BEING A PASSENGER

Being a passenger. Living for the moment. The weather. *On the road*. So to speak. A summer. One or more underway. Here inner space on wheels, there the countryside. Something in the making. Friendship or its opposite. Little things. They look around and within.

What did Abel see when he looked within, thinking back on what had happened with Danko and the others? There being no proof, there was nothing for him to see. At first he squirmed a bit—the stomach, the shin—but that soon passed, and nothing remained but a dull feeling, and then not even that. Before leaving Carlo's office, he had tidied up good and proper: no matter what, don't forget somebody's got to get rid of the mess. Carlo stood at the door with an ax in his hand, swinging it a little: should he help or not? Then he sent Ida over. She said not a word, never once looked at him: they worked side by side in silence, sweeping, carrying out the rubbish, splinters of glass in milk and marmalade, putting the furniture back in place. The desk had a scratch; nothing could be done about it. Thank you, said Abel when it was over. Again she failed to react; she went back to the shop. He went to Kingania and lay down on the roof. The next morning he was covered with dew, his hair smelled of tar, and he had a scratch in his throat, but two days later, when they set off, he had forgotten that too.

They never let him in on their route, nor did he seem to care. He had learned to drive, but the others did the driving: he sat on his side of the seat—sometimes in the sun, sometimes in the shade—and peered up at the buildings. Later the scenery changed: an unkempt river valley, woods, flat fields for hours on end, new towns, accompanied by music and more or less the same radio news every hour on the hour. Not much talk. Not only did the musicians avoid talking to Abel; they had nothing to say to one another. The two in the front seat occasionally exchanged a few quiet and for the most part functional sentences: where is such and such, what do we do now, right turn up ahead. Otherwise Abel slept, his head resting against the side window—or made believe because whenever they stopped he opened his eyes immediately. What is the name of this place and where is it located?

Except as a potential driver he was totally superfluous. He never helped to carry things or set things up at the gigs: they did not need his help; they could do it themselves. A bump on a log, a fifth wheel. He could have got out long ago, but for some reason: no. He was still there. All they had to do was say, Fuck off, and off he would go, politely, without complaint. Yet he preferred to stay on. As if he enjoyed watching. How men behave. Their drinking and smoking rituals, the way they moved, the way they fished during a break in the woods. The unabashed romanticism of the gleaming body parts: close-ups of hands whacking the fish, gutting them, impaling them, roasting them. That he was totally useless for such operations was taken for granted; they simply caught an extra fish for him. He seemed to be observing them as they ate. You'd think he didn't know how to eat fish. Janda was no fool: he could tell that Abel was constantly watching him, of course he could, but for years his strategy had been to pretend he didn't notice, and there was no reason to change it now. As for Kontra, he couldn't have cared less about him, but he didn't care much about anybody, and of course good-natured Andre got along with everyone. I'm just a simple village boy; you can tell from my dialect. When you're cut off from your country, your language remains at the level of a child's. Religion was important at the time, but that was not why he was unable to write anybody off or hate anybody or the like. He was lucky enough to have been born a good man, Kinga had once said; that's the long and the short of it. But . . . but . . . he stuttered, I never looked at it that way. A country kid with a gift for music too obvious to ignore. Everything has its price, he liked to say, and it's not true I've got a bone to pick with *this* life; it's just . . . Still, he would have gone back had the others not persuaded him to stay, appealed to his reason and their solidarity. We need you: you keep us honest and together. Don't exaggerate, he mumbles (blushing).

Depending on the promoter the gigs came with hotels, private rooms, or the van: a one-time dormitory mattress with a blue floral-patterned cover—later to become Abel's property—spread out over the back after the seat was lowered. (Once it was the room where the liquor was stored: a filthy double bed between crates. What do you say? Janda asked. Yes or no? Kontra, who had subjected the contents of the crates to close scrutiny, gave him a nudge with his elbow. They took as many of the most expensive bottles as they could carry.) In double rooms they would pair off as follows: Kontra with Janda, Abel with Andre. Though the fourth bed, the place for *our driver*, was often unnecessary. Some gigs he went to, others he did not. He would disappear after the first song. Where to? Into whatever town they happened to be in. To do what? Nobody asked. Later he would recount bits and pieces of strange encounters to Omar, but it was impossible to tell how much was true and, if it was made up, *who* made it up.

Some cities never sleep, others are like crossing a meadow; some consist exclusively of fords, others, after devastating fires or floods, have been given broad thoroughfares; some churches are like fortresses, others like pleasure domes. Motorcycle bars are everywhere. Strange as it may seem, Abel had no inhibitions when it came to choosing a drinking establishment. He was no longer helpless, he was merely different: he stood out everywhere. He stood out even if he did not go in, if he stayed outside, in the street. Whether the streets were crowded or quiet, someone almost always stopped and talked to him. People, except the musicians, seemed to feel the need to talk to him.

One evening he was coming out of a bar when an old woman went up to him and said, There you are! No, sorry. You're not him. She looked him over once more to be sure. No, you're not my son.

Would you . . . Could you come with me anyway? I'm scared to death. This is no place, no time of day for an old woman, but I've got to find him: he's an alcoholic, you see, and you look like such a nice young man.

They walked together for a while, she somewhat bent, he with his hands in his pockets, she tottering along, he walking as slowly as possible. She did not dare enter the bars; she asked him to go in her stead or peer through the windows: You're nice and tall, you can see if he's there.

But he didn't know what he looked like.

Like you!

But he did not see anyone who looked like him. Later it came out that the son was no son; he was her lover. Abel looked at the woman more closely. She looked seventy.

What you must think of me now!

Not at all, he said. Shall I stop a cab for you?

She nodded and disappeared.

At another time, in another place: a little man standing in the bushes at the edge of a park, briefcase in hand. He too had been ill-treated.

It all began when my wife made believe she didn't understand what I was saying. It was double Dutch, she told me, a jumble. Try another language. But I don't know another language, and I ask you, what's so hard about understanding what I say? You understand what I say, don't you?

Absolutely, said Abel.

The little man began to sob.

I talked about it at work. What did I expect? Commiseration? At first they nodded sympathetically—yes, yes, marriage—but later they started pretending *they* didn't understand what I was saying. I know, they were just having a laugh, making fun, but then they couldn't stop. They went on like that all day, making believe they didn't understand me, so I stopped talking, but on the way home, squeezed together with everyone on the bus, I suddenly burst into tears and had to get off, and since then, said the little man, staring into the dark bushes, since then I've been wandering and wondering whether the sentences I utter in the belief they are leading me step by step to the truth are in fact leading nowhere. But this time I'm not going to ask you if you understand. God only knows what it's supposed to mean. Forgive me. I'd better be going.

He took two steps and paused.

Forgive me, but do you think you could take me to the nearest bus stop? I'm actually quite frightened. It's strange, I know: I'm an adult, after all.

No problem, said Abel.

And so on. One man wanted to buy a stolen car in the middle of the night and needed an interpreter. (And you believe that? Alegria asked his grandson. Yes, said Omar. Why not.) One of the last to come up to him was his father.

Brother, said the man. Scraggy, unshaven, ill-smelling. He may have been slightly younger than Andor, it was hard to say: life had taken its toll, and it was dark. Sometimes no more than a single fold is the same: the path between nose and mouth. Brother, said the man who had come up to him, why do you go weeping and gnashing your teeth through these dark streets?

Abel did not weep, though he did perhaps gnash his teeth a bit; for the most part he simply wandered.

In this neighborhood?

It's not forbidden, is it?

Uh-uh.

Well . . .

Brother! cried the scraggy man, grabbing him by the sleeve. Strong fingers, dirty nails. Got any spare change for me?

Abel rummaged in his pocket and came up with some money: coins, two crumpled banknotes. The man looked over the offering and picked out the lesser banknote and a couple of coins with the tips of his fingers. Or know what? He swept everything from Abel's hand into his. Tenderly. The guys over on the corner would have robbed you anyway. Or if not them, the guys one corner down. I might as well take them. God bless you, brother. And off he went in the direction Abel had come from.

There were no guys on the corner. Nor did he meet anyone farther on except two cats, one black and one brown, spotted, sitting motionless like two tiny stone lions on either side of a garage driveway.

When he got back to the hotel in the middle of the night, the musicians were still in the bar. He could hear them laughing from the entrance.

That evening they had had one of the strangest gigs on the tour. They knew from the start it wouldn't be anything but a money-making proposition. No real concert: they were just the musical bell announcing the end of the rounds of a panel discussion on "What Needs Fixing Back Home." The moment it looked as though people were going to jump down one another's throats, someone would announce, "And now for a bit of music!"

You ask me why we have no more to contribute than a few anecdotes? (Janda at the bar, posing affectedly with his cigarette.) Well, what is history if not the marginalia between two extremes?

And we stand there like idiots! Kontra shouts passionately, pounding on the counter.

Right! says Andre. It's a confirmation of all the clichés ever said about us. How come nobody can tell the truth! That's not so hard, is it?

Janda, affable: Ah, but what is the truth?

He laughs; Kontra joins in. They clink glasses.

Andre, tragically earnest: How do you account for the fact that our intelligentsia either makes things worse or does precious little to alleviate the situation and then thinks nothing of going abroad and making a fortune out of our misfortune?

Janda, laughing affectedly: I regret—correction, *rejoice* to learn that actors have at last been accepted into the ranks of the intelligentsia.

Subdued mirth.

And now—Kontra raises his index finger—for a bit of music! Tootle-tootle-tootle, brum-brum-brum, che-che-che. They laugh, play make-believe guitars, pound on the counter; they stop. Janda picks up a cigarette end that has almost gone out and flicks away the ashes; it makes an unexpectedly loud noise.

The bastards . . .

What do you say? Andre says to Abel, who, unsure of himself as usual, is standing off to the side. Another drink?

They had drunk more that night than they ever had before, Janda especially. They—that is, Abel, the only one who stayed sober—had to carry him to his room. His eyes were open, but whether he could see was uncertain. The next morning was the first time nobody was in a state to drive but the boy.

Shit! said Janda, lying down on the back seat and falling back asleep. Abel drove carefully, trying not to jerk. Even so, later, Janda: Stop! I've got to barf.

They stood for a long time in a no-standing zone, the cars speeding past behind them, while Janda threw up into the ditch by the side of the road. They saw a police car coming in the opposite direction. Abel and Kontra thought about the driver's license that was still in Kontra's wallet, but luckily nothing happened.

FALCONS

Later, however, something did happen. A scandal.

Though the evening started out differently—quite promisingly, in fact. Another town, a bar that had once been a cinema and still had a curtain, a platform, a balcony, and a few posters. A pleasant atmosphere, all in all, and an audience larger than any they had had so far on the tour. Despite their poor physical condition and the fact that they heard a lot of their native language around them—which isn't necessarily a bad thing—they were more or less up. Abel sat, as always, alone, on the sidelines: a table had been placed for him near the steps to the platform.

For a while nothing happened. Music. At first people tend to listen attentively; with time—it's inevitable—they start talking and the glasses start making noise, though it's not clear whether the bartenders aren't doing it on purpose, the clinking noise. I'm on edge today, Janda told them. His head ached; having to drum didn't help; he even lost the beat a few times. He was sweating. Break time, said the ever-observant Andre.

Janda nodded, headed towards the bar. Need a drink. He landed next to a cowboy type: lumberjack shirt, jeans hugging the slimmest hips you ever saw. A leather pouch, hanging from the neck, filled with what? Native soil?

Hey!

The voice and posture betrayed a certain degree of inebriation, but the gaze was penetrating and clear.

Hey! the cowboy said to Janda. Play the falcon song, why don't you.

Thanks, Janda said to the bartender and went back to the stage.

Later—and, as it happened, during a daring rhythmic experiment—there it was again: Not that! The falcons!

He never called out in the breaks, only while they were playing. At first he kept going on about those falcons, but later added other words: sons of bitches, highway robbers, lazy bastards, traitors.

Janda to the others: Am I crazy or are you hearing what I'm hearing? Maybe I'm imagining things. I'm not at my best today.

The others confirmed they'd heard the guy too.

Forget him, said Andre. We'll just stop three songs sooner than usual.

So on they played and on the guy hollered. And groaned loudly and yawned outrageously. With an occasional *deadheads* or *assholes* or *double-crossers* thrown in.

Janda put down the metal can he was pounding on and, while Andre and Kontra played on, went over to the owner and said, That man at the bar—where is he? somewhere or other—well, I want you to kick him out. The owner, a man with a soft face and blond hair falling over his earlobes, nodded, but it was easy to see he would not do a thing.

Could he kick the crazy guy out now? Janda asked two songs later. His voice was unsteady by then.

What was he talking about? the owner asked. This was a bar; bars are noisy.

Janda looked around. Falcons, you motherfucker! the voice babbled. Janda turned in the direction it was coming from. Each time he lost his cool, the voice jumped out at him, luring him into the dark, the balcony. The balcony bore clear traces of the former movie theater: rows of plush seats, stray couples smooching. Janda stumbled in the dark; the people sitting downstairs, including the musicians and Abel, looked up. A malicious laugh came from some-where. Janda turned and then, finally, he saw him: scraggly hair plastered against a drunken horse face, grinning. Janda grabbed his collar with his long, bony fingers.

Listen up, piss face! One more peep out of you and I toss you over the balcony. Then I go down and kick the shit out of you, you fucking bastard. And you won't be the first, get it?

Nana nana na na na, Andre was singing down below.

Without looking, Janda could see the expressions on the back-row couples' faces. He shoved him into a seat, let the collar go, and started back down.

Filthy stinking Gypsy thief! Lily-livered fascist pig! the voice called after him.

Whereupon Janda swung round, yanked the guy out of the seat with a crash and dragged him along the row and down the narrow stairs. The guy did nothing to defend himself and had stopped talking, but it took forever for Janda to get him from the balcony to the back door. By now nobody was paying the slightest attention to the music: Andre and Kontra were just marking time. But they could not stop either. Then all at once the cowboy began to sing.

Weep, don't you weep! he howled. Mourn, don't you mourn! Just give a call, and . . .

When Andre heard that, he laid down his instrument, but be-fore he could go Janda had managed to shove the guy through the back door.

. . . all the falcons will give their lives for you! Call, just give a call . . .

At which point the door shut.

The owner stood in Janda's way. Sore at *him*! Now look what you've done, damn you!

All I did was what you can't: keep order. And make music.

He went back to Kontra and picked up the can.

Nana nana na na na.

It was about this time that Abel went out.

The atmosphere is all insults and violence the minute more than two of us are in a room together, said the blond girl—correction, young woman standing outside. Abel had just happened to stop next to her while he decided: right or left. She spoke the mother tongue.

Where are you from? she asked him to his face.

At first he did not seem willing to answer, but in the end he did: The others are from B.; he himself was from S.

You don't say! S.? Really? She gasped for air. That's where I'm from.

Only then did he look at her.

ELSA

Intermezzo

Round face, broad mouth. One of the canine teeth (the one on the right) is crooked. Blue eyes, wide open, looking up at him: Do I know you? No, she said, almost disconsolate. I don't remember you.

Her name is Elsa. Actually she came from a nearby village: P. Heard of it?

He nods.

It's . . . Gosh! . . . She laughs. Then her eyes seem to well up with tears. Big eyes. She looks away, places her hand on her stomach. Only now does he notice she is pregnant. Background noise from the bar.

What's your name?

Abel.

Abel. I don't feel too well. Not enough air in there. Will you see me home? It's not far enough to take the bus, but I'm a little afraid in the dark.

Street, outdoors, night, Abel and Elsa. A completely different atmosphere. As dead as the bar was full. You can hear your own footsteps. They don't speak again until they reach the first traffic light and are waiting for it to turn green.

I went to a convent school, Elsa says as they move on, led a regimented existence. I'd go straight home after school. We kept cows. Besides, decent girls didn't wander around the city. (She laughs.) Every day we waited for the bus at the stop in front of the hotel on the Ring. Remember that stop? On the ridge of the hotel roof there were two statues, angels, one on each side. A baroque façade. One day one of the angels—the left one or the right one depending on where you stood—lost its head. A stone—or was it plaster?—angel's head came off, just like that, in the middle of the afternoon, and fell into the crowd waiting for the bus. Down it flew and hit—nobody, by some miracle. Landed in the space opened up a second before by somebody navigating his dog through the crowd. Fell in the spot where the dog had just been. Pow. An angel's head. Slivers of angel's hair spreading over cigarette stubs and spittle. Thudding along, rolling to a stop. You hear about that?

Does he nod or shake his head? Neither maybe. He is looking down the whole time, looking at her feet. Elsa is wearing gym shoes.

She'd only just come, she continues her story, with her husband. Dave, who pronounced his name as if it were Doyv, is a cameraman. They were making a film, a documentary, and they took Elsa on because she knew English and was dirt cheap. At first I didn't understand him. His accent. Later it got better, but I still didn't understand. When they asked him why he was doing it, he said, War is fun. What are you, an idiot? I asked. You've got no sense of I, he said. You mean of me, I said. He laughed. No, I as in irony. You had to turn around whatever he said. It wasn't always easy. God, what a thin-skinned lot you people are. What did you expect? Sometimes I really gave it to him. By the end of the filming Elsa was pregnant and they got married with the crew as witnesses. The ceremony took place in a meadow. She danced with flowers in her hip-length hair, her dress covered with grass stains, but she danced and laughed and cried. The camera shook: there is a video of it. And through it all I'd go and throw up. Once he videoed that too and me licking the last bits of vomit off my lips and starting to dance again. They kept making us kiss, and he kissed me, kissed my vomit-tasting lips.

Now Elsa was in her fifth month and no longer threw up, but she did laugh and cry in quick succession or, sometimes, simultaneously, and all day long. The minute I wake up I have to cry. Or laugh. It comes of being happy and sad. I'm partly unaware of the causes, partly aware. The officials were handling Elsa the way they handle everyone. There's no point in complaining, I know. If you're a man, you're a mafioso; if you're a woman, you're a whore. That's the way it goes. There are women in the office. I'm in my fifth month and married, and they give me a three-month residence permit. It runs out in my eighth month. Get it? And that's the women.

By the way, I finally asked if we were going to get married. It must have been a terrible burden on him, hearing me cry every day like that. Though he never said a thing. But when you think about it: you've known somebody six months, and when she's not barfing she's bawling. Now it's a little better: he's away. He was offered a job. Another disaster somewhere. He's off for a month or more. He's got to earn a living, after all.

Every morning I go out. Buses make me sick, so I walk, walk all over, to the park, through the shops, though I don't buy anything. At some point my feet feel cold, so I go back home, take a bath, watch the water running down my stomach. The rest of the day I lie on the couch in front of the window and look out over the city. We live on the second floor. In the morning clouds of steam rise out of the basement laundries; smoke rises out of the chimneys and turns into clouds. But no matter how nice they are to look at, man cannot live on smoke and steam. Is this what I should be doing? Does it make sense . . .

She belches.

Oh! She puts her thin, white finger on her lips. Sorry. I'm pregnant. It happens. End of sentence: . . . to go along with it?

Contact with *the local women* had no charm for her. I know it's not nice of me, but I find them so . . . *simple*. Know what I mean? Oh, here's where I live.

They were standing in front of a high-rise.

Do *you* have contact with other people?

A few.

From home?

No.

She places her hand on her stomach and belches again.

Sorry . . . Want to come up?

He just looks at her.

Sometimes I even miss the church, says Elsa. I'm getting so conservative. Would you stay with me? I can tell I won't be able to sleep. (Pause.) Just to talk.

Sorry, says Abel, but he had to get back to the others: they didn't know where he was and they might want to move on tonight.

She stands in front of the house; he leaves with long, rapid steps, bent slightly forward.

Such was the story of Elsa, whom I knew for one hour.

What time was it—shortly after midnight perhaps—when Abel started back, more or less, to the hotel? It is one of those less-than-spectacular cities: everything is new and looks like everything else—the same shops on every corner. Besides, the whole time he had walked next to Elsa, he looked at his feet: sidewalk, dusty black shoes. But let us radically shorten the hour or so that passed until he arrived at the relevant corner. This time he met nobody new.

At first he failed to recognize the street in back of the hotel: he had never seen it before from this perspective; no, he must have, because there was the van. And coming from behind the van was a groan that sounded like a couple making love in a run-down house entrance. Or like two men kicking a third, especially Janda.

Apart from the *incident* the concert had gone off as planned. Janda left the platform without acknowledging the applause; Andre and Kontra packed up and got paid. That took forty-five minutes or so. When they got back to the hotel room, they found Janda on the double bed watching stock-car races, gritting his teeth. He had been drinking but was so furious that he had remained sober. Andre decided it was better not to say anything. What are you so upset about, the guy's an idiot, the kind you see on every, etc. They joined him, watched the races, then a bad horror film, screaming women, flashing knives. Later there was a knock on the door. The boy, most likely.

Come in!

He doesn't.

Well, don't then. (Janda, muttering)

I'll go.

Andre went to the door, opened it, and I must be dreaming, I'm not standing here in the doorway, I'm still glued to the TV: there's this guy standing in the hallway with a knife flashing in his hand. Doesn't say a thing, just stabs me.

The tip of the blade slipped down along the collarbone, making an indescribable noise, then the knife fell with a ping, despite the carpet, and the next moment the guy was gone. Only the knife on the floor and a bloody shirt.

Kontra's voice coming from inside the room: What's up?

This guy . . . The wall jutted out in such a way as to hide Andre: they could not see him. This guy . . . with a knife . . .

What?!

Andre tottered a few steps back into the room. His shirt was slit open from the collarbone to the chest, drenched in blood. Must have been aiming at the neck ar . . .

He could no longer stand and slid down the wall, squatting on the carpet. Without a word Janda stepped over him and ran out, Kontra on his heels.

The boy on night duty was reading over his class notes when they stormed past him to the front door: locked. Impossible!

Open it! Janda roared, pounding on the door. The frightened boy at the desk pressed a button; the door slid open; the men flew out into the street and—nothing.

Kontra stood stock-still, but not Janda: he raced to the corner, around the building, and found the cowboy pissing against the van.

Now the checkered shirt was lying there motionless, arms out. It's okay, said Kontra, pushing Janda away. The dirty rat! Janda roared, trying to kick the lumberjack shirt.

It's okay! Kontra screamed. Janda was trying to regain his balance by hopping. It's okay, said Kontra, this time as if speaking to Abel.

Janda ran past him to the entrance door, pounding on the glass again, this time from the outside. The young man at the hotel desk peered out of the illuminated cube of the foyer in panic and merely shook his head. Janda let out a howl and ran back to the place where Abel and Kontra were still standing with the inanimate cowboy at their feet.

I don't care what you think, said Janda to Abel. You get in there and bring him out. He's wounded.

The man at the desk was still trembling when Abel appeared at the door and showed him his room card through the glass. Luckily he doesn't know I'm with them.

Andre's wound was long but not deep. He had taken off his shirt and was pressing toilet paper against it. Not even in a situation like this would he dirty a white towel. The toilet paper stuck to the blood.

Abel went first with most of the baggage; all that was left for Andre was the double bass and a small bag. They took the back exit. Getting past the front desk would have been problematic: the young man was having a grating conversation with someone they could not see.

They left the torn, bloody shirt in the bathroom. The knife was there too.

Bags, instruments, jackets higgledy-piggledy behind the backseat. Kontra—No, you (Janda) aren't driving; I am!—steps on the gas. Sssss, said Andre. The instruments! The van is racing around a traffic circle with a fountain in the middle. When they came into town, the fountain had sprayed a gale of water onto the car, smearing yellow road dust all over the windshield; now it is off, so Kontra activates the window-washing mechanism and the water shoots out with a whoosh, as if things had gone far enough and the noise were meant to wake them all up. There is a man crossing the street in front of them, and if they maintain their speed they will run him over. They don't: Kontra is a good driver and whizzes past just behind his back. Fuming, he stops in his tracks and tries to say something but can't: he's concentrating on holding his urine in. And then the car is gone.

When they have just about left the city, Abel: Could you stop please?

Kontra can't believe he has heard right; he glances in the rear-view mirror and drives on. Andre sees that the boy is sweating and trembling.

Could you please . . .

Janda in the seat next to the driver: Keep going!

Andre is about to say something, but just as he opens his mouth, a stream of blood seeps through his T-shirt. The shirt is gray, the growing blood stain on his left shoulder russet.

Later: no more city, just fields; no moon, clouds perhaps: you can't see anything but the asphalt lit by the headlights. Now you can stop.

Kontra turns onto a country road and drives quite a distance until he stops and switches off the lights. Now, finally, darkness. They sit there, the four of them, breathing.

Shit, said Kontra.

Andre: What . . . What did you . . .

A fumbling on the boy's side of the van, after which the door opens. A crunching noise: he has put his foot outside. A torrent of aftershave sweat flows over Andre. Then the door to the luggage space goes up and he takes something out.

Andre: What are you doing?

The door goes back down.

Andre: Turn the light on.

Kontra immediately turns the inside lights on. A shining interior in the otherwise nearly total darkness. How can it be so dark? You can hear the leaves moving on the plants. Abel has disappeared.

Andre climbs out of the van, calls out, Abel?!

No response.

Janda to Andre: Get back in.

Andre: What have you done?

Get back in, I tell you.

What is he doing?

He's left, says Janda, now completely calm.

You turn us in and I'll kill you, you little queer, he had thought a few minutes before. And then he had the feeling he had *heard* what the boy thought back: Just keep calm. Janda glanced in the rearview mirror but did not see him: he had just bent forward.

Let's go, Janda says now.

Kontra just looks at him.

Janda turns the inside lighting off.

Now Kontra gets out, goes over to Andre. To help him look into the field. To see nothing. Andre, still bleeding from the shoulder, is stumbling among the cabbages.

Abel?

It is hard to keep your balance when you have to keep one hand on a bleeding wound in your shoulder. Andre teeters, an ankle cracks—Ow!—and he falls to his knees on some cabbages. It is a good thing Kontra is there and can pull him up and get him going. He bleeds all over Kontra's arm. Janda has slipped into Kontra's seat, turned the engine and the lights on. He sees: Andre, Kontra, cabbage. No Abel.

He is gone.

Shit, says Andre. He is nearly in tears. What have you done?

He can hardly stand. Not the ankle: he is suddenly nauseous.

Come on, says Kontra. We'll get the first-aid kit.

The first-aid kit is as good as empty: a few Band-Aids. Andre knows that but goes along with him anyway. Kontra tows him to the back seat. Hey! Kontra barely has time to climb aboard before Janda is off. Andre groans. You're crazy. Absolutely out of your mind.

Later, when it was a bit lighter, they stopped and bandaged Andre's wound. Finally. After a while it was time for a cigarette. Kontra rummaged for his jacket in the mess in the back and: Damn it to hell!

Janda: What's wrong?

Kontra cadged a cigarette before answering: The boy took my jacket. It had my tobacco in it. Oh yes, and my papers.

He looked over the passport Abel had left behind. Oh, he said, he was born on the twenty-ninth of February.

Congratulations, said Janda.

I don't hate the man who stabbed me, thought Andre. I hate *you*. I want to go home, he whimpered in the back seat.

All right, said Kontra. I'm driving, aren't I.

As for Abel: The jacket fit him like a charm; he did not notice he had taken the wrong one until he went to pay for a hot drink at a lonely filling station after dawn. He asked for the key to the toilet and held up the open passport next to his face in the mirror. The similarity between the passport picture and the life-size face was tolerable: we could be cousins. That makes my official name now Attila V. I had no idea he was from my father's country . . . Though it makes no difference.

Kontra was the only one who had a valid visa, and it was good for years. Now I can go everywhere.

PART VI

THE IMPOSSIBLE

Marriage

STREET SCENE. MERCEDES

Sometimes, like pus, things thicken. The always somewhat curious, so-called everyday and seemingly gradual processes that help us to approach our, how shall I put it? life-until-we-die, suddenly speed up and go out of whack. It can't be explained, an unemployed chimney sweep was told by his mistress of many years, or he simply failed to understand. How love comes and goes. He did not want it to live on, it seemed; he merely wanted an explanation going beyond the because you or I are/am so and so, because such and such took place. Nothing took place, and each of us is as we are, so such things don't matter. It can't be explained, said his mistress. Shortly thereafter she married a man she had known for only several weeks, and the chimney sweep set fire to four roofs and a kiosk. Mercedes stood in the street with roofing tiles raining down on her.

To say that everything in Mercedes' life had run, as the expression has it, *according to plan* would not be quite accurate. She had a good childhood: her parents were hippies and she spent her diaper years on a Caribbean camping site at the state's expense, her bare abdomen the basic motif in the picture. Twenty years later she fell in love. His name was Amir. He was so handsome and so black that in the twilight or when it was very bright or very dark she could scarcely make out his face and the rest of his body. Part ebony statue, part noble and mysterious prince, he would come to her late in the night and crawl all over her in the dark. They were together for five years, during which he grew ever more handsome, noble, and mysterious. In the first year he spoke five times more than in the second. She learned about trees that are planted upside down and have wood made of water and when you go to the artificial lake at night and think you see one ablaze you find it completely unconsumed the next morning. It is black magic. By the end he had pretty much stopped talking. To her at least; he apparently went on talking to others. He was a good talker, clever and engaging: he was chosen to lead the group. The group included people whose names are completely forgotten, as is the fact that they would monopolize the conversation. Up and monopolize the conversation. As their leader he would moderate far into the night, after which he would go to her and wake her with his weight. What was he doing with a white woman? the group would ask him. None of your bloody business, he would say. You're nothing but a pet to her, they would say. He asked her not to speak during intercourse, not to groan. She isn't worthy of you, the group would say. You know that as well as we do. The reason you go to her in secret, at night, is that you can't look at her yourself. Snakes, he would say, snakes make obscene gestures with their tongues. I don't want to see your would-be tolerant parents again, he said: They treat me like a talking ape. He did not say anything at the end; he simply stopped going. She turned pale for want of sleep. She scraped the inside of her thighs climbing over the fence of his hostel. Every thrust was like sandpaper, but no word did she utter, no groan. He disappeared three weeks later. Clueless, she carried the baby three weeks too long. When it was born, it had one small blue eye and one large black eye. She named him after his father: Omar. My name is Omar; that means solution, exit, means.

Later she started on a doctorate. Her professor was a sallow old man with a face like a cave of stalactites and skin that hung like icicles from his eyes. He was as ugly as he was intelligent—and as vain. After his second wife died in the quiet and discreet way she did everything else, Mercedes moved in, because that made it easier for her to do everything for him. When shortly before his sixty-fifth birthday Tibor discovered he would soon follow his dear Anna, he said to his young partner, I do not wish to be disturbed in the weeks to come. I shall die soon, but before I do I want to finish my book. She nodded, her eyes, as always, looking tear-swollen. I would set down his meals at the study door as if he were . . . He had time only for a final chapter. The editor said it was very good, it just had nothing to do with the rest of the book, the history of rhetoric; it had something to do with death, with fear and fury, and was unusual, even gripping after a fashion. This last sentence, for instance, I wonder how he arrived at it: God is a bespittled dog's toy . . . A May diagnosis, an August death. Of course, according to a usually well-informed friend of the young widow, he didn't so much as leave her a roll of toilet paper; it was all she could do to reclaim her own furniture. Luckily she managed to get the manuscript and the diaries out of the house before the children from his first marriage came on the scene. In his diaries he deals with much the same issues as in his books and manuscripts. At times he records the day's weather, a wry observation, important business calls: U.E. gave me a ring. Not once in five years does he mention his partner or her son. But apart from that, Mercedes maintains she has nothing to complain about. All in all, much as there is room for indignation and grief, I was then and am now: happy. Take Omar and my job at the private school: I love being a teacher; besides, there's a fee reduction for teachers' children.

On the day we are concerned with, the *fateful Monday*, the worst hell—summer—was behind her: they had moved into a new apartment; the school year had begun. Now she had two periods free, and with a bouquet in her hand and a book under her arm she was on her way to see a sick friend. A genial elderly colleague had, quite *out of the blue*, engaged in a quasi-religious argument with the headmaster of a denominational school—denominational, but otherwise quite decent! (Mercedes)—on the topic of Darwin vs. the creationists. It went on for weeks with the result that her colleague, his name is Adam Gdański, had landed in a psychiatric ward. Mercedes was of the opinion that while they had no business denouncing him as a doddering lunatic when he was so close to retirement, there might be additional reasons for his nervous breakdown: What do we know of the lives of others?

What was going on inside the cab driver whose nameplate was on the dashboard? Maybe he had had a bad weekend: first she said he could have his son for both days; then she changed it to Sunday only, and so on, with the result that he went and stood under her window and shouted, though not loud, Your new guy's a cop—and yet on Monday morning he was back on the job. His first fare asked for the railway station. He took the street he always took, a street where earlier that morning a building had gone up in flames. Red-hot roof tiles were still shooting up in the air and whistling down onto the sidewalk, where they shattered and slid into the road. The taxi, however, as witnesses later reported, sped right up to it, breaking only at the last moment, as if the driver, Tom—his name was Tom—had failed to notice what was going on until then. The rear of the car swerved and collided with a police car coming in the other direction. The driver, Tom—this was his third accident in short succession—went into reverse and tried to turn, but landed on the sidewalk instead and with such force that although he braked hard . . .

I've had it! I've had enough of this. Enough, you hear? I'm sick and tired of it! He leaped out of the car without turning off the engine, paid no attention to the policemen running up to him; he only shouted to a group of rubbernecks, I've had enough! Enough! And there on the sidewalk between him and them, with roof tiles still landing all around, sat: Abel Nema's future wife.

Bouquet in one hand, reaching out with the other, trying to catch hold of something; nothing there; she keeps trying anyway; maybe she can stop the tiles; the book falls, a large picture book; she sits on it, *eye to eye* with the bumper; stalwart in a way; back straight; the broken ankle under the car, invisible. Am I dreaming or has a taxi just rammed into me? The hand with nothing in it is still fishing in the air and suddenly it catches something, another hand; she holds it tightly, she is about to faint. A stork has tweaked

her ankle; no, a car has shattered her ankle. That can be very painful, but you often feel nothing at first: it's the shock, the trauma.
You think it's the bomb, she told people later; it all fits: flames,
water spurting, glass shattering, blue lights flashing, screams. The
driver was still screaming, tearing his hair out, running around in
circles, the police approaching him, arms extended, as if trying to
catch a chicken. Here I was, taking flowers to a sick friend, and
all at once the world caves in and you're sitting on a tiny island
amidst the rubble, surrounded by rubbernecks and constantly
photographed.

The flash of a passerby's small point-and-shoot camera went
off straight in her eye. She came to, realized what the problem
was, saw herself sitting under a purring car that was breathing its
warm, stinking fumes onto her. With her left hand she was holding
on to somebody for dear life. She looked up.

Oh, it's you, she said and then nothing more.

ABEL

The last time they had seen each other was three or four months before. It was a Sunday. She, friends, and family were marching in a demonstration for more tolerance. Omar was enthusiastic, she in another world: the diagnosis had been known for four weeks, and try as she might she could think of nothing else. Tibor is dying, Tibor is dying, Tibor is . . .

As for Abel, he had just had a long run: he had been running after a certain Danko or the laptop under Danko's arm until he got caught up in a pack of dogs and took a tumble. Later, making his way home, he suddenly found himself back among all those people with their signs and could not at first comprehend what they were about, only that they were impeding his progress, when suddenly: Abel! Omar cried. So you're here too?! Abel's here!

So he is, said Mercedes. (Tibor is dying.) Hello.

Omar was carrying a blue balloon; Abel said he couldn't stay any longer: he had to . . . —what he said was—go to the station.

But it's practically around the corner!

So it is, said Abel, brightening up. I had nearly lost my way.

How is that possible? Omar asked his mother afterwards. I'll ask him the next time he comes for a lesson.

But there was no next time.

My Russian teacher has disappeared, said Omar several days later. I'd prepared ten or twelve questions for him. Where is he? This isn't like him.

Mercedes (Tibor is dying, Tibor is . . .) dialed the number he had given her. A butcher's shop. Sorry.

Sorry, darling. (Tibor is . . .) I just don't know.

We don't know, said the musicians, back at Kingania after their interrupted tour. They arrived much sooner than planned and were somewhat taken aback to find *her* there.

She was sobbing. The camp had been *absolutely humiliating*: after a stint in the kitchen, where she made fun of their under-developed sense of spice—This is a camp for *children*, madam! *Madam* they called me!—they'd switched her to housekeeping, but she wasn't going to let them do that to her: she'd cleared out, literally, in the middle of the night, six kilometers on foot to the nearest station, gnashing my teeth in the starlight. She hadn't even asked to be paid. And now this. What happened? How come you're back so soon? Where's the boy? What's that wound on your shoulder? What did you do? Did he do that? Why? What have you done with him?

No, said Andre. It wasn't him.

We haven't done anything with him, said Kontra. He just left.

I know, said Kinga to Janda, who had remained conspicuously silent. I know you had something to do with it. You're the one.

That was how it always began: You're the one, I know, you, you, you! But this time he did not let it get to him. He had promised.

Be reasonable, Kontra had said to Andre, who whimpered at first, then grew hysterical. You can't drive that far by yourself. At least wait until the wound heals.

And something else, said Andre, trembling all over. You breathe a single word to anybody, and I'm gone, out of here. Tell him that!

Okay, I will.

The two things weren't connected, Kontra, the new spokesman, lied. The first was just a potshot after a concert, and the boy—he just upped and left. He'll be back: he's got my passport.

Chch! Janda could not help uttering. He—and the others—pretended it was just a sneeze.

Let me see! said Kinga, grabbing Abel's passport from Kontra and looking at his picture in it. She burst into tears again and marched off, taking it with her.

Where are you going?

Bam. The door closing. Not long after, she was back with a copy of the passport photo, a copy for *Texts*, in black and white, and hung it up in the kitchen.

Just so you don't forget him.

Janda, still silent, walked into the kitchen and, perfectly calm, tore the picture off the wall, crumpled it up, and threw it into the trash. Kinga waited until he had left the kitchen and retrieved it. There were coffee grounds sticking to it. She cleaned it off but could not remove the spots completely. She hung it back up, spots and all. Later she went out, and when she came back the picture had disappeared, ditto the trash, and there was nobody to pick a quarrel with. So that was the end of that.

We could have the Red Cross search for him if need be, said Andre later.

Search for who? asked Kontra, dismissing the idea with a wave of the hand. A grown man goes where and when he pleases. And for how long.

Kinga had had a lot to drink and had curled up on a mattress, sniffling occasional soft *madam*s . . .

Later—it was autumn by then—they came back to life somewhat. Kinga got over the *madam* thing, and—having stealthily followed the news and heard nothing about a body turning up—the musicians started talking to one another again. Maybe he had only played dead or fainted: nobody had bothered to find out. Kinga knew they were hiding something, but she had too many problems of her own to attend to and had lost all desire to probe.

She had just come out of the *bathroom*—an autumn morning—her now-clean nether parts in greasy jeans with a shiny greenish trim along the pockets, her fingers still warm from the steam, when suddenly there he stood in the door.

Hello.

She rejoiced; she could rejoice again: You're back! He's back!

She threw her arms around his neck; he swayed; she took his face in her hands: Where have you been? How do you feel?

Hard to say. As always. Slightly the worse for wear. On the road a lot lately.

Where on the road?

If I remember correctly, he didn't give a particularly helpful answer. Just on the road. And unfortunately he would have to leave again. He had only come for his things.

He had been in town since the night before, and once more before daybreak somebody had offered him a place to live. The next ten questions—Yes, but who, where, how, why?—never made it out of Kinga's mouth: she simply stood by as he gave Kontra back his jacket and everything in it. He had spent some of the money, not much. You will get it back.

Thank you, said Kontra and gave him his things.

Thank you, said Abel and took the two black traveling bags.

He kissed Kinga on the cheek; he nodded to the musicians.

They nodded back.

He had arrived by train as he had the first time, though this time it was evening and he came from a different direction. The Bastille gleamed in the sun going down behind the platform. He went to Kingania, but no one was there; he went back to the station, left his luggage in a locker, and went into the city.

In The Loony Bin a stocky newcomer was twirling his glitzy G-string before his face. Abel looked past him, perhaps up to the swing, where a drag queen dressed in angel-white was swinging back and forth over the dancers' heads. The music was deafening, but otherwise all was still. No one spoke more than was absolutely necessary. Now and then he held up his empty glass, and the waiter came and filled it.

Later it was morning and everyone had left; only Abel remained in the corner he had sat down in at the outset, buttoned up to the collar. The iron door to the courtyard was open, admitting a rectangle of bright sunshine and air to the perfumed filth inside.

Nobody told him to go; the clean-up crew worked in silence. Thanos, picking up glasses, came closer and closer to his niche. He looked at him while taking the glasses from the table, but still said nothing. There was a glass, half-full of a brownish liquid, perched on the upholstered seat next to Abel and overlooked by Thanos. He gave it to him.

Thanks, said Thanos. What's wrong? No place to stay?

Right.

I see, said Thanos and took the glasses away.

He came back and offered him a cigarette.

Abel shook his head.

You're not taking care of yourself. You had at least six of the house's most lethal offerings. You should be dead by now.

I can't get drunk.

How come?

Shrug. It tastes like water and has more or less the same effect.

You're handsome, said Thanos.

What do you expect me to say?

A bit too old, eh?

Pause.

And you're more the observer type, aren't you.

. . .

After all these (how many?) years Thanos asked one of his regulars: Where are you from?

The answer came after a long pause.

I see, said Thanos.

A vacuum cleaner went on in a back room somewhere.

So you're looking for a place to live, said Thanos, and offered him an illegal attic flat for a ridiculously low rent.

Abel thanked him and slipped the key into his pocket. He took a cab back to the station from Kingania.

OMAR

Oh, it's you, said Mercedes.

For a while she could say nothing else. Others came up to help pull her out from under the taxi. The flowers scattered white and green over the sidewalk. The pain had now kicked in; she held hard onto his hand; her forehead was sweating.

Later they gave her a needle in the back of the hand and things got better. She realized she was in a hospital room and asked after her things. He had brought them: her bag, her phone, even the book and tattered flowers were lying on a chair. The damage to the flowers reminded her of the damage to her ankle: she didn't want to look at it, but she didn't want to tell him or anyone else to throw out the bouquet.

Would you do me a favor?

Give her the phone. Before they took her off to the complicated ankle operation, she had a few calls to make.

Six days a week from nine to three Omar's grandfather does not speak on the phone, because during these hours, his *working* hours, in his *study*, he turns it off, though in fact it makes little difference, because the child's grandmother is on hand or, if she isn't, the answering machine is. For reasons that have never been explained the only response she got on that day was a recorded message: Your call cannot be completed as dialed. She had no trouble reaching Tatjana, but she was out of town, on assignment somewhere. Impatient voice: What's up? I'm in the middle of things. Not that important, said Mercedes. Erik or, better, Maya would have been a possibility, but for reasons that have likewise gone unexplained Mercedes' choice fell upon her son's former Russian tutor, whom she hardly knew and who, incidentally, had disappeared under circumstances worthy of a novel, then turned up again as the passenger in the taxi that ran into her without visible cause at the site of a fire that broke out for reasons as yet unknown: she asked him to do her another favor, namely, pick her son up from school.

He was not surprised, nor did he waver. He said yes.

And please try to get hold of my mother.

And she sank into sleep.

Omar was waiting in front of the school on the third step, so they were the same height, eye to eye. The child's had a cold gleam.

(Well? Did you find it? Omar had asked.

What? Abel had asked back.

The station.

Po-russki, pozhaluista.

Vokzal.

In a complete sentence, please.

Ty . . .

Nashël. From *nakhodit', naiti.*

. . . *nashël vokzal?*

Da.

Do you want to leave?

Abel had written the sentence out in Russian and said it aloud. Omar had repeated it after him.

Do you want to leave?

Net, ia ne khochu uezzhat'.

Did you want to pick someone up?

Did you want to pick someone up?
No.
What did you want to do there?
I live nearby.
I live nearby.
Then how could you not have known where to go?
Then how could you not have known where to go?
I was lost.
I was lost.
In the park?
No, before that.
No, before that.
I don't understand, Omar had said. *Ia ne ponimaiu.*)

Now: Hello, said the grown-up shyly. I'm here to pick you up.

I know, said the child with the charisma of his unknown father and the calm voice of his wounded mother. He hoisted his backpack over his shoulder. I don't want to go to the hospital; I want to go home. I'm hungry. Thanks, I can carry it myself. Why take a taxi? It's only two bus stops. What's the matter? Haven't you even taken a bus before?

No, said Abel. *Ia nikogda ne ezdil na avtobuse.*

The child looked at him. One: Speaking Russian means hooking up with something that was in the hope that it still is. In other words, currying favor. Two: Now the child was forced to smile and shake his head: How can anyone be so . . . ! Apart from that, he remained stern.

Here it is, said Omar to the bus and climbed in. Abel had no choice but to follow. Omar moved back to the middle of the bus. A sudden crush, body to body. Abel concentrated on the crown of the child's head, but at a certain point his hand started to slip. Just as it was about to slide off the pole, Omar said: Here!

They got out, walked through the park. The soccer field was in use. Omar saw out of the corner of his eye that the man next to him was dripping with sweat. And this was the first cool day of the year. What's wrong with you? He did not ask. But if this goes on, I'll forgive him sooner than . . .

. . .

They no longer lived where they had: they had a flat of their own in a nice tree-lined street not far from the park. There was a block and tackle on the building: *for the piano*. Abel recognized some of the objects—they had been pointed out to him on a previous tour—in their new configuration: the African statue on the chest of drawers. The child went into the kitchen; Abel tried to reach the relevant individuals.

I know who you are, Miriam said, interrupting his telephone stutter. A good strong voice. What is he doing now?

He's taking down a pot from the kitchen cabinet. He wants to make a noodle-and-corn casserole.

Good. You eat with him, and I'll go to the hospital.

He hangs up.

There is something inexplicably pleasant about the whole thing. Oh, it's you; no, we won't go straight to the hospital; we're not taking a taxi; I know who you are; eat with him; will you help me?

The child with a can of corn in one hand and a can opener in the other. Abel opens the first can of corn in his lifetime. Butter-soft metal. Something inexplicably pleasant.

Later the kitchen clock looms into Abel's field of vision, and he thinks of the traveling bags he left in the trunk of the taxi. With everything in them: black clothes, what was left of a book with pictures of naked boys, which he always carried with him because he knew Kinga would go through his things, and the nearly expired passport of a no longer extant federation. He should find out where they were, though he could just as well forget about them: they were gone, gone once and for all, so there was no reason to hurry: he could just as well stay here and deliver himself into the hands of this bright-eyed family.

Ready?

Abel gave a devoted nod. When he gave the child back the can, his eye caught the numbers printed on the lid: 05.08.2004. For a moment he thought it was that day's date.

. . .

Thank you, said Miriam, when she finally arrived. It was wonderful of you. Though Omar is no troublemaker. He's a big boy. Did you eat? Did you have a good time?

Omar had poured the food into two soup plates and placed them on the table in silence. His former Russian tutor took a seat in silence. An odd couple. For the most part they ate in silence.

   I am sorry I had to go away so suddenly, Abel finally said, and could not say good-bye. You are right: I should have; it was the least I could do, and my punishment was that I lost my apartment, my computer, and all my jobs. I tell you this not to play on your heartstrings: it serves me right, I deserved it. But I disappointed you. Can you forgive me?

   The child took a drink out of a large red crystal glass. The light of the kitchen lamp on the cut-glass surfaces and the glass eye above them. He put the glass down and took up his fork and spoon again.

   Of course I *can*.

Yes, said Omar. We did have a good time.

   After that Abel borrowed a map and traced the route on foot to his new apartment. Twilight, The Loony Bin closed for the day, empty sidewalk, brick wall, wind, and odd squeaks he could not place at first. He recognized the building, the next to the last before the dead end, because of the two bags standing in front of the door. *Somebody* had delivered them—along with the foam-rubber mattress he had borrowed from Andre—to the address he had given the cab driver. Later, when he was standing on his platform five flights up, he saw where the squeaking noises came from: trains shunting.

That is how new perspectives open up. He stood on his platform, hip-high in the iron cage, the wind nearly pressing him to the wall, a quaintly shaped dusty room behind him with nothing but a wardrobe and a radio spattered with whitewash in the so-called kitchen, and the so-called bathroom consisting in fact of two enamel basins with rust-colored water on the floor, and *in the middle* an old mattress and the two black traveling bags he had given up for lost. He pinched his eyes together: the bullet-shaped silver container trains rolling past on the tracks below him were emitting the last reflections of light.

BETWIXT AND BETWEEN

Crises

Barely six months later they were married. It is not particularly extraordinary, though back then there was no sign of it. He has returned, surfaced from obscure depths, at just the right time, a hero come to the rescue: he holds hands, opens cans (well, one, *one* can), nurtures prospects, and behaves as never before in so adult and normal a fashion; he phones after a suitable interval to inquire after the patient's progress. Oh, says Mercedes absently. She has other worries by then.

The time for her to burst into tears no longer seemed in the distant future, she thought, literally, as she was being lifted off the asphalt on a stretcher and the pain shot straight up to her skull. Or to faint. But faint she did not, nor did she burst into tears: she was much too confused at first and then too woozy from the painkillers. She calmly observed the effect of the morphine on her body, and just as the pain began to rise again she informed the nurse and got another shot. Morphine is related to heroin. You feel you are outside your body. For the next few days, weeks even, she was as if next to herself or somewhere else, she couldn't quite say where. Her entourage registered certain let's call them mood swings: for a time she would tolerate everything (television programs, the building site directly opposite the hospital, her only protection a piece of canvas over the window) with a patience bordering on apathy; then she would have a bout of ill humor she could scarcely mask (the headmaster pays a visit, she nods, yes, sure, back on her feet in no time, but her hands are waving him away: take your flowers and go), to say nothing of the temporary reduction of her vocabulary (What is that thing, piece of crap, piece of shit?), the unprecedented outbursts (she tries to hit the wastepaper basket under the washbasin with a book), the curt, categorical orders, yeses and noes, and when she had to repeat something it would come out a roar the second time, in short, a clear-cut case of postoperative depression.

What was the matter? What was the matter, anyway? The city would emerge inside out from behind the canvas. Was there a single spot in the city in which pits were not being dug to an infernal accompaniment? The nice trees along her street had lost their leaves—Where had autumn gone? How was it that summer here had recently started merging seamlessly with winter?—were just standing there, giant brooms. Without leaves it was obvious how ruthlessly they had been pruned to make sure they would not grow too high, too wide, too round for this nice street. Why did the veils have to fall from my eyes?

Home again, she did almost nothing but sit on the couch with her foot on the marble tabletop. The table had been standing on the street the day they moved in—a greeting, as it were; someone may in fact have purposely left it near their furniture on the sidewalk: free for the taking. This too? the movers asked. She looked both ways—no one in the vicinity—and in the end nodded. The marble top was light-colored and almond-shaped and had a black crack running along its length. She stared at the crack, immobile, for several weeks. Her narrow but stable network of family and friends, however, never stopped coming and going. Unlike many people I have no need to be alone, so I should feel love or at least gratitude, but now everything got on her nerves. Erik, when he burst in like a bullet train to announce: There's never been less reason for depression! We're as vital as vital can be! Our late-nineties boom is unprecedented. Of course it can't last longer than three years, and when the bubble bursts, there will be, quote unquote, a terrible *bloodbath*, but until then . . . The only thing that needs settling is whether we should bomb B. or not. Anyone with the slightest self-esteem thinks we should. Do you?

Don't know, said Mercedes. Never thought about it. My life is cracking up like an arbitrarily run-over ankle.

Is it true you've given notice?

Yes. I mean, no. But I will. As soon as I have a clean bill of health. If that day ever comes.

I don't think that when they told you to keep your ankle elevated they meant for the rest of your life, said Miriam.

No, seriously, said Erik, things are going so well at the moment that I've been seriously thinking of giving up the time-proven principle of exploiting the never-ending stream of trainees and taking on a bona fide editor. It's yours for the asking.

You're a dear, said Mercedes (Erik blushed), without budging from the spot.

Miriam: I really mean it—if you don't start doing something with that foot, you may never walk again.

Sitting doesn't do any harm.

Insert: the expected maternal lecture about adult behavior and its responsibilities. How old are you anyway? Twelve?

I've been good, hard-working, optimistic all my life, all thirty-three years, and now that my life is cracking up like an . . .

You've said that already.

And if I have? Can't I repeat myself if I want to? Can't I just sit here till I get better? What's wrong (Miriam dismissed her with a wave of the hand and picked up her handbag) with that?

At this point the phone rang.

Hello! Mercedes shouted into the receiver. Oh, it's you . . .

Omar came out of his room and stood in front of her.

Thanks, she said into the phone. Coming along. Nice of you to call. She would have long since thanked him for his help, but we had no number for you. Would he give her one now? She'd like to pay him back some time, when things were better, a dinner perhaps.

When is he coming? asked Omar after she had hung up.

Can I help? asked Miriam from the door.

Thanks, no, said Mercedes.

How about next Thursday, Omar proposed

Hm, said Mercedes.

To tell the truth, she was only being polite. For the time being I have no deceit—correction, desire to see people.

When? asked Omar.

When what?

When will you?

There he stood, the white of his glass eye like the marble tabletop: similarly veined and with a similar gleam. He was born with a tumor in his eye. I was a bit ashamed at the time.

Soon, she said, soon.

Before a few days were up, Omar heard the tapping of crutches on tiles as he opened the front door.

What's going on?

Guess who's coming to dinner.

Who?

They had noodles again, but this time Mercedes made them, with a hot sauce.

Which do you like better?

They are both good.

Yes, but which is better?

The child was still stern with him: I *can* forgive you, of course, or, rather, *that* is now a thing of the past. Which did not mean there were no more questions to be answered. The thing was: who should ask them?

It was a strange, very quiet meal, as if none of them wanted to come out with . . . with *something*. He was never particularly talkative; it was up to her to keep the conversation going. And the child, when he felt like it. This time: hosts of angels seemed to be parading through the room, but—and this is the funny thing—it was not unpleasant. The whole time she watched Abel *inquisitively*, one might say, and then, when Omar went to the toilet and they were alone, the wounded ankle lying between them on a separate chair, she said, her voice very light: By the way, the hearing about my accident is scheduled for two weeks from now. You've received a subpoena too, that is, thanks to the post office's forwarding service my deceased partner Tibor B. received a subpoena.

At the time she thought it would only be the pain: she sat on the asphalt, then on the stretcher; she was lifted into the ambulance with a clatter. It was a miracle she had been able to hear his answer to the policeman's question about who he, the helpful taxi passenger and witness, was: Tibor B., home address . . . After which he got into the ambulance as if he belonged to her already.

Does that speak for or against him? He didn't know Tibor was dead when he claimed to be him. He learned it a few hours later, from Omar.

Oh . . .

Yes, said Omar. I went off on holiday with my grandparents, and when I came back he was dead and we had moved.

I am sorry, said Abel now. (He may even have blushed slightly. Who would have thought it.)

It's all right, said Mercedes.

Omar came back: What's wrong?

A short pause. Then—I didn't realize it, Mercedes—Abel told the child what had happened: I made believe I was someone else.

Oh, said Omar. *Pochemu?* Why?

It had grown noticeably darker in the room. The marble table now had a lunar gleam to it.

It is simple, said Abel. The country he was born in and had left nearly ten years before had in the meantime been split into three to five new countries. And none of these three to five countries felt under any obligation to provide him with citizenship. The same held for his mother, who now belonged to the minority and could not get a passport. He could not leave here; she could not leave there. They phoned. He also had a father; his father was the citizen of a sixth and independent neighboring country, though he had disappeared almost twenty years before and had never been found.

Oh yes, and because he had failed to respond to a conscription notice, he was officially considered a deserter.

Oh, said Mercedes and Omar. So that's it.

Yes, he said and apologized again.

If you ask me, Tatjana said later, that was the moment. Mercedes is the type who can't resist a guy who's in such a bind he takes on the identity of a corpse. The shady, the ridiculous, the tragic. So that's it.

They said nothing more until they said good-bye. A man in the dark. White hands, loosely clasped.

SPRING

Last spring—before it all—Mercedes had gone to a secondhand bookshop near her school. A tiny shop with barely enough space between the door and the cash register for a small person like her to lie down in, should the occasion arise, yet you could wander around it lost until closing time. The reason why was that it was so packed with books: they were piled up everywhere—on shelves, on tables, on the floor—and there were so many that no ordinary mortal could cope with them.

Just ask, the owner advised her. Self-portrait of the artist as the Anointed One, his cognac-colored Christlike mane disappearing under the counter, behind which he sits with a perfectly straight back. What are we looking for?

Mercedes had something like a bilingual edition of Rimbaud in mind.

A good choice. The man, who looked like Dürer, pointed her in the right direction. It's not far.

The gazelles are only a two-day walk from each other, thought Mercedes with a smile as she balanced her way through the dusty chaos. The sides of the book towers rubbed against her as she passed: stripes of white dust on a dark dress. She heard rustling in the other aisles. Other customers or mice. Rats. Doves. Mercedes, who had an aversion to certain animals, got gooseflesh.

Found it? The owner's voice. *All things being equal* you should be standing right in front of it.

She looked at the shelf, and what did she see in her line of sight but a bilingual Rimbaud. She laughed. I've got to tell the gang about this guy. Could there be a secondhand bookshop that has everything anyone is looking for? (Call Alegria.) At this point somebody came into the shop: she heard the door open, the owner talk to somebody. On her way back she followed the voice. By the time she reached the cash register, the customer was putting his change in his pocket.

Oh, hello, said Mercedes to her son's Russian tutor. And since she had the impression that he hadn't recognized her, she said, I'm Mercedes, Omar's mother.

Abel nodded. Of course. He knew that. Hello.

The money in the trouser pocket, the book in the pocket of the black coat. It did not quite fit: a strip of the bright cover peeked out. You could see it from far away: the man was carrying a book. Mercedes paid for her *Saison en enfer*, and then they walked part of the way together.

Mercedes is short: she does not come up to his shoulder; he hunched a bit while walking next to her. This posture made him look older than he is. Or younger. A teenager at a loss for what to do with his body. He reminds me of both an old man and a boy. The first time she had met him anywhere but at home, their first conversation alone. They walked in the direction of the park, an April in open winter coats: everything was wet, though it was not raining. Nature awakening in the middle of the city.

Uhm, said Mercedes. How are the lessons coming along? Is Omar making progress?

Excellent progress, said Abel.

She was glad to hear it. She had heard he tutored other children as well.

He did.

He must enjoy it then.

He did.

She enjoyed teaching too.

No response.

How is the dissertation going?

Another pause. During which: the remarkably synchronic sound of their steps and, by way of contrast, the arrhythmic jangle of change in his pocket. Men who carry their change in their pockets. Mercedes' feeling about that is ambiguous. In fact, *everything* was somehow *on the one hand—on the other* at this point. Here the elegant rhythm of his steps, there the cacophonic, proletarian jingle-jangle of the coins. His answers too. (Above all: there *were* only answers—he never once asked about anything. Later too he would ask a question only when there was absolutely no way around it. How do I get to the station?) On the one hand, there was the voice: the best of both masculine and feminine in richness and melody; on the other, you had to pull everything out of him and when you did you never knew whether he was being ironic or was merely lost. When asked how his work was progressing, he would respond after a brief yet undeniable pause: *All right.*

I didn't finish my dissertation either, said Mercedes. Oh, sorry. I meant: I didn't finish my dissertation. And only now that I'm teaching do I see that I never had an idea of what scholarship is or, rather, had any interest in it.

He gave no response to that either. What could he have said?

Say something in Russian, Mercedes said later, at home, to her son.

That won't work, said Omar. You can't just say something.

Then say: I love my mother.

Ia liubliu svoiu mamu.

That sounds so nice, said Mercedes. What do you talk about?

Omar shrugged, which was uncharacteristic of him, and said, Oh, this and that: grammar, Russian customs.

I think he likes him, Mercedes said to her parents. He never imitates people he doesn't like. *He* is always shrugging like an adolescent.

So you've noticed that. (Alegria)

Mercedes: Tibor has no time to spend with the child, unfortunately. He lives for his work.

Miriam, nodding: As only absolute egotists like him can.

Alegria made believe he was lost in thought and had only just come out of it: Who?

Abel and Mercedes walked as far as the psychiatric hospital and said polite good-byes. Then he turned left, she turned right, and the rest is history.

It was there on that street corner that everything was for the last time *as it should be*. Not a bad point in both their lives: everything had a place and was in it. But then he lost his bearings, got mixed up in a violent business, and disappeared, and their relationship did not exactly thrive. Now they had a chance to start over. We've been going in a circle or, no, the circle has changed: I am different, not completely, though in minor but important ways, and him? That was as yet to be seen.

Mercedes had not seen the passport with the troublesome date, but on the basis of the information she had at her disposal the ten years would soon be up. So on the one hand, there was the time factor; on the other, they had to proceed with caution. Keep in mind: What do we know about him? What does Omar know? What do we sense? What is there to see?

The ensuing weeks gave plenty of opportunities for observation. This time I want to learn French as well as Russian, said Omar. Mondays Russian, Thursdays French. Fine, said Mercedes and relayed the message to Abel. He accepted without surprise or hesitation. Mercedes, for her part, fell back on Erik's offer: I've got to pay for the lessons, after all. At first, she worked from home because of the ankle, which paid off: she could brush up her French. I just sit in the corner, quiet as a mouse, and listen, though I watch too.

What does he look like? How does he hold himself? How does he move? When he's eating, when he's teaching, when he comes and goes. The nature and state of his visible body parts? Apart from a few black hairs on the lower finger joints an all-but-flawless skin; signs of physical labor: none. Perfect fingernails, though perhaps somewhat longer than one might expect. A minor irregularity in the lower incisors: sudden pressure from the wisdom teeth. Hair like crow feathers, not what I would call a hairstyle. Is he good-looking then? Sometimes I would say: yes; sometimes you just can't tell. The same face and yet . . . It's a matter of perspective, and of perspectives there are many: light, time of day, topic of conversation. A face like the moon: craters, darkness, and then full, white, beaming. The beam comes from the eyes. Oh, those eyes.

When you invite him to stay for supper after the lesson and ask him questions, he answers. Courteously, concisely, and to all intents and purposes sincerely.

Where does he come from? What's it like there? Or, rather, what was it like? The climate, the architecture. Was there a theater? Was it only for touring companies? Were there hotels, houses of worship, car dealerships?

A metro system? (That was Omar.)

So you can't visit your mother?

My father disappeared too, said Omar.

Mercedes has recently become interested in refugee issues: What are the legal problems, the specific ills? Though he isn't the best one to discuss those things with; it's not surprising; how would you feel if you were him; I'm ashamed to ask. Let's go back to presumably harmless topics:

What had he been doing since the last time they had met? Had he moved? Where to? What did he live on? (Observation: He takes taxis more often than *somebody like him* might be expected to.) Did he have money? Where from? No papers, but money? Is that possible? (Are you with the Mafia? Mira asked him one day over the phone.) What people live on is often a mystery. (What was that drug thing?)

What do you find more interesting: teaching or research?

They are both good.

Yes, but which is better?

Mercedes misses the children. I wonder if they miss me?

Why do you like him? she asked Omar out of the blue one morning. He knew exactly what or who she meant. He shrugged and said wisely: I just do.

Later, when she was a bit more mobile, she tried other things: We're going to the seaside next weekend. Would you like to join us? Have you seen the wooden cathedral since it opened?

Can you tell me about the icons? Mother has vertigo. Will you take me on the Ferris wheel?

He's not such a stick-in-the-mud after all: you can talk about art and books with him. He's quite up on the permanent collections; he hasn't been to the newer things yet. We're going next Friday. Come along, why don't you.

He always said yes. They saw each other at least twice, for the most part three times a week. And at a certain point you willy-nilly begin to feel the difference: between the sort of days you spend with him and the sort of days you don't. On the days you spend with him you don't have to think about anything; on the others you have to think about him. Mercedes could not tell which was better. Then too there's the psychological angle: I wanted to like it, *him*, though why not? The cornerstones in her life had resumed their proper places, but there was a new tension among the parts: it was a new building and still settling. She sensed the return of the well-known, vertiginous state of being someone's secret lover.

CE JOUR

And one Monday she turned up at the *jour fixe* with him on her arm. The *jours fixes* had started up again recently under the patronage of the Erik-Maya couple in a café near the publishing house. The times call for social interaction and debate. If you (Mercedes) don't mind. Why should I mind? She searched her inner self and was surprised to find: the pain was gone. To be honest, I've pretty much forgotten how things were *in that house*.

She had spent the weekend before that Monday hard at work. One of her authors—his name is Maximilian G., but here we (Erik) shall call him simply Mad Max—phoned her before she had had breakfast and asked in a tremulous voice, Can we meet? I know it's Saturday, but I . . . (I've had a terrible night.)

A nice guy, said Erik, with a head on his shoulders, but out of his mind. Thinking himself to death. We're the same age: we sat next to each other in school for twelve years, and look at me, look at him. Hair gray and thinning, and that scalp, those teeth—the whole body! Bent back, crooked fingers, a cigarette constantly trembling between them. Racked by a coughing fit every fifteen minutes. Carves each page out of his ribs: there's less and less of him. One day a breeze is going to come and sweep him out of the window and he'll drift off through the sky like a leaf.

No problem, said Mercedes in a soft, soothing voice. I'm calling Grandma to see if she can babysit for you (Omar)—no, let me put it differently, if she'd like to keep you company.

Or, said Omar, I can go to the zoo with Abel, the way we'd planned.

I don't know . . .

It's too late anyway. He'll be here any minute.

Just then the doorbell rang.

See?

A minute later they were gone: I somehow hadn't the time to put in a but. And then—what a metamorphosis!—Mad Max had taken Omar's place at the dining table and was staring with feverish eyes in the direction of the manuscript while Mercedes set about, for the third time, reading aloud a long sentence whose meaning at first unfolded, as is only fitting, from dependent clause to dependent clause, groping deeper and deeper, but then, shortly before the end, something got tangled and suddenly you couldn't tell . . .

There are times when I seriously wonder, MM said bitterly, whether any thought can be kept right side up.

His hand lay on the table, and his fingers were trembling so badly that a nearby glass of iced tea was affected: the echo of a distant quake.

It's only a matter of language, I'm sure, said Mercedes softly.

Of course, said MM. It's always a matter of language. Mercedes was shocked to notice that the trembling had spread to the rest of his body, like a current running through him. He stood up, the chair sliding back with a screech.

I need a smoke. Sorry, he said, but instead of standing at the open window, as might have been expected, he sat cowering on the windowsill, leaning against the frame: shoes, socks, trouser legs, the body slouching on its spike of a behind, folded over like a rag doll whose gray cardigan nobody has thought of taking off for years, and even then he seemed to be freezing. White ash wafted from his fingers into the street. If he happened to fall, I'd have no way of stopping him.

I think I understand what you mean, said Mercedes.

You do? He threw her a biting glance. Round eyes, pointy nose. A bit contemptuous too. It was not until that moment that she realized: he was contemptuous. That hurt. A voice like a whiplash with an undertone of ratlike whistle: What do I mean?

In her soft voice Mercedes ventured out along the crumpled sentence, smoothing it into a correct, though every bit as long one of her own, and yes: he tossed the cigarette stub out of the window—she blinked: she had not expected that either—and went back to the table, the smoke pouring out of his mouth and onto the pages.

Shall we say it like that? Mercedes asked.

The child and his companion came back shortly before dark. Introductions: Omar and Max knew each other; the good-looking man was new. Hello, he said, smiling politely, his head slightly cocked. MM stared at him in amazement, no, in deference. The temperature, the texture, the pressure of a hand free of nicotine stains. The minute it took Mercedes to see the newcomers into the next room MM simply stood there, and when Mercedes came back he said, You know, I think I'll do the rest of it on my own.

I respect you, he said in the doorway, his eyes shining out of their sockets, the dandruff out of his hair. I thank you and I apologize. I'll pick up the cigarette stub. If I can find it. If not, I'll pick up another one. Any one.

He smiled, she smiled; then, still smiling, she turned away from the door.

Well, did you have a good time, the two of you?

To make up for the botched weekend Mercedes took Monday off, got a few boring errands out of the way—nobody irons the way the Thai washerwoman irons—and waited for the afternoon lesson. It proceeded as usual: they drank tea. Afterwards she set off for the *jour fixe*, he for home. They were headed in the same direction and walked together.

Usually (always) she was the one to initiate the conversation and keep it going; this time she said nothing, so they walked in silence. When they were about halfway to the café, a couple of tourists came up and asked directions. He translated the question; she answered it; he translated her response; the tourists thanked them. Then they went back to their silent walk. He said good-bye on the corner of the street where the café was located. Their handshake was so discreet as to be non-existent. She started off, but stopped short after two steps, sssss, and stood on one leg. She had done too much walking that day, and there was a stabbing pain in her ankle.

What could he do for her? Call a cab?

There's no point. It's right there.

Well then, he would accompany her.

She was so small and light he could easily have carried her, but he did the conventional thing and gave her his arm. She held on tight.

Well, well! Erik shouted from the head of the table. Whom have we here! (Abel lowered his eyelids in shame; Tatjana raised one eyebrow.) We all remember you of course, and I can't tell you how glad we are to welcome you back into the fold. You haven't forgotten my wife, Maya, I'm sure, and this is Max—ah, I see you two have met—and my old friend Juri—whom you haven't met—and my eternal adversary Tatjana, who, as is to be expected, is in the process of twisting her to my taste overly red lips into an expression of disdain. What are you drinking?

How is the long-awaited *universal project* coming along? asked Erik while the espresso and cognac were being brought.

Thank you, Abel said to the waitress.

Hm? (Erik)

Sorry, said Abel, I didn't . . .

Erik repeated the question. The comparative linguistics project.

Abel took a sip of espresso.

My computer was stolen.

Oh, said Maya. How did it happen?

So what? said Erik. People make backup copies, don't they?

This person did not.

Oh.

Silence.

How is Omar? Maya asked.

Fine, thank you, said Mercedes.

Which was about the only thing she said the whole evening.

Where were we?

I understand you very well, said Tatjana (feigning a lack of interest in her best friend and the man she had brought) to Mad Max. First we wrestle with our own stupidity, then with everyone else's: it's not easy.

Yes, said Erik. We sympathize, but don't commiserate. You get what you deserve. *You tempt fate; you pay the consequences.* You wait and see.

Smack! Down came his paw on Mad Max's bent back. There was a boom behind the rib cage. MM coughed. From the smack or something else. He coughed, he nodded, he laughed a sad laugh in agreement.

Max has just finished a book. (Erik, by way of explanation to Abel)

What I'd like most is to go off somewhere, said MM, up and go, for a year or more. That's how long it took the wounds to heal after my last book. I wish there weren't so many imponderables—cough, cough—money, first of all.

And the fact that you're completely lost outside your daily frame of reference.

I'll go with you if you like, said Tatjana.

MM gave her a frightened look.

Do you want to kill the poor man? whispered Juri in her ear. What's he done to you? She made believe a hair or a flea had got in her ear, dug into it with disgust.

And so on. Erik dicted; Tatjana contradicted. Mad Max chafed between them. Maya took Juri upon herself with a polite conversation about trivialities. Mercedes and Abel sat in silence in the corner between window and entrance, surrounded by the usual café clatter. Mercedes sat there benumbed, her ankle prickling under the table, yet there was a perfume in the air she had never noticed *here* before. It was the scent of the man next to her, not concrete, no, the *aura of his presence*, and suddenly she said without looking at him, Have you ever thought of marrying?

WHAT WAS THE QUESTION?

Erik was in the process of making a point, getting *to the heart of the matter*: he took a running start, caught his breath, which gave rise to a brief pause—and just then somebody burst into laughter at the other end of the table. It was the man named Abel, who had sat there like a clam the whole time and had suddenly come out with a laugh the likes of which no one had seen in him before, a toothy laugh. Everyone at the table turned to look at him. Erik, deprived of the limelight and his train of thought, frowned in a fit of pique. What was so funny?

Nothing! said Abel, waving his empty cognac glass apologetically.

The waitress misconstrued the gesture. Another?

That would make the fourth or fifth, Mercedes realized. Count drinks before not after proposing. He laughed again and shook his head. A misunderstanding! He put the glass back on the table.

His having laughed like that was unfortunate, though what did you expect if you ask that kind of question at a crowded table? I don't know. Since the other end of the table was still quiet, he could say nothing.

. . .

(All sorts of things.

All sorts of what? [That must have been Erik.]

He, affably: It was my answer to Mercedes' question.

And what was the question?

A private affair, she had said quickly, which had put an end to the conversation until the ever-amicable Maya could come up with another topic.)

He waved a Go on from where you left off to the others, don't mind me, leave me alone, let me twist my umpteenth empty glass on the tabletop and enjoy the scrape while pretending to be looking out of the window.

Anyway, to finish my sentence . . . said Erik, and finished his sentence, and started another, but attention flagged, his too, because no matter what he said or did he could not take his eyes off the two of them.

She stared red-cheekedly into the coffee cup before her; *he* pretended to be looking out of the window. But you couldn't look out of the window: there was nothing to see, it was dark, your own reflection at best, but Erik could tell he wasn't looking at that either. And so, blind—he couldn't tell whether anyone noticed—he stretched his hand out, took hers in it, and kissed it. There were four people engaged in conversation at the table . . .

A friend of mine was recently sitting near a window in a café when all at once a man fell past the window: he had jumped from the department-store roof right into the crowd.

Did he hit anybody?

Really now . . .

Not so far as I know.

. . . and did not notice; Erik was the fifth. I mean . . .

Kissed her hand! It was so old-fashioned, unexpected, hackneyed that I was overcome with envy. Not jealousy. Simple, honest envy for an unlikely gesture.

Took her hand and kissed it, then put it back down next to him. Now her hand was on her knee, his on his. The rest of the evening they said not a word to each other. Thank you, yes or thank you, no? What a situation to be in, the thing to do would have been to stalk off, but with her ankle the way it was, well, at least hobble off, but even for that she would have had to talk to *him* again; besides he was in her way, hemming her in and had stopped listening to anything but his own heartbeat.

Later, though, he was courteous enough to give her a clearer explanation. At least I thought so at the time. (Mercedes, with a dismissive wave of the hand.) Erik offered to drive her home, but by then he had called a cab.

I have something to tell you, Mercedes said to Omar the next morning. We're getting married.

Really? said Omar. Not particularly surprised.

If you have no objections, that is.

I have no objections, Omar said with dignity, and spread some butter on his bread.

Mercedes laughed and kissed the hand holding the knife.

Careful, said Omar.

Their appointment was for a Saturday morning at nine twenty. He was late, had to fumble for his identity card, and smelled funny. Irritating as it was, he had withstood the humiliations of the bureaucracy in the previous weeks not so much, as the saying goes, with fortitude as with *elegance*, as if they were an outmoded yet stylish cape rather than a lead apron (no matter what comes of it, said Tatjana, *your* conscience is clear), so he really could be forgiven *that* now. He has everything you need: he's youthful and paternal, he'll look good on your arm in a government office. Yes, we do want to marry, yes.

Afterwards they went to the park, the way people go to the park to have their picture taken, Mercedes treading crunchy paths in shoes not designed for them, the bouquet swinging loosely in her hand. Now and then Tatjana said, Stop! and they stopped: by trees, benches, statues, a bridge, a small lake—according to availability. Tatjana would spend an eternity twirling the dials of her manual reflex camera while they stood as in the old days in stiff poses on the bank of an artificial pond surrounded by little green piles left by the ducks and geese who for reasons of their own had stuck it out there. Fat white birds waddled through the picture. Newlyweds with poultry. A goose deposited a pile right next to Abel's shoe. Omar started giggling. Abel responded in kind. The arm Mercedes was hanging onto quivered accordingly.

Get it over with, will you? How long do we have to wait? I'm getting tired of this!

Her words encouraged the birds to squawk. She stopped suddenly; they followed suit. Finally: click. She let go of his arm and started off, weaving her way carefully between the piles towards the edge of the grass, where Tatjana was standing. She tossed her the bouquet.

Catch!

She threw it with all her strength—she was annoyed—but not strongly enough: it fell into the grass before reaching its goal. Not that Tatjana had made a move: she followed the bouquet's trajectory with interest, but when it landed she went back to dismantling her tripod. Omar picked up the bouquet.

Catch!

He threw it to Abel; Abel caught it and threw it back. The women ahead, the men behind tossing the bouquet back and forth and giggling. Mercedes glanced down at her shoes, now much the worse for wear, and decided they were a lost cause; she also decided against tears and for turning and holding out her arms and crying, My turn! Omar happened to have the bouquet; he laughed and aimed it at her chest: yellow pollen on a black dress. She kept it.

Try again! said Tatjana.

But the bouquet . . . Most of the petals have come off.

Then throw it away.

But in the end she did not throw it away. It was what it was.

In the last picture of the day they are standing in the shadow of the hedges in front of the bird preserve, their black clothes all but invisible against the dark green leaves; only their white faces, collars, hands shine through. Mercedes is holding a tattered bouquet—flowers with heads hanging—and peering over the hedge into the picture, its head tilted as if to show interest, is a peacock.

Before Erik could ask What's wrong? he had to ask It can't be true, can it? What the Bad Witch Tatjana's been saying.

What's she been saying? Mercedes asked amicably.

Have you actually married the guy? Note I'm not asking you why, though I've asked myself; I'm only asking Why wasn't I invited?

Even my parents weren't invited.

How come? Miriam asked her husband.

Because it's only a fictive marriage.

And if it is? She's our only daughter. It would have looked all the more genuine.

The father of the bride shrugged: So what?

I do, pictures—after that it was hard to go their separate ways, so they stayed together, strolled through the park, sat on benches, ate waffles, later hot dogs, and finally, leaning forward slightly: ice cream. Mercedes had to laugh: our wedding feast. The rumpus of rock and roll wafted past from somewhere, compliments of a boombox. The park had filled up over the previous hours: picnickers, sunbathers, dogs, frisbee players. There was a match in progress on the soccer field. Men Abel's age. Look, said Mercedes to Omar: an old woman with a snow-white ballerina bun carrying a birdcage. The bird looked like a sparrow. Two boys Omar's age staging a race between their painted turtles in the grass. A dog walker in a rainbow-colored hat. A squirrel in a tree behind the wedding party. Mercedes offered it the rest of her bouquet; it just stared at her. He'd rather have the turtle, I bet, said Omar. The church bells chimed. Tatjana shoved her sunglasses up to her forehead and looked at the clock; she opened her mouth to say something, but just then the bells started chiming again and she shut her mouth. She waited patiently until it was over, then said, it had been swell but she had to be going.

The remaining threesome walked to Mercedes' building. The groom said good-bye at the door.

See you on Monday.

See you on Monday.
See you on Monday.

Three years, right? That's how long you've got to wait for a passport. It's automatic. So why am I worried?

Pause.

He's terrific with the child, and everything else about him seems okay. He's a quiet, courteous, good-looking young man, and yet . . . I don't know. There's something about him, something . . .

Yes, said Alegria, I understand.

They went their separate ways and met again the next day for the lesson. Since it was the last day in the month, Mercedes gave Abel the usual folded banknotes. He thanked her politely. Then he accepted her invitation to stay for supper.

Omar was working his way through a geography he had never seen: ocean, sea, coast, waves, breakwaters, island, peninsula, promontory, lagoon, mouth, delta, stream, river, rivulet, brook, lake, pond, marsh, plains, grassland, woods, birches, poplars, oaks, firs, undergrowth. He spent a long time on the taiga. Bears. Then he moved on to elevations: hills, mountains, ranges.

The grown-ups said almost nothing.

When Omar had finished, Mercedes asked him whether he would like to visit the country whose language he was learning and see its geography with his own eyes. He could go as a tourist.

Omar thought for a moment and said, It wasn't actually *necessary*.

For the most part things remained as they were. The void of sorts that follows a goal achieved. When the only thing happening for a while is time passing. Lessons two or three times a week, meals, pedagogically valuable leisure time. *Our fixture* also did anything he was told to do, was asked to do as a necessary camouflage. At first he was quite reliable. Though most things you had to take care of yourself. I am my own husband: I use his toothbrushes, his shirts, his deodorant. It's not clear how much of it all he picks up.

Does it matter? Tatjana asked. *You're* calling the shots.

Aren't you the clever one, said Mercedes with a wry expression.

She bought a few black men's shirts (What's your size anyway?) and wore them as pajamas. So there is always something in the hamper.

The perfect criminal, said Alegria. I'm proud of you. It looked as if the peace would hold out for a while this time round.

LIFE IN THE HILLS AND
ON THE HIGH SEAS

His name was Gavrilo, Gábor, or Gabriel. He came out of his mother and into the new century. Well, not quite. It was actually a bit earlier: otherwise he would have been too young for the war. He wrote his fiancée rose-colored postcards from the front about nothing, his only noteworthy experience having apparently been that lying in the heat under some orange trees, terribly thirsty, they were forbidden on pain of death to pick the damned fruit. He returned home, took a wife, tilled the soil, and begat three daughters; there is no record of his having ever uttered a memorable word. But when the next war broke out and he, a father three times over, was called up he made for the hills.

I don't know where he is, said his wife amidst the household paraphernalia strewn about the courtyard. As calm as if her house were searched every day. Haven't seen him for months.

Who gave you that belly then, you whore? asked the officer between blows. He gave her a thorough thrashing and in the end raped her too before—no, not killing her—letting her go. While *he* was up there with his beauty, nature, drinking fresh stream water, she said later.

When they threatened to tear the house down, the village idiot—who was no idiot at all, just a clubfooted alcoholic—proved to be the only man in the village. Without being asked, he reported to the authorities that the child in my grandmother's belly was his.

Now there's cause for celebration, said the officer, and poured an entire bottle of a sixty-percent alcohol concoction down his throat. He should have died, but didn't; he survived and stayed on the farm with my grandmother and her now four daughters. Thus did a gimp save our farm and our lives, for the next few years at least. My grandmother affectionately called her youngest the little whore and forced her to eat her vomit, but that may just have been the way in those days.

As the war started winding down, Gavrilo started coming down the mountain. Several villagers claimed to have sighted him: he was somewhere in the vicinity of the village, but apparently could not make up his mind to return for good. Perhaps he had sprouted a set of antlers, but in any case he simply could not come back after making it through the first winter, which was particularly severe. And following the officer's *investigation* neither his wife nor any other family member had visited him in the woods.

Years passed, and he turned into something like a mountain spirit, an Old Man who would be seen roaming the ridge when the moon was full. He had no papers any longer and therefore no statistical existence. Missing in action. The gimp took his place in the family, and things ran smoothly except for the fact that he was still an alcoholic of course; besides, one good deed in a lifetime is enough for a day's leave from hell. And what more can a gimp ask for.

Gavrilo too seemed satisfied with his lot up there in the hills. He starved and froze and had to steer clear of people and larger beasts, but otherwise he wanted for nothing. It took several years for the report of the new country to reach him, and perhaps the border patrols were giving him trouble or perhaps there was no direct cause, but one day we received a letter from him. It was written in coal on a dirty piece of cardboard. It is impossible to recapitulate the content—the war widow promptly used it to kindle the fire in the fireplace—but the essence of it was that my grandfather Gavrilo had, heaven only knows how, turned anarchist. Down with the police, the military, the parliament, the government, the bureaucracy, the Eucharist, in short—down with the useless and dangerous toy known as the state! Such was the message on the dirty piece of cardboard. Long live nature, freedom, thought, beauty, and joy. Long live the individual, long live man!

After the disappointing summer, the boy's disappearance, and a series of *half-hearted attempts* with younger lovers Kinga came to the conclusion that it was becoming time for her to do something with her life, and she finally put the *accursed story* of her grandfather the anarchist down on paper. The first draft was too short: four pages in all; she reworked it and sent it to a magazine.

Apart from pointing out the spelling mistakes, the fatheads wrote that they unfortunately did not find the story convincing. It didn't *grab* them. What is that supposed to mean?! Was it too subtle for them, or what? The only way a thing will grab that kind is if it grabs them by the *balls! We* on the other hand are affected by everything. The other day I was walking along the street when I was overcome by the smell of trees and food like in front of a factory cafeteria, and I was both euphoric and depressed out of my mind. But that's not *sexy* enough! It's too far from the world of our experience. Oh, you miserable bastards!

After this recent disappointment she took to drinking even more than usual; she would stagger bawling through the streets. Then one afternoon she looked at herself in a puddle. The puddle had formed in a hole in her courtyard. There was a crack in the asphalt at the bottom of the hole; it looked like God's eye. I saw myself in God's eye, an insecure creature, and fell to my knees. There was a horrifying crash and a howl like a she-wolf's. When she had had her howl and calmed down a bit, she pulled herself together, washed her face, combed her hair, and began to act human.

But not long thereafter—two weeks later, three at most—it started up again. Oh, how I miss the mountains! She would stand at the window for hours on end, sobbing; she would paint mountain crests on the windowpane with her greasy fingers. When the sun wandered round to them, they would glisten like silver. Oh, Andre once said: sailing ships. Something like that, she said.

Most of the time, however, she was too restless to stand in one place and paint mountains or sailing ships. I am restless! she would shout and run for hours back and forth along the not particularly broad path between the hills of disorder. From the time the parties *chez Kinga* had dried up, more and more had drifted from the edges to the center. If the get-togethers had gradually *fallen through the cracks*, nobody seemed to miss them. For a while it was fashionable to pretend it was still the eighties and we were the in-crowd in our small town, but what's over is over, as Janda said, and not even Kinga seemed to mourn the passing of her salon. She did not mourn at all; she ran up and down. When something lay in her way, she kicked it aside with her bare coal-black feet and moved on. Meanwhile spring had come. The sun is shining, nature burgeoning; I'm the only one who's still unhappy. Why? How come? she would mutter. Everything's going downhill. Everything's going downhill.

The musicians, when they came, spread out over the room, as in the good old days: Kontra patiently rolling joints, Andre making himself useful with the instruments, Janda reading the paper.

In C. only 0.9 percent of the population claims Orthodoxy as its religion, Janda read.

Andre: Oh?

Kontra was licking a cigarette paper.

Everything's going downhill, Kinga muttered. Everything's going downhill. Everything's going downhill.

They've made the guy who assassinated Che an ambassador.

Andre: Hm.

Ssssst. Kontra lit a match.

Downhill, downhill, downhill.

Duško T. . . .

Andre: The swine . . .

. . . has been found guilty of eleven of the thirty-one charges filed against him.

Everything's going downhill. Everything's going downhill. Everything's going downhill.

Janda: That's enough, Kinga.

Everything's going downhill. Everything's going downhill. Every-thing's going . . .

Kinga, *please* . . .

. . . downhill. Everything . . .

Janda, angrily closing the newspaper: CUT THAT OUT, YOU HEAR?!

DON'T YOU TELL ME WHAT TO DO!

Sh! (That was Andre, of course.)

How long have you been saying that?

I don't know . . . Days, weeks, months? I can't stand it anymore! I can't help it! I'm sick!

Then go to a doctor.

Go to a doctor go to a doctor, she mutters, still pacing. Go to a doctor. Where do you think we are, anyway? WE SEEM TO HAVE MISSED SOMETHING, *COMRADE!* Go to a doctor. If I were one of those . . . one of *them*, I could see a doctor, get a prescription for two cheekfuls of brain pills, and go into therapy. But I'm me, and for me there is no therapy! You've got to stay what you are or are becoming: a mental case dangerous to society. She stopped and gave the men a meaningful look: There are women capable of mur-der just before they get their period.

Try it, why don't you, said Janda. You'll see where it gets you.

My grandmother—not the one who was raped, the other one—hanged herself when she was forty-eight.

Well, it's less painful than slitting your veins.

Asshole!

Stop it, will you!

Here, said Kontra, holding a joint out to Kinga.

She smoked it for a while, quietly, defiantly; later she had some drinks and started screaming again: I can't sleep! I can't sleep! I can't get drunk anymore! I can't get drunk anymore! Though she was pretty far gone by then of course, reeling through the chaos, stubbing her toe on a heavy book lying on the floor, howling like a she-wolf: Ow! Ow! Ow! Ow!

Janda rose with a sigh and tried to block her; she kept walking in place, pumping her black feet.

Janda, softly: It's not true there's nothing to get mad about. (Out loud.) But all you can think of is: me, me, me!

She stopped moving her feet and pounded him on the shoulder with her fists: you, you, you! Is that better? No, it's not better. It hurts!

Good. You deserve to suffer, you dog. Dog, dog, dog!

He whacked her with the newspaper, grabbed her by the hair, and pulled her up. Could he pull hard enough to stop her feet from trampling the ground?

Stop it! (Andre)

Kinga, roaring: Aaaaaaaaaaaaaaaaa!

Stop it, I say!!!

Andre and Kontra separate them; Kontra takes Janda away—just to be sure—and Andre stays with Kinga. Somebody has to stay with her. She flinches at every touch. If he does not touch her, she touches herself and shudders. Uuuuh. Oh, Daniil, she sighs.

Who's Daniil?

My lover.

You have a lover named Daniil?

In my . . . in my dreams, know what I mean? In my dreams I have a lover named Daniil.

I see, said Andre.

Have you got a secret love? What's her name?

Ilona.

She's going off the deep end, said Andre to the other two.

Pure hysteria, mumbled Janda. But he knew it wasn't true. No one, not even Kinga, can have permanent PMS. The truth is: she's going off the deep end. She can't stand children anymore. She can't stand people in general. Or shopping. Cleaning. Not at home for sure. The men have to do everything for her. She does not wash her body for days. She stinks. It gets so bad I have to stick her in the basin and scrub her down. Or I let her wallow in her own filth for a week or two, till all the food is gone, and see what she does, whether she finally does go out shopping or rolls over and dies. We have to see to it that she shows up for the only job she still has. Then at night she runs up to her tiny reflection at the end of a long hallway and talks to herself. Madness.

Much as it pained him, Janda could not help thinking of Abel. Since he had moved out, months ago, he had made only one or two appearances and then only to see her *outside*. He avoided the musicians. Not that we missed him. He did give her money and a telephone number, though she never called him. She appeared to have given up (on him too). Who would have thought it.

Now Andre called him.

Hello, said Abel, as if they had spoken the day before.

It's about Kinga, said Andre. Her birthday is coming up.

I know, said Abel. Her fortieth. Of course he was planning to come.

When he stuck his head through the skylight, she was standing on the chimney, a figurehead and siren, roaring into the night: Tootooooot! Tootoooooot! From today on it was no longer Kingania; it was . . . the *Titanic*! She could not come up with another ship on the spur of the moment. So that's what it is. The name of this ship is: the *Titanic*. The roof is the upper deck, the living room the lower deck! And the city's dark waters swirling around! The locks to our stern close at eight! All hands on deck! Till daybreak!

Her jeans were freshly washed; she was wearing a red blouse; her face was made up, her hair combed; there was an artificial camellia behind her ear. The camellia had a sad droop to it, but she herself was laughing. Her lips glittered fire-red; her upper lip was shaven with the same razor she used for her underarms, and what difference did a few nicks make: she was standing legs spread wide over the chimney, waving her arms and laughing uproariously.

Do you realize she's locked the door? asked Kontra.

You don't want to disembark on the high seas, do you? Hello there, my pet, she said to Abel. You here too? Floating past: Got to take care of my guests.

Later it turned out that she had hidden all the plates and silver. She held the only utensil, a painted wooden spoon, in her hand and made the rounds with a pot and the spoon, spooning Janda's red and hot concoction into mouths. She also had a bottle of schnapps in a case strapped to her back, so she could administer it immediately afterwards. Tsssh! *To put out the fire!* The guests had to drink straight from the bottle, because all the glasses had disappeared as well. Or is that a problem for you overcivilized fuddy-duddies?

Abel sat with his back against the fire wall; she was holding out the spoon to him. He shook his head; she chortled and moved it closer to his lips. He shook his head; she burst out laughing as if she had been tickled, and smeared the chili over his lips with the spoon. It ran down his chin, fell into his collar, and crept down to his stomach, tracing a red stain on his shirt. Kinga laughed. She took the bottle and poured schnapps into his face, washed it off—like old times, remember? the bump—and ran off, still laughing.

Later she insisted that the music spread to the upper deck. All hands on deck! Band included!

No, said Janda, but in the end the band did move upstairs to the foot of the chimney and played as softly as they could. She danced with a burning candle on her head. The flame flickered, the wax ran into her hair, she cheered, she smelled of burning. Later she made believe she would use the roof as a running board. Yoohooooo! The candle went out and fell off her head; the musicians—first Janda, then the other two—stopped playing in the middle of the song.

Play on! she cried. Don't you see the iceberg?

Janda disappeared down the hatch; the other two and most of the guests followed suit. Abel stayed where he was. Scared I'll jump? She laughed. Dance with me!

They began to play again downstairs, or at least Andre and Kontra, as far as Abel could hear: they had to do something while Janda looked for the key to the iron door. The boy had never danced in his life; he was not about to start. He did not stand. She gave him a few tugs but gave up in the end and dropped down next to him. Ouch! She had landed on the candle. She laughed.

At the lowest point in the evening Kinga and Abel were sitting alone against the fire wall, surrounded by the silhouettes of the city. Trees in some of the courtyards. Shadowy iron installations. Cranes in the distance against the background of the slowly oranging sky. A herd of giraffes in the savannah. She turned to him, sat astride his lap, and started wriggling as if trying to find the most comfortable position. It was an earnest, concentrated wriggle. The warmth of her body wandered slowly through the hard jeans. She pressed her knee into his side, embraced his head with both arms, pressed his face to her breast. Cradled herself and him. Little bastard. Lifted his face from her breast, took his head in hands smelling of chili, smoke, dirt, burnt coffee, burnt hair, wax, and alcohol. His ears between her fingers. Since he still did not open his lips, she gave him a bite; he grunted—a reaction at last. She took advantage of the opportunity to stick her tongue into his mouth. Her mouth tasted of what her hands smelled of; his tasted of nothing. A trickle of blood. She sucked it away. He looked up over her hair to the sky. It was almost dark.

Answer me one question, Antonius, said the voice next to his ear. Which do you prefer: oysters or snails?

He looked at me blankly.

She bumped him with her pelvis. Eh? Her face was one big eye. Hm?

She moved back a little, smiled. He smiled too and said softly, It has nothing to do with you.

When a laugh near tears falls from a face.

Asshole, she said, getting up off him, and disappeared down the hatch. He stayed.

Later the others came back and watched the sunset, shivering. Kinga was not with them. He went downstairs.

She was standing in the kitchen, looking perfectly sober, making coffee. He pulled up a chair. They did not speak.

Where's the key? asked Janda. Some people wanted to leave, and the main entrance would be locked by then.

She made believe she had not heard; she went on making the coffee, humming.

Kinga! said Janda sternly. Where is the key?

What key, dear?

Janda had neither the time nor the desire for a discussion: he knew from experience that a discussion would get him nowhere; he went up and stuck his hand in her jeans pocket.

It was like catching a piglet for the slaughter. She screeched, thrashed about, and rolled on the kitchen floor while the party guests formed a semicircle around her. Shit, said Kontra. Andre just stood there stone-faced. Not until Kinga's blouse ripped did anyone intervene. Seconds later the kitchen was in an uproar: somebody plowed into Abel's chair and a loose leg came off with a crash, but even before the wreck had reached the floor he was moving off from the fray. Kontra was busy shaking a soda bottle; Andre was the only one who saw Abel making his way to the door. At the very moment the fizzy water exploded over the scufflers, the boy opened the door and left.

That was the day before he received the marriage proposal. They did not see each other again for a long time.

KITE FLYING

The wedding took place at the beginning of spring. Some time in May, as soon as the weather permitted, the small family took a trip to the seaside.

It was a day of sunburn and sneezes: the sun shone brightly, but the wind was still nippy; you sweated and froze simultaneously. Mercedes' bare feet were cold in the sand, but grit your teeth: your honor and status were at stake, your fatherland and family album. The kite was fluttering in the wind. Omar held the string; Abel stood behind him and made believe he was ready to help, but his hands never touched those of the child. In the picture the left hands are cut off; the faces show intensity and joy. Mercedes spoiled far more than half the pictures by acting the ardent photographer to get her subjects to laugh, which they did, but only because something Abel was wearing kept tickling Omar's ear. You're tickling! Whirling grains of sand raining onto the child's goggles. A fine day. And suddenly:

Well, well, is it really you? *Kurva*, Abelard, what brings you here?

She kicked sand onto his calves, jumped onto his back, wrapped her legs around him, punched him in the sides. The kite went into a turbulent, clattering spin. Not in the family album: picture of a stranger, a woman, wrestling her husband to the ground.

What brings you here, you motherfucker?

A glance at the child, who was trying to bring the kite back under control. The woman with the camera paid her no heed. Abel had sand in his mouth.

We're flying a kite, the child informed the stranger. Or, rather, we *have been*.

He had pushed his goggles onto his forehead: one eye is made of glass, but that is not noticeable at first glance.

Kinga looked at him as if he were a thing.

Hello, said Omar. My name is Omar.

Hi, said Mercedes, who had come up to them by then.

Off to the side, near the water, a young man—he belonged to Kinga—was stretching his neck in their direction, but then he took to stamping out the foam as it swirled around his feet, and stayed where he was. For a while they all just stood there. Then Mercedes said, Can we help? (Who are you?)

Kinga to Abel: Who is that?

Mercedes, amicably: My name is Mercedes. Pleased to meet you.

She held out a small, brown hand. Kinga stared at it. A wedding ring. She took Abel's hand: the same. Thin, yellow-gold. Mercedes drew her hand back to shade her eyes.

Kinga: Is that why you don't come anymore?

At the word *that* she may have tilted her head slightly: because of them. Her mouth stank of tobacco and bad teeth. She had a hairy wart on her chin. She was looking more and more like a witch: she had the angry look, the hiss, the tendency to leave without taking leave. Her companion looked back once or twice as they walked off. Perhaps that was why she had given his arm a tug.

Who was that?

An old friend.

What makes her so angry?

A few days later they met at a café. She was wearing earrings and had combed her hair. He looked better than he ever had. *Marriage agrees with him.*

How long?

Two months.

How come you've kept it a secret.

I haven't kept it a secret.

Pause.

Hm, she said. So we've done it. You love each other, I presume. She's so cultivated-looking—no barbarian she. And very much the little woman. *Little woman*—it's just made for her. So polite, so polished, so educated. Open, considerate, tolerant. With parents to match, I bet. The apple does not fall far from the tree. She hasn't got a clue, has she. Does she fuck well at least?

No.

No?

It's not a real marriage. It's for the papers.

Moron. You fly kites with her kid.

His name is Omar.

Pause.

Is it for money?

???

I've done the arithmetic. I owe you nearly six thousand.

He waved it away. That doesn't matter.

What does matter, then? What kind of guy are you? Eh? Nothing matters. I don't think you're good; I think nothing means anything to you. Money, people. Why do you keep disappearing? What are you? A fata morgana? No, you're no fata morgana, my boy; you're a person. And other people worry about you. You can't do that kind of thing! Without warning. Is it Janda?

(???) No.

What's he done? What's he said to you? You know he's an idiot. Or don't you? A nice guy, but an idiot. You can forget whatever it is he's said. He's got nothing to say. Don't listen to what he says. I'll give him a punch in the kisser.

It has nothing to do with Janda.

Then what does it have to do with? What's your problem? Tell me.

Abel shook his head.

What's the matter? What is it?

No response.

Maybe somebody should give *you* a punch in the kisser. The guys have been talking about it for ages. I say, He hasn't done anything. They say, We know he hasn't done anything, but there's something about him.

He smiled.

Would you like that? You would. A good thrashing, eh? That's just what you're after. What have you done anyway?

Abel stopped smiling. Pause.

I make you uncomfortable.

No.

We don't make you uncomfortable?

No.

A bunch of drunken, down-and-out nobodies?

He shakes his head.

Then tell me: what am I to you?

You're mine. My beloved. My godmother.

She gave a coarse laugh. Her face was the color of the bones just beneath her skin, more visible now than ever. Her nostrils flared when she laughed. There was a hair protruding from the left one. She grew serious again:

You charming asshole. Always learning. Though you were polite to begin with. So polite it made people want to smack you. Did you get knocked around a lot when you were young? Well, now you know why.

(What do you think you're doing, climbing through a window into the house of strangers? Decent people use the door! What a way to behave—knocking on the window and then. What have you got to hide? What kind of secrets can two seventeen-year-olds have? What do you do, the two of you, when you're alone in this room that can barely hold a table and a bed, where there's only one shelf for books near the ceiling and only one chair. Why don't you answer me? After all the sacrifices I've made for you. Why don't you speak? For years I've had the feeling nobody has said an intelligent word to me. Is it any wonder I'm growing old and feeble-minded? Don't shrug! Don't you dare shrug! Who do you think you are? . . . Forgive me. I didn't mean to hit you. I'm just so wretched.)

Kinga: I could have married too. An elderly man wanted to marry me. But I can't. I'm not the marrying kind. Know what I mean? I can't. I never thought I'd sink so low in ten years. It's *this place* that does it to you. I'm so low I don't even have the strength to give up. I don't need your money. I pass it on. To this one or that. You can't stand one another. I know. I tell them you can't do anything about it, you have no heart, you can't do anything about it.

He looked for change, put it on the table.

Sorry. I always do it. I'm always attacking you. Of course you have a heart. Now you can't even look at me. Don't take it seriously. You know I'm crazy, don't you? Maybe you don't. Go, go. I'll be able to cry better.

What do you know! So he's no impotent homo after all?

What in the world are you talking about?

You're right, said Tatjana. It would be premature to draw conclusions. Though I do like the idea that she *could have been something like his wife*. It opens the door for a love triangle.

Go ahead, then, said Mercedes. Turn it into a story. Or: so what? What does it boil down to anyway? Encounter with a loutish stranger, unexpected and irritating. These things happen. People meet people.

How come you brought it up then? (Tatjana)

I wish I never had.

The weather was magnificent: downright hot between the gusts. He had rolled his shirtsleeves up past the elbow, to just the spot where a vaccination scar showed, and Mercedes thought, Now I've seen something of him. The longest stretch of skin so far, in fact: almost an entire arm. Next time we'll go swimming. Or I'll invite him home and ask him to take his clothes off. I can always say, What if I'm asked about your body? Where your moles are. And swimming probably won't work: Omar has a thing about water; he just looks at the sea. It may have to do with his eye socket, though he's been told water won't do it any harm.

I know, he said, that's not the reason. To Abel: Do you know how to swim?

Yes.

I don't. And I'll never learn.

You know, said Mercedes as they were driving home—she at the wheel, Abel sitting next to her, watching the sea disappear slowly behind the landscape—you know, today is the first time I've ever met a friend of yours.

The reason was, he said, still looking out of the window, that he had no friends. Only her. Her name is Kinga. We hadn't seen each other for a while.

I don't have any friends either, said Omar from the back seat.

I'm your friend, said Mercedes.

After that they were silent.

Swimming didn't work; the weather had other ideas: winter made a comeback, ruffling the crowns of the trees along the nice street, whistling through the freight trains at the station. Swimming was simply not in the cards. Besides, said Abel, he was busy next weekend unfortunately.

It would not have been amiss for the child to ask with childlike curiosity, What are you going to do? But Omar did not ask, and so we (Mercedes) did not find out. Why does that get to me now?

All of a sudden something appears. A *moment*. A rich aunt by the name of Providence has made me a gift of a gigantic husband-jigsaw. Piece by piece I work my way in from the edges, honing my powers of observation and endurance; trial and tribulation it may be, but I can't stop now, not yet, even though the result is predictable and, let's face it, pretty disappointing: a two-dimensional picture riddled with cracks. Or—to vary the metaphor—it's as if you were going somewhere in a dream and the *something* you were after was always around the next corner. That's how I feel, Mercedes thought. No matter what I discover, a part of the story remains concealed around the corner. A crazy game. Or rotten. I can't quite tell yet.

While we're on the subject, said Erik, I have a new item for you. Actually, no: the Eriks of this world do things differently.

Listen to this, he said, keeping his voice down and shutting the door behind him, though they were the only ones in the room. I've got something new for you.

He took a deep breath, then exhaled noisily: You remember, don't you, there was that fishy story about a certain *work* with no backup on a stolen laptop. Well, I didn't want to go on about it at the time, but *in a situation like that* (???) you can't help wondering: How could it have happened? What is it? Hard luck, incompetence, fatalism, lies? What does experience tell us? Experience tells us that most texts which are not backed up never existed in the first place and disappear through outside intervention. Did anyone ever read a single line of the *work*? Was the laptop really stolen? Did he even own a laptop? Where did he buy it? How much did it cost? Does he actually know all those languages? Who can test him? (Mercedes opened her mouth.) Let me finish! Okay, let's say it's just my jealousy speaking. True, I can't prove he didn't write a dissertation on whatever topic it was. But he never got a degree, did he?

???

Triumphant: University Library, Dissertation Catalogue, Foreign Languages—nothing.

Pause.

That doesn't mean a thing, said Mercedes. What are you shadowing him for?

I'm not shadowing him; I'm interested in his work. I'm sorry. I just thought it my duty as a friend to . . .

I thank you from the bottom of my heart, said Mercedes.

At that very moment a team of seven experts—linguists, neurologists, and a radiologist—equipped with the latest and most powerful technology was charting the brain of Mercedes' husband. There are many approaches: CAT scan, MRI, contrast-medium procedure, etc. What they all have in common is that the subject lies in a coffin-like tube, with his head immobile. There was nothing physically appealing about them; nor did he find them particularly interesting, he said when they finally located him. (Heavens, we looked all over for you! Were you out of town?)

There's someone I'd like you to meet, said the team leader, taking Abel by the arm. His grip was paternal, strong, and he did not let go until they were standing before a wizened, furious-looking graybeard.

Mr. N., I'd like you to meet Mr. L. Mr. L., this is Mr. N.

Pleased to meet you.

Eezmeetyu. Or *Peezmee.*

Mr. L. is from Switzerland, a former L5 speaker. Four of his languages overlap with yours.

B-b-b-b, said Mr. L., his eyes bulging with effort. B-b-b-b. *B-b-b-bazmeg,* fuck you, *mein Sohn.* He nodded and rolled his eyes at me. Understand? *Bazzmmm . . .*

See what I mean now? We can do a lot of good here, and there's some money in it too.

Abel had a test on the weekend after the beach trip. The next day he gave Omar a colored printout. It is the rainbow in my brain. Some parts are highlighted, others not. Each of the highlighted fields has its own color. From L1 to L10, L standing for *lingua.* Omar spread his fingers and, placing the fingertips along the back of the glossy piece of paper as if it were a tray you had to balance precious glasses on in the midst of a battle, carried it into his room, and pinned it over his bed.

My grandson falls asleep under the gaze of his stepfather's brain, says Miriam. I can't explain why, but there's something eerie about it.

Eerie? Really? Alegria asked.

Mercedes studied the reproduction with mock solemnity. Hm, she said, hm, and kept looking at Abel, as if comparing the internal and external versions. Everybody laughed.

At least the issue of whether or not he knows the languages had been put to rest.

I thank you from the bottom of my heart, said Mercedes to Erik and the others who expressed their concern (which *most* of them felt called upon to do). Thank you, said Mercedes. And now let me be. I am a single mother, and he is my fictive husband. I have no time and no cause to observe him.

But to be honest, she never stopped waiting for something to *turn out*. People who for years pass themselves off as doctors, priests, postmen. It was not the kite story or Erik's questions that set her thinking; it was *that laugh*. Since then everything had been a sign: a late arrival, a sigh, a pause before a normal, bluebeard response. His oddities, his lack of presence. Hints of obscure origin had been turning up lately. He says he can't make it next weekend, then comes on Monday, completely transformed. Appearance and scent. A distillery. Perfume or alcohol. What's strange is he doesn't seem to smell of it himself; no, his clothes, his hair, and to a lesser extent his skin seem to have taken on the smell: he seems to be wearing it like a coat. It was the smell he had had two years before, when she wore a tight black dress with a white collar and carried a bouquet of white daisies in her hand. A smell of illegality and sex.

Omar, who wanted to spend virtually the whole weekend in the park *observing people* (= waiting for him to happen by), had a cold and was therefore unfit to give his views on the smell, and he didn't see anything unusual in the downtrodden expression or murky red eyes. They were drinking tea.

Ogurtsy i vodku! Omar cried out, but Mercedes did not understand and the request went unanswered.

On Tuesday or Wednesday she suddenly stopped what she was doing and made a call to her husband's former department, the one where she had done her studies too.

Of course, dear, said the friendly secretary, the middle-aged *Ellie*, of course I remember. Could she call back in an hour.

I did a little research, dear, said Ellie. I looked and looked, dear, and couldn't get over it. I remember him perfectly well—a handsome young man—and then I realized what the problem was. The *auditors* are in a separate file.

I see, said Mercedes.

A separate file, dear, said Ellie. And how are you?

To sum things up, Mercedes thought on Thursday, while she pretended to be working. One: Erik was right. Auditors don't get degrees. Two: She could have had the information before they got married. A single telephone call. And let's, three, admit it: She'd thought of it. It was only reasonable to make inquiries. Why hadn't she done so then and why had she now and what were the consequences? None: it didn't matter that my husband never officially enrolled as a student, and it didn't matter that he concealed it, just as it basically didn't matter whether she knew his old friends or not. She didn't care a rap about any of that, to be honest. Then what did she care about? What did matter?

That afternoon the French lesson took place as usual. Looking at him now that she knew somewhat more about him, what did she see? A man who appeared untouched by all the strains and apparent excesses of the last four years, as if since the day she first *took cognizance* of him on the threshold to Tibor's sarong they had left not a trace. A smooth, white face, sober, innocent, clear, aged twenty-four. Wouldn't hurt a fly, wouldn't upset the apple cart, butter wouldn't melt in his mouth. That face was even more irritating than the new one. She had originally intended to ask him if he wanted to stay; now she let him go.

No sooner was he out of the door than the phone rang.

Yes, she said. No. He's just left the house. Five minutes ago. Of course. No, sorry. He'll be out of town over the weekend. Monday afternoon would be fine. Yes, I'll be here. Fine. Thank you. Of course. No problem.

She hung up. Pale.

What is it? asked Omar.

We probably won't be having a lesson on Monday, she said.

What is it?

We're having company.

Who?

She looked at the clock, thought a while, then dialed.

Call me back as soon as possible, she said to his answering machine. It's important.

She hung up. Omar waited for her to answer.

Immigration, said Mercedes. They're checking up to see if we're a real family.

Oh, said Omar. I see.

. . .

Over the next hour she looked at the clock ten or twelve times. It took no more than fifteen minutes by foot, at his speed at least. Assuming he'd gone straight home. But could she assume that? What could she assume? Maybe he'd do some shopping on the way? And buy? A loaf of bread, a string of sausages, a container of milk, a bottle of whiskey appeared before her mind's eye. Good, another ten-second delay. At midnight she phoned again. Answering machine.

Was it going too far to stay up all night? Not all that much time had gone by; it wasn't yet *urgent*, but I thought I recognized a certain feeling coming back. She was reminded of the time—almost eleven years ago it was now—she'd climbed over a wall and through a window to get into a bed that smelled of pot and sweat, *his* sweat, and of someone else, a third person, an additional pain, but that scarcely mattered now. Omar slept soundly.

Abel did not call back on either Friday or Saturday. I might have known. No, don't come on Sunday; come on Monday. He's never missed a lesson. Except when he disappeared for months without a word. She kept leaving messages. Come home at once. *We're having company!* Maybe she should phone the usual places: hospitals, the police. Or do nothing. Cook up some story when they come. And each time they come. The husband who never was. The plot for a romantic comedy: *The Fictive Marriage.*

Though maybe she should drop in on him. Go to the cul-de-sac near the tracks. Ring the bell. Omar looked at her with interest: walls, sky, new vistas, fine cloud-giblets. Like a tree in bloom. Or mold. It smelled a bit like mold. Besides the other unhealthy smells. So that's how it smells where my husband lives. Then there were the giddy noises from the near and far environs, amplified or deadened by the cul-de-sac: bars, trains, streets, the wind. Otherwise: nothing. The intercom—does it seem to work?—was dead.

Mercedes pressed the button next to the name FLOER—(supposedly) the tenant who had lived there before him, he had told her that at least—then pressed it three times in the rhythm of Mer-CE-des, as if they had agreed beforehand on a family code. The thought of a family code and then the thought that he had a key to her apartment but she had no key to his made her furious for the first time. At *all this*. How can you treat a person like that! How can you . . . What?

The neighbor, Omar repeated. Try the neighbor.

The only other name of a person on the board: the lower floors were apparently all businesses. *Fictive* businesses. The neighbor's name was Rose. Rose and Floer. Is that normal? She looked around, gave everything another look: normal? Yes? No? Pinch me.

Somebody was coming. Two figures were tottering in her direction from the end of the cul-de-sac: a man and a woman in skimpy, shiny futuristic garb and loud makeup, feeling their way through the bright Sunday morning. Literally: their arms stretched out before them, they staggered over to the parked cars. They did not notice the woman and boy at all. Giggling, they stumbled up to one of the cars, fell in, and drove off, leaving a familiar smell behind. Mercedes looked in the direction they had come from. She had just about made up her mind.

To go there, knock on the iron door, stand face to face with Thanos, go in. It was pretty much empty at this time, they would be sweeping up, just a few scattered customers who for reasons of their own had decided to spend the whole weekend there, until Monday, when it was closed.

But she did not; did not even press the neighbor's button. You can look over at Abel's balcony from his balcony and inside through the glass door. In case he has been lying there for days.

Let's go, said Mercedes to Omar. He'll call.

THE VISIT

For some it is determined by the season, for others by the situation, and for many no one knows. Sometimes they simply can't go home. Then they stay for days, our guests, as if I (Thanos) hadn't rented some of them their apartments. The Loony Bin is rarely closed between Friday at one and Monday morning at nine. They sleep, drink, work, have sex in shifts. Like the owner and his staff they shut their eyes when and where they can, for an hour, thirty minutes, in the store room, the office. Grace ends on Monday morning at nine, when the last of them are put out onto the street, blinking in the always dazzling light. Thanos is too tired to go home: he collapses onto the moist red plush in one of the private rooms and snores. The iron door to the courtyard remains open. Thanos sleeps so soundly that anyone with the nerve to slip back in could serve himself at the bar. Make off with the valuables. But nobody comes or drinks or makes off with anything. Thanos wakes up in the early afternoon, showers, dresses like a human being—that is, puts on a gray, custom-tailored suit (he is overweight)—and goes to visit his mother in a nearby nursing home.

. . .

Hello, says Greta A.—thin, infirm, sitting up in a hospital bed under a tree at one side of the park—to her illegitimate son Thanos.

What's the matter? How come you're out in the street?

Somebody rolled me down here.

How come?

At ten to eleven. Some of us are still in nighties, as you can see.

Yes, but how come?

They found a suspicious-looking package in the common room. Somebody must have left it there yesterday when M. and E. were celebrating their engagement. We even had some reporters. Finding the love of your life at eighty-one! So there's hope for us all—for you and, heaven knows, maybe even for me.

A bomb scare?

The photographer must have forgotten something, or it's a press packet or a sweater. Sunday's always a busy day. But people get so crazy about these things nowadays, and here we are.

You senile imbeciles! (an old man in the window of the old-people's home bellows down to the street).

All but Uljanow. He—and I quote him—couldn't give a shit. There are pigeons up there sitting on their nests.

What?

In the tree up there. Or other birds. The hullabaloo is making them nervous. The droppings are fast and furious.

Want me to move you?

No, I don't care.

Pause. A rustling in the trees. Activity not far off: a few rubbernecks, park regulars, homeless people have come up to the roped-off area to see what is going on. Greta gives a loud yawn and puts a frail, liver-spotted hand over her mouth. A woman on the other side of the rope stares at her. Greta stares back. You're next, love. On the other side of the roped-off area a man in black is arguing with a policeman.

You can't walk through here, says the policeman. The street is cordoned off. A bomb alert. It's for your own safety.

But I live here. I live right there, in that street, with my wife;

I have to walk through here; I don't know any other way to get there; I may get lost if I have to walk around the block; not only that, I'll be late; I'm late as it is . . .

Abel Nema had awoken at about the same time as his landlord, listened to all nine messages on the answering machine, and called back.

Sorry, he said. I'll be right there.

A half hour before the appointed time Mercedes was in no condition to respond.

Sorry, said the policeman, turning away. I've said all I have to say.

Abel just stood there for a while, looked around, then turned back to the policeman.

Politely: I'm sorry, but you see that fat man standing next to the woman in the bed under the tree on the other side of the roped-off area? That's my father and grandmother. I've really got to . . .

So now it's your grandmother, is it?

The policeman looked in the direction Abel was pointing.

That's your father?

Who are you waving to? asked Greta.

A friend, said Thanos. Over there.

I don't see why you can't get there by going around the block.

That's the first time I've ever seen a *friend* of yours, said Greta, waving too.

Sorry, you'll just have to.

He's good-looking. You'll have to introduce him to me.

He's just a client, Mother. A renter.

I'm going to die soon, said Greta.

The birds chirped.

What's he doing? Trying to break through the cordon.

I don't believe this. Are you deaf? Out of it? What's so hard about walking around the block? Look, show me your papers. Don't look at me like that. You know what I mean. You know very well what I . . .

What was a body to do? Run away, *again*? Abel weighed the possibility. He was out of shape and the cop was no pushover; he might even be the same one as last time. They did look somehow familiar to each other.

Well? I'm waiting.

The only other possibility was a deus ex machina, and suddenly there it was in the form of another policeman emerging from the old-people's home, waving his arms: False alarm! False alarm!

Abel, his hand still in his inside pocket, took a step to the side—Sorry—and took to his heels.

Hey, where are you going so fast!

But he was gone. And couldn't have cared less about his *father* and *grandmother*, of course. The duped policeman watched him go, furious. The spectators applauded the escape artist. Uljanow spat out of the window but did not hit anyone.

Finally! Mercedes flung open the door. Why didn't you use your key?

But she did not repeat the question, because it was not the man we were all waiting for; it was two strangers, a man and a woman.

May we come in?

My husband . . . It looks like my husband is going to be late, unfortunately. He had some business to attend to, work to do, tests to take, and the traffic . . .

Tests?

Yes, it's . . . it's . . . (Why are you so inarticulate? Why are you turning red?)

Psycholinguistic tests to determine the effect of multilingualism on the brain, said somebody in the background. A swarthy boy with an eye patch. I've got a picture of it in my room. Want to see it?

A glance at their notes: Omar, right?

Right. Shall I bring you the picture or will you come with me?

A car (a taxi?) ran into my husband on his way home from work, from a test. Run over. Stopped by the police. Got lost. Changed his mind. He . . .

. . . is fiddling with the key in the door. The door flies open.

She did not ask him anything, not even in a whisper—the other three were still in the child's room—she just stared.

I know, I know, he said in a loud and cheerful voice. Late again. Sorry, darling.

. . .

I was speechless. That *darling* followed him into the living room, which he entered self-confidently, calling out, Omar! I'm home! in the same nonchalant tone. He apologized again, this time to the officials: the street had been cordoned off because of a bomb scare and he'd had to take a detour. Looking straight at them—the woman, in particular—with his incredibly blue eyes.

And so it went. He was perfect, as was Omar. They gave an impeccable performance: sitting together on the couch, behaving naturally, giving each other clues, yet making sure Mercedes was not left out, which was not easy, because she was so stiff and quiet.

This is where we go to fly kites, where it is exactly I can't remember: my wife does the driving, I don't have a license; for better or for worse, my head is full of other things; we each do what we're better at: theory for him, practice for her. Here we are at the zoo, here at the museum; these are our wedding pictures; no, that's not my father-in-law, it's my wife's deceased husband—correction, partner; no, he's not Omar's father; he's just standing in the shade; a chestnut tree, I think; I don't remember where; a fine man, I knew him well; he was my professor; comparative linguistics; of cancer, completely unexpected; the bathroom is the second door on your right, and while you're at it you can match the scent of the aftershave I have on with the aftershave in the medicine cabinet; and if I don't know where the sugar cubes are, you can't use it against me: show me the man who . . . ; we don't use sugar cubes; our lives are sweet enough without them, my wife always says.

Polite as always, friendly, at times even charming; never distant, bordering on the elegant—and that is where things start to falter. There seems to be something *not quite right* about him. He's plausible to the point of implausibility. Though why does he dress so poorly: the rubber soles, the bell bottoms—they date back to the eighties. The jacket looks like he paid for it out of his first clothing allowance at one of those thrift shops we all patronized at the time, like the salesgirl took one look at him and took twenty-five percent off the rock-bottom price. Then she dreamed of dancing the night away with him, dreamed of it for years. But here, now, it didn't tally with *the rest*: the wife, the child were on a completely different *level*.

Mercedes, who could read the woman's thoughts as if they appeared on a monitor above her head, put herself in gear. She set him up as a genius and herself as his inspiration, and he, either because he caught on or by chance, flashed her a gracious, you-flatter-me smile. Now that, the woman had to admit, was on the mark. What was going on in her male colleague was hard to fathom. To be honest, he seemed rather dull. Whereas you could tell she was being torn this way and that: would she too fall under his spell or would she warn the young woman against him?

How long have you known each other?

She: Seven years.

He: Actually (pause: he waits until he has everyone's attention to make his point) we first *saw* each other more than ten years ago. On the day I arrived in the country.

True, but only for a very short time.

Long enough for him to have recognized her immediately years later.

She smiled.

Who chose the aftershave: you or you?

He, smiling: I buy my own toiletries.

Not surprisingly, therefore, he leaves the cosmetics to her. Though he's up on her childhood, father, mother, friends, and work.

What size dress does your wife wear?

With a warm smile: 32/34. That is Omar's size as well.

Do you get on well with your stepfather?

The child, serious, dignified: We're kindred spirits.

This seems to have produced a shudder in *her*. Turning directly to her: How would you characterize your relationship?

He (jumping in before she can answer): From the very first . . . (Another pause: everyone looks at him; he starts again.) It was love at first sight.

I was furious, I could have burst. The tension of the last few days, for one thing. And then he says *that*. They were standing in the entrance hall, a little family, the boy between them, waving good-bye to the officials as if they were on a train waving good-bye to their grandparents, the man with an arm around the woman's shoulders and a hand on the child's, and no sooner did the door close than he removed both hands and *turned out the lights* to save energy. Oh, the melancholy silence. How well she knew it. If we had a real relationship, if there were the slightest spark of intimacy between us, there would be a real scene right now. What was that supposed to be, eh? What kind of playacting? But she, Mercedes, was so beside herself she couldn't get a word out.

I wonder if they're sitting in their car and watching the entrance to see if you stay, said Omar.

Good thinking, my boy. Let's play marriage a while longer and have some cake. People stay together after this kind of thing: they turn the lights on, turn the water on, set the table. Let's stay together for two more hours—the grown-ups won't do much talking—until it's dark.

I'm tired now, said Omar. To Abel: Will you tuck me in?

He tucked him in, though he no longer needed to be tucked in. Mercedes could hear them talking from the living room. Was he telling him a good-night story? Omar was not interested in fairy tales. He wanted the truth!

What is true? Alegria once asked him warily.

I don't know, said Omar. You don't know until you hear it. *He* told him only true stories, Omar claimed.

Will you tell me one?

They're hard to tell. They're the most everyday things. He takes walks.

Does he like to take walks?

Like to? I don't know. But he takes them. Nights mostly.

He takes night walks?

When he can't sleep.

Does that happen often?

I don't know.

So he goes out walking.

Right.

And then?

Meets people sometimes.

What kind of people?

People who want to buy cars, say.

Cars? At night?

Right.

You believe that?

I do.

He tucked the boy in and came back into the living room. Only a small lamp was on. Will you sit for a while? Turn the lamp so it lights up his face? Or simply go on with the interrogation.

It's probably too late to ask, she said, but is there anything else I should know?

He didn't think so.

Pause.

Have you heard anything from your father?

No.

Pause.

How's your mother?

Getting along.

There is no emotion in his voice. How come that gets to *me*?

Silence.

Do you think they're really watching the door?

No, I don't, he said.

And then he vanished. Mercedes can't remember having seen him to the door. Had she gone to the bathroom? Had she heard the door open and close from there? Not that I knew. Could he simply have vanished into thin air? Could he still be here, hiding somewhere?

On that odd—there was no better word for it—evening Mercedes turned on all the lights in the apartment. She looked in on the child and then—it may sound crazy, but fear is fear—into the broom closet.

The marital bed remained untouched: she slept on the rug next to Omar's bed.

What are you doing there, Mother? the child asked the next morning.

SMALL THINGS

What does experience tell us? Experience tells us: It won't work this time either. Why should this time be different? By the light of the following day the constellation is clear. Though not perhaps equally clear to all participants. People do not know the same amount about things not exactly the same and as often as not have quite different and obscure expectations. Not even the best of intentions on both sides can forestall trouble. I don't say he's doing it on purpose, *torturing* me on purpose, but Mercedes was, to be frank, pretty much fed up.

To be frank, she said to her face in the mirror the morning after, I'm pretty much fed up.

What did you say? Omar asked from the entrance hall.

I was wondering whether we'd passed the test.

It's too early to know, said the child in his wisdom.

Let's hold tight for a while. Go on parlaying Français, but keep the weekend under wraps. Hear time pass in the form of asynchronous tolling and hammers constructing a roof and hope or let hope rest depending on which seems in keeping with the possibilities. We'll have to stay married at least one more year, no matter what. That's only decent. My wounded pride over his departure is not worth considering. But Mercedes was now a bit *subdued*. They were still perfectly polite and friendly to each other, of course, but there was a break in their common excursions. She had always been the one to make the proposals, and for the time being she made none. Nor was he about to make any.

What's *he* up to?
    Who *he*?
    Your husband.
    Nice of you to ask. Healthy. That's what counts.

A few weeks later they held what they called the *blast*. Mercedes and her father celebrated their birthdays on the same day. It had taken a bit of doing, she having been born a minute after midnight of the following day, but why be pedantic about it, said the doctor and gave his blessing for eleven fifty-nine: father and daughter on the same day, how nice. He was sixty-five, she thirty-six. They could not set up an umbrella in the garden: the constant wind. But friends of all ages together with the inevitable relatives streamed in from all points on the compass. A few of the latter—some disingenuous, others innocent—inquired after the birthday girl's reputed but as yet unrevealed husband.
    He's coming later. He had something to attend to.
    Today of all days he had another test.
    We are particularly interested in the motor and auditory speech fields in the left temporal and frontal lobes, known as Broca's area and Wernicke's area, though the organs governing memory and emotion—the hippocampus, etc.—also play a significant role. Thus the explanation the subject's stepson gave to his audience.
    How big you've grown. And how clever.
    If there's one thing I can't stand, it's precocious brats.
    The human brain is an amazing map, one reputed to show everything. Traumas form enclosed, tumorlike regions.
    Your garden is a veritable oasis. It must take a lot of work.
    Unfortunately we've had an influx of crows.
    I've heard there are villages that have more crows than people.
    Peck sheep's eyes out.

Joggers.

It's like in the . . .

That fat old chauvinist pig ruined T.H.'s career.

We bear the tragicomic burden of having three brains: the reptile in us, the tiny mammal . . .

Most religious ecstasies have probably been epilepsy.

Do you know where the bottle opener is?

Yes, yes. Thank you, thank you, thank you. Just for toasting!

I expect poetry to enhance my humanity. When I want to be entertained, I look at . . .

Oh, there you are! He's here!

He was the last to arrive and brought no gift. Apologized politely for being late. He'd come as soon as he could.

After six hours of tomography . . .

What's it like to lie there for six hours, my boy?

(Alegria, aside:) Could she have repressed death fantasies? Though why would she want to kill her son-in-law? The motivation is as yet obscure.

Can you kill somebody with a CAT scan?

You can kill somebody with a slide projector.

That's a novel idea.

In most cases Father uses poison.

Enjoy your meal!

He looked exhausted. He took the plate Miriam offered him, and gave his other hand to Omar, who pulled him over to a couch. Abel did not touch the food: he kept the plate in his lap for a while, then slipped it under the couch.

Hello, was all anyone could get out of him: he spent the whole evening talking to a ten-year-old.

Eleven, said Mercedes. And what's wrong with that? They must have things to talk about.

What did you talk about? she asked Omar later.

Eskimos.

You talked about Eskimos?

Yes.

The whole evening?

No. Later on we switched.

Switched to what?

We spoke Russian.

What I mean, Erik shouted, is that the call for faith in a single abstract god is too much for our brain. Once practical matters like the weather, fertility, or success in battle lost precedence . . .

And when did that happen?

Group experiments have shown that . . . only because they belong to the other group . . . utterly arbitrary . . .

Yes, yes, yes, yes.

Tostidi, Tatjana, who had sat down on the other side of Abel, heard the child say. She has Russian ancestors.

His tutor nodded. *Tsiruet.*

Later Omar went to bed. Mercedes saw her guests to the door. (Thanks for the food and the subdued light.) Abel was standing in the middle of the room when she came back; Erik was standing near him, almost touching him with his protruding stomach. Erik was swaying. He was very drunk.

What's going to happen? Maya had asked her husband earlier on.

What? asked Erik. He did not look at her. After a loud and strenuous discussion about language and politics he had positioned himself in the only chair near the drinks and, keeping an eye on the couch opposite, counted the glasses Abel emptied—and followed suit.

Maya: That's number six.

Oh, said Erik. I must have lost count. I thought it was five.

The discussion had, as always, been basically with Mad Max and Tatjana, except that this time he would turn to Abel after every third or fourth sentence and ask, What do you think, Abel?

Each time Mr. Deca-Ling seemed to emerge from great depths to say, Sorry, what was the question?

Erik would repeat the question, whereupon Abel—every damned time!—said either I can't say or I have no idea or I don't know.

There's nothing to know! the frustrated Erik finally screamed. It's not about knowing! I'm asking for your *opinion*!!!

Ssh. (Maya)

Why are you screaming, my boy? Are you in pain? (Alegria in passing)

But Abel had gone back to Omar and the discussion was over. As if I didn't exist. It was then Erik settled into the chair near the drinks, mumbling, Disgraceful! . . . Disgraceful!

Mercedes: Questioning look.

Maya: Wave of dismissal.

Mercedes looked over at her husband. Nothing: listening to what the child was saying. But his face, let's look at his face, and for the first time Mercedes would describe it as: sad. The eyes red. With drink or with tears? The computer? The test? Tatjana sat to the left of him, *unnoticed*, making believe she was listening attentively to Mad Max and not the two of them. So it wasn't Russian they were speaking . . .

Mercedes sat on the arm of Erik's chair. She claimed she had some work-related issue to discuss, the consequences of this or that telephone call.

Erik did not respond. Facial expression: defiant. Or trying to keep from vomiting. His eyes glued to Abel and the child.

As if none of it had ever happened . . .

Excuse me? said Mercedes politely. I didn't catch that.

Erik (suddenly loud): What I'm talking about is this endless . . . this arrogant, ignorant . . . (Mumbles incoherently again.) How can a person . . . (Scarcely audible.) Not of this world. I mean . . . : You've *got* to learn new things!

Mercedes: Hm . . .

Making a constant display of strangeness like a . . . like a . . . shield. Why must you be so complicated? So dark? You seem permanently hurt. WHO hurt you? ME? Not that I'm AWARE! (As if calling out, restrained, over a great distance:) I did everything I could. Really. I. Did. Everything. I. Could.

Mercedes (about to say): But . . .

Erik does not let her say her piece.

But I bet that even when they stand before their Maker they will be hurt.

Who? Who is standing before his Maker? Who is hurt?

Erik (screaming): Okay, I'm the one. I AM HURT!

Ssh, said Maya. There's nothing to get upset about.

When he saw Abel was making to leave, he bounded out of his chair and stood in his way.

His protruding stomach almost touched him; he swayed; he seemed to have trouble keeping his large, bull-like head on its neck; his face was wet. He laid a heavy paw on Abel's shoulder. Less out of familiarity than out of the need to steady himself.

Can you tell me . . . Can you tell me just one thing, pal? Just one thing. He moved his face up close and said in a wet whisper, the tiny needles of his spit bombarding Abel's face, What . . . What was the title . . . of your dissertation?

They looked at each other, so close they could easily have kissed. An intimate scene. Abel's eyes wide open, clear. Sorry, he whispered back. Could you please stop touching me?

The moment Erik let him go he took a step back to re-establish the requisite distance or, no, to turn on his heel and go. Erik, as if nailed to the spot, did not move. He merely muttered, What sort of a . . . What kind of a . . . are you? Eh? What kind of a pigsty did you . . . ? Can you . . . Can you ever . . . A freak . . . Mercedes has a thing for freaks; collects them like . . . like . . . those little (waving his hands in the air) tiny things . . . Those tiny things, I can't think of the word right now, the fucking word . . . Help me. You must know it. You're the word man! . . . Oops!

He would have fallen had Maya not stepped behind him and held him up.

That's enough. We're going home.

What happened? Mercedes asked.

Nothing. Help me to get him out of here.

When she returned a minute or two later, Abel was nowhere to be seen.

Where is he?

Tatjana gave a pointedly disinterested shrug.

Mercedes went into the dark garden and listened. Abel?

Nothing. Crickets.

IN FLAGRANTE

He forgot his coat. Mercedes did not notice it until the next morning. Hanging in the entrance hall. ID, money, key ring with his key and hers. Some pocket fluff, the green shreds of a napkin used for a handkerchief. ID: surname, given name, birthplace, birth date. Address: same as hers. But the keys, both and, are here. And money for the taxi fare. A long, nocturnal stroll? Or could he be lying somewhere close by, in the bushes? A glance at the garden: candle stumps, the usual morning-after detritus, nothing.

Mercedes and Omar stayed until afternoon; helped tidy up. Miriam found his plate under the couch, untouched, its contents looking petrified, as if it had been there for ages. She did not mention it. Omar did not mention his name. They drove back to town.

Then: the usual. Days of silence. Nor did Mercedes phone.

I'm willing to apologize, said Erik at work. Just give me his number.

No need, said Mercedes.

As you please, said Erik with a shrug.

Omar would stand at the window, turning his head this way and that.

What are you doing?

Shut one eye, said Omar, and you see a fuzzy, two-dimensional picture of your nose on the right or left side of your field of vision, respectively. When you open the eye, your nose disappears from the world. It may not be world-shaking, but: I will never see the world without the shadow of my nose. I jut into the world.

Since this discovery I notice that whenever I'm sitting and thinking or not even thinking, just sitting, after I lift my eyes from a book, because every now and then, often, you have to lift your eyes from a book, I shut an eye and follow the notably bumpy line of my nose. In short, thought Mercedes, there's no way around it; it's true, it's so obvious that it would be ridiculous to deny it: I love you.

She thought: I love you; picked up her bag—I'm going to work at home—and went to the cul-de-sac by the tracks. Took out the key; opened the door. The stairs are steep; halfway up, the light, which you need even on sunny days, goes out. Feeling her way through the dead, silent building. You'd think nobody lived here. Her usual fear of the dark, of the unknown. Homely-sounding noises at last. From the top floor. A radio. Pausing somewhat out of breath and listening for the source. Unclear. Cautiously leaning her ear against the door. Cool color. The music is from somewhere else. Deep breath. Unlock. Entering her husband's apartment for the first time.

Immediately overpowered, stops in her tracks, marshaling I wonder what forces to cope with: all that. The smell (bitter-sour), the temperature (sultry), the shape of the room (split), the noise (muted music behind the kitchen cabinet), the furnishings (none but a few black garments and dictionaries strewn about like meteorites landed on a dirty-gray terrain), and overarching it all, lurching through the bleak castle keep of hopeless solitude, the light bouncing off a passing train.

Slow motion: outside, the strange machine, big as a house, loaded down with freight, inching its way painfully along the tracks; inside, a woman standing in the door, a man sitting at a desk on the only chair, between them, sensitively gearing his tempo to that of the train, a naked boy turning on his own axis. He is exhibiting himself to his audience—now made up of two—from all sides: vanilla-colored back, behind, legs, arms, sides, chest, stomach, genitals . . .

Oh, said the boy, when he reached the point where he could see Mercedes. For a while they just stood there. Then the boy burst out laughing; stood there with his beautiful body and laughed. The expression on her husband's face is blocked by the body; she cannot see it; all she can see out of the corner of her eye is that the black bundle in the chair does not budge.

Sorry, she whispered, lowered her eyes, and left. She wanted to drop the key somewhere, but there was nothing to drop it on, no normal table, only the floor. She did not want to throw it down, so she bent, her back to the two of them, and laid it on the floor. The door handle, then outside at last. Nothing moved behind her the whole time.

He had gone to see Thanos for a replacement key and stayed on somewhat longer than necessary, two days altogether, not leaving until closing time on Monday. He took the boy, whom he had picked up there, home with him.

And now, he said when he supposed his wife had had time to climb down the stairs, get the hell out of here.

You don't need to be so coarse, said the boy. It's not my fault.

Put your clothes on and go, please. Or don't put your clothes on. Just go.

It was a whole day before he went to see Mercedes.

He apologized politely for the unpleasant situation.

She said nothing.

From the outside he looks like a perfectly normal man—correction, a perfectly normal *person*. Correction: delete the entire sentence, because Mercedes realized immediately that even the first part, *from the outside*, made no sense when applied to a *person* (man), so there was nothing left, nothing that would hold water. *Sometimes I doubt whether a single thought* . . . She felt herself swaying as she stood there. She wanted to look him in the face, but kept having to focus, as in a moving train. My eyes had begun to hurt, and suddenly he seemed no longer to have a specific sex, he was a hermaphrodite. The *person* slid off her tongue, down, mixed with her spittle.

Finally she managed to say, You could have told me. (It wasn't written all over him, after all.)

Sorry.

Would you mind not saying Sorry all the time!!!

That was conceivably the loudest she had spoken in years.

Another period of silence followed.

She would make good on their mutual agreement, she said. That is, stay married to him for more than a year. But it would be best if he kept his distance from her young son from then on.

Thus for the second time Omar A.'s language instruction came to an abrupt end.

Everyone has a talent, said Mercedes. Mine is to love the impossible.

Granted, you like someone for obvious, that is, external, or hidden, that is, unknown reasons. Up to a point everything goes smoothly, though or precisely because he does nothing special. He basically does nothing at all; he simply exists, one way or another. And suddenly or gradually he becomes a chain of irritations and offenses. Unpleasant situations a polite person would not impose on his fictive wife. But that is not the point. I can be understanding for the most part; in fact, being understanding is my main damn character trait. Though it was also important that Omar . . . But I mustn't use Omar as an excuse. The least you can do is set your own house in order, no matter how painful. The fact is: I got caught up from the start; I fell in love with someone who I sensed wanted no more than to be alone, a marginal figure, to avoid getting at all involved. The only reason he learned his ten languages was to be more alone than with three, five, or seven. Having sensed it, I am to blame, and *that's why* I'm not angry with him. But what she failed to understand, said Mercedes, was why he had kissed her hand and taken her home and helped her up the stairs, and here, at the door, when he might have given her another hand-kiss or just a handshake, to seal the bargain, what had he done? She just wanted to get it out into the open, put it into words: naturally, she wanted to say, naturally it was only *a bureaucratic affair in connection with his status* . . . when he bent down and kissed her on the mouth. Nothing out of the ordinary, nothing spectacular; it was simply: good. Surprising, promising. A *talented* kiss. Then he left, and I thought: what a gentleman.

I won't go so far as to say he was being calculating: hand, home, mouth. But he could not possibly have been unaware he was giving me hope, and did so over and over, only to disappoint me over and over. Friendly and polite as he was, that was not nice of him, not in the least. Somewhere along the line it stopped hurting and became a strain. For four years it was mostly that: a strain. Now all I want is to put it behind me. So much for this marriage. I'll call you if I have reason to, but I had none.

The most frequent grounds for divorce are: (1) infidelity, (2) infertility, (3) criminality, (4) mental instability. Only the best combine all four. Tatjana laughs.

You don't need any grounds at all nowadays, says Mercedes. Say yes, say no, and that's that.

For a while no one says anything. Then Tatjana: Do you realize you could have the marriage annulled? The grounds could be: incest, bigamy, marriages between minors or the mentally ill, marriages contracted by deceit, such as sexual impotence at the time of betrothal.

If I have the marriage annulled, says Mercedes, he'll lose his passport.

Shrug.

PART VII

BINDING AND LOOSING

WHO DO YOU THINK YOU . . .

It went wrong, again. Significant details that refused to come together or did, but followed their own queer logic. Mercedes finally gave up. They would leave the building together. The women were considerate and adjusted to his tempo. He would go to the park, sit on a bench. The usual shouting, ringing, and barking all around him had no effect: he was soon asleep. Now he wakes up to find the *crazy guy* sitting next to him. Just what I needed.

It's been a long time, but there's no doubt about it: it's him. He looks basically the same; so do I. We're even wearing the same clothes. More or less. A bit more crumpled, maybe. Crumpled up asleep on a park bench, Monday afternoon. He wakes up, blinks; he's disoriented: where am I, when, and who are you? It is seven years since they last met. They have been living around the corner from each other and accomplished the considerable feat of never having met. Who managed that? Was it far-fetched or was it only natural? Konstantin had never forgotten him and occasionally thought of keeping an eye out for him, but: nothing. And now.

No one else would have sat next to a man sleeping on a bench and stuck it out despite the rumbling stomach—oh, the imponderables of strange kitchens—how long? until the man finally woke up, and would then have taken up from where they had left off as if they had seen each other a few hours before. So you're still here.

It would be too much to list all the things that had happened to Konstantin in the interim. Things had gone on as they always had: a long line of inconsequences and injustices temporarily in a midday meal at the soup kitchen. Yes, hunger had its part, but the main thing was to occupy his time until evening, when he hooked up with a few characters he might otherwise have avoided like the plague, but what can you do. Start out the day humiliated so it can't get any worse. But I don't want to impose my sorrows on you. Nor does he bring up the conditions surrounding their separation, either the *incident* or its aftermath. No tearful lamentation, not a word. He just sits there—a bit too close for comfort, a spot of tomato sauce in the left corner of his mouth—and asks, What are you doing here (old pal)?

For a moment—the warmth of Schadenfreude suffusing his body—Konstantin hoped the answer would be, I'm living here now. But it was immediately followed by compassion: I am a humanitarian who likes nothing better on a day like today than to find a person worse off than himself. And then? Take him home with me? Begin again? And again? Why? Because what would the alternative be?

Let's take it easy, though. Have a closer look at the face. What's that? Have a fall? Been in a fight? What did you do? Or did you do nothing? Were you just, as we so often are, at the mercy of the everyday? And what's this? Looks like makeup. One has moments of absolute clarity. Konstantin had one now: how could I have failed to see it? The man has a dark secret of the sexual sort. Though word has it he's married. How come you and not me got one of those fictive marriage passports, you lucky dog!

Abel—what did you expect?—did not answer any of his questions. Voiced or not. Nor did he say what he was doing here. Sitting on a bench, can't you see?

Had a hard night?

Abel moved his head between a nod and a shake. So-so.

What follows is rather hazy. What they said, that is, he: Konstantin, sliding back and forth on the bench because of a twisted stomach—no, intestines; Abel, the same, but for different reasons.

Everything okay? asked Konstantin when Abel bent forward after a few rattly breaths, propped his elbows on his knees, and stared down at the dusty ground strewn with cigarette ends. His neck was covered with sweat.

Hm, said Konstantin and waited, silent, until the wind had dried it.

Listen, said Konstantin, I don't want to keep pestering you, but . . . Well, the thing is, I've overdrawn my account by eight hundred. You can overdraw it up to a thousand, but the bastards won't give me any more money. Could Abel lend him something? A hundred, say? And then I wouldn't bother you ever again. What do you say?

First just the wind in his black locks, then he lifted his elbows, sat up straight, and, without looking at Konstantin, dug into his pocket and came up with a few coins and a key. He fished out the key, shook the coins into a pile in his palm in the sun, and held it out.

You've got to be kidding, said Konstantin, his face suddenly red.

Sorry, said Abel. It's all I have.

Konstantin's head looked ready to explode, Aaaaaaaaaa, unable to speak, waving his arms in the air, splashing the air, until he finally found the right gesture and struck Abel's outstretched hand from below. The coins fell down among the cigarette ends. Even though they made almost no noise, the homeless looked over.

Think you're being funny? Ha? Ha? What do you think? Who do you think you are?

Abel put his empty hand into his pocket and walked off.

Look at that dirty traitor! Konstantin shouted, his spit spraying all over. Look at that inhuman swine, wallowing in his filth, refusing to accept what he is, thinking he's better than he is. But you are what you are and what you were, like the rest of us. Run from it as you will, they'll always be with you, they'll track you down inside your own four walls . . .

The rest was lost to the taxi.

. . .

Tachycardia: eighty-three point five; hot flushes: eighty-one point five; feelings of anxiety: seventy-eight four; shudders, shakes: seventy-five three; feeling dazed: seventy-two two; sweating: sixty-two nine; chest pains: fifty-five seven; shortness of breath: fifty-one five; fear of death: forty-nine five; fear of loss of control: forty-seven; abdominal problems: forty-five four; feeling faint: forty-three three; signs of paralysis: forty-two three; depersonalization: in thirty-seven point one percent of the cases.

The leather seat is slippery wherever his hand has touched it: he is sweating profusely. Attempts to suppress the coughing end in a long, drawn-out belling that comes from under the sunken chin, ghost-like, animal-like. The superstitious eye of the cab driver in the rearview mirror. What kind of metamorphosis is going on in the back seat? This weird-looking but not bad-looking guy comes out of the park, ducks into the back, grinding his teeth and breathing deep like he's just been shot in the stomach or staggering away from a duel, ready to lie down and die. Look, pal, if you're fixing to barf all over the back seat, out you go. Or, depending on his mood: Shall I take you straight to the hospital? But no, neither. Just a pair of fearful dark eyes in the rearview mirror. A fragile man in a turban, young or young-looking, displaying the terrible readiness-to-suffer of the new arrival. Should I die here, he would clasp his hands and cry. His first tears in this country. The flowing tears of a child. Someone else would have to call the ambulance. A resolute red-haired woman with a cell phone. But not to worry, kind sir. This is only a mild attack. It will be over in no time. Panic is not . . . Panic is . . .

The first time you think it's a heart attack, but no, you're too young to think such a thing, during the night after your graduation party, I love you, but I don't love you, maybe it was just a nightmare, one you don't remember because it leaves only a feeling behind: I'm about to die. You huddle on the floor, your sweaty forehead in the dirt as if in prayer; how you got your clothes off, every stitch of pain—correction—of clothes, you can't remember; all you can feel is you're choking on nothing or everything. Press your head against the back of the driver's seat. There, it will be over in no time.

The driver feels a bump behind him but does not dare glance back. What's happening? If even some minor thing happens, he'll jump out of the cab into the callous traffic, under the wheels of his fellow drivers, a turbaned bowling pin. But for the moment he jerks the steering wheel to the left to drive away from the bump, from the fear, and the car skids, causing a wave of nausea to rise into Abel's throat, but he keeps his eyes shut and presses his head harder into the seat until the thud of the pressure against his eardrums wanes. He has to repeat, We're here, this is the address! several times before the driver hears him.

He lifts his head—the back of the driver's seat impressed on it, looking as if it had just come out of the pool, though an otherwise perfectly normal, average face—fumbles in the inner pocket of his coat and, extracting a few of the banknotes the divorce lawyer lent him—did you really think I'd give them to a lousy scrounger like you?—pays, gives a slightly larger than normal tip.

For a while he just stands there, the wind making winglike motions with his black coattails, which the driver watches as he turns the car around. Today I saw a man who must have just fallen from heaven or risen out of hell: when he got into the cab, he was not a whole man; he battled for his form in the back seat, grunting and sweating, and later, when he stood in the street, I could tell he could fly, a black-and-white man. The name of the driver's wife was Amina. She stared at him with her large eyes, saw the sweat on his honey-colored neck.

The first time you think . . . In time you get the hang of it. The wind is as soothing as a peppermint; standing in the wind for a while is good. Only a few moments. Then Abel went upstairs.

WHAT IT IS

When he left the building in the morning, the radio alarm next door, which had gone on an hour before, was still echoing through the stairs. Now it is afternoon and quiet. Quiet to even the most acute of ears. For instance, standing at the door and rummaging for the key, Abel can tell there is something or, more probably, someone moving about in his neighbor's apartment. Halldor Rose is usually out on Monday at this time. Now: what sounds like footsteps, scraping. Abel registers it, then puts it out of his mind; unlocks his door, shuts it behind him, takes his sweaty clothes off, and puts on the ones he washed two nights before. They have something of a laundry-bag smell to them.

And now?

The computer is off, the screen dusty. You would think no one had been here for ages, and yet it is only a few hours. The last strange weekend was still fresh, as was everything else. It was as if Monday, Tuesday, Wednesday, and Thursday had happened and today was Friday. It was actually still Monday, and not so late in the afternoon. The cut on his foot was throbbing. I should sit down. Or better: lie down.

Before they get out of hand, things are for the most part unspectacular: you live one way, then another. Of Abel Nema's attempts at life until now we might mention the various prisons and forced relationships. For example, the summer junket with a few hostile friends and so on.

Yes, let us begin again with the tour or, rather, with its abrupt end, which caused such a to-do, as was only natural, given the circumstances. Nothing is known about the night after his departure from the cabbage field, but later he looked at his face in the dirty mirror of the filling station toilet, comparing it with the picture in the passport, then went out and looked around to see what was there. Not much: a street, trees. Houses farther on. Now: destination everywhere.

But in the end all he did was what he had done on a different scale before: he crisscrossed the country or, rather, the bordering countries, as far as he could go without having to show his passport. I have a new identity, but I do not use it. Kontra had money in his pocket and even a bank card, but Abel preferred hitchhiking. What does that mean? It does not mean he ever held his thumb out. He simply walked along the road and people stopped and asked him whether they could give him a lift.

Where are you going?

Anywhere.

Once in the car, he would glue his cheek to the side window and his eyes to the sky and landscape.

Is this your first time here?

Mhm.

What does it look like where you come from?

Very similar. It is the same climate zone.

They would talk about plants and animals. He, said a middle-aged black man, had been born here, but he had a *certain affinity for the vegetation in the land of his forefathers*. He was *tending* a banana plant in his garden. Later he asked, as others did after him, whether Abel needed a place to stay. He introduced him to his wife and two children, a nine-year-old girl and five-year-old boy, and himself made up the bed for him, a convertible sofa with an ugly pattern in the basement playroom, where he slept when he was drunk. An air-traffic controller for the army.

The next one was, in a word, *dull*, a man my age with a small, chewed-up mustache, who drove around the region just to give people rides. He spoke a virtually incomprehensible dialect, not that he had much to say. He put on a cassette of a cabaret performance that Abel understood not a word of at first but got more and more of until finally he found himself laughing at even the less funny jokes. Mustache laughed along in gratitude.

Number three was a woman cab-driver, a plump blonde who took him out to the country after her shift. I prefer village life. And you? Where are you from? *Originally*, I mean. No, you have no accent. How did I know you're new here if you have no accent? That long? Do you want to stay the night and tell me about it?

And so on. He went from hand to hand like a baton in a relay race, as if it had all been organized *somewhere*, pre-arranged: there was always somebody there. The last one, a sad old man, took him all the way to the coast. It was now another sea. He sat on a bench on the drafty concrete promenade, a row of flags batting behind him in the wind, wire cables beating against metal flagpoles— pling, pling—the loose poster corners rustling on a nearby advertising column. The poster announced events taking place in the convention center behind the flags. He knew that kind of center; he could apply for a job there. Better be on the safe side and say you know only four languages, six at most: otherwise they'll take you for a . . . You have the possibility of starting a new life: *neu, nieuw, nouveau, nuovo* . . . But he did not want a job. For the first time, oddly enough, he felt something like homesick for the city he had lived in for the last few years. He bought a coach or train ticket, took the shortest route back, and met his future wife again.

Both saw a sign in the chance encounter: as good a reason as any. Her friends were a disaster, but then there was the boy; besides, *she* had everything it took: she was both boyish and motherly, and you could stand arm in arm with her when summoned by officials. Everything went well for a while: he/it was flawless at first. Apart from the sex. He realized that; you'd have to be blind not to. To be honest, he had even thought of sex as a possibility—his good will was genuine—and stayed away from The Loony Bin for a time. But it was an unnecessary sacrifice: all in all, that was not what had gummed up the works. At a certain point it had developed one too many glitches, and it was better to carry on at a distance. Though he would go to her birthday party, of course.

He had had a test that day, you might call it our *most spectacular* so far: it is like a simultaneous chess match except that instead of chess partners you'll have conversation partners. It is terra incognita for us: until now we have been limited to producing static images, and our goal must be to trace the *processes*. They fell silent when he entered the room. The Pope had made his appearance. People everywhere, no air. Could they open a window? They opened a window. Street noise. A column of buses crossing a bridge in the middle of the room. We'll have to shut the window. Will somebody shut the window, please? Thank you. In principle, the exercise is simple, which makes it all the more difficult to put into practice. Let us know when you feel tired, though getting tired is part of the experiment: we want to see how the ability to switch languages varies as fatigue increases, if you understand what I mean. He nodded. Buzzing in the room: Mr. Deca-Ling had nodded. Students manning tape recorders and EEG machines. On it goes for several hours, poor boy, from L1 to L2 to L3 to L5 to L7 to. Within and between language families; from which to which is easier, harder; when does he start mixing up words; which language is the first to go; all go one after the other. Can. We. Stop. Please. Applause, congratulations, really just, just, extraordinary, thank you, thank you, thank you, good-bye, thank you, shall I call you a cab?

Six hours of tests, then back to the station district for a quick shower, forty winks time permitting. He looked at his mail. A senseless habit. He had official letters sent to Mercedes' address; nobody wrote him private letters but his mother, and by the time they had crossed land and water she had told him most of their contents over the phone. The box was bursting with the last few days' worth of junk mail. He opened it, and everything fell out, the whole colorful pile and with it the crumpled envelope with Mira's handwriting. He inserted his pinkie as he was making his way up the five flights stair by stair, a minor diversion. He left a trail of tiny bits of paper.

A sheet of paper, a page torn out of a newspaper. Disappeared in July seven years ago: Ilia Bor, young doctor, during the call of duty, under unexplained circumstances, remains never found, friends and family mourn.

So I can really stop looking for you *now*.

He would probably go back immediately, Abel thought, sitting on the bench in front of the conference center; still, he looked around to see what I'm giving up here. Nothing: river, cement, flags, posters. Until he finally! realized what was on the poster he had been staring at all this time: Tomorrow morning, Lecture by Elias B.R. on "Post-Traumatic Stress Management."

He stayed up all night on the bench. River noises in the night. Water lapping against the embankment. Ships, possibly. Something from the city perhaps: lights, sounds, quite far off. The endless pling-pling of the flags. Later the sun came up. Of course. Mist. The first passersby. Some may have looked over at him. Sitting there like a Buddha.

He stayed awake the whole night and just before it would have been time for him to set off in search of a toilet to freshen up, face and hands mainly, to find out how to get to the lecture, he fell asleep. He slept through the entire thing. It was afternoon by the time he awoke. He had a sunburn and a cold. He made a (fruitless) attempt to clear his senses, tipping to the side and lying there in the breezes coming from the water. People came and went; he lay on the bench, unable to move or look to see whether *he* was there. The first time I have been ill since childhood. The first time Abel Nema gave some thought to the fact that people, he, could *really* die. That it could be *experienced so close up*. Might even be desirable as the simplest way out. Lie there until I dry out into a rolled-up leaf and am blown down among the stones.

No, I won't get off so lightly. This isn't even the sea, damn it. Just a river, an estuary. He sat up, worked himself back into a normal position. Face burned, neck itching, he shut his eyes. He made up his mind to recover, and within a half hour he had. True, he still felt a little weak. He needed to drink. Drinking is always good. He went into the first café he could find; it was an Internet café. He paid for half an hour and Googled the name on the poster.

He got several hundred hits: publications, lectures, references. The man had been active for five years; he could well have been my age, but was not. After a few tries, a biography with a picture: a middle-aged man, glasses, beard. He had only a minute left. He hesitated, then typed—fingers trembling, quick!—*Andor Nema* into the search field. Just as the clock was running down to 0, he saw the same 0 flash on the screen: 0 results.

Mira's letter in one hand, the key in the other. Schmaltzy music seeping out of the flat next door. He opened the door and shut it behind him.

Later he found himself huddling on the floor. How did he get his clothes off? He could not remember. A pockmarked light through the window, a wild wind outside. He bent over his pounding heart as he had done long ago, when I was still living in a wardrobe. He beat his forehead against the rug, dirt particles sticking to his skin, then drizzling down. Gasping for breath, coughing, drinking water from the tap, hard to swallow, more coughing or none, which only made it worse. Finally he managed to pull himself up far enough to make it over to the balcony. He leaned against the grill, into the wind, breathed through the mouth, and watched the trains through the bars, watched them pull, pull, pull coal, wheat, refuse, people. Now I am better, now I am better.

He went back into the room, took a shower, and went to his wife's party. The rest has been told. He returned on foot. When it got bad, he would stop, lean against something, and breathe until it got better. Once he pressed his head against a telephone booth. The impression had the shape of a butterfly.

Since then he has lived a secluded life. Half the time in The Loony Bin, the other half translating droll stories. The world is full of madmen. He keeps his head above water. About the only thing he hears is music from next door. Does it bother him? No. Not at all. He doesn't care.

OTHER QUESTIONS

The schedule for the next few days is clear. One: get new papers. It's no fun, though perfectly doable if you put your mind to it. Not that it can't wait until tomorrow. Or the day after. Or, say, Thursday, when I've got to go out anyway (two): to meet Omar in the park. For a year now my only set appointment in the week.

See you Thursday, Omar whispered into Abel's ear on the stairs of the courthouse, hiding behind his profile. Abel did not answer; he merely gave his hand an extra squeeze.

Here's the deal, Omar had told his new French tutor the year before. You get your money without teaching me. My stepfather will do the teaching. We'll be in the park on that bench over there, weather permitting. You can watch from your window. I'll spend forty minutes with him. Then I'll come back to you and tell you in five minutes what I've learned, and you can pass it on to my mother if she asks you.

I don't know, said the tutor—her name was Madeleine—I don't know if under . . .

We won't budge from the bench. We'll just be talking.

It's dark by then in winter, and you can't see. Sorry, said Madeleine, wrapped in a coat. You can't go on like that. Come inside with me. Once Mercedes came for Omar early. Madeleine hid the man in her windowless bathroom. A bad idea: what if she needed to use it. She did not. She apologized later for having put him out.

What crime have you committed? she wanted to ask, but did not. Later it was spring again, and they went back to sitting on the bench.

Can I ask you something personal? asked Omar. Or, rather, *may* I?

Yes and yes, said Abel, smiling.

Who is the person you've loved most in your life?

Reflex action: Ilia. Don't say it. Say what comes next: You.

For me it's Mercedes.

Abel nodded understandingly. Of course. She's your mother, after all.

Pause.

Why? asked Omar.

Why what?

Why do you love me?

I don't know. I just do.

Hm, said the child. I said the same thing.

. . .

How long will this go on? Omar asked last week.

I don't know.

You keep saying, I don't know.

Because I don't.

At first I thought it was a sign that you were wise.

And now?

Now I don't know anymore. I know less and less as time goes on. I used to think my head would burst one day, burst from brains; now I don't think there's any such danger. It must have something to do with the fact that I'll be coming into puberty soon. My personality will probably change too. I may not feel like sitting here with you. I can tell even now that you need me more than I need you.

Pause.

I apologize, said Omar. I didn't mean to hurt you.

You did not hurt me.

Yes, I did. Admit it.

All right. I admit it.

Pause.

It is not easy, you know. It is complicated.

Yes, I know, said the boy. I apologize.

No, said Abel. I am the one who should apologize.

No, said Omar. That's the way things are. That's life.

He turned his hand, which was resting between them on the bench, palm up. Abel placed his hand on it.

While we're at it, said Omar after a pause, I should tell you that I'm not particularly interested in languages. I can learn them, but I have no feeling for them.

Je sais, said Abel. That is all right.

Smiles.

Three days to Thursday. Abel stayed in bed.

Whenever a new situation arose in the cul-de-sac, there was this nothing time. It was neither pleasant nor productive, but there seemed to be no alternative. Usually he closed his eyes the way you do when you want to concentrate, conceive of something different from death or not so much different as at least a tolerable solution if not the final one. Later he would lose consciousness or fall asleep, the difference between the two being difficult to ascertain in someone who never dreams. When he came to (woke up), he typically had a new idea: for a new job or something else, a new person.

Nothing of the sort this time round. He stayed awake. There were still steps going back and forth behind the kitchen cupboard. Music would turn on, then off, as if someone were searching for something and not finding it. When you can't sleep and The Loony Bin is closed, you might as well go out for a walk. Block after block until you no longer know what next. Asking directions in your own city. In just under a dozen modern languages. Or not asking directions. Leaving it in God's (?) hands until rest or exhaustion takes over and the issue is taken care of for the day. But this time for objective reasons—a cut on the foot—that was impossible. The edges of the wound under the ball of the right foot had coalesced with the handkerchief he had wound round it and, through the handkerchief, with the sock. That meant, if nothing else, that a new cloth would have to be applied. Or a way to heal it found. He once did manage to heal a cold, but that was easier. Perhaps completely new, though somewhat occult perspectives opened up at this point. In the end, however, he did nothing: he simply stayed awake and waited.

Later the sun went down again, and he at least moved over to the balcony.

The balcony actually consists of two balconies, two tiny boxes divided by a partition with holes in it. When his neighbor comes out for a smoke, they sometimes meet.

What are you working on?

Translations. And you?

Chaos research.

What are you smoking?

Holy sage.

What does it do?

Last time it gave me a canoe trip down the Amazon. If you like that kind of thing.

I can't get high.

You just haven't found the right medium.

Maybe.

Would you like to try?

I can't even smoke.

Well, in that case. Sorry, I think it's starting up. I'd better go in.

That was basically it.

(Excuse me, I don't want to . . . But you've been kneeling here naked on the balcony groaning for quite some time now. Is anything wrong?

No, no, said A.)

A Sorry came out of the darkness behind the partition. A woman's Sorry. Had Halldor Rose turned into a woman? No. I am his sister Wanda. Could you come over for a minute? Unless you're busy, that is.

I'm not, actually.

THE SKY OVER OUR
CUL-DE-SAC

She was standing on the threshold by the time he hobbled his way
to the door. The resemblance was striking: blond hair, red cheeks,
hooked nose, thick eyebrows hanging low over green, birdy eyes.
She gave me a stern look.

My brother Halldor, your neighbor, has been missing for several days. I don't know whether you noticed. Actually, he *was*
missing. He's back. Back and claiming . . . He claims he spent the
last three days in heaven. Heaven as in Kingdom of. Understand?

Because of the foot he was basically standing on one leg. She
looked him up and down. Had he, H.R.'s neighbor, noticed anything strange about him?

Abel considered the question conscientiously and said, No.

I thought you two were friends.

???

Come with me, said Wanda. I want to show you something.

Refusing was out of the question.

It was the first time he had seen the apartment. Bed, desk, monitor.

It was on when I got here, said Wanda. At first I thought it was the television set, but it was the screen saver. The thing is full of files with scientific stuff I don't understand and pictures of naked, big-breasted women there's nothing to understand about, though I can't get over how the tastes of clodhoppers and geniuses, insofar as they are men, fall together on that score. That's just the way things are, I guess. She'd looked for something personal, which you may or may not condemn, because the first thing they do when you're admitted to an insane asylum is go through your personal items, hoping to find an indication, a . . . letter . . . But I found nothing, not a word, just formulas and meat and that thing there. She had been staring at it for hours, during which time it had repeated itself ten times over, and now her thoughts were going around in circles too. In short, I don't understand a thing, not a thing. Can you explain it to me?

Once several weeks before, Abel had to stop working because something had flown against the window. A bird. A dead bird on the balcony. What to do with it? Or merely stunned. What to do with it?

No, it was a something. A flying robot with orange ping-pong balls at the end of what were supposed to be legs and a tiny camera attached to the front with insulating tape.

Sorry, said Halldor Rose over the partition.

Abel bent over the partition and handed the something to him.

Thank you, said H.R. It has a steering problem.

Abel looked down at it and asked what he had wanted to film.

Its wobbly flight towards the wall, the tracks, but mainly heaven. Want to see?

He's taken pictures of heaven, said Abel to Wanda. In the rectangular-pixeled clips, each lasting a few scant seconds, heaven is green, the earth orange. Now and then the tracks come between them. The clips are so wobbly and disjointed that the tracks seem to be traveling over the heaven, hopping between clouds.

There! said Wanda, pointing triumphantly to the screen. Abel's head and hand flashed for an instant on the bottom half of the image.

Yes, said Abel. That.

Look, I appreciate your concern, but please try to appreciate my situation as well: I have been having a hard time of it for a long time now; I am just coming out of a new panic attack. To be frank, I would like nothing more than to lie down and sleep for the next ten years . . .

This was obviously not the tack to take. Wanda pursured her interrogation unwaveringly.

And what are these?

Plastic baggies she had found in the kitchen. Containing what? Spices? Seeds? She read out the words on the small white labels: *Acorus calamus, Lophophora williamsii, Salvia divinorum, Psilocybe cyanascens, Amanita muscaria, Atropa belladonna.* Well?

I presume they are psychoactive plants, said Abel accommodatingly.

I'm well aware of that, she said. Belladonna. Every peasant knows belladonna. But I know nothing about the others. The bag with the Mexican cactus is empty. Nothing but a bit of fuzz. If he took it all . . . Can you die from it?

Abel really didn't know.

Wanda tossed the baggies onto the desk, crossed her arms over her chest and looked around the room: How can *you people* live like this?

No matter, she said in the end. He's not dead. He's not only alive; he seems perfectly normal—except for insisting he's been to heaven. We're not even religious.

She looked out of the window. At his heaven. Abel's telephone rang. It is not clear whether she heard it; she gave no indication of doing so. One of the baggies slipped off the desk. Abel picked it up.

There were six of us at home, said Wanda to the windowpane. I'm the oldest, Halldor the youngest. We're all potato farmers. We talk about nothing but the potato crop or our children—and about the crisis, of course. Our only dealer, a French fries manufacturer, has cut down on his purchases. Our barns are full. Luckily we've got the family: for eight months we've stopped taking salaries and started eating potatoes. How long can a family of twenty live on four thousand five hundred barrels of potatoes? Before they rot. We're not complaining: if things work out, we'll be millionaires; we can't talk about anything else. But Halldor, Halldor can't talk about anything but his chaos and none of us understands one fucking—sorry—word of what he says. That's how things are. We love him. He's our . . . God, understand? And we're not even religious. He is what we cannot grasp. The things we say to him sound like gibberish. He's our idol: we've been loving him and spoiling him ever since he was born, though we're afraid of him too and even hide from him. We visit him less and less often when we're in town. I've never been to this apartment before. How long have you known him?

Three years.

Have you seen anybody here in all that time?

No, but he hadn't paid attention.

It breaks my heart, said Wanda, looking back out through the balcony door, a disjointed heaven flickering behind her profile.

Later Abel went back to his apartment. The answering machine showed one call.

Only seven—no, nine—people in all know the number. Do I want to receive a message from one of them at this moment? What does experience say? Experience says it is better to know immediately what there is to know. He pressed the button.

Friday, said the voice. Such and such a train.

When Ilia died *once and for all*, it hit him with a force that knocked him out of his orbit and landed him with a thud on the hard, gray ground, whence in effect he was never to rise again. The phone call he had just received gave him the same news about Kinga, but had almost no impact: I find it painful, but it is the truth.

They had lost sight of each other for quite some time. She had not called since the kite incident. He did think of her at times but felt nothing. On the day he learned of Ilia's death she was the first person who came to mind. After the fit had passed, that is. Go to her place. Put his head in her lap. Gulp down all the medicines. French-kiss. But then the birthday party seemed a less painful way out. Later, when he had recovered from all the *scandals* that the decision had entailed, he did go to Kingania, but they were no longer living there. He pressed his ear to the door and heard that nobody had been living there for a while. Her name did not come up on the Internet, and all the references to the musicians dealt with old gigs. Maybe she had moved out of town. So that was that. That was the end of their relationship. In the year that followed he had talked to practically no one except for an occasional word with the neighbor and Thanos.

Later the phone rang.

May I speak to Abel N.?

He could not quite tell which of the three it was.

She jumped out of the window, said the voice. In case you wanted to know. (It sounds like Janda. Heart pounding.)

I do want to know. When?

A week ago yesterday.

Pause.

When is the funeral?

There isn't any funeral.

Silence.

What are you going to do? Throw her in the river?

We're sending her ashes home. (That is probably Andre.) She wanted them to be dispersed.

I see. When?

Don't know yet. We haven't put the money together.

That was why they had called.

How much?

Don't know. Five hundred?

Pause.

Can you tell me when? What train?

Pause. A breath. No: a pause.

We don't know yet. We'll let you know.

He did not believe them, but said, All right.

My condolences, said Thanos. How much do you need?

He owed him two months rent as it was. Those strange stories are less profitable than they're made out to be.

. . .

Neither thin with the head of a bird nor stocky with a rectangle of a forehead, neither Janda nor Andre. No, it was Kontra who came for the money. They met in the street: neutral grounds for the transaction. Alone, out of context, he made an odd impression. Abel threw a glance in the direction of the corner to see if the others were following him, but no one else came.

She'd thrown his can out of the window, Kontra told him, the one he liked to play on. They'd had an argument about something, the usual, and she screamed, So I'm crazy, am I? Well, I'll show you crazy! And bam! down went the can into the power company courtyard. Before it had stopped clattering, Janda grabbed her by the collar and started slapping her: forehand, backhand, forehand, backhand. And before long all four of them were in it together, rolling around on the floor. But then Kinga fought her way out and sat under the window with her back against the wall, sobbing, her gums all bloody. And then Janda broke away and Andre, who was still on the floor, tried to grab at his foot, but missed it and lay there sobbing and screaming: You're out of your minds, all of you! Off your rockers! Clinical cases! He had a scratch near the eye; it was bleeding; he rubbed it. The next time, he said to Kinga, who was swallowing her blood, I won't try to stop the two of you. You can kill each other if you like. I'm going home to my family! Kontra stayed. Later he went downstairs, climbed the wall, which was protected by jagged glass, dropped into the neighboring courtyard, and retrieved the can. He sat in the kitchen, trying to hammer it back into shape. It was clearly done for, but he kept tapping away. There they sat in the gathering darkness. Tap, tap, tap. He stayed the night, but he too left the next morning.

A stormy love lasting twenty years, said Kontra. I don't think they ever saw each other again. Soon thereafter she married a refined, elderly homosexual whose apartment she had cleaned and who had asked her to marry him before. He was a window dresser in a large department store and collected ugly carved furniture. He had set aside a room for her, and she could live there when she wished, but did not have to. I don't have to, she told Andre, whom she once ran into in the street. That was the last any of them saw of her. She had also told him she had an insurance policy and a doctor had prescribed some medicine for her and in a few weeks she would build up a deposit in her body. But before the weeks were up she had jumped out of the kitchen window into the courtyard on the other side of the building.

Pause.

How were the other two doing? Abel asked.

As was to be expected, said Kontra. Andre's got his family. His daughter must be two by now.

Abel did not know he was married.

No way you could have, said Kontra.

The time had come for him to hand over the money. Kontra stuffed the banknotes into his pocket and kept his hand there. He said good-bye and was gone.

Kinga had once said, How can I explain the reverse side of our courage to someone who hasn't experienced it? It's so frustrating; it's like explaining colors to the blind. But you can't change these things: you either have it or you don't, and then you understand it or you don't, though it doesn't much matter in the end: I understood it and what good did it do me?

Abel sat by the phone for a few minutes, then put his hand in his pocket and took out the baggie he had picked up and failed to return to H.R.'s desk. Amanita muscaria. Your everyday fly agaric. He could still hear Wanda's comings and goings behind the kitchen cupboard. One: papers; two: Omar; three: ashes. But then he made up his mind to stop waiting.

CENTER

Delirium

And I—I, that is—did not kneel down on the clammy linoleum between toilet bowl and bathtub, nor did I pray to a god to help and
pardon me or pardon and help; I took the milk, poured it into a
basin—my only bowl—stirred in the contents of the little bag,
and waited. After waiting a certain interval, I drank the milk,
now marbled in brown, and spoke: . . . no, fell, according to the
documentation, into a half sleep after twitchings, dimness of eye,
nausea, and numbness of foot. I awoke to find myself strewn over
the earth.

What and where am I? Not in the open: this ceiling is no firma-
ment, no. It is as dark as a basement, but the wind is as noisy as the
upper stories. It never stops: the building is in a wind canal or on
an elevation that is not entirely natural. Yesterday's mansions are
the quarries for tomorrow's underprivileged—correction, unculti-
vated—correction . . . society. He who builds on rubble. Though it
may also be that the whistling is all in my ears, wherever they may
be at present. Siberian shamans say it is like lying chopped up in
chunks. Where is my leg, my head, my hand? Is this stone member

mine? This archaic torso? Fallen are the Parthenon's heroes, the heathen idols, crumbs all, pillaged to the winds, shelves full of feet, left, right, nostrils, elbows. Only God can piece them together. This is not my calf, these are not my testicles, those breasts would do me proud. Though most have been enlarged with styrofoam. Cracks galore. I am puzzled: Have I always lived in a warehouse of antiquities?

I have been here at least once before. How could it be otherwise? My mother was a teacher and made it a point of driving the barbarian out of me. Rocococococo, I say, stroking my stylized hair. Circumstances permitting, of course. Provided there is a hand, for instance, and hair. Stone curls encrusted with pigeon droppings fall into my eternally open eyes. Yet I cannot see down to my feet. I am as stiff as after a shot in the neck. It comes from all that sitting. Not that I need my feet. I distribute my superfluous limbs to the needy of this world. Though I would not mind retrieving my hands. I need to work. I work a great deal. That alone, I realize, does not (by far) make an honest man of me; I have simply grown accustomed to mentioning it. Nor do I presume that it has any significance here, now. What does?

There are windows, but they are not for seeing through. They are too high up under the ceiling and the lower half is always frosted. They have no handles either, of course: it is the janitor's duty to remove them; the first thing he does every morning is to take off the window handles. They weigh down his pockets, they clink, they dig into his thighs, he can barely lift his legs, yet he can duck behind a door in no time flat before you can ask him anything. All that remains is the chirping neon light on the ceiling and us. My next-door neighbor is a Hermes binding his sandal. Now I ask you.

A certain time passes. Nothing happens, nothing moves. That we must tolerate their observing us for centuries is not out of the question. Sweet little boys on a school trip, gnawing on their pencil ends, making small sketches in large pads, taking notes they cannot later decipher and, all too soon, rustling out in their oversized clothes as I look longingly after them. Gone, they are gone. Back to styrofoam and stone.

Later night falls, and I come to life as in fairy tales and go along the row of Apollonian youths and maidens. I use *go* in its broadest sense. *It* goes. Darker and colder. My teeth chatter. They are strewn about everywhere, small yellowish stones with black dots. Skinny old women play dice with them. This one here is my mother. Haven't seen her in ages. You look older. You too.

Her head is round; she backcombs her hair, the style of her youth. Taken in by that fox of a Magyar she was. It was the way he walked that got to me, and his voice. He could disguise it better than anyone I've ever known; he could be a little girl telling the man from the gas company through the door that her parents had told her never to open for a stranger. Not that we couldn't afford to pay the bill, but did we laugh! And that's how it was with everything, and it was just the time for it, but then, but then.

The names of the other two were Granny and Vesna. They are the same age and have the same white dresses and white rococo hairdos kept in place by yellow plastic combs. They are sitting in a white room at a white table; two are throwing dice, the third is knitting. The wool is yellowish.

This is a nice little shirt for you.

They warm their souls on things like these. Which is understandable: it is freezing cold here.

Thanks, I say, but it's too small for me. It will hardly cover my hand.

Don't worry, my boy.

They laugh: Don't worry.

The wool my mother is using is dirty. It has black, oily sludge in it, as if she had fished it out of the river. All kinds of muck gets caught in the stones under the bridge. It stinks. I don't want to be clad in muck. In the end I won't have any choice, of course. Be polite. Wear a nettle shirt on Christmas Eve. Pustules sprouting underneath. Sleep in a bed of thorns. Stop scratching. We're eating. It's disgusting.

Complaints, nothing but complaints! You don't seem to understand the situation, dear. We should be happy the building doesn't fall on our heads. The raccoons go in and out. To say nothing of the wind. We stop up the holes in the walls with oil cans from the relief agencies. Later, when they're empty, we use them for planting tomatoes and hauling water, which is on between seven and nine A.M. only. That's what we're up against. It's like living in a camp.

It *is* a camp. For widows like us.

I bear no grudges. I'm just glad to be alive. At my age that's enough.

And there are little things to take pleasure in.

Right. We take pleasure in the little things.

Sometimes we sit facing the sea.

There is no sea here, I point out.

They do not respond. Mother knits. The other two shake the dice cup.

I don't particularly like these women. I hope they don't notice. I hope they die soon. You are guilty even when you are innocent.

They laugh forgivingly, though a bit unnaturally. That is because they have to pretend they did not hear these thoughts. But they did. They know everything. No matter how well-behaved you are, they throw your teeth on the table.

Instead of kissing her hand three times a day. After all she's done for you.

Further proof that it's wrong. Children are not innocent.

I'm no child.

No, quite a tall man.

That is and remains incomprehensible to a mother: the body that has become. I was in labor twenty-four hours. Or was it five days? Did I die of exhaustion when it was over? I don't remember. It's so long ago. My son is an old man.

I'm thirty-three.

No one responds. Either yes or no. Maybe they're right and I've grown old without noticing it. I wish I had a mirror, even a piece of one. But: nothing. It's possible the poison has made me old. Does that mean I have a right to stay here? Is that what I'm supposed to acknowledge? Hey, may I stay here now?

To be honest, I have no desire to stay here. Though who knows what's outside. The glass is frosted. Is there black rubble or are there majolica monuments sparkling in the sun? What does the silence mean? That man has left the earth or that he has reached a stage in which his life in the cities is as soft as a whisper. Maybe the smell outside is poisonous, or the odorless atom, or maybe it smells the way it hasn't for ages or never did: of pure ether. Or maybe it's the great ocean outside, as they all say, the ocean whose banks we sit on when we're old, sunning our faces and taking in the roar on an endless row of benches. Maybe that is eternity and this is where time makes its accustomed rounds. Though maybe that is nothing as well. Finding out for sure involves too great a risk. Though it is a risk I will eventually take. I will open the window, cast an infinitely short glance at the nothing, and become part of it. Someone will carefully close the window behind me. With a broomstick.

I back unobtrusively into the vicinity of the window to test the terrain. Not surprisingly, there is no handle: it is not so easy to open the window to the nothing. Or to the something. One cannot tell which. The windows to the outside are tight and tightly shut, while the inside doors hang crooked on their hinges. Now you can see the desolation of the second world. Instead of trying to repair the out of order, they make it all the more out of order. It stinks to high heaven. As if the air were full of poison spores. I am afraid to breathe.

The old women give a satisfied sniff: lunch is on the way. We skip lunch because we're watching our weight. Or because there is none. Oh well, no lunch. But there's always breakfast. And at night we have biscuits and tea. Sweet tea with lemon and tiny yellow worms in glasses: the cellar is full of them. Luckily it can't damage our teeth anymore. Afternoons are the hardest: I'm most hungry between four and ten. I fall asleep with a smile, because I know that in the morning my hunger will have gone down. In the morning death is an infant.

All that is very well, says Grandmother, but the question is: What do we do with him? Now that he's here. Unannounced. Not very considerate, I must say.

But it's offset by the fact that we get to see him after so long.

Nonetheless, it would have been good to know how long he intends to stay. I don't know if we can afford it. The food a man like that consumes. If I were in his shoes, I'd think about easing my family's burden. Maybe he can find something in the canteen garbage next to the telegraph office. Apples baked in ashes are a delicacy.

I'd be perfectly happy to have a look, but I don't know where the telegraph office and the canteen are, so I make believe I haven't heard.

We can't afford him, Grandmother says. A tall man like that. We've done very well without men up to now. We're like sisters. It's better not to have men here.

But if we reject him, he could die. (Good old Vesna.)

They say nothing for a time. I try to make myself as small as possible: I sit hunched over on a wooden stool. Hard wood, hard bones. For the length of the visit I try to be a nice, solid person who respects his elders and is discreetly devoted to his wife, without indicating a sexual proclivity, ambiguous or unambiguous, for the former, let alone prepubescent stepchildren. This is meant to produce a fully integrated impression: our values have been more than accepted; they have become flesh and blood. Fortunately there are no mind-readers among them.

He was never examined.

An exhaustive file is set up for each new arrival. There are no exceptions. Typical ailments include impotence, dehydration, depression, and heart and stomach disorders. You're in for it if you get cancer along the way. The cure is an iffy business. Though it's never too late for an examination. The question is, who does it?

It always comes down to us in the end.

How could it be otherwise? We're the only ones here.

He's your son.

When I call forth the milky scent of his belly just above the pubic hair, when I summon the scent between his shoulder blades, the scent of his neck, of his nipples, of his elbows and hands, my head starts to spin and my mouth fills with water.

That is a normal reaction. It can even be pleasant.

Yes, pleasant it is. What bothers me, though, is that no matter what I do I can't get my fingers warm. I rub my fingertips till they're ready to come off and to no avail. I don't want him to jerk every time I touch him as if I were applying current.

It's only a weak current.

Still.

It may even help him. A weak current leads to desensitization.

Yes, but only if applied by infusion. Shocks are passé.

Has the current been restored?

I don't trust it in general, says Vesna. The patient is said to be cured, but he's a completely different person.

What's so bad about that? I'd have been glad for the opportunity. (Granny)

I did what I could. I always tried to shield him from harmful influences.

Then you should have been consistent and raised him as a girl, starting with our wonderfully comfortable ladies underwear. Now he's neither fish nor fowl.

All the more reason to skip the physical and go straight to the EEG and the autopsy. To measuring the brain and the organs. That's very interesting. The bodily juices will be weighed separately. Grams of bile, number of cells. He weighed no more than 1,375 grams at birth.

That's not true.

How do you know? asked Granny rudely. I'll just have to keep my mouth shut.

Don't talk about these things in front of the child, says Vesna. It will only frighten him.

I'm not so much frightened, I say, as paralyzed. I feel I'm all head, a brain with a forehead drenched in sweat. And so I'm forced to wander, wander against my will.

Poor boy. He's running a fever.

Wrap him in a wet sheet and smack his behind. I guarantee the results. But don't forget to remove the sheet or he'll catch cold and die. What would people say then?

Maybe this is a good time to tell Granny here to shut her sadistic trap.

Pour ice water on his neck until he has inflammation of the brain membrane.

Will you shut your sadistic trap, damn it!

The brain swells and presses against the skull.

Naaaaaaaaaaaaaaaaaaaaaaiiiiiiiiiiiiiii . . . !

The force of the scream finally pushes me away from them, and I start screaming too, screaming as I've never screamed before and as long as I can. I shut my eyes, so I can no longer see them. I can still hear the dice rolling in the cup, but the sound grows weaker until at a certain point it stops entirely, and I stop and let myself be pushed along by the momentum.

Much later I cautiously open my eyes. It is dark again, which is good. I glide through a windowless hallway. I still don't know whether I have a body and how it is made. I fortunately managed to avoid the examination. I don't remember the last time a doctor examined me. Am I afraid of injections? Can I stand the sight of blood? To be honest, things are not so bad. For the first time in ages I feel no pain.

I keep floating along, but the hallway grows more and more narrow and up ahead, at the iron door, it seemingly comes to an end. I try to spread something like my arms and use the walls to break my progress but am whisked through the door into greater darkness.

It seems like water, but it isn't. It has white things popping up in it: stones, metals, bones. Part of a harrow. I don't know how I know that. Have I ever seen a harrow? A dog's collar. A red jug, its enamel chipped. And once more: statues. Feet and knees, mostly. A knee goes round the world. A mutilated penis.

Now I know what it is: it is the earth under the city. No panic, Houdini. It just makes the matter around you porous and stuffs your mouth. You can die from it, as you can die from ingesting lava. We'll be highly disciplined about it: take our time, refrain from coughing, talking. The slightest noise plays into the enemy's hands. Try to find a way up. Then follow it. But first take these coins, lying amidst the crumbs at arm's length; scratch them over with your fingernails. Then you'll have them when you need them! You'll be glad you pocketed them. Never leave even superannuated money. My father couldn't hold on to money. It comes on its own to me. I'm good at keeping it too. I've never been broke, at least.

Now I see where to go: I see the light of the old beer cellar up ahead. The place where we had our graduation party, remember? Two corners down they'd broken two windows, but I didn't know

DAY IN DAY OUT 363

it at the time. Will you all be there again? My heart is pounding as I enter.

It's different from what I had expected. No rustic medieval vault, just an ordinary club with posters and oil paintings on the walls. My father is sitting under the disco ball in his white wedding suit, the vest showing his trim torso off nicely. He is the entertainment: he wears a white carnation in his buttonhole and plays the synthesizer. So that's what you've been doing all these years.

Your father, my boy, said my mother, is a dubious character. You'd think he was still a bachelor the way he prowls the streets at night meeting other dubious characters he supposedly shares secrets with and we supposedly have no knowledge of. They love him; they know everything there is to know about him; they call out to him, all palsy-walsy, Hey Andor, that your son?

What do you know! My son is here. My son has come. My wife threw away all the pictures, so I've got nothing to go by, and still I recognize him. He's the spitting image of me, though he looks a little older than I did when I was forty and we saw each other for the last time. He dresses in black lettuce leaves, his head sticking out of the top like a gloomy radish. His face is consumed with lust, cracked with despair; the furrows in his forehead are clogged with ash-gray earth. His eyes are a bloody net and his tear pits! Why, they're like lizard bellies, no, really. And the trembling jaw that gets worse and worse and threatens to roll away like an old skate. Hey there, my boy, tell me how you're doing before you burst into tears. Want a drink?

I didn't answer. I can't get over how easy it was to find him. My head is spinning. I feel moldy milk in my throat. A drink would hit the spot.

But my father can't get one for me: he's playing his synthesizer, all white and shiny in the spotlight and surrounded by glitter. It is very hot where he's sitting.

Well? he asks in his chatty way. How's life been treating you? Are you married? Am I a grandfather? Or are you a lone wolf like me?

To be honest, Father, I'm gay, I tell him at our first meeting in twenty years. I meet boys in a nightclub or on the street. Once I asked one of them to stay with me for twenty-four hours. He stayed with me for twenty-four hours. He put his head on my shoulder and stayed that way. The sun went round the earth. I didn't know if he was awake or asleep. When the day was up, to the minute, he stood, went through my clothes, and took what he wanted. All my money, down to the last cent. He glanced at my passport picture and name and gave me a look of amusement. Then he left. I've never told this to anyone.

I see, says my father. Impotence has become a national epidemic. I understand, my boy. I understand all too well. I did what most men do, especially the thinking variety: I married to have children. A son. You.

I can't say you overexerted yourself on our behalf.

I just couldn't show it. And what could I have done? It was impossible to talk to those people. They had old hates and new hates—anyone was fair game. I'll kill any man over eighteen who crosses this bridge—those were their words.

As far as I remember, that began after you left.

He had nothing to say to that. He knew I was right. But he's not the kind to justify himself. He hopes time will take care of things. Five minutes is enough for him; five minutes, that's it.

If you've come to see me just to lay a guilt trip on me, you can save your breath.

First of all I haven't *come to see you*, and then I'm thirsty. Is that the toilet door behind you? How I'd like to drink some water from the tap, get to know somebody.

One thing I'll say for you, my boy, says the father speaking for the first time like a father, one thing: you've made it on your own all these years, without kith or kin. I admire you for that. It was never an issue for me. Fighting depression is never an issue unless you know what's involved. And you know what's involved only if you've been depressed yourself. Either you are or you're not, and then you know—or don't. If you, one, claim to know what it is and, two, claim never to have been it, you're lying. The way I've just lied. I've been at least once on the front steps of that something, and I'll never forget it: it was on the twelfth of June 19—.

Yes, I said. I remember. The summer holiday was beginning.

You left us without a word. You've been here ever since. A person nobody talks about. Playing the piano. Pop songs. "Yes, We Have No Bananas." Once you stood in for somebody. Until then I didn't know you played the piano. Maybe you only made believe. Later you switched to synthesizer. You traveled all over Europe to clubs where workers from home got together. You wore a white suit, stretched a leg out to the audience between the synthesizer's rickety knock-knees, and tapped your foot. You wore white slippers and mustard-colored socks. The socks curled down over your ankles. You left the camera in the bus, so the pictures of us in the quarry were lost, the two of us in the vast, gray space against a dark background. Mira got rid of all the other pictures. After a while I could scarcely remember your face, but I'll never forget that ankle: my father's ankle on the scale of a monumental statue moving up and down with the tapping foot.

He smiles as he plays his schmaltz. Good music makes good minds. My father's songs made my father. On and on he plays, completely oblivious to what I am telling him. Seeing his son for the first time in twenty years after leaving him behind in a city where a war later broke out and never having tried to learn whether we were alive. If I were a good son, I'd punch you in the nose. No guilt trip. Just a fist to the place where the nose, my nose, begins between my violet eyes. Drive your nasal bone straight into your craven brain. I could do it even though—it bears saying—I don't hate you. At a certain point—we were halfway through: it was after the fifth or sixth woman—I realized I had started to ride with you. Somebody was practicing the synthesizer—making a lot of mistakes—in the back room of a club, and my heart started pounding because I thought we had found you. That's when I realized I was hoping we wouldn't find you. Children are so just and unjust.

Father laughs and plays "Rosamunde." That's nice of you, son. Though nobody with hands of chalk can break anybody's nose.

???

You've got beautiful hands if I may say so as a man. Piano fingers. And the stick-to-it-iveness to go with them.

What's that you're mumbling?

Watch out with that What's that you're mumbling, son. You don't want to get on the wrong side of me. Stick to nice quiet games with those chalk hands or they'll crumble into nothing. Under the piano bench, on the podium, in the dusty streets. He obviously can't use them to punch his father. It would be like makeup on my face. Gone at the nearest sink.

Oh, I say. So that's how it is.

Yes, he says. That's how it is.

We stop talking. Piano music.

Am I right in assuming there's nothing for me to do here?

Nothing whatsoever, son. But stay a while, listen to the music, have something to drink.

He plays something; I listen. Father and son.

I'll be going now.

He smiles and plays. I turn my eyes away.

Either that or the revolving stage he is sitting on rotates away, and behold! my eyes open wide and I see that this cave was merely a small place amongst many, a tiny isolation cell. All around, endless paths open up in a distorted 360-degree panorama. You can choose. If I walked for a long time, I'd pass through a street that got darker and darker until I came to some pigsties. Then to a brothel. That would be worth considering. The wise man follows the path of least resistance. It would be a quick solution at this juncture. Though I don't know if speed means anything here. Is my time more limited than usual or on the contrary: have I come to the forecourt of eternity? Some of the paths are quite narrow at first glance, too narrow to let a whole man through. A magnetic card at least, but unfortunately I haven't got one: my wallet was stolen recently and with it went my library card, but that doesn't matter anymore because the relevant slits open automatically as you come up to them. They reveal shady districts reputed to be dangerous, unchanged since Ur and Babylon; I feel most at home there. I inherited my eyes and insomnia from my father, so like him I have always lived two lives: I worked by day and walked by night, visiting clubs. And yet my background is completely different: the provincial middle class, if you please. It's a wonder I even know there are two kinds of people. The menwomen laid siege to heaven, etc. Our punishment is that we are now chopped up like clods of earth. I was lucky at first: I met my other half when I was only twelve. Unfortunately, as is so often the case with child stars, the success formula did not survive into maturity, but where the red plush goes up to the ankles it is nearly as good as it was when the salty slush froze our coarsely made shoes, our cheap socks, our toes, and we walked on and on. If die I must, then I would it were here. I could use a little relief about now, but I have the feeling I must take care of something first. Meet my wife probably. You've got to meet your wife now and then, regularly or not: it's required by law. *At home*, mostly, for dinner, so my smell will linger; less often at a café. Then we talk; then our un-common son tells us what we did all week: geography, biology, mathematics, humanities. I say little, for my part. That's because I don't do much. I have no objection to that. It's sometimes the most honest thing to do. That's what I think. Nothing. Or, rather, not entirely nothing: nothing is nothing. I am fed, but I also feed myself and organize the rhythm of my days and nights.

Stop talking, says Bora. She is standing barefoot on a threshold. The zipper of her raw-silk dress is torn under the armpit; her strong white arms are making beckoning movements. Get over here. We're all waiting for you.

Who is *we*?

She points to a gigantic table set with silver and damask. We are: Anna, Olga, Marica, Katharina, Esther, Tímea, Natalia, Beatrix, Nikolett, Daphne, Aida, and myself. Twelve women of various ages. The youngest is naturally the one who committed suicide. Her name is Esther. You're number thirteen.

Is it okay to be the thirteenth?

Everything's okay in paradise, says Aida. Black hair, white skin, voluptuous red lips, looking provocative, good enough to eat.

In this case paradise looks like a sultry greenhouse full of tropical plants. With steamed-up glass, of course. It is the plants, the people, the food that make the steam. There is a lot of food. The women keep serving it. They alternate between sitting and serving. A dish of caviar, a sugar bowl. The next one takes it away and brings a basket of fruit in its place. Fresh from the fridge, replete with dewdrops, very picturesque.

This is the night of perfect plenitude, says Bora, who is running the meeting because of her seniority. You are our guest of honor and can eat all you like.

Thank you, I say, but I'm not the least bit hungry. To be honest, I'm not even sure I have any digestive organs left.

Don't be an asshole, says Natalia. Just do as you're told.

She yanks me into the empty chair next to her. There are other empty chairs around the table, one between each two women.

You've sat in each of these chairs at least once.

I see, I say. Is that how it is in paradise?

Exactly.

If this is paradise, I say, where are the four rivers—Nohsip, Nohig, Sirgit, and Setarhpue? Where are the walls, the towers, the garden, the throne, the glass sea? No, you try to blind me with a few potted palms! I don't want to be ungrateful, I'm not ungrateful, but couldn't there at least be some open-air spaces? Other people fly over boundless meadowland; yesterday I was still wandering through the dark nooks of my room. Couldn't you at least open the ceiling? There must be some sophisticated hydraulic device. In spite of appearances to the contrary and what people say about me I would not be averse to a little beauty, in the form of nature, say, the Creation. All I need is a green meadow. I used to take walks in the park. But for various reasons that is no longer possible. Besides: what is a park? The absence of natural landscape. Just as a greenhouse is the absence of natural greenery. That is the crux of paradise. The tame animals you hear so much about—they're all on plates and trays. And the fruit that never goes bad. I bet it's made of wax.

Have a bite, says Marica. Then you'll know.

But do I want to know? I lost my sense of taste ages ago. Hard, soft, wet, dry—that's all I have left. Besides, I go on in a loud voice because I feel sure of myself in this domain: No one needs to tell me about paradise; I've been a regular there for years. Eros, earthly or heavenly, can be degrading: flesh is flesh. But I know one place where it is not. It is called The Loony Bin. There the most sincere and well-mannered people in the world celebrate the demon who arbitrates between God and man. They are as beautiful and ugly, wise and ignorant as the rest of us; they just put more into it. I am the exception. I always try to seem more down-at-heel than I am. I should be ashamed of myself, but I'm not. I beg forgiveness for any unpleasantness I may cause, but all things considered there is nothing to forgive.

The women give me sad looks. Sweet, wide-eyed Nikolett breaks the silence. I can't believe he has no love in him; he simply lacks humility.

Too true, say the women.

All too true, I say.

For which he deserves to be roundly punished. (That was Anna. Her voice is deep and coarse. She is the fattest of them all.)

Though, to be honest, I don't imagine any of us is willing to do the honors. (Beatrix. Never at a loss for words. Hamster cheeks.)

And his father has unfortunately disappeared. (Katharina. Thin, careworn, a woman of few words.)

He has nothing to hold against me!

They nod in agreement: He was a bastard, God bless him. So you'll just have to look after yourself. (The mercilessly sage Olga)

Control yourself. Be civilized. Get a grip on yourself and behave like a gentleman for a few hours. (Tímea the Firm)

You can do it. (Esther the Mild)

He's got it, all right, though he keeps it well hidden, that combination of elegance and ungainliness everyone finds so appealing. (Daphne the Playful)

So please do our—correction, your duty.

But what have I been doing all this time? Is it just because I'd like to go to the club?

Nobody cares about your dirty little secret!

I hope you don't mind my saying so, but that's what makes it clear how provincial you basically are.

Even the way you suffer is provincial. One of us is in a mental institution and another is dead. I'd give that some thought if I were you.

The purpose of suffering is to overcome it, redemption in a

word. But your suffering just causes more suffering. Get thee to a monastery, Abelard!

Who said that. I stare her down, but she's not the one.

I must admit I've thought of it. A monastery, I mean. One of those nice touristy ones in the mountains. Visitors could have tours in ten languages. The frescoes of the main church exhibit a mixture of Byzantine and Western elements. The faces look closely related or the same a hundred times over but in different garments, a wonderful face with masculine, feminine, and childlike features. Actually, it is *his* face over and over. In an environment like that you don't easily forget what brought you. It's as if I were making nonstop love to him and watching his face hundreds of times over. Sometimes right next to mine, like grapes on a cluster, sometimes off in a corner. A crack runs through your nose, one cheek on one wall, the other on the other. I will never see my way to praying, but I can spend the rest of my days making love while watching his face.

Silence reigns for a while. Have I finally made a dent in them?

Your father, says Bora finally, was a remarkable lover. None of us had much experience, so we can't compare him with others, but he was remarkable for his time.

Everyone, muttering: Yes, yes.

And you? Are you married?

Yes, he is.

But he doesn't sleep with his wife.

What kind of marriage is that?

All I can say is, everybody's gay these days.

Not really, I say, but they don't let me go on; they start babbling among themselves.

I raise my voice, which is not my way, and say, Will you pipe down!

They immediately fall silent. Good. Now that I have the fruit basket before me, I will do a little experiment.

If this is paradise, I say guardedly, then wax fruit should taste like fresh fruit. Let me take a fig rather than an apple. I raise it to my lips under the attentive gaze of the guardians of paradise.

At first I feel only the wax against my teeth, but before I can get all hot and bothered—I knew it all along! Where can I throw it? I don't care what you do to me! We won't stand for your hysterics!—the taste of paradise explodes in my mouth. Applause. Close your eyes. Let yourself go. That's the way. Don't worry. A net of women's arms will catch you. Hands stroking your head, hands smelling of soap and womb, one after the other stroking your thick, shiny hair.

Would it be possible? Could we go back? Make a new start and follow a new path? Bora? Just take a damn bath and change smells. She forgot to bring a towel for the guest; he could take hers: it is old, beige, and slightly wet. Pressing his traveling clothes against his midriff, hiding his nakedness one last time, he goes barefoot through the kitchen, the door, the rug. Lies next to her. Within viewing distance of the house. A forty-year age difference. Happiness is a loose womb. What kind of sentence is that? I don't know. Let me come closer. But she is already pulling me to her; she is experienced; I slide easily into her innermost district of warmth. Her stomach reminds me of Mother, but hers is darker, harder, very hard even: I feel I'm pushing against a wooden basin. Her vagina is like a kernel. That's not fair, given it's my first attempt. I look down and lo! it really is wood, a piece of carved wood, polished, the Y of a stylized yoni chiseled in, the navel too. I knock on what is called the abdominal wall to see if it is hollow. What is it, a sarcophagus? The mummy laughs, a laugh I know. I look up and see: Tatjana's face. She is lying in the position of the lying Buddha, the shameless hussy. Only her head moves: she has put it in her hand and is laughing. Is her hair made of snakes? Woodcunt! Where is my paradise?

You probably believe in Santa Claus.

Why not, you stupid f . . . !

She laughs; I'd shrug if I could. The reason you hate me is I don't fall for your tricks: I won't put you up or put up with you for half my life. You've got to do everything for yourself, from beginning to end, and our little boy doesn't like that. Which doesn't mean I'm not willing to fuck you. Not for your sake but because I want to. Though of course I'd be doing you a favor too. It might—perhaps— make you human. I can't guarantee anything, you understand. It would certainly be nicer, for the moment it lasted, than sticking his prick in a piece of split wood and leaving it there forever. Hey, stop banging my pelvis, Abelard. You'll rip it out!

Don't call me that, you hear!

Your wife thinks she's your wife, the statue said, unmoved. She also thinks you have a secret. But you have no secret. You're dead, that's all.

At least I'm not made of wood!

No, but what are you made of? Can you tell me that?

Somewhere sirens seemed to be singing: *Au ciel tout est bien. In heaven everything is fine. Im Himmel* . . .

That sends shivers up my spine, shivers up my spine, shivers up my spine. Who will release me from this unworthy situation?

They really are gruesome, those sirens, someone says.

Omar?

Or only the wind again.

Awake. Nothing more to hear or see. The wooden virgin is gone, ditto the palms. Peace and quiet for the first time in hours. In the mountains on the way to the sea their train would pass through white walls of fog. *Between*time. It feels good. To be honest, I'm beginning to have my doubts about whether I'm up to all this. What did I have in mind? Nothing maybe. Taken in like millions of others by the legend of the positive, disinhibiting effects of drugs, dance, sexual ecstasy, and the like. And now I've got to do battle with *every last one of them*. How many more will there be? Only those I would or should meet are nowhere.

Things here look rather like my wife's favorite café. It wasn't as hard as I'd thought. That's how life is: all you have to do is stand around and hate—correction, wait and the problem will take care of itself. Usually it's right there, on hand; it has positioned itself in such a way that the moment I walk in I can't miss it. Just to make sure, it gives me a friendly wave. Not this time, though. *You are nowhere.*

Generally speaking, I find this spot strange. Many details work on their own, but don't go well together in the end. It's as if space had gone out of time. Is space older than now or time earlier than now? Warm or cold? Is there a coal-stove smell or no smell at all?

How can so many people have no smell? Because there are a lot of people: they're everywhere, all over the floor. You can hardly make your way through them. It happens more often than I'd like. Suddenly the scale is vast.

Go ahead and step on them, if you like, someone says. They're like daisies: they'll stand up again. It's not clear how late we're going to be, how long we're going to have to wait here on the siding. Let's hope nobody runs into us from behind. During the night, at full speed. What a mess that would be. All we can do now is try and make ourselves comfortable.

What? Or, rather, what have you lost here?

His name is Erik. He's the only one it can be: holding court at the head of the silly table between entrance and window he commandeers for their weekly get-togethers. The others are there too even though I can't recognize them. Say something rude and leave them like a fart. Or say nothing at all. Just leave. Like a.

I look around insofar as I can see above the heads of the people at the table. Again there seem to be corridors, paths, possibility. But now be smart and make the right choice. Far away the homeless are bedding down in the moldy grass in a black-and-white film. Bedding down and bedding and bedding down. Something's wrong. Bedding and bedding down. I'd better go. Where they're bedding down. A pity I still know nothing about moving physically forward in space under the current conditions. Man must struggle. It is only decent. Sometimes he is afraid, but that is unnecessary. Have no fear of blackwhite. It will be good there. Poorer than poor, ugly, smelly, but good. One thing is comforting: there seems to be no rush. Time is waiting for me there. Bedding and bedding down.

Cannot. Cannot budge me from the spot. Feel glued down. Silly prank. The homeless bed down in eternity, yet I cannot get to them. I am not destined to. What am I destined to? Is there no way to oppose it?

Why don't you find a nice spot for yourself? Erik's wife says kindly. Look. There's a full twenty centimeters over there on the red plush seat!

Now I am sitting there, squeezed between strange thighs.

Twenty centimeters is less than you think. If I move, that's it for my pelvis. I'm in an impossible position: I can't even move my head. I'm stuck with them. They're going on as usual, but this time it's even less comprehensible: a mutter-rug. Give me a kangaroo court any time.

Hrm, hrm. No disruptions, please. (Clearing of throats, rustling of paper.) Thank you. Everybody comfortable? Thank you. And the boys, how are they? Thank you. Shall we begin? Let us begin. Thank you.

I turn to the aforementioned boys. Are they standing in alcoves along the wall amidst pitchers and stuffed foxes, motionless for hours on end? Their heads to one side or the other? Their beautiful sandaled feet casually crossed? Flutes in their hands, at their thighs? Ah, could they but love one!

Is the idol ready? Then we can begin. Thank you. Who are you? Three giant heads, identically sculpted, with identical features, no features. What are you made of? Stone? Soap? Camel dung? Though it's all the same. I do not recognize this court. I will interpret for myself. I can trust no one. Apart from that, I know nothing. I will be unable to corner my witnesses because I know absolutely nothing. I would defend myself if I were guilty, but as it is . . . Could I please have a bulletproof booth and a microphone? I have a right to good health till the end. Most people most likely live better lives than they deserve. No really, I was just joking, everyone, just . . .

Name?

Celin des Prados.

Who is answering for me? That is not my . . .

Age?

Thirty-three.

Who . . .

Color of hair? Eyes?

Black. Blue.

Listen, that was only a . . . I just want my wife . . . A cup of coffee, a cognac, per . . .

Good. Let us begin.

Rustling. Coughing. It is very bright here. My eyes are tearing.

Plus the constant turning to see (anything). Because I can't move my head anymore. Who's making that racket? The press? Interested parties? Defendants?

Hrm. Hrm. Rustling. Sorry. Thank you. Let us begin. Is the person making the accusations present?

Here I am.

Erik.

I should have known. Objection! The man is biased! He is in love with my wife and hates me to boot. I once humiliated him, but that's not my fault. It's not my fault that he's a clueless idiot at the peak of his powers. He doesn't know a thing about me, not a blessed thing. You've got nothing against me!

Will the accused please hold his tongue! Verbal attacks directed at witnesses are unacceptable as evidence. Behave yourself! You're a grown man! And not among Hottentots, you know . . . You may proceed.

Thank you.

Thank you, judge. May I cite the deposition of witness W.? She states, I accuse A.N. of being a substance dealer. When I was not looking, he slipped a bag of poisonous mushrooms into his pocket, hoping to cover his tracks. He is a Balkan substance dealer. Just look at him.

That's a lie! My commercial interests lie exclusively in the realm of artifacts and ephebes. I sift the sand of the ruins of fallen cities. I throw the teeth away and keep only the coins. My sexual orientation is completely irrelevant.

Under the circumstances the circumstance that the offender is a kiddyfucker is of the utmost relevance, whether he exercises his predilection in word or deed or by omission.

If that's how you look at it, we are all of us guilty. (I laugh.) It's ridiculous!

Do you deny having taken part in mass rapes?

I do! We are all willing participants. Though I am not a participant at all. I am merely an observer. An observer!

That is irrelevant. In for a penny, in for a pound. It is often difficult after the fact to ascertain which individuals are to blame, in which case they are all to blame, or, if that is impossible, because there are simply too many, then an individual must bear the brunt of the guilt. The choice of the individual may well be arbitrary: witness the scapegoat phenomenon.

We'll run you out of here, you limp prick of a pervert! What do you think of that!

The person who has just spoken is sitting to the right of center, a thin man in uniform with a mustache covering his thick upper lip. I find you repellent, yet I'm glad you're alive and have found a place for yourself even if it makes a monster out of you, says this man of the center, the presumably wise and scrupulously courteous old Protestant, though he goes a bit too far and expresses gratitude for each shit-ass remark. The man on the left is a sarcastic, self-righteous bastard. Not a very original performance, but what can you do? The invisible audience laughs, of course.

Congratulations, I say with dignity. Evoking the reproductive organs is always a sure thing, albeit less than elegant.

Boos and catcalls from the gallery.

And they said, I should bite his balls off, and I bit his balls off. Is that yours too?

No.

How do your balls feel when they're swimming in somebody's mouth?

They don't swim. They're too big for that. The hair makes it like taking a bite out of a dog.

Have you ever bitten a dog?

No. Nor the opposite.

Are you afraid of dogs?

Is that relevant?

Please record that the defendant, also called the idol, refused to answer the question. Thank you.

The truth is . . .

Yes? Go on. We're listening. Thank you.

The truth is . . .

Yes?

The . . .

Yes?

You must formulate it differently, my bodyguard whispered. He is my former professor, mentor, and predecessor. He is dressed as a postman. So you're here too.

Thank you, I whispered.

What was that?

I merely said thank you.

May we proceed? Thank you.

Well, what I meant to say was, I did not torture, I *was* tortured.

Mumbling in the front rows.

Proceed. Thank you.

At first they only talked, but then a few of them came and beat me. They kicked me in the shins the way my mother did the last time, when she was too small to reach my face. But I don't care. I've stopped limping. It's the principle of the thing.

Were you frequently the subject of such sadomasochistic treatment?

Fairly frequently.

Did it afford you pleasure? More than other practices?

It was what was available.

So you took only what was available.

You might put it that way.

How else?

Excuse me?

You said, You might put it that way. How else might one put it?

Please strike *put it that way* from the record and substitute *say so*.

Done. Thank you.

Perhaps we can take a short break and follow it with a long leap. Thank you.

Excuse me? Could I perhaps—as long as we are taking a break; how long will the break last?—have something to drink? My mouth is dry. Another problem: I don't know where my sacroiliac is, but my back is killing me! My tailbone is caught in my neck. Excuse me! You there!

No response.

Cigarette?

No, thank you, avuncular friend and jovial bodyguard.

Now he looks more like my father-in-lieu—correction, father-in-law. No cigarette. Some water would be nice. Schnapps. Heroin. Mushroom stew.

Strange, says my bodyguard, how often it happens.

I don't mean to ask, but do so anyway: What?

That capital offenders have so few small vices.

I have no response.

Apart from sex, of course. It's a good way of nabbing them.

I've noticed that as well. The trial has become highly sexualized.

What did you expect? It's all about coupling and war.

I must agree.

We are silent for a while. The standard rustling and coughing continues around us. Finally I say, It would be nice if my wife could be here.

You have no wife.

Yes, I have. I am married.

That doesn't count. *I* am married. Have been these forty years. Not ideal, perhaps, but it counts.

I feel like giving my wife long French kisses, I tell him. A youngster may have a powerful flick of the tongue, but I have the advantage of being much bigger. I can practically take her into my mouth, store her in my cheek like a stolen crocodile tooth.

He says nothing for a while. Have I gone too far? She's his daughter, after all.

Fine, he says. What is her name?

I don't know just now. I have even forgotten my own name.

Impossible. You know it very well.

No.

Yes, you do. You know what's outside too.

What is that supposed to mean? I pretend I didn't hear it. Fortunately things start up again.

Could somebody please put out new ashtrays? Thank you.

Excuse me. May I say something before we proceed?

You may.

Well, what I want to say is that I'm a little man. A little man. I've done nothing but work for the last ten years, words rolling past like panels on a conveyor belt. My job. All I cared about was working as efficiently as possible and keeping alive. Nothing more.

Can you omit the *Nothing more* in future? Thank you.

I did my job.

What did you do?

I've my . . .

Yes, yes, but what did the job consist of? Can you go into detail?

I taught languages and translated and interpreted.

Was it regular work?

Pretty regular. Pretty much every day.

So it might be called your profession.

Yes.

Did you have an employer?

No. I freelanced. I've freelanced all my life.

Am I correct to assume you have never had a valid work permit? You have never paid a penny's worth of taxes, correct?

My income was too low.

I bet it was.

I never had health insurance.

Do you have health problems?

No. Yes. I don't know.

Have you ever been diagnosed with schizophrenia, paranoia, manic depression, or dementia?

Pardon?

Have you ever been diagnosed with schizophrenia, paranoia, manic depression, or dementia?

That's my own business.

YES or NO!

No. Not diagnosed.

Occasional dizziness? Sexual ailments? AIDS?

I fail to see how that . . .

Tropical diseases?

No, damn it! I've been to no more than ten or twelve places in my whole life. All in temperate zones. Meadows, furtive fields.

Did you say *furtive* fields?

Fertile, furtive. One of the two.

Do you suffer from dyslexia? Are you prone to slips of the pen?

(Laughing:) Oh yes. I make them practically every day.

Please record that the idol . . .

That is not my . . . !

. . . has demonstrated a heretofore unnoticed tendency that is commonly referred to as sarcasm.

(Giggling:) Do you mean camsarc?

Wipe that smile off your face, shithead!

Well, I can proffer several explanations. I have a file in the Institute for Linguistic Research that is as long as I am tall.

My, my! How impressive!

Laughter in the courtroom.

Now I've lost my train of thought.

Your work.

Yes, thank you. I translated stories. Heart-rending and funny, gripping and droll, sentimental and skeptical. Human stories, children's stories, animal stories. Faith, hope, charity. That kind of thing.

The courtroom is suddenly still. I can feel I'm doing well. I proceed. My voice takes on a lilting, sonorous quality, melodious and masculine: Once there was a couple very much in love, but hours would go by before one could understand a single word of the other. She was deaf and dumb, he a spastic. Their names were Ling and Bo, and they lived together in a home for . . .

Giggling from the sidelines. The boys?

Blahblahblah, says the man on the left. A tragic fate! Realistically portrayed! Plays on the fartstrings. What kind of crap are you feeding us? Think it'll get you off the hook?

Cries from the gallery: Down with stories! Down with lies and kitsch!

My face very white behind the glass, my voice distorted with emotion: The world as word! My only comfort! Why can't you understand that? (Whining:) It's unfair.

The leftist, blasé: Laying it on thick, aren't you. Who do you think you are?

Good-for-nothing! Doom-monger! (Shouts from the gallery.)

The leftist, sardonic: Hustling like an ant, aren't we. A dinky, harmless creature. What can I tell you? I've done nothing but work for the last ten years. Wouldn't hurt a fly. And the cobweb in your hand? A pathetic hairnet your life is caught up in. The best thing you could do is squash it into something more effective. Applause in the courtroom.

I too would bow if I were physically up to it. One thing I can say for your jealousy, I tell Erik. I lower my voice and aim my words directly at him: it's a private matter, between him and me. One thing I can say for your jealousy. For someone as thick-skulled as you it provided a few good similes. Which doesn't make it any less of a torment to be within range of you. Especially now. I've done nothing to deserve it.

The applause diminishes.

Okay, says the man in the center. Time for a break. Thank you.

Listen, I say, could we possibly speed things up? I know it's not done to speak of the body, but I'm worried about the consequences of days of sleep deprivation. I could as easily wet my pants as suffer dehydration: you can never tell when your body is going to betray you, and you can understand I wish to avoid that. But apart from personal matters I consider it my duty to point out that this is basically a self-perpetuating mechanism: we could go on forever, which process, apart from being deadly dull, would end in a perfectly predictable, never-changing result: nothing. That's right, all this will end in NOTHING because you bigwigs are incapable of and will always be incapable of returning a verdict. Either you lack what it takes or it's just plain impossible.

You are wrong: it is possible; we have got what it takes. This is one of those things that work whether you believe in them or not. For all the doubts one may have about the legitimacy and methods of this court one must not lose sight of its deep, humanitarian goal, that of creating a worthy precedent. As for the tedium involved, we can only concur: you bore us. You advance not a jot, you run around in circles, you keep missing the essential, though, if you will allow me a personal observation, I cannot help thinking you are deliberately making yourself out to be duller than you are, and that alone is grounds for a few hefty clouts. Still, I'm not your grandmother, thank God. All I can say is that you are like a centrifuge: your bits and pieces stick to the sides, while your middle is empty. You are right: we have had enough of this, and don't try to tell me it was something *back there* that caused the split. That counts as an excuse for only the first three years, which is how long we allow for homesickness. After that we declare that all self-tormenting adherence to the God knows anything-but-glorious past must give way to integration and thus the future. In your case, therefore, all excuses are long since invalid. The time has come for us to bring our deliberations to an end, whether you like it or not. Has anyone in the courtroom anything to add to the charges?

Konstantin: His head the size of an apple. (In a faltering falsetto:) He willfully refused to lend me money!

That is an important point. Thank you.

First, it is untrue, and second, I needed the money myself. Does the judge have the authority to remove this gentleman and his demagogic rhetoric from the court?

Boos from the gallery.

Before I wring his neck, let me add.

Whispering and whistling from the gallery.

Aha! Now we're getting there!

I don't know what you're talking about, I say rudely.

I bet you don't!

Well, I don't. Haven't a clue. I'm a mild-mannered man. I have no desire to pick a quarrel with the authorities. I am obedient to the point of servility. I show my papers the moment they're requested. I answer all questions politely, to the point, and with what would seem to be absolute honesty.

Blahblahblah. We know that. An unblemished record—except for matters sexual.

There we go again. I laugh uneasily. You are trying to throw me off with your casuistic chains of causality. You are violating juridical norms. I may be ignorant about most things, but language I understand, and I know when I am being made an ass of. All things being equal, I would leave now. Simply leave. Elegantly, without a word. Unfortunately that is at present physically impossible: although I appear to have a body for the time being, someone else has power over it. I might as well be in a cage, like a dangerous animal. I cannot therefore defend myself. That is unfair. Unfair, I repeat. That is not what we were promised! That is not what we were promised!!!

Hrm. Well, I . . . (Rustling.) I think . . . Hrm.

How is it, I break in, how is it there is no one to speak *for* me. I demand my own witnesses! I too, improbable as it may seem, I too have friends. Real men, in part. I like to watch them at work. My mouth goes dry at the sight of the veins straining under their arms. Unfortunately they hate me. Though who knows. It's not love, in any case. Is that significant, now or ever? But the woman who is with you or with whom you are, my godmother, she will speak for me. The same holds for my wife and my stepson. Unfortunately I have a bad conscience when it comes to the aforementioned. I have partially forgotten why. But is there such a thing as forgiveness or is there not?

Silence. We wait.

Or is there not? I say.

Nothing.

Erik sighs.

Is it my mother-in-law? says the man in the middle. I think that would explain everything. We are coming to the verdict. The verdict was placed in a sealed envelope before the trial began. May I have the envelope? Thank you.

Agitated fumbling in an invisible room. The tensely awaited ceremony is imminent. Funny. Only now, at the end of it all, has my heart begun to pound. I feel like begging for a few more hours. A few more hours of this torment! Excuse me, but I . . . Excuse me! I have something to say! And say it I will. You can turn the mike away from me, but it doesn't matter. It's all one big sham, the lot of it: the booth, the mike. There is no way you can turn my voice off once I start talking. I want, I want . . .

Well?

All the charges against me are false! I have done nothing!

We know.

Then what do you want of me?

All right, then. Let's forget all the rest. Just answer the following four questions: Were you smart? Were you fair? Were you brave? Did you strike the proper balance?

No.

No.

No.

No.

Who is answering for me?

What do you expect then?

Long silence.

With dignity: *As thou art neither cold nor hot but lukewarm, we shall spit thee out of our mouths.* Before reading the verdict, we wish to make the following statement: Crime begins in the imagination and is as such an integral part of our humanity. But that does not excuse . . . I refuse to tolerate the diabolical grin of the accused! What is there to laugh about?

You cannot execute me.

Is that so? And why not?

I am a virgin! (Screaming:) I have *preserved my purity* for the one and only one *groom*!

The bigwigs confer. I laugh.

Finally the man in the middle says, We cannot reach unanimity as to the relevance of this claim, which we cannot verify. Granted, there was a time when it was assumed the devil could not inhabit a virgin—a sore point for the entire Joan of Arc incident—and therefore, just to be sure, we are returning a verdict of: mass rape.

Voices, chairs moving back, patches of applause, tongue clicks. The voice of the usher over the loudspeaker: Form a line, please. Boys first.

I am a bit fearful, but I can't help feeling expectant as well. What will the boys do with me? Will I feel anything, or is my behind, like every other part of me, made of chalk and plaster?

Shut your trap! says a fat, red-haired lad I have seen before. First we'll read out the torture procedures. We've classified them according to countries or, rather, culture, but naturally there is a great deal of overlap. The Chinese cut your nose off. The Mongols prefer to skin you alive. In Spain the practices are called the bathtub, the sack, the wheel, and the operating room, while the grill, the B-telephone, and the barbed stick are known the world over. Electric current, water, plastic bags, truncheons, excrement, and motor oil all have their place, as do contorted body positions and assorted bindings. Hanging upside-down leads, in the minds of most peoples, to enlightenment. The excision of body parts is practicable in individual cases. Nothing life-threatening: a finger, an ear, a tongue, you dirty thief, you ungodly preacher, you maligner of all we hold dear. Wiring lips closed is another traditional possibility. Think of all the problems it would solve. Be honest. By severely limiting food intake, it minimizes waste products and thereby the danger of self-soiling. Not that you need to worry about your clothes: you'll be naked for most of it. Will you look at that shriveled-up little cock!

All right, I say. I choose the boys.

Shut your trap! We're not through yet! Even as we read, new techniques are being discovered. We're always behind the times. We can't go back to a point we've passed—you must know that—so get those sweet boys out of your head. We must move forward, and when if not now. You were never thought of as a sacrifice. You will do it all yourself. Scientific studies show that ten percent of mankind derives pleasure from inflicting pain. Everyone here, friends and strangers—they're all yours, yours to do as you will with them.

Janda's face is like a pincushion; he is squatting, hunched over, in the corner; his gums are bleeding.

You can fuck him if you like. Just keep away from his mouth. His teeth are the teeth of a rusty saw. His bones are sticking out, but his intestines are soft—they dry last—so he can hold out for another ten days or so.

You know what? I say (my voice quivering against my will). You can fuck *yourselves*, that's what!

So you don't want to come clean, cast off your impotence, and feel the glorious power that comes of moving beyond yourself?

No!

What else are you good for, you lowest of the low! You deserter! You virgin! You traitor!

And proud of it! I say. And once more, roaring this time, ready to carry on for centuries, I cried: PrO-OWOWOWOWOWO WOWOWOWOWOWOWOWOWOWOWOWOWOWOWOWOWOWOW OWOWOWOWOWOWOWOWOWOWOWOWOWOWOWOWOWOWO WOWOW . . .

You stupid fool! Screaming is part of the deal.

I don't care, I say, screaming on: PrOWOWOWOWOWOWOWO WOWOWOWOWOWOWOWOWOWOWOWOWOWOWd. Come on and stop me. Stop up my mouth! Kill me!

No sooner had I thought that last thought than they were gone and I was lying on the ground. That is, I think I'm lying and I think it's the ground. No one says—because I do not say—another word. I am alone once more in the barren sand of Agirmoru Put. The peace and quiet feels good. More than ever I feel a need for solitude. I cover my face. Much time passes.

Later I open my eyes or had them open the whole time. I seem to be alive. What right have I acquired thereby? I have acquired the right to linger in gray ruins. They look as though they had had smallpox. Swallows' nests. I could crush them with one hand. It does not look as it should, yet I know what it is. Does it still have the equestrian statue, the pigeons, the theater, the tourist paths? Yes, no, I don't know. I can see nothing but the plague column and hear nothing whatever. I am the only one here.

Wrong. You are here. You are here too.

Have you any idea what I went through to locate you? Where I looked and how long? Under how many names? I tried everything.

Everything you could have become: priest, doctor, conciliator, or their opposite—commander. You were nowhere to be found. And now. Here you are, sitting by the road on an old milestone, a cement dustbin. Are you young as you were then or would be today, or old as you could not yet be? I can't tell. Everything about you is perfect: your clothes understated and elegant, your body in them. Be careful. Don't lean against the wall: you'll get your fine coat dirty.

How are you? As well as can be expected. I can't complain.

You just sit there, saying nothing. I dreamed I saw my father, said Grandmother, but he didn't speak. Dead people don't speak in dreams. You always used to speak. Now your lips might as well be painted on. Perhaps you're not you at all, just a doll that looks like you put out in the street as a joke. Or one of those mannequins thrown out of the shops in great numbers back then. Later they were everywhere: in dustbins, on balconies, in every conceivable position. Some were armless, legless, living their own lives. Hands reaching out of cellar entrances, impaled heads instead of road signs, torsos floating belly-up down the river.

Finally a blink. Submissive, demurring like an animal. You stand, you walk. I follow.

It is almost like the old times. Except I can't get close to you. But I don't want to. It's better this way. I can see more of you than I did then. The whole of you, from head to foot. Though from behind. But it's easier too. It's like a classical dream. We're walking through the streets. I know it's our hometown even though it looks different. Are there other people around? I don't see anybody. Alone in a deserted country. Home. It is our duty to love it. I say, To hell with it! I'm a bit hesitant to say it aloud, though nobody hears it but you. It's pleasantly eerie that everyone has vanished suddenly. Just you and me.

It's a strange role: I'm not usually the one who speaks. And yet I'd come a long way, not that it showed at first glance. I'd read a thing or two in my leisure time when it was cold out. If you asked, I could give you quite a demonstration of what people call general education. You don't ask, of course. You walk on, ignoring the intersections, both right and left. You're right: there are no alternatives; one must follow a road to its end. I hope this one has an end because to be honest I'm not partial to long marches. Why not take me home? We can slip into the warm bed in the shadow of the oil heater and read novels of outer space. Am I talking nonsense? Am I a child? Yes and yes. Take me in!

I know you're not the kind to be bargained with. You keep walking and walking. There's the old bridge. The river sometimes brings red sand down from the mountains. I've completely forgotten to mention that our town had many bridges. We used to cross them all the time. This one is the only one left. It's full of refuse: household appliances, a synthesizer, a few of the mannequins, oil canisters, buses, a pig. I don't understand how people can complain about how bad things are when they are so wasteful. Do you? . . .

Looking closely, I see you're moving rather stiffly. Has that got anything to do with your mannequin past or were you born that way? You had a weak heart and were exempt from PE. Even when I'm dying, the machines show my functions to be normal. I'm uncomfortable talking about myself, but I do wish you'd pay me some attention. I had other opportunities, you know. There are even people who find me attractive. Unfortunately, you can't really tell with the boys: I've got too much power over them. My age and all. Though true power comes from submission. I hereby submit.

We never went this far out of town, you and I. See that charred tree over there? Beautiful, isn't it. And what a funny-looking hut, all jerricans and burlap bags. Or is it a barricade? You don't find that particularly witty? Sorry. I want so much to make an impression I sometimes overshoot the mark. Though I've never had a weapon in my hands. In school they gave us pieces of metal with wooden handles for hand grenades, and the toilets stank like these camp latrines on either side of the road. Not a pleasant memory. Fortunately I haven't had anything to eat recently. I lost my appetite at some point on the way here. Though usually the first thing you pardon is native dishes.

Now I understand: you're the one who roams the rubble landscapes between the four rivers, where the roads are overrun with potholes and a reddish desert sand peeks out of the cracks in the asphalt. Oh, how I'd like to gaze up at the stars, but you make me look at my feet. My ankles hurt. My shoes are run down. There are mine warnings everywhere. We can't leave the road, succumb to the temptation of the orchards: Come, let's lie under a tree. We've got to stay here, where ragged children—are they black or just tanned a deep brown?—line the road, shoveling dust into the holes with their hands: Look at us, we're repairing! The wind blows it out again at once. The airstreams of a jeep speeding by. The most practical means of transportation in the precarious road conditions frequently encountered after military conflicts and long-term mismanagement. You can crank little slits in the side windows and stick tattered banknotes through them. The airstreams whisk them away, and there's less danger of their getting run over if they chase after them in the fields. Which they always do, shouting *pao, pao,* as they go. It's the only word they know. They call everything *pao:* bread, trees, stones, father, mother, sisters. Us too, of course. Is that my real name? *Pao?* They line the road, *pao, pao,* their arms so long they can reach out to the middle.

Here. I've found a few old coins. They may still be worth something. They're all I have. You walk in front of me and never turn; you don't see my good deed. I share my ancient inheritance with the needy of the world. I'm a little worried it won't suffice. I don't know how many coins I have: they have no weight in my pockets. I give more and more away, dropping rusty coins into tiny hands like seeds into the earth. My eyes are veiled with tears. I am not moved; I am afraid.

Then it is over: the children have disappeared and with them the road. We are back in town. The sun is going down. The muezzin is calling. It's the first time I've heard it since then. Standing in front of me and having turned at last, you lift an empty hand. I know what you want. You won't get it until you've spoken to me. One word. Just one word. I love you. I hate you. But I love you. Couldn't you say it at least once, softly—no one can hear us here—in not precisely these words: I love you too.

You just stand there, holding your hand up. If I stand here with you for the rest of time, what will you do?

I know, you hear? I *know* you loved me too. You loved only me. Me instead of God. And so much that you had to bar me from your heart. There's the truth for you, you ingrate!

You wait patiently. I have done with my insults, nor are apologies in order. You know everything about me. You are right: I won't cry. I take the last two coins from my pocket. One belongs to you.

À chacun sa part, I say, placing it in his hand.

You open your mouth. Is there a black cave beyond it? I look in, trying to conceal my horror. I do not cry, though from now on you will speak neither to me nor to anyone ever again. You take the iron wafer and for a brief moment of bliss I glimpse your tongue. The greatest joy I have ever felt suffuses my body. Eli! Eli! Eli! I gave him my flower; shortly thereafter my beloved died. I do not know how it happened: I was not there, I was not the one. He fell into a peaceful sleep—for when the heart stands still, one dies—but before he died he deflowered me. More I could not ask for.

Fine, I said at last after spending a long time by myself. Good. I will show my gratitude and speak. I will deliver a long and firmly grounded hymn to language, which is the order of the world—musical, mathematical, cosmic, ethical, social—and its most grandiose delusion. That is my field. A man can produce two hundred facial expressions to convey his feelings. An infant can generate approximately the same number of sounds. Later he learns his mother tongue and forgets the worthless residue. That is known as economy. He learns through mistakes as well as correct utterances, deriving rules from the former when corrected. That is known as: the universal linguistic instinct. *From the frying pan into the fire.* Now translation we may define as an aspect of communication, communication as an aspect of interaction, interaction as an aspect of action. Thus translation, insofar as it rests upon intention, is: action. I went into all this at length in a work I envisaged in forty volumes, but it was lost before I could complete or begin the first. These things happen. Strictly speaking, however, it is no great loss: one can read about it in numerous other works. In winter, for example, when the heating fails or one's flat is beleaguered by noisy strangers. Libraries are usually quiet and sometimes even warm. In theory I have nothing to add; in practice I have officially mastered ten languages, though I actually know many more. My native language alone gives me entrée into circa twenty-five dialects, some of which are defined as independent languages, given that a

single nuance in a single expression can evoke an entirely different world. In addition to Štokavian I speak Kajkavian, Čakavian,
and Ijekavian, and with equal fluency. I could learn the dialect
of any village in the world. Whether extant or not. (What did the
last three Livs speak among themselves? What can three remnants
speak? By the way, we may assume that they were women: women
hold out till the end. Are they to be envied for doing so? Sometimes
I say yes, sometimes no. Anyone in the world could come to me and
speak and I would understand. Even if it were utter nonsense. Gibberish invented on the spot. *Kerekökökokex*. I was granted this ability one day, with no explanation. I thought I was dying, but I did
not die; rather. Unfortunately—beware the gods bearing gifts!—it
has certain side effects. A hearing problem, for instance: in any
public space, no matter where, I perceive all speakers at the same
volume. I hear the other interpreters in their booths, all the people
in the café, the park. As a result, I often have trouble answering
their questions. There is simply too much input. Not always, but
frequently, and more often than not it comes unannounced. I am
not trying to defend myself. It simply makes no sense to keep it a
secret anymore. I have thought of going to an ear, nose, and throat
specialist, but I have no insurance for one thing, and for another
I know it would serve no purpose. I am in good physical shape: I
have a stable thorax and can produce a stable breast tone. I am a
healthy, fertile man. I say this not to boast but to dispel the various rumors about me, and doubts. Whether I am who I am or can
do the things I claim. Though do I make the claims, or has another
made them and I merely failed to refute them? And how could I
convince anyone? Once you reach the top of the ladder, you can
refer only to yourself. I could of course call upon God, who may be
said to understand all languages. How could he but otherwise? He
knows everything—past, present, and future—which is why he
holds his tongue, while I am pressed forward by my lack of knowledge. Or whatever. Ecumenical—correction, economic as well as
biological forces. Let's just say that I have had more than my share
of both good luck and bad. How can so much happen to an individual? And in a mere ten years? Some people have nothing happen to them; they want nothing more than to have nothing happen

to them. I am not one to go whaling for want of anything better; nor have I a desire to suffocate eight and a half kilometers in the air. I lack my father's adventuresome spirit or the inquisitive, probing mind of my friend and idol. Not everyone is cut out for such things. I could have lived my whole life in the same tree-lined street, a closeted homosexual teacher in the provinces, and been perfectly content. For ten years nobody has heard a peep out of me. I neither complain nor make demands, as others in my situation are wont to do; I have taken up learning instead. Having moved from a confined and stagnant childhood in the provinces of a dictatorship to the all-encompassing provisionality of the absolute freedom conferred by a life without valid papers and hence to absolute self-reliance and all that it implies, I felt that the only path open to me was to concentrate on the cultivation of my talent and assume no responsibility for the obscure remains of anything else. Today I know nearly all there is to know about the disciplines in which languages come into contact and even about those in which they do not. Something always remains in the dark. Learning more means learning more about the existence of the dark realms. Hence the care with which one must convey one's thoughts. Five thousand commonly used words per language more or less. Later my research enabled me to learn as much about my brain as a layman can. I had access to sources in all languages, but I am also a hard worker and enjoy doing my homework, so I acted as my own consultant. Did you know that the temporal lobes, where language resides and, incidentally, one experiences God, have precisely the same structure as the regions of the brain connected with aggressive behavior? Or that going berserk is a type of insanity produced by hallucinogenic mushrooms? Well, it is. Ecstatic and violent ideas go hand in hand. Fortunately we have a beautiful civilization in the frontal section of the brain. A ten- or umpteen-fold language barrier. I have myself perfectly under control. Unfortunately it leads to a marked asymmetrical left brain: I can't hold a cup or a slice of bread longer than a few seconds with my left hand, but I'm right-handed anyway. When I was young, I would think grand thoughts about the universe and suchlike; now I've practically stopped thinking altogether. I live like an amoeba, a highly resistant, economical form of life: the place I take up on the earth is no larger than the soles of my feet, the impression my body—lying, sitting—leaves on a mattress, a shoebox of a flat six flights up. And I practice peace day in day out. I support myself with poorly paid but honest work. I repeat what is said to me in one language in any other. I generally do so with my head between two other heads, which some call the ostrich position and others—stereo. Communication is the sign of the times: anyone with something to say is welcome; we speak, therefore we are. We form sounds that come together as groups, bouquets of sorts, that may constitute a word or may not, but no matter: that's what I'm there for. The most preferable shape for a table is round, alternatively, oval, because it saves room, which is not insignificant, given that all-encompassing togetherness has physical limits among others. The fact that matter needs room can lead to not-inconsiderable conflicts. The interpreter must also translate the menu: the soup is called *royal*; there are speeches beforehand; later everyone talks at once, as is their wont. No matter what they say, even if it is murder, I must repeat it, and the reprieve lasts exactly as long as it takes me to open my mouth. Has it not occurred to me that by preferring one nuance to another I could have a short-term or even long-term influence on the course of world events? By failing to close a sentence, for instance. It would be good to pronounce an ENDLESS SENTENCE, but is that not too much for an individual?

All in all: I have nothing to complain about. Not that I quite understand what it means, but most of the time I was: happy. Apart from the ruptures—I don't know, can one say: in time?—when it suddenly became intolerable, neither life nor death but a third thing man was not made for, when a flood of repulsion, of fear overcomes you and carries you off not to pain, no, not even that, but to nothingness, nothingness, nothingness, until at a certain point, like water, it slows down and passes into an *idyllic* splish-splash, and I, the flotsam and jetsam, remain behind on the shore.

Brief pause to allow me to utter the following words—which in their entirety, not one by one, are for various personal reasons *holy* to me—with the requisite space: Sometimes, I say, I am filled to the brim with love and devotion, so much so that I practically cease to be myself. My longing to see and understand them is so great that I wish to be the air between them so they can inhale me and I sink into their every cell. Then there are times I am overcome with repulsion when I see them before me, their cadaver mouths eating and drinking and talking, and everything in them turns to muck and lies and I feel that if I have to see and hear them one second more I'll give the next face I see such a drubbing that there won't be anything left when I am through with it.

Okay. Now it's out. Yes, damn it. I know what's out. What's out is that I'm not going any farther; I'm going back, taking the train back, and I'll mow down anybody who has the misfortune to get in my way. Plunder and rape are not my style. Torture doesn't do a thing for me. But I could easily, with nary a word and no hesitation, take aim and kill. Friend, foe—you name it. I would be totally unbiased. Racism, prejudice of any kind, is alien to me: man, woman, young, old—they're all the same to me. I'm a fair machine. And merciless.

I'm surrounded by gray walls, nodding like an old man.

So that's how it is, that's how it is. I long to go back. Twenty-four hours a day. At the same time I know for certain that if I did go back and saw the streets, the houses, the chestnut trees—and whether I saw the traces of the destruction or whether they were all gone—it would all be as fairy-tale perfect as it once was under the incomparably blue sky of home, and if I saw what is to be seen or what is not, all the barriers I carry around would fall on the spot, as if I'd eaten poisonous mushrooms, and I would knock it all to pieces, cursing the heavens as I went. In such a state I am capable of greater exertions than usual. I can smash the city with my fist, make the labyrinth go up in smoke. I know no other way to go about it—I'm too weak for that—but I'm strong enough to tear it down to its foundations. It may well take centuries, but it may also be over in a day. And *Blut und Boden!* I roar through it all. Blood and soil! The dog stink! The river stink! The pestilential stink of water corpses, pressed together like joints of pork in transit. Damn it all! Damn it to hell! I swing my fists—Damn it all! Damn it to hell!—but after each blow the skin on my knuckles grows back only to scrape off again. I must swing even faster so the skin can't grow back. Maybe the loss of blood will help to stop me. Or maybe the sandstone will suck me up until the whole city is sucked full and sits there quivering like blood pudding, food for the gods.

I don't know why I'm sobbing. Oh, for a roll of toilet paper. First the expense and then the infinitude it brings to mind. SHIT-FINITUDE. A grown-up man without a handkerchief. Without hands! Without a nose, damn it! It is merely the aroma of memory. The shitty aroma of shitty memory.

Until I came here, I was sad. Well, not sad. I was never nostalgic; I had no illusions. Or, rather, only one: the love of a child. It no longer matters; hasn't for ages. What I'm trying to say . . . What I'm trying to say, I say now, quite loud and clear, is that I have a new country: shame. Here and now I have practiced peace, day in day out, yes. Because it was possible. And if the price was my story, in other words, my origins, in other words, denying myself, I was more than ready to pay it. But all too often I was a barbarian. To the good and not so good. Love lived on in me only as longing. I had luck, skills, and possibilities, and while it can't be said I totally squandered them I am lost today. My shame was simply too powerful. Shame at being in the wrong place, or in the right place but the wrong person. All my strength went to that shame, from dawn till dusk and on through the night. Insistent, indescribable shame. That I come from where I come from. That what has happened happened.

Pause. Then barely audible: One day the gifted man I am lost hope. The moment hours or years later when I realized that the moment in my life when I was most myself—the moment of greatest purity and satisfaction—was the moment when I climbed through the window at the back of the theater. That and only that is true.

Very long pause. Then, softly: I'll put the coin down here. If you want it and happen past, you can pick it up. I promise not to do anything to you. I can do nothing else to relieve my pain.

No sooner had I put down the coin than I heard a bell ring. O my God, must it be? A din so painfully disturbing. The Introitus, the Kyrie, the Gradual, the Tractatus, the Sequence, the Offertory, the

Sanctus, Sanctus, Sanctus, Sanctus, God is with us, with us, with us, with us. Here they come, all of them, my succubi, dancing around me. They're carrying items for me to recognize them by: a chain saw, a hiking stick. Wanda, who is half of her brother, apple-headed Konstantin, Eka with the baby. The blond Eka is carrying a plaster angel's head under her dress and hugging her round belly so it doesn't roll out in front of the people, smash half the city, and cost a pope's throne. Then comes my wife, whose name is Mercy, dancing—a joy to behold!—cheek to cheek with my gold-turbaned godmother and singing:

> *Min bánat engele for*
> *Ki häret sillalla tur*
> *On vér qui vivír*
> *Mu kor arga kun tier*

And above it all, the bells they toll unceasing. On it drives us and on, away from our outlandish universe; we fly, light as dandelion down. Is it death definitive? How far can it drive us? Shall we plunge into the void? Is that possible? No, impossible. No, impossible. No, im . . . I will not die, damn it. Or not damn it. Little by little they overtake me; eventually I am alone once more. Weightless I float and could stay here, merely by failing to open my eyes. For the next, say, three thousand years. After that we shall see. As a child I read a lot about being a visitor from the past. Whenever I think about it, the tears gush forth beneath my closed lids. Thirteen years ago a crying got stuck inside me; now I have the feeling it is ready to pour out. Peace, peace, peace, peace.

Now: only waiting. In embryonic anxiety. Shall I tell you a story, one last story to put you to sleep or wake you up?

I know this voice. It belongs to my son. The desire to see him is stronger than shame and fear. But I keep my eyes shut: I do not wish to frighten him.

Yes, I say softly. Yes.

The name of the story is: The Three Temptations of Ilia B.

Ilia B. was a pious boy. From the day he was born he thought of nothing but God. He perceived his life only in relationship to God and cared only for Him, yet he did not care for His creations: he loved neither the heavenly bodies nor the earth nor the creatures that people it; other people did not exist for him. In short, Ilia B. was a cold bastard of an egoist incapable of love. Though affected in general by the natural and historical disaster that ravished his country, he felt no personal connection to it: Godseekers have no homeland; they find meaning only in God's house.

Later he became a doctor. As a member of a religious relief organization, he was to be found in regions of the natural and historical disaster, lancing festering fingers, performing cesarean sections without anesthesia, and treating tuberculosis with aspirin. One day a cell of his organization was arrested for missionary activities. A nun was raped to death and thrown at Ilia B.'s feet, and not even he could bring her back to life. A priest had his tongue cut out; Dr. B. had to gag him to save him. He had also had to defend himself: his chin and neck bore traces of knife wounds, which he had stanched with cobwebs and chalk. After weeks in prison, during which he provided covert daily treatment to the remaining fellow relief workers (discovery could have meant death), they were released and allowed to return home. They underwent thorough examinations and were found to be physically and otherwise sound.

Some time later Ilia B. was invited to a party by friends of his fiancée. Scores of men and women expressed sympathy for his plight and admiration for his bravery. He responded with courtesy and restraint, telling them what had gone through his mind, whether he had been afraid of dying, what he had felt when the nun's body had been thrown at his feet and the priest's head laid in his lap. Nothing. No. Nothing, nothing. He had thought and felt nothing the entire time. He had not feared for his life. He had prayed. Our Father, who art in Heaven. Unworthy as I am of Thy presence under my roof, shouldst Thou but say the word. He had planned to do a residency at the local hospital, to marry, to have children.

After the party, the last night of his life, there were no taxis to be had. Ilia B. and his fiancée strolled through the streets in the hope of finding one. They did. Later, however, they had a run-in with the driver: I.B.'s financée accused him of taking a roundabout route, whereupon he made them get out in a dark, out-of-the-way street. I.B.'s fiancée—contrary to her nature: she had had a bit to drink—stood in front of the car as the driver started off. The car stopped, the driver got out, went up to the young woman, stabbed her in the stomach with a knife, and drove off. Ilia B. held the injured vein with one hand and dialed the emergency number with the other. He went with her to the hospital, where she was immediately operated on. They offered to let him sleep at the hospital, but he said he preferred to go home and would return later. When after two days he failed to return, his fiancée asked her mother to try and locate him. He was found lying in his bed. He had died the night of the incident: several hours after the onset of death flies had laid eggs in the corners of his eyes.

Yes, I say, as softly as possible. That's what happened.

Look at me, said my son.

I opened my eyes. He is hovering under the blanket, his legs tucked under him.

Your name is, he says, fading like an old photograph, your name is: Jitoi.

Abel Nema alias El-Kantarah alias Varga alias Alegre alias Floer alias des Prados alias I: nods.

Right, I say. Amen leba.

I have now arrived at a perfect calm. I sigh the better to feel it: the lightness in the rib cage. Everything is light now. No longer in a cast, no longer in concrete, no more brain clots wandering around in the corners. I can feel it: my life will soon come to an end. My decade in hell is over. What is my guilt? Whom did I hurt? No one I know of.

And off it staggered, a body swaying in pain. Walking or crawling or something of the sort on its way to the tracks.

PART 0

EXIT

Metamorphoses

AWAKENING

Going on about some lights or other and high as a kite, he walked off the balcony, five floors, bam, onto the sidewalk. So promising a mind. All others present must have been beyond caring or otherwise engaged, or else how would it have happened that nobody thought of stopping him from climbing up on the railing? What made him do it? Some thought it was a hallucination; whatever; suddenly there's this guy tightrope-walking the railing and, bam, he's gone. There weren't any lights; he didn't say a word; there wasn't anybody to talk to; he was alone; and he crawled there, he didn't walk; he was happy to crawl, though he wasn't in pain: it was the only way he could keep his balance. Because he got dizzy so easily, he would go out into the little barred box he called his balcony and just sit there. People down in the street could see him all year round, burnt by the sun, dried by the wind, a weather-beaten statue. They couldn't get over how tasteless it was, this skeleton throwing some clothes on and sitting out on the balcony, but not many people walk down a street that dead-ends at the tracks, so not many people got worked up about it. He would sit up there watching the trains being shunted back and forth. At first the distances kept changing and he had to reach over to the door handle as if he were three people or one among giants, but the railing was Tom Thumb–size, a breeze to get over. He took advantage of a time when the distance to the wall happened to be short and his leg happened to be long and simply made the step *over*. It was good; it was like when as a child or even now he had the feeling it was only one step to the coastline on the horizon. He was careful when placing his foot between the tracks to keep from twisting his ankle and possibly bringing the house down with him, given that the other, smaller foot was still up there. But no matter where he had come from, whether he had clambered over the wall, squeezed through the barbed wire, or simply climbed down from a train on the wrong side, he was now standing between the tracks with trains moving back and forth to the left and right of him, so later he had the feeling he was moving backwards when he was walking forwards. Sometimes he stopped taking steps, yet on he went, now backwards, now forwards, as if in the midst of a grunting, squealing herd: when he stopped, the beasts carried him on. Later he saw that the clouds never changed, and realized that heaven is a never-ending loop, which meant he would presumably never get out of this. It was the kind of flash that causes despair to rise up in us, as if the spinal column or esophagus were a custom-made lift for it, but then he said to himself, Well, now that's over with, and calmed down, let go, sometimes walking, sometimes letting himself be carried along. And from then on he was no more to be seen . . .

The toxic effect of a somewhat less than lethal dose of amanita muscaria lasts approximately thirty-six hours. One subsequently falls into a what is often an equally long sleep. At first he had all sorts of dreams, later only one, in which he kept trying to get onto the balcony and from there onto the tracks. The attempts having failed one after the other, the story took an unforeseen turn, and he died each time, though remaining obstinate. At one point he finally managed to jump over the wall, and then it was just trains for hours, trains, trains, and then nothing at all.

One Friday morning Abel Nema woke up because he heard bells ringing. About thirty bells rang for about thirty years. He kept his eyes shut. The sun was shining on him. It had found this person there. His eyes hurt a little, the result of an occasionally extreme roll of the eyeballs, but that was all; apart from that, it was as though nothing had happened. As though nothing had ever happened. He sat on the balcony, running his closed eyes over his body: nothing. At some point the bells stopped and the trains came back. Their screech and rumble. Their smell in the breath-fine wind brushing against his face. He opened his eyes.

And nearly lost his balance under the pressure of the unexpected brilliance and breadth of the sky before him, though he was sitting and the lower half of his view was obstructed by bars. The top horizontal bar was at just about the level of his forehead. The brick wall between the bars looked older than before to him. He could make out thirteen pairs of tracks behind it with very old and very new trains running along them. Beads on an abacus. After that thought he thought about his neighbor the physicist, who had failed to calculate what was being calculated there. Or, on the contrary, had succeeded.

Hello, said Halldor Rose at that moment on the other side of the balcony partition. I'm back.

Because what's it all about, anyway? Halldor Rose had said to his sister Wanda a few days earlier.

My experience of God, that's what.

Oh my God, said Wanda.

Let me finish! I understand that each time someone experiences God he ends up in a psychiatric hospital, and it was very nice of you to get me out. What I don't understand is why with brief interruptions for food and sleep, I have to be taken through potato fields and silos. What are they supposed to mean, those mountains of potatoes people keep pointing to conspiratorially—young, sprouting, curling—a metaphor for life, is that it? Am I to draw conclusions from the configuration of the spots on the skins or the flight of the dust over the fields? Am I to make something of how crooked or straight the rows are or the shape of the leftovers on the family table, where I sit at one end, opposite Wanda, so I can have a good view of her and she of me? Am I to study the coffee grounds on the sponge in the sink and, what? read something in them? What it's all about basically is that I've been forcibly detained in this bleak idyll and condemned to lethal boredom for no other reason than that I refuse to deny my experience: God. If Wanda is of the opinion that the whole thing is a drug-induced state of insanity . . .

Temporary, just temporary, said his mustachioed brother-in-law, holding out a schnapps.

No, thank you. I don't drink. If that's the case, why doesn't she just leave it be? Why does she insist that I deny my, I quote, *ascension story*?

I'm not really up on all this, his brother-in-law said, but didn't you yourself say you wanted no more to do with it?

No, said Halldor Rose, frowning. That was not what I said.

And all at once he saw how the whole thing had begun, and on the following day he plotted an escape from the potato wilderness with a guile and efficiency no one would have expected of him. The French-fries driver let him off on the same bridge he had picked him up from the week before. He did not go straight home; he went to the theoretical physics research institute where he worked, where no one was particularly surprised or happy to see him, and where they told him that since there was no rush and the weekend was about to begin he would do best to take things easy and give himself a few days to rest from his labors: they could sort things out on Monday. Okay, said Halldor Rose, and left. That is why he was now sitting on the balcony. Hello.

Abel peered at him through a crack, saw two lips surrounded by a week's worth of stubble and a mop of long, shaggy hair fluttering diagonally above them while they said, Beautiful day, isn't it?

A swarm of birds flew from left to right.

Abel tried to move his tongue, but it felt dry, so he only nodded: Yes, a beautiful day.

Thank God, said H.R. through the crack. I'm back. It's been a week, I think.

You're telling me.

He had been sitting on the balcony, and since, after exchanging a few words with his neighbor over the partition, he found no reason to do otherwise, he stood—he had no trouble standing—and went back into the apartment.

Went back into the apartment and could scarcely recognize it. He had a vague memory of the passing efforts in recent years to bring order and cleanliness into the chaos though without, as was clearly visible, success. While the room seemed less cleft than he had remembered it—he counted up the corners: there were only five, one more than normal—what he saw was a broad field of virtually complete neglect. It was of no help that the number of objects was few: they were all shabby and patently dirty. It smelled too. Making his way through the black piles, mostly of clothes, he knew they had not ended up where they were as a result of the delirium: they must have been there beforehand, most likely for a long time. He was barefoot and advanced slowly, placing the sound foot flat and forming a hook of the wounded one, as if the crumbs on the floor were broken glass. On, in, and under the rug: endless dirt; the former tenant's unused kitchen radio encrusted with grease and dust. He turned it on. A crackling sound came out from under the crust. And now the news. The H. case has been postponed once again, this time because the defendant, S.M., has come down with the flu. Incumbent heads of state enjoy immunity in the new, more moderate anti-genocide law, etc. He turned it off and sat in the bathtub, which was coated with yellow and black grease. He gave his body a careful wash, listening in on himself the while, but the result was the same—a miracle we might call it: there was not a drop of poison left in a single cell of his body; the drug had been dispelled and with it everything else. His sense of perception—his senses in general—and his consciousness were absolutely clear for the first time in thirteen years. I see, smell, and taste as other people do. And while like anyone else in such a situation he felt the flutter of a small joy and a great fear arise in him, the fear had nothing more to do with the other person. That was gone. It was gone.

But take it slow. Proceed with caution through the minefield. The new peace is all too fragile: one rash move, one false sound and everything could be over, back to before. The only sense that appeared to have suffered was the sense of hearing: he could not hear Halldor Rose's movements next door or the whale songs of the trains in the distance, though the door to the balcony was—a rarity—open. Instead he heard a hum in his ears like the hum of a computer in an empty room or a constant, far-off wind that goes sssssssssh, sssssssssh. It couldn't be the computer, though: he hadn't booted up for days.

Now Mercedes, she could hear the trains with the utmost clarity: they were nearly as loud as his voice. It was as if they were tuned to each other in a kind of atonal piece, but that was not what really mattered. What really mattered was that she heard something she could not place at first. Only after she had hung up and rushed back from the kitchen, bathroom, bedroom, where she had run in her excitement—the phone rings, I answer it innocently enough, and believe it or not—to the living room, where she paused between the cracked marble coffee table and the old chest to rest her gaze on the wedding picture still standing there, did she realize what it was: he had a barely noticeable, barely audible, yet discernible accent.

He himself had observed it, shaken his head, made a few faces to loosen the speech organs. H-krm, he said. It sounded like a belated case of voice breaking, though it was most likely dryness: he had drunk nothing for days; each of my cells a tiny desert. He drank some rusty, lukewarm water from the tap, but it did not help much. It lay *down below*. Something you could not wash away. He basically knew it made no difference what he did: drink, do exercises. The metamorphosis had taken place entirely without his complicity and was barely perceivable: a slight tickle in the vicinity of the vocal chords, that was all. He did not dare look in the mirror. If that's how it is, if I am going through a metamorphosis, then I don't want to see myself in the process. There were two things he dared not do: speak and look in the mirror. Later he overcame the former by phoning Mercedes. But not only did she hear something new in *him*; he heard something new too: he thought he discerned an accent in *her*. But that could not be: she was speaking her native language. What had changed was his hearing: for the first time he perceived the hoarseness, the coloring in her voice.

What is it? she asked. Have the papers come through?

H-krm, he said. No, not yet. I . . .

She waited.

Could I speak to Omar?

He's not here. Would you like to leave a message?

Pause.

Tell him I'm sorry about what happened on Thur . . . No. Tell him I'll call back.

Fine, she said and hung up.

My hands are all wet.

LAST TURN

The day before, Mercedes and Tatjana had got together.

Some things have happened, and I have to tell you about a few of them at least.

Fine, said her friend.

First, the Erik thing.

Aha, said Tatjana, tapping her spoon noisily against the cup: refractory milk foam. What's up?

What had his day been like? Probably like any other day. When the family woke up, he was out in the garden, barefoot in the bumpy natural lawn, venerable trouser-legs rolled up above the knees, studying the goings on of a molehill. Later, sitting in an old wicker chair on the boarded terrace and carrying on a conversation with his daughters, he wiped the dew off his feet with a small, rough towel he used only for that purpose. In the kitchen he kissed his wife's hair, and she dropped against his soft stomach, rubbed her nose on his shoulder, taking on and in his scent: under the soap and recent sweat a hint of the intercourse they had had a few hours before, and above all the aroma of the formerly frozen rolls he had heated up for them.

(I can just see it, Tatjana sighed.)

On his way into town Erik ran over a hedgehog. The innards lay on the street: a tiny, blue kidney. Not a pretty sight, though not perhaps significant for what happened later on in the day. What really matters, as he always says, is first, to acknowledge the moment and second, to consider it in the light of eternity. I am the animal that (in principle) can build cars, whereas the animal with needles on its back lies dying at the side of the road, and that is that.

(Hm, says Tatjana.)

At ten thirty he had a meeting with an author in this very café. The manuscript they were discussing was titled "The Fool as King: Mentally Retarded Rulers and Their Governments." Or, said Erik, to put it in my own words: Is it better or worse for us if the man in power is a moron?

Hm, said the author.

A minute after they sat down at the table it was clear that the meeting would go nowhere. Mutual personal antipathy was immediately followed by professional apathy. For vacuous, randomly strung-together, linguistically slipshod, pseudoscientific claptrap like that I don't need to hire an author. A close-mouthed wait for a breakfast ordered too soon. Suddenly Tatjana as deus ex machina appeared on the scene. Pretending not to see him, she took a seat at the bar. Her hair, back, behind, legs eyed by the author, who does not know her. By Erik as well. Objective physical pleasure mixed with a consequential subjective aversion born of experience.

Sorry, said Erik to his ogling table partner. I've just seen someone I need to have a few words with.

To Tatjana: I'm sitting with a tedious, arrogant moron. Talk to me for a few minutes, will you?

Tatjana swung round on the bar stool and gave the author a friendly wave. The author waved back.

Fine, said Tatjana. What shall we talk about?

What are the appropriate topics in such situations? Mutual friends. One (Erik) could ask, for instance, how Mercedes is doing, whether she was really, as she claimed, in good spirits. She'd been looking strange lately.

Whereupon Tatjana licked the milk foam from her very red

upper lip and said, Know what you mean. You wonder why she isn't relieved to be rid of the guy. I would be.

That is how Erik learned that Mercedes and the man in black had separated.

Oh, said Tatjana, sticking her index finger into the cup to gather up the rest of the sugar. I didn't know you didn't know.

(Yes, says Tatjana. It's true.)

Then Erik made believe he had to rush off. When he got to the office, he stood staring at Mercedes' back so long that she finally noticed him. She gave him a wave; he waved back and went into his office. After spending the major part of the day pacing back and forth, he returned to Mercedes' office.

I have two things to say to you, said Erik, as the office was closing up.

Can they wait? asked Mercedes. I've got to go. Omar.

Number one. Erik stood in the doorway, his fists in the pockets of his trousers, making creases in the material. Number one, I am hurt and disappointed that you told me nothing about your divorce. We're friends, after all. Number two, I have just spent the worst six hours of my life, and the result is: I love you. Marry me.

(Tatjana bursts out laughing.

Wait! says Mercedes.)

She looked at the sweaty man at her door, then repeated that she had to go.

Haven't you heard what I said?

I have.

Well?!?

He was practically screaming.

I'm willing to give up everything for you, give up the white-gold lifebuoy on my ring finger that has kept me free from despair, two charming girls who worship me, a loyal, intelligent wife plus salubrious house and garden for your cramped apartment crammed with kitschy bric-a-brac, your strict vegetarian cooking, and your weird little kid who despises me, plus dinners with your vain and cranky, mediocre penny-a-liner of a father and your talent-challenged desiccated snob of a mother, plus the constant surveillance of your battle-ax of a best friend. I am willing to give my all to you—it's about time you had a normal, healthy man in your life—and you say, distracted and a bit disgusted . . .

Sorry, said Mercedes softly, slipping past him and through the door.

(Tatjana laughs.

Wait, says Mercedes.)

Omar was at home by then. What's up? he asked.

Nothing. Erik proposed to me. He must have been drunk.

She laughed. The boy looked earnest.

Erik's an idiot, said Omar. Don't marry him. He'd give me a hard time.

Mercedes laughed.

Why are you crying? Omar asked.

Yes, said Tatjana *now*. Why?

Mercedes, thoughtful: I'm not crying, but I'll probably have to look for another job.

That's life, said Tatjana. You win a few, you lose a few.

Hm, said Mercedes. She looked out at the street. Maybe this would be the right time to have another child.

Maybe, said Tatjana.

A daughter.

Aha.

It would be good for Omar. To have somebody. Though he's stopped claiming to be the smartest person on earth.

Pause.

I've loved no more than three men in my life, said Mercedes. And even though I may seem to have got nothing out of the relationships, I've always come away with what was most valuable about them. First a boy, then a manuscript.

Sorry, said Tatjana. I'm afraid I don't understand what you're getting at or, rather, I understand all too well and let me tell you: *This* takes the cake!

Wait, says Mercedes. But her friend was already on her way. I'm through with you, you dumb broad! You got on my nerves from day one! I never had any feeling for you! said Tatjana in more or less so many words and stormed out of the café.

Everything okay? asked the waiter.

Everything's just fine, said Mercedes and paid for both of them.

Not very much happened after that. A worker from G. found a wallet containing a picture of his beloved, lost twenty-two years before, under the floorboards of an office when the factory he had been working in at the time was torn down. A man and a woman who had posed as inspectors for Immigration Services or employees of Child Welfare were arrested. In the middle of a soccer game in a small village in V. two men stole the ball and ran with it through the shadowless village streets, tossing the ball to each other and laughing, ran with it all the way home, at which point the furious crowd caught up with them and beat them to death; a radio DJ was shot because he refused to play a song that a listener had requested; an eighteen-year-old sliced his penis off and his tongue out in a fit of religious fervor; and Konstantin T. was caught trying to purchase a false passport. He spent the night before his extradition in handcuffs on a kitchen chair. He had been gagged because he kept complaining, sobbing convulsively, his nose slowly filling with snot.

The following morning, a Friday, Abel put on his coat and went out. The door of The Loony Bin was open, but there was a sheet of paper on it that said: Closed Until Further Notice.

How long?

Thanos shrugged. Want a drink? Clear as water, he said as he poured.

Abel took a swig, noticed that it made him drunk immediately, and left the rest.

Well, well, said Thanos. Well, well. Anything else I can do for you?

Abel had gone to Thanos, my fatherly friend and patron, to ask him one last time for money. I stopped looking after the wound on my foot last week, and now—together with the others, which I'm not particularly worried about—it has made it hard for me to . . .

Don't say that; just say you've got to see a doctor and unfortunately have no insurance.

Even though it would have been a bit shabby, he could have mentioned that he had got the wound here and lost his money here, but it turned out not to be necessary.

Is that enough? Get well soon.

Nobody else would have done it, but he walked home after the procedure—nine stitches, after all. For one thing, the anesthesia had not yet worn off, so it was like having a cloud for a right foot. But he also wanted to see if he could do it, if he, as he suspected, could find his way without getting lost, first to the registration office, which was only a few blocks away, to pick up the new papers at last, and then to the bank. He never again made it to either.

They were the only ones in the small playground. Not a park, just a tiny, desolate triangle of so-called green space left over when two streets came together in a point. One of them sat on the crumbling edge of the sandbox, drawing in the sand; three were squatting on the playground carousel, two were hanging on the jungle gym—bim bam—like two bell clappers. Their games were wordless and serious: they spun, they drew, they dangled without taking their eyes off *him*. It was plain to see—he too could have foreseen it—that things would end badly. He did nothing; they did nothing; yet it was clear. They had developed from petty car-radio thieves into full-fledged toughs: the previous winter they had set a homeless man on fire. The man in black walked past the two who were swinging and crossed the green space in the direction of the carousel. The two who were sitting on it ground the soles of their shoes against the cement, and the carousel screeched to a halt. He took a step to the side, still hoping perhaps to get past them, but the moment he shifted his weight to the wounded foot—no cloud that!—his knee buckled with pain. The fresh stitches tore open, and moisture began seeping into the shoe.

Upsy-daisy, said one of the two standing in front of him. The two behind him had jumped noiselessly down from the jungle gym and were grabbing him under the arms, as if trying to support him.

Upsy-daisy, said Kosma, clapping the sand from his hands. He was taller and even fatter now, his eyes, nose, and mouth tiny in a big, red face. Upsy-daisy, said the tiny mouth.

Abel indicated with his body that he could stand on his own now—thanks for your help—but they did not let go of him: they held him on both sides, their fingers boring into his underarms.

Sorry, I've just spent most of the money I had on me. You'll find what remains in my left inside pocket. It's all I have. He was in a hurry, he added.

They did not budge; they merely stared at him.

Shit, said Kosma. Fuck. I know you.

Now he knew who they were too. The terrible seven, except they had gone down to six a while back.

Before all hell broke loose, Abel had time to wonder whether he was ready *for that*. Had he come to the point where he could die without a peep, because that he would die seemed as clear as day. Ready or not, you're done for.

Kosma took a step forward and kicked him in the genitals. He would have fallen, but his two guards held on to him. Later they asked to be released from simply holding him. Do what you like, said Kosma. Let him go. He collapsed slowly, as large statues collapse. From the moment he hit the ground nothing is known.

Later that day Mercedes received a call from the hospital.

EXIT

It was not easy to cut him down: the tape was recalcitrant, and the tomboy had nothing but a penknife. The tall thin one held on to his shins; the fat one cradled his head in her hands. They laid him down on the asphalt, then picked him up again immediately, carried him for a few more steps, and laid him down in the grass, carefully letting the back of his head roll out of the well-padded hands. His eyes opened for an instant: a blue sky, then a red one, then black darkness. Is that good? Yes, it is good. That's good.

He could easily have been dead. An improbable piece of luck: the blade entered between the fourth and fifth rib, two centimeters deep, and came to a stop without wounding any of his vital organs. The only real harm came from hanging upside-down.

That's good.

The room is full: doctors and at least ten speech therapists, one for each language. The moment they realized who he was—someone had recognized him, the MRI person—he was given a private room. Meanwhile the family had been notified and was present. Mercedes' eyes.

That's good.

It seems to be the only thing he can say. Slight hemorrhaging in the front lobe, extensive hemorrhaging in the temporal lobe. How much he understands is unclear. As a result of the hemorrhaging your husband is suffering from aphasia.

What is aphasia?

That is ggggg . . .

Aphasia, says Omar. From the Greek *phanai*, to speak. Loss of the power of speech but also, in the figurative sense, of the power of judgment.

To make a long story short: he's lost his languages. You've got a bright little boy there.

The amazing porcelain white of his right eye encompassed the entire hospital room.

What do you mean by: He's lost his languages? All of them?

That's good.

It often goes together with amnesia, unfortunately. We can't yet tell for sure. How are you, Mr. N? Your family's here!

Mercedes does not dare touch him. Omar lays a hand on Abel's right arm. Unfortunately it is the paralyzed arm. The face moves only with the greatest of difficulty. I might as well be in pieces still. Sounds forced out of a mouth half-numb: Good, good, good!

Some speech capability can usually be restored over time, though this is the first time we've had a case of decalingual aphasia. It's a great challenge for us.

(Fuck you!) That's good!

. . . thirteenth expedition in search of noah's ark begun the maw of all malice shall be stopped psalm one hundred and seven fourteen signed x.y. head of the institute for creation science and the expedition's initiator the theory of evolution gives a woeful view of our life and undermines society if I am a mere chance product of the primordial brew what is the meaning of the entire . . .

Yes, leave the television on. To talk to him. That's good. We get foreign stations too. You have no idea what this means for us. Lay people can't possibly grasp the scholarly interest in the case. It's one of the most interesting neurolinguistic cases ever.

That's good!

But we're very hopeful. It could turn into a project of its own: the Abel Nema Project, the ANP.

Gooooooood!

Funding permitting, of course, but given what's at stake . . .

Goooooooo!

This is a good injection: it works in no time. There are times you can't tell what's going on in brain-damaged patients. They'll fly off the handle out of the blue . . .

Good!

. . . or toss and turn in a panic. The most harmless things can seem to threaten them, so don't be frightened. Suicide thoughts are a frequent phenomenon, unfortunately, and I promise we'll keep him away from all stairs and windows. You've probably noticed that the doors have no handles. It's for security's sake. We have a long, hard road ahead of us, but a beautiful road as well,

Gggg!

a road of hope.

Gg!

Every day, every step forward, no matter how small, is a victory.

Gggggggrrrr . . .

Yes, put your hand on his forehead, young man.

Omar removes his hand from the cold, clammy forehead of his once and still stepfather and picks up the warm, sticky hand of his sister. He adjusts to her walk. They toddle through the park's wet grass together. He talks to her as if she were an adult. She does not say anything yet; she merely nods or shakes her head or cocks it and lifts an eyebrow, depending on what is appropriate. What she never stops doing is: smiling. She has her father's mirrorlike eyes and long limbs and her mother's friendly cheeks and trusting mouth. Her brother has grown taller and slimmer. The beauty streaming from his perfect face and entire body, even the invisible parts hidden by clothing, is so overpowering that closed rooms, metro trains, and small shops fall silent when he enters, and, even out of doors, women and sensitive men will twist their eyes painfully to take furtive glances at him. He appears not to notice because his left field of vision is nonexistent and the little girl toddling along on his right takes up all his attention. Except when he casts a glance back to a certain bench, to see whether *he* is still sitting there, his head slightly tilted, smiling peacefully, like the Abel Nema of former times, and following them with his eyes. Amnesia has in fact set in: he remembers nothing. When people tell him what they know about him—his name is Abel Nema, he comes from such and such a country, and once spoke, translated, and interpreted ten or twelve languages—he shakes his head with a polite-apologetic-incredulous smile. He understands everything said to him; he can move normally, if somewhat more slowly than most people; he can even speak. Contrary to expectations, he has recovered but one language, the local language, though in that language he can generate only simple sentences: he can say if he wants something to eat from the nearby stand and can also ask the children if they would like something. He can say other things too, but it obviously takes a great deal of effort on his part. What he most likes to say is still: That's good. The relief, no, the joy he derives from being able to say it is so palpable that his loved ones give him every opportunity to do so. He always utters it with gratitude: That's good. A last word. It's good.